REGULAR SHOW™

A CLASH OF CONSOLES

CALGARY PUBLIC LIBRARY
JUNE 2018

D1096820

ROSS RICHIE CEO & Founder • MATT GAGNON Editor-in-Chief • FILIP SABLIK President of Publishing & Marketing • STEPHEN CHRISTY President of Development • LANCE KREITER VP of Licensing & Merc
PHIL BARBARO VP of Finance • BRYCE CARLSON Managing Editor • MEL CAYLO Marketing Manager • SCOTT NEWMAN Production Design Manager • IRENE BRADISH Operations
CHRISTINE DINH Brand Communications Manager • SIERRA HAHN Senior Editor • DAFNA PLEBAN Editor • SHANNON WATTERS Editor • ERIC HARBURN Editor • WHITNEY LEOPARD Associate Editor • JASMINE AMIRI Assoc
CHRIS ROSA Associate Editor • ALEX GALER Assistant Editor • CAMERON CHITTOCK Assistant Editor • MARY GUMPORT Assistant Editor • MATTHEW LEVINE Assistant Editor • KELSEY DIETERICH Production
JILLIAN CRAB Production Designer • MICHELLE ANKLEY Production Design Assistant • GRACE PARK Production Design Assistant • AARON FERRARA Operations Coordinator • ELIZABETH LOUGHRIDGE Accounting Co
JOSÉ MEZA Sales Assistant • JAMES ARRIOLA Mailroom Assistant • HOLLY AITCHISON Operations Assistant • STEPHANIE HOCUTT Marketing Assistant • SAM KUSEK Direct Market Repre

REGULAR SHOW: A CLASH OF CONSOLES, May 2016. Published
by KaBOOM!, a division of Boom Entertainment, Inc. REGULAR SHOW,
CARTOON NETWORK, the logos, and all related characters and
elements are trademarks of and © Cartoon Network. (S16) All rights
reserved. KaBOOM!™ and the KaBOOM! logo are trademarks of
Boom Entertainment, Inc., registered in various countries and categories. All characters, events, and institutions depicted herein
are fictional. Any similarity between any of the names, characters, persons, events, and/or institutions in this publication to actual
names, characters, and persons, whether living or dead, events, and/or institutions is unintended and purely coincidental.
KaBOOM! does not read or accept unsolicited submissions of ideas, stories, or artwork.

For information regarding the CPSIA on this printed material, call: (203) 595-3636 and provide reference #RICH – 665292. A catalog
record of this book is available from OCLC and from the BOOM! Studios website, www.Boom-Studios.com, on the Librarian's Page.

BOOM! Studios, 5670 Wilshire Boulevard, Suite 450, Los Angeles, CA 90036-5679. Printed in USA. First Printing.

ISBN: 978-1-60886-800-1, eISBN: 978-1-61398-471-0

REGULAR SHOW™

A CLASH OF CONSOLES

CREATED BY
JG QUINTEL

WRITTEN BY
ROBERT LUCKETT
& RACHEL CONNOR

ILLUSTRATED BY
ZÉ BURNAY

COLORS BY
FRED STRESING

LETTERS BY
SHAWN ALDRIDGE

COVER BY
ZÉ BURNAY
WITH FRED STRESING

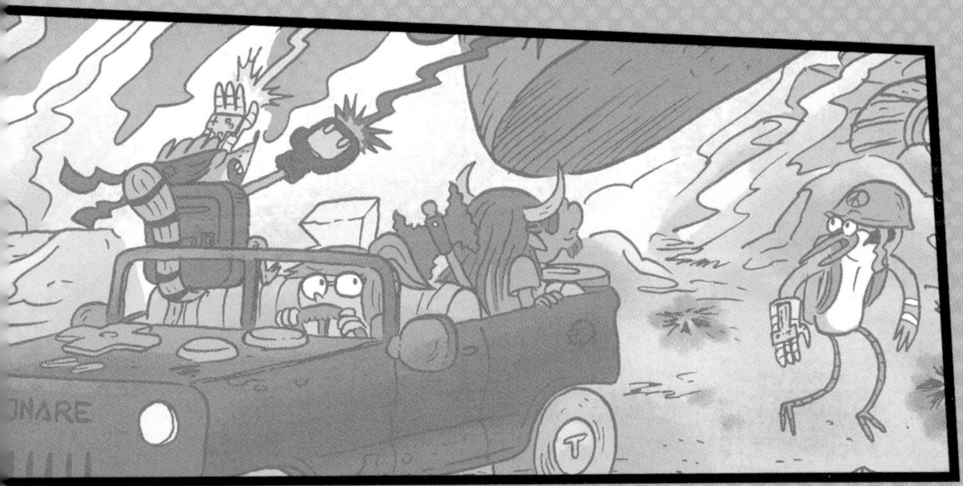

DESIGNER
GRACE PARK

ASSISTANT EDITOR
MARY GUMPORT

EDITOR
SIERRA HAHN

SPECIAL THANKS TO MARISA MARIONAKIS, RICK BLANCO, CURTIS LELASH, CONRAD MONTGOMERY, MEGHAN BRADLEY, RYAN SLATER, AND THE WONDERFUL FOLKS AT CARTOON NETWORK.

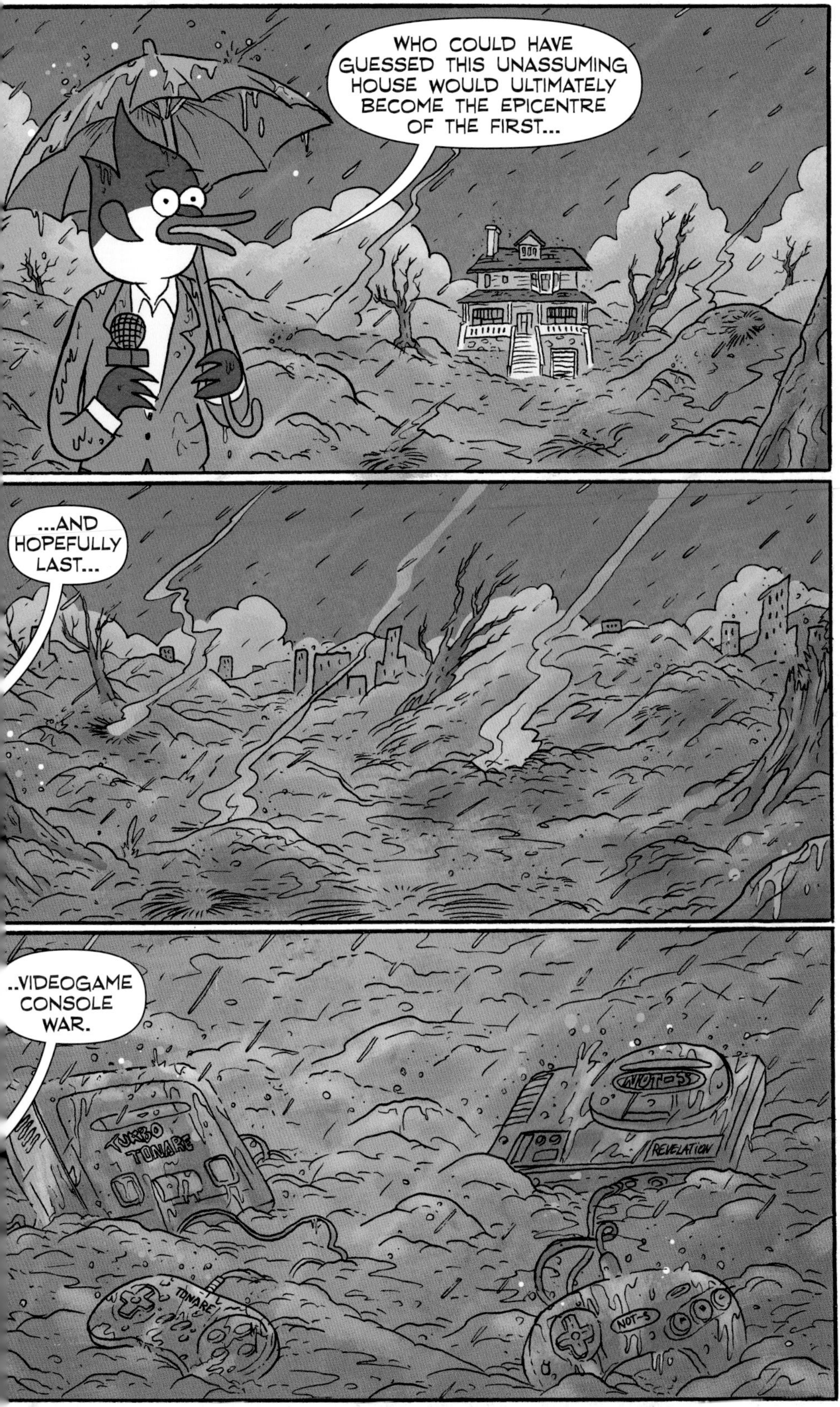
WHO COULD HAVE GUESSED THIS UNASSUMING HOUSE WOULD ULTIMATELY BECOME THE EPICENTRE OF THE FIRST...
...AND HOPEFULLY LAST...
..VIDEOGAME CONSOLE WAR.
TURBO TONARE
REVELATION
TONARE
NOT-S

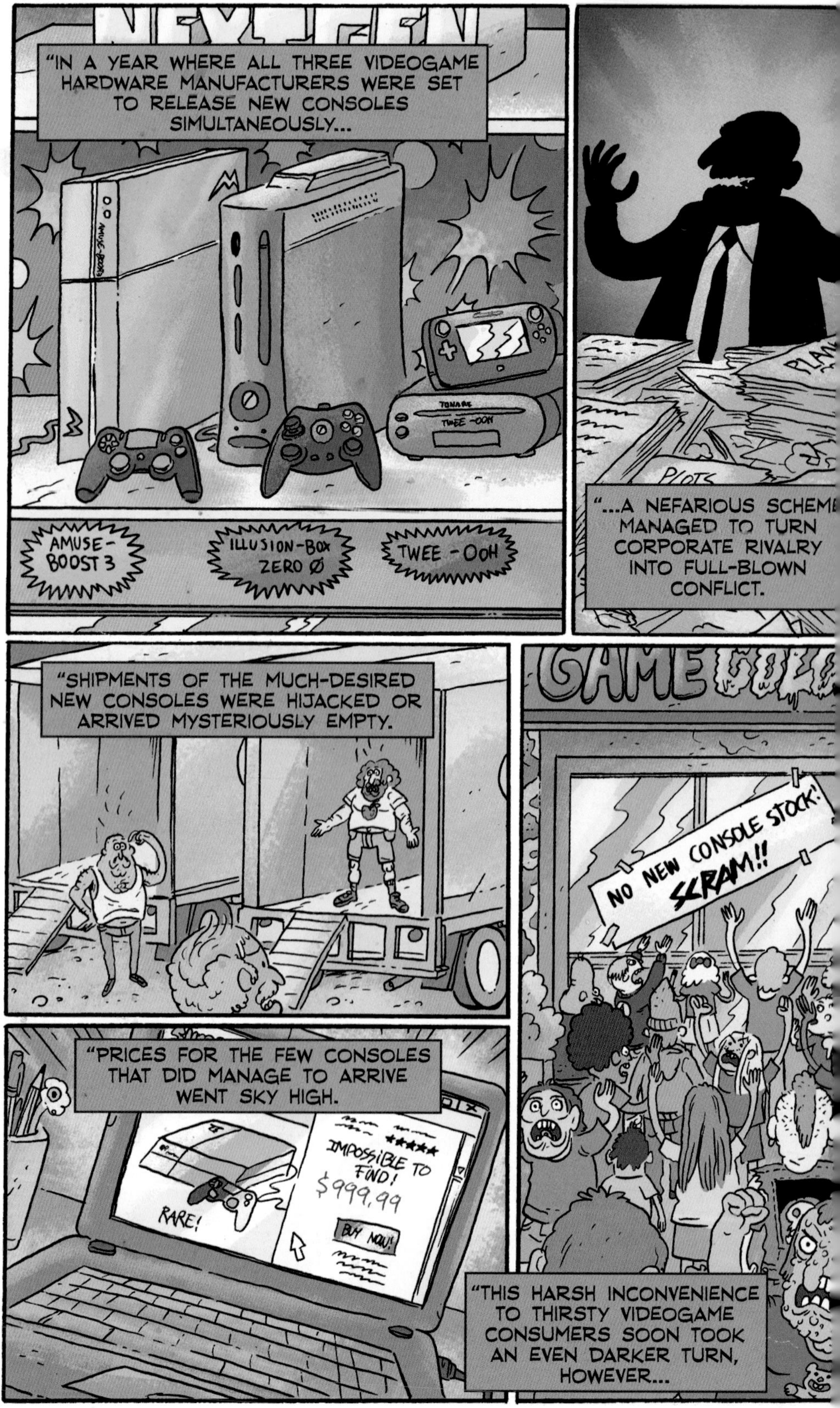
"IN A YEAR WHERE ALL THREE VIDEOGAME HARDWARE MANUFACTURERS WERE SET TO RELEASE NEW CONSOLES SIMULTANEOUSLY...
AMUSE-BOOST
TWEE-OOH
AMUSE-BOOST 3
ILLUSION-BOX ZERO Ø
TWEE-OOH
PLOTS
"...A NEFARIOUS SCHEM
MANAGED TO TURN CORPORATE RIVALRY INTO FULL-BLOWN CONFLICT.
"SHIPMENTS OF THE MUCH-DESIRED NEW CONSOLES WERE HIJACKED OR ARRIVED MYSTERIOUSLY EMPTY.
"PRICES FOR THE FEW CONSOLES THAT DID MANAGE TO ARRIVE WENT SKY HIGH.
IMPOSSIBLE TO FIND!
$999.99
RARE!
BUY NOW!
GAME
NO NEW CONSOLE STOCK!
SCRAM!!
"THIS HARSH INCONVENIENCE TO THIRSTY VIDEOGAME CONSUMERS SOON TOOK AN EVEN DARKER TURN, HOWEVER...

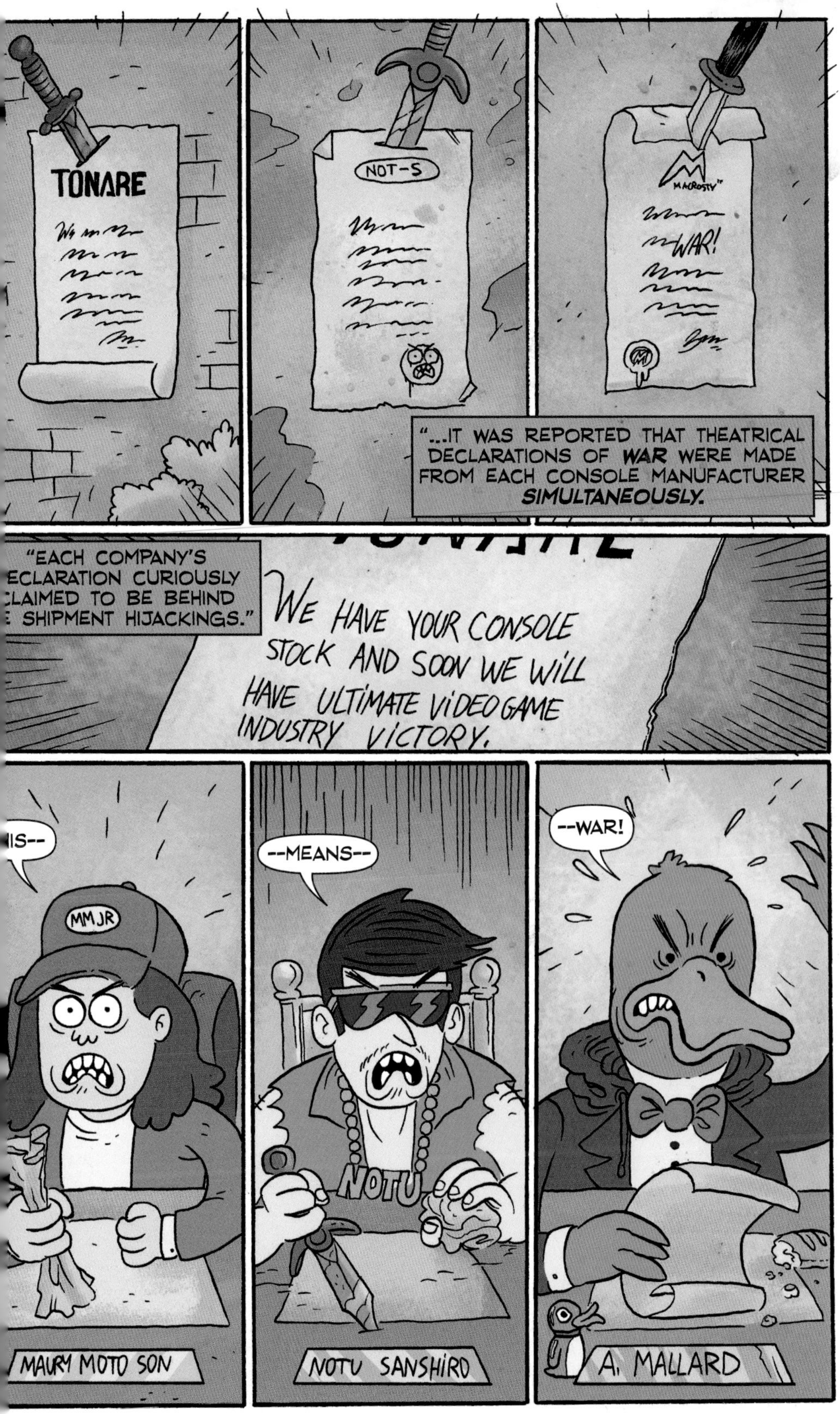
TONARE
NOT-S
MACROSTY™
WAR!
"...IT WAS REPORTED THAT THEATRICAL DECLARATIONS OF WAR WERE MADE FROM EACH CONSOLE MANUFACTURER SIMULTANEOUSLY.
"EACH COMPANY'S ECLARATION CURIOUSLY CLAIMED TO BE BEHIND E SHIPMENT HIJACKINGS."
WE HAVE YOUR CONSOLE STOCK AND SOON WE WILL HAVE ULTIMATE VIDEOGAME INDUSTRY VICTORY.
IS--
MMJR
MAURY MOTO SON
--MEANS--
NOTU
NOTU SANSHIRO
--WAR!
A. MALLARD

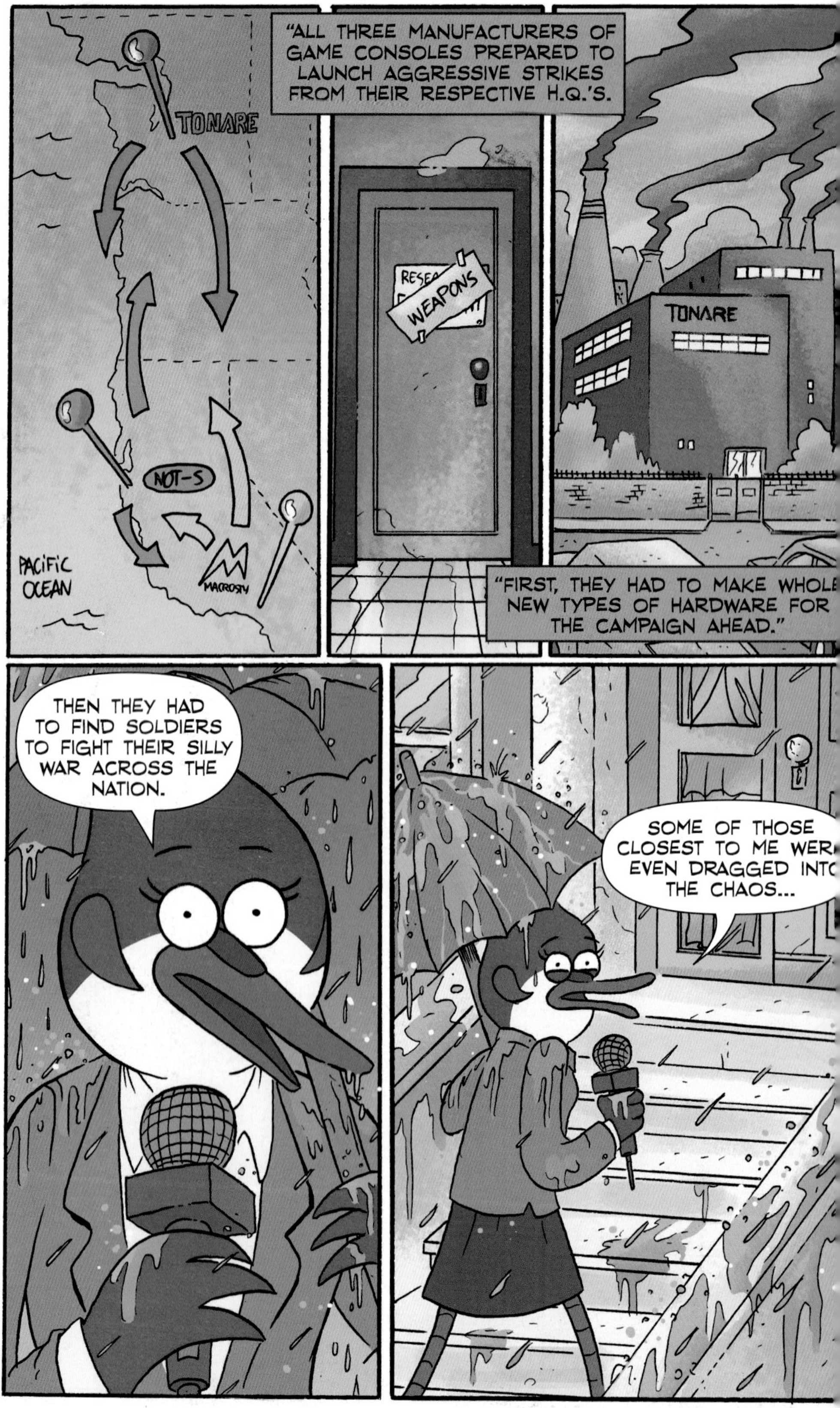
TONARE
NOT-S
MACROSTY
PACIFIC OCEAN
"ALL THREE MANUFACTURERS OF GAME CONSOLES PREPARED TO LAUNCH AGGRESSIVE STRIKES FROM THEIR RESPECTIVE H.Q.'S.
WEAPONS
TONARE
"FIRST, THEY HAD TO MAKE WHOLE NEW TYPES OF HARDWARE FOR THE CAMPAIGN AHEAD."
THEN THEY HAD TO FIND SOLDIERS TO FIGHT THEIR SILLY WAR ACROSS THE NATION.
SOME OF THOSE CLOSEST TO ME WER EVEN DRAGGED INTO THE CHAOS...

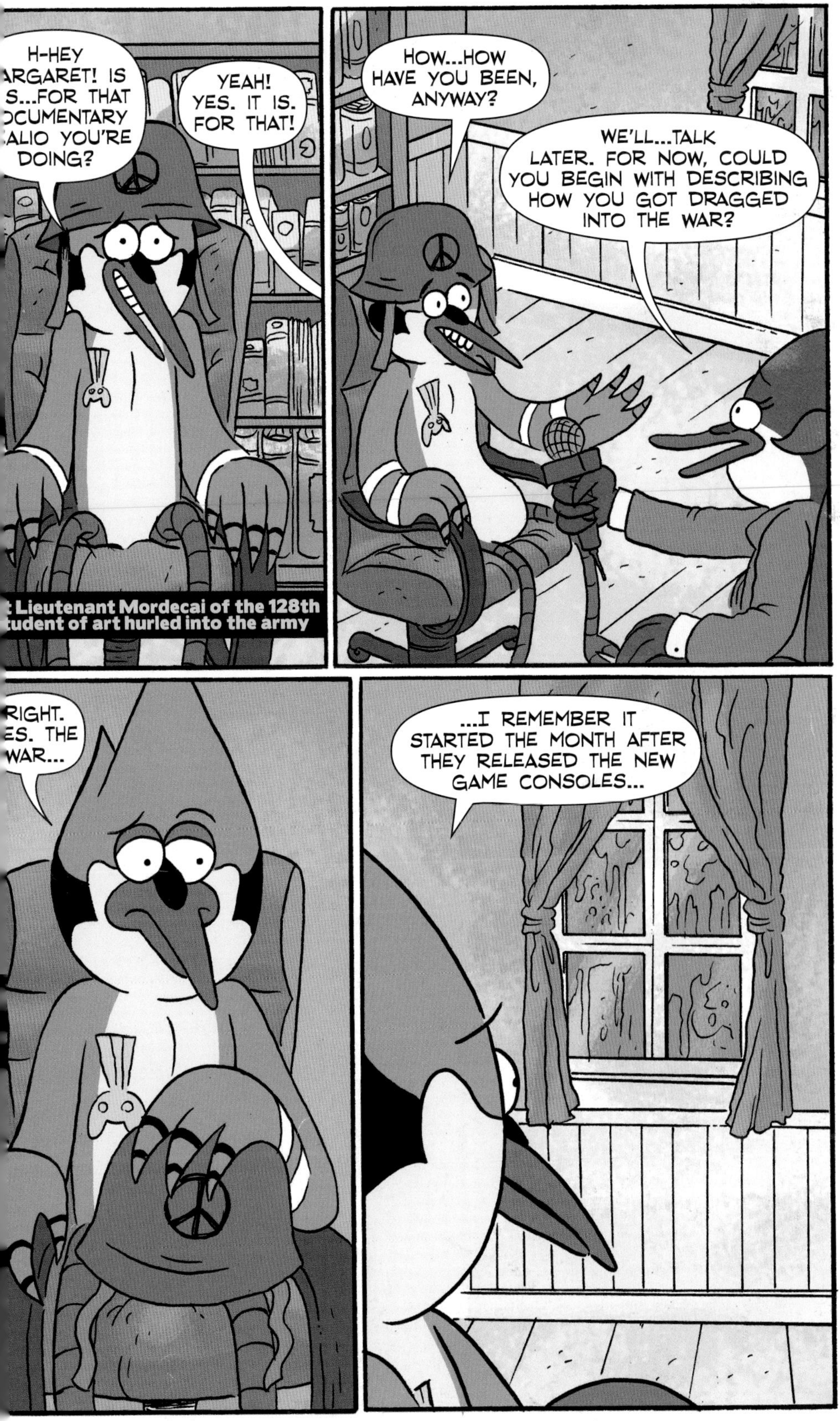

H-HEY
ARGARET! IS
S...FOR THAT
OCUMENTARY
ALIO YOU'RE
DOING?
YEAH!
YES. IT IS.
FOR THAT!
Lieutenant Mordecai of the 128th
tudent of art hurled into the army
HOW...HOW
HAVE YOU BEEN,
ANYWAY?
WE'LL...TALK
LATER. FOR NOW, COULD
YOU BEGIN WITH DESCRIBING
HOW YOU GOT DRAGGED
INTO THE WAR?
RIGHT.
ES. THE
WAR...
...I REMEMBER IT
STARTED THE MONTH AFTER
THEY RELEASED THE NEW
GAME CONSOLES...

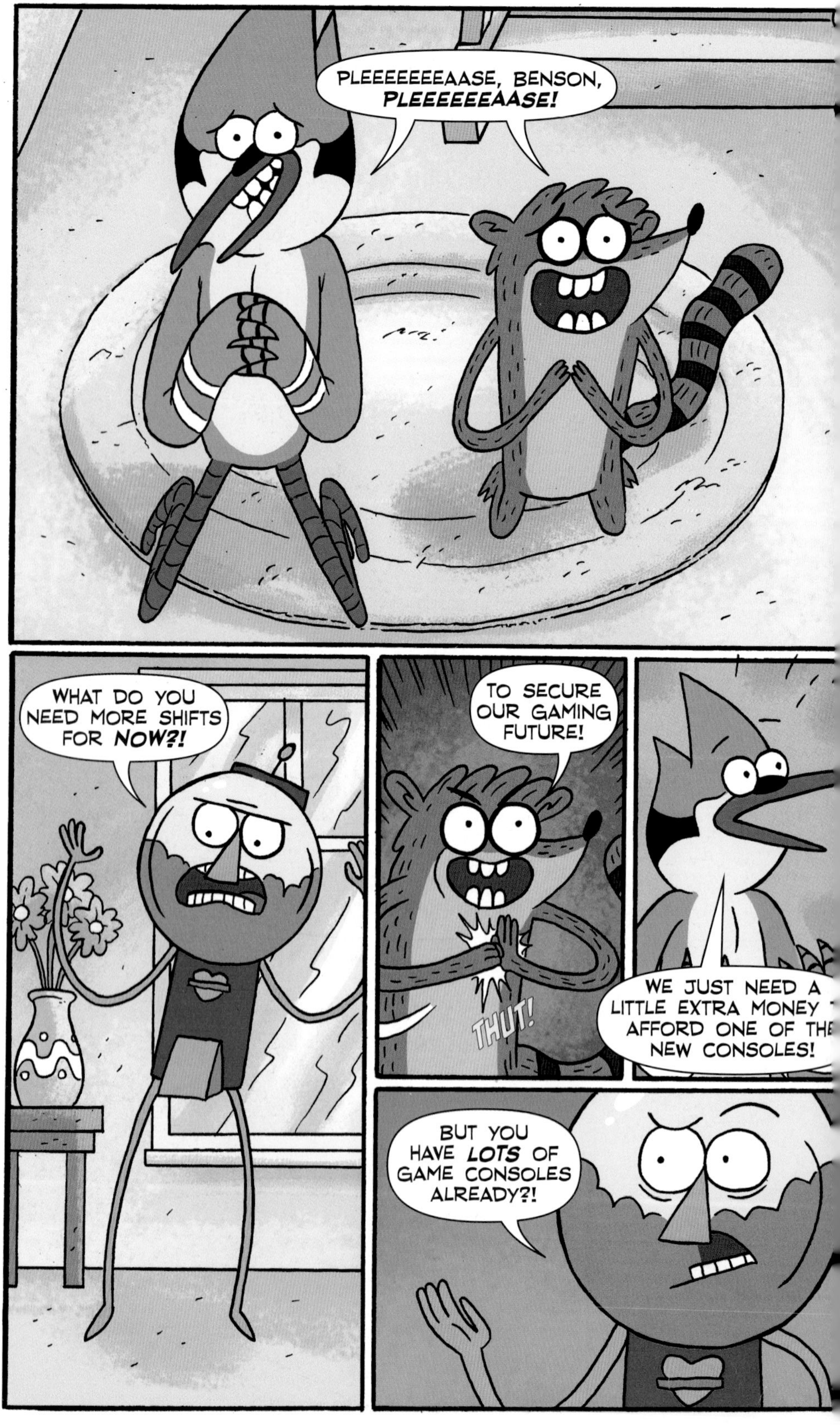
PLEEEEEEEAASE, BENSON,
PLEEEEEEAASE!
WHAT DO YOU NEED MORE SHIFTS FOR NOW?!
TO SECURE OUR GAMING FUTURE!
THUT!
WE JUST NEED A LITTLE EXTRA MONEY T AFFORD ONE OF THE NEW CONSOLES!
BUT YOU HAVE LOTS OF GAME CONSOLES ALREADY?!

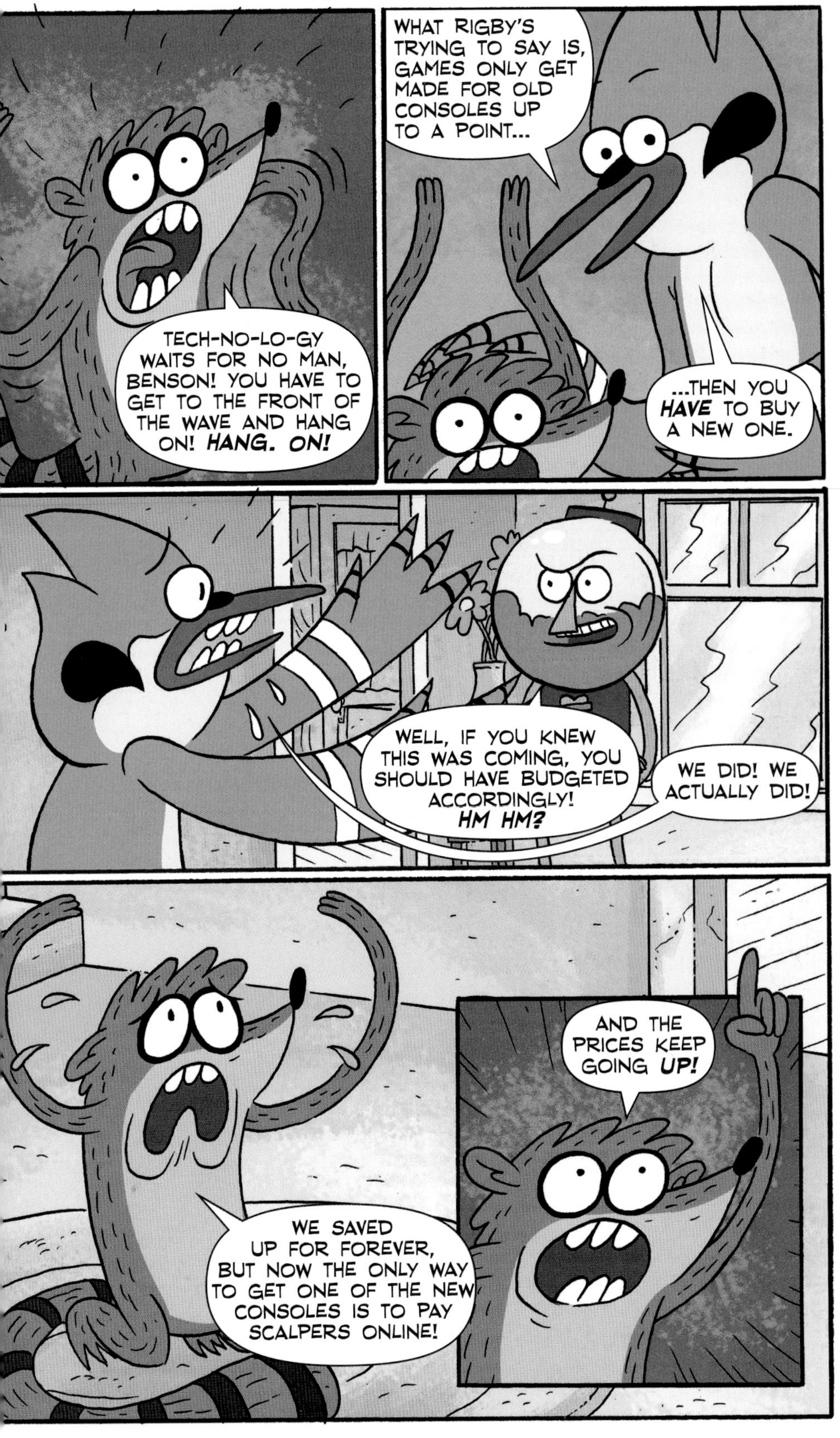
TECH-NO-LO-GY WAITS FOR NO MAN, BENSON! YOU HAVE TO GET TO THE FRONT OF THE WAVE AND HANG ON! HANG. ON!
WHAT RIGBY'S TRYING TO SAY IS, GAMES ONLY GET MADE FOR OLD CONSOLES UP TO A POINT...
...THEN YOU HAVE TO BUY A NEW ONE.
WELL, IF YOU KNEW THIS WAS COMING, YOU SHOULD HAVE BUDGETED ACCORDINGLY! HM HM?
WE DID! WE ACTUALLY DID!
WE SAVED UP FOR FOREVER, BUT NOW THE ONLY WAY TO GET ONE OF THE NEW CONSOLES IS TO PAY SCALPERS ONLINE!
AND THE PRICES KEEP GOING UP!

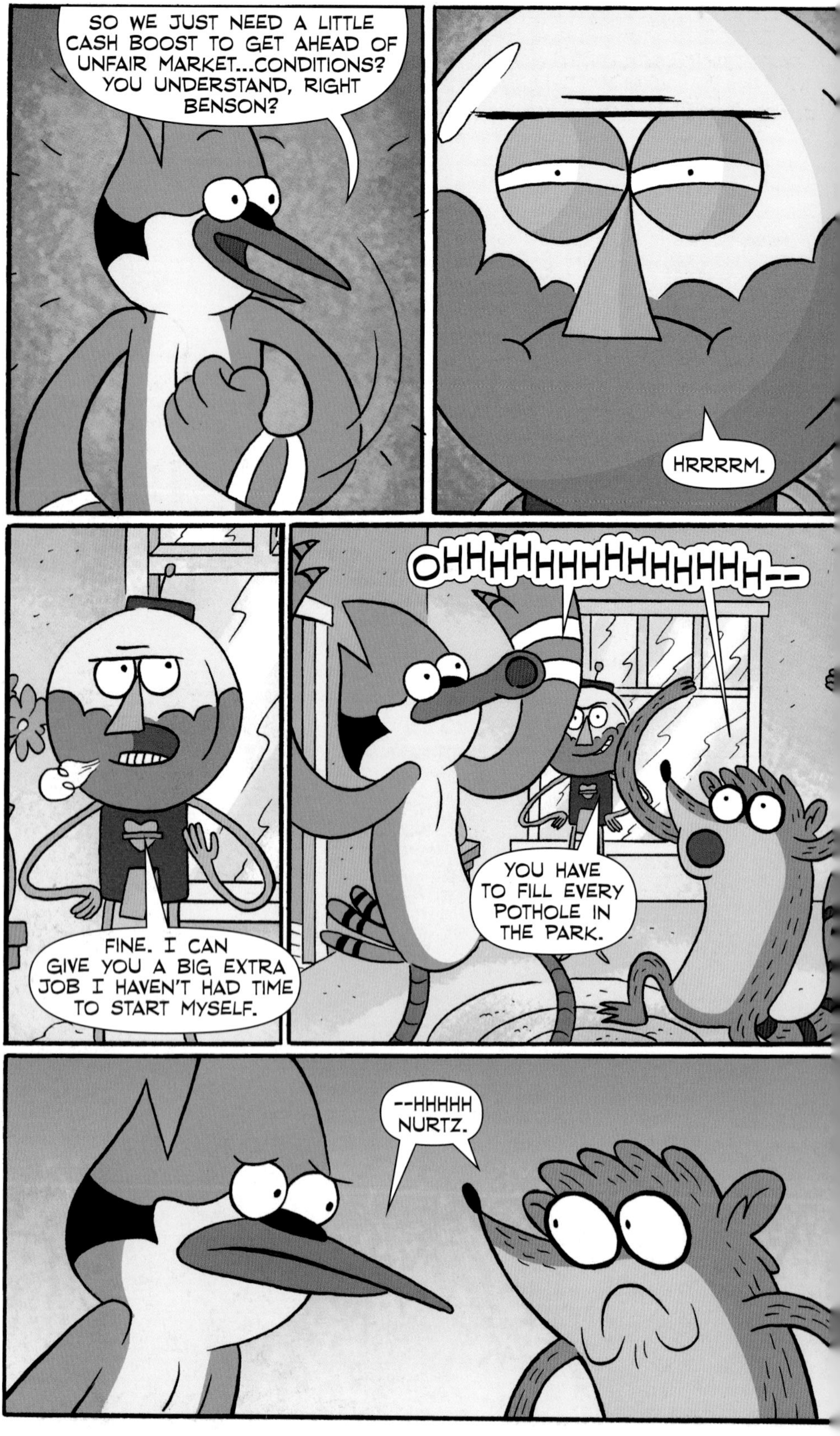
SO WE JUST NEED A LITTLE CASH BOOST TO GET AHEAD OF UNFAIR MARKET...CONDITIONS? YOU UNDERSTAND, RIGHT BENSON?
HRRRRM.
FINE. I CAN GIVE YOU A BIG EXTRA JOB I HAVEN'T HAD TIME TO START MYSELF.
OHHHHHHHHHHHHHH--
YOU HAVE TO FILL EVERY POTHOLE IN THE PARK.
--HHHHH NURTZ.

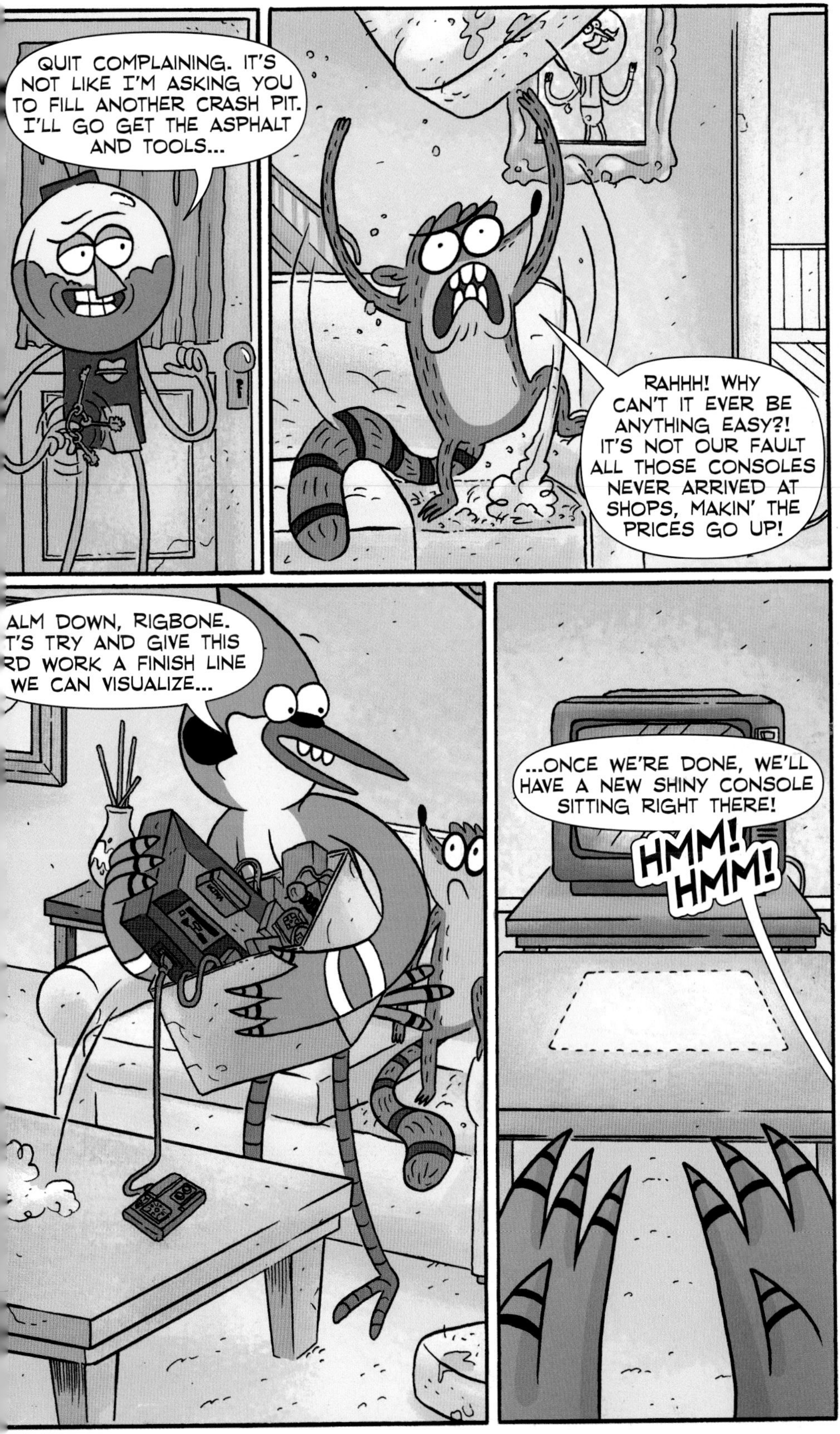
QUIT COMPLAINING. IT'S NOT LIKE I'M ASKING YOU TO FILL ANOTHER CRASH PIT. I'LL GO GET THE ASPHALT AND TOOLS...
RAHHH! WHY CAN'T IT EVER BE ANYTHING EASY?! IT'S NOT OUR FAULT ALL THOSE CONSOLES NEVER ARRIVED AT SHOPS, MAKIN' THE PRICES GO UP!
ALM DOWN, RIGBONE. T'S TRY AND GIVE THIS RD WORK A FINISH LINE WE CAN VISUALIZE...
...ONCE WE'RE DONE, WE'LL HAVE A NEW SHINY CONSOLE SITTING RIGHT THERE!
HMM! HMM!

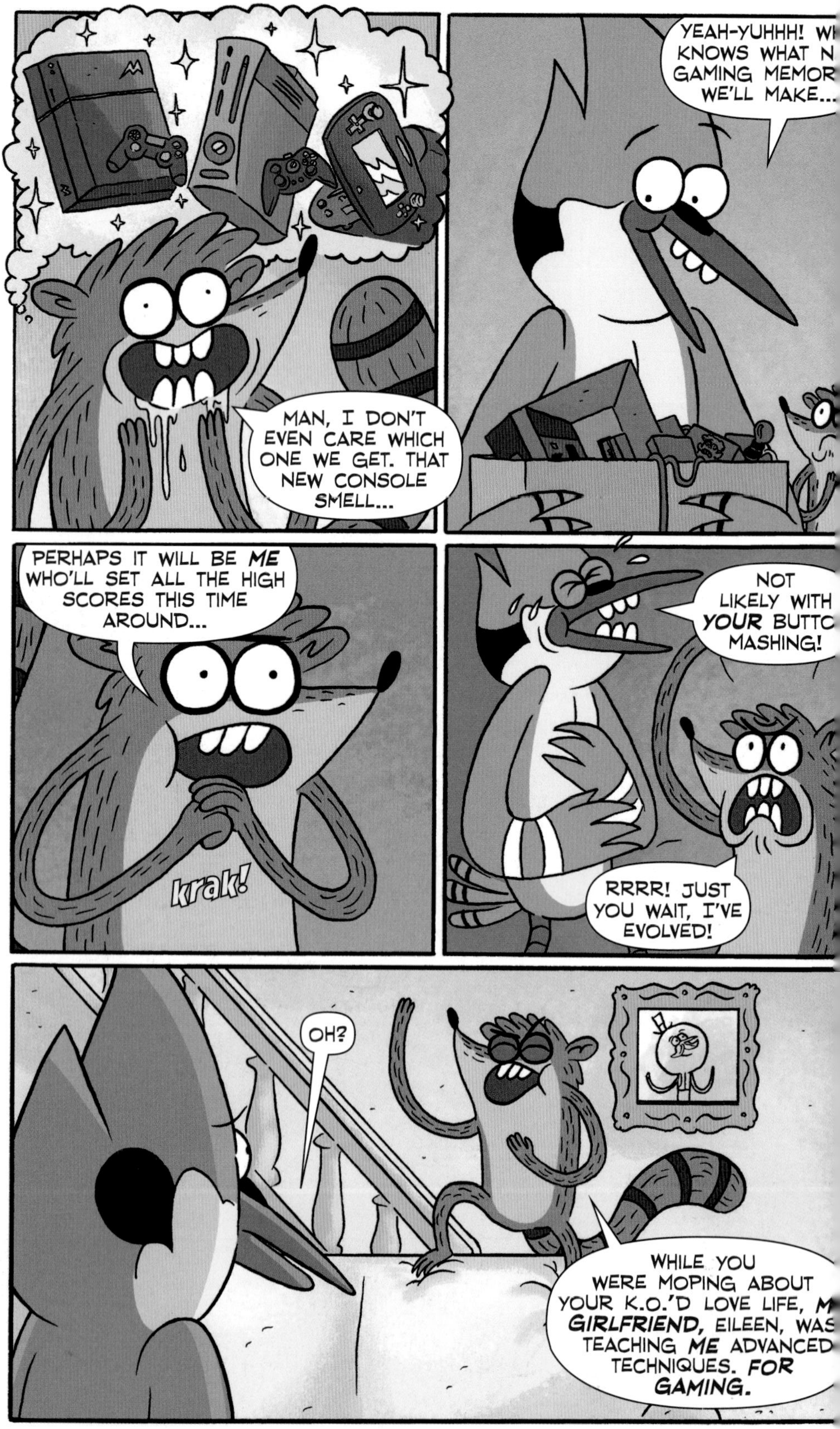

MAN, I DON'T EVEN CARE WHICH ONE WE GET. THAT NEW CONSOLE SMELL...
YEAH-YUHHH! W
KNOWS WHAT N
GAMING MEMOR
WE'LL MAKE...
PERHAPS IT WILL BE *ME* WHO'LL SET ALL THE HIGH SCORES THIS TIME AROUND...
krak!
NOT LIKELY WITH *YOUR* BUTTO MASHING!
RRRR! JUST YOU WAIT, I'VE EVOLVED!
OH?
WHILE YOU WERE MOPING ABOUT YOUR K.O.'D LOVE LIFE, *M GIRLFRIEND,* EILEEN, WAS TEACHING *ME* ADVANCED TECHNIQUES. *FOR GAMING.*

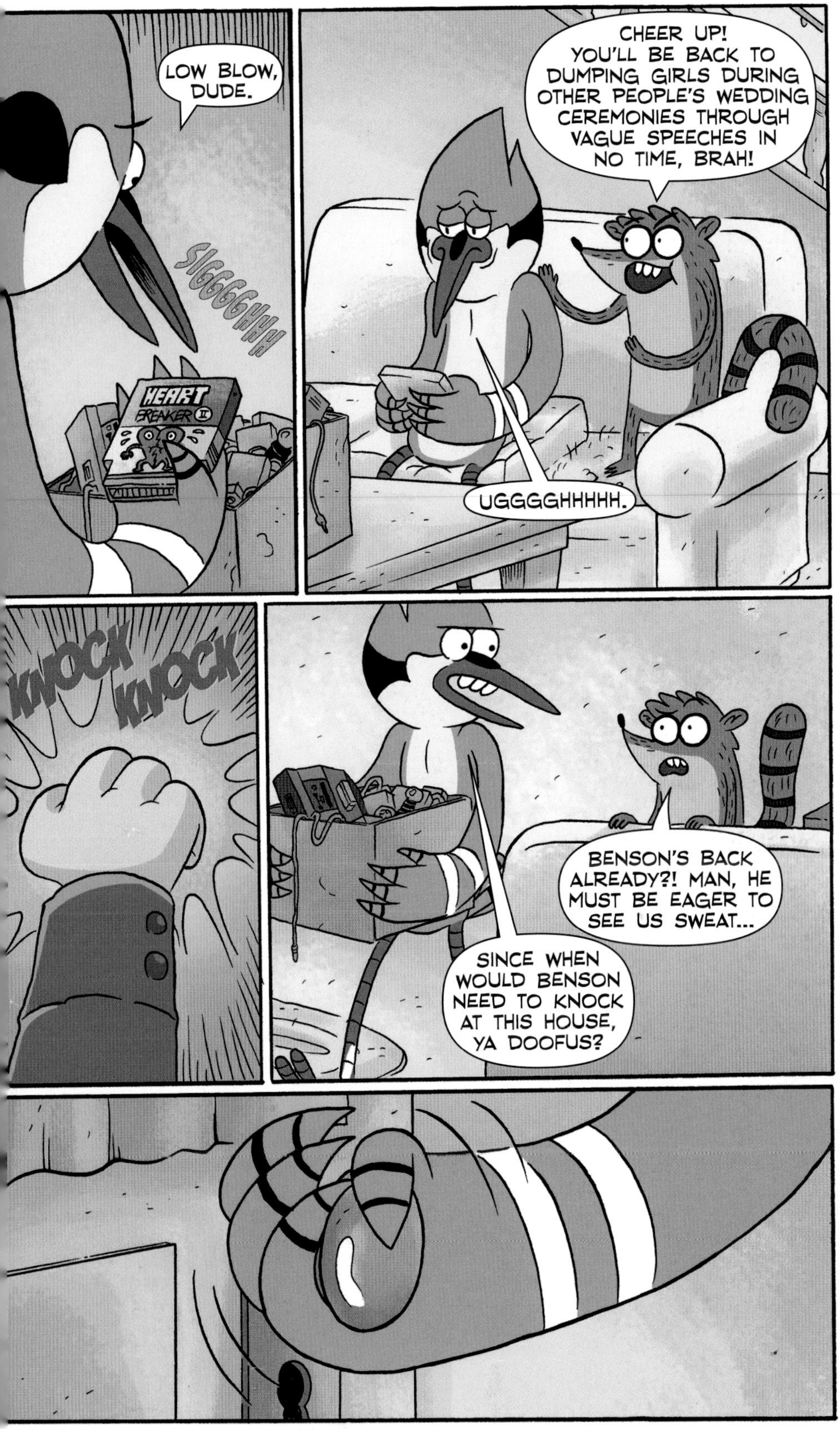
LOW BLOW, DUDE.
SIGGGGHHH
HEART BREAKER II
CHEER UP! YOU'LL BE BACK TO DUMPING GIRLS DURING OTHER PEOPLE'S WEDDING CEREMONIES THROUGH VAGUE SPEECHES IN NO TIME, BRAH!
UGGGGHHHHH.
KNOCK KNOCK
BENSON'S BACK ALREADY?! MAN, HE MUST BE EAGER TO SEE US SWEAT...
SINCE WHEN WOULD BENSON NEED TO KNOCK AT THIS HOUSE, YA DOOFUS?

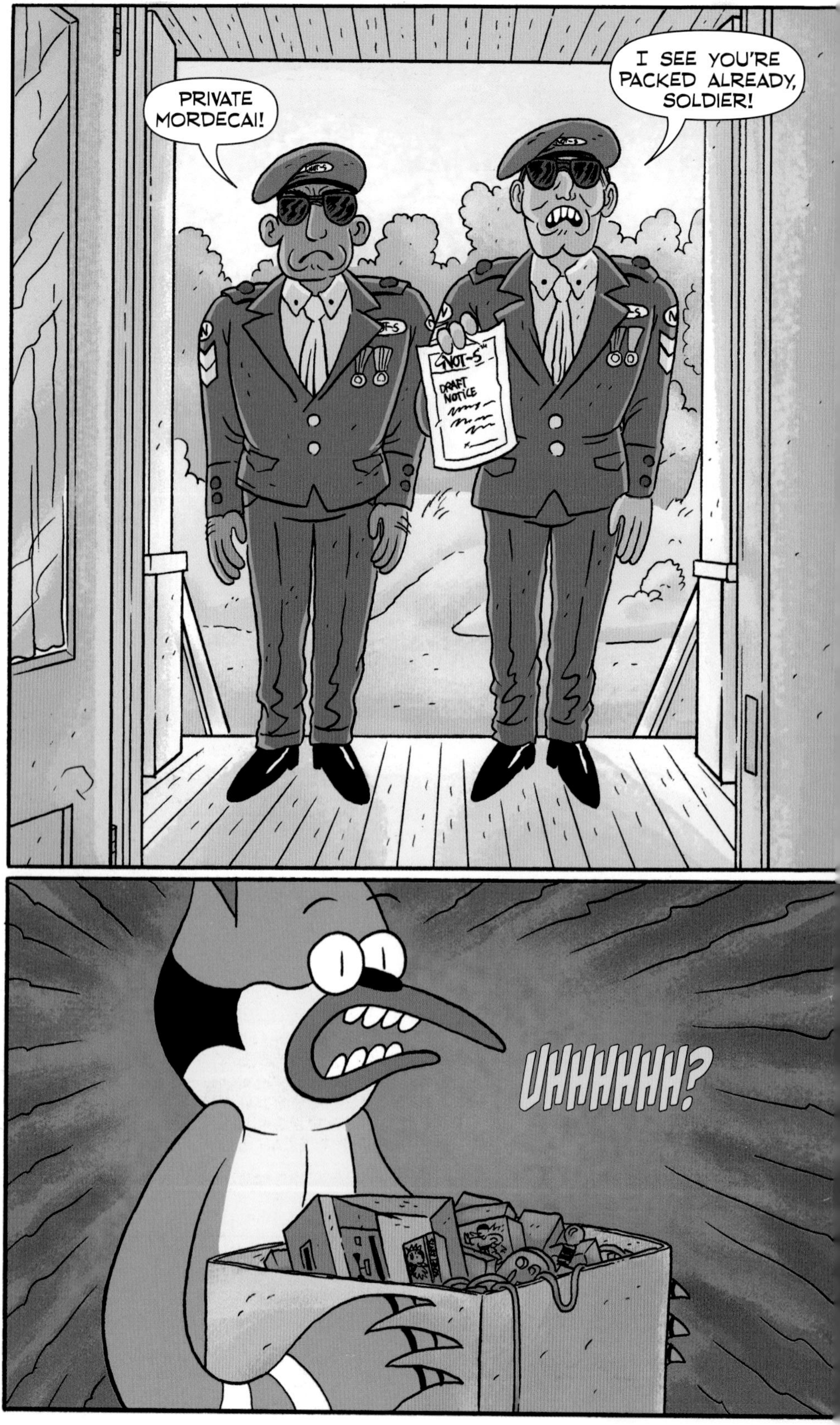
PRIVATE MORDECAI!
I SEE YOU'RE PACKED ALREADY, SOLDIER!
NOT-S
DRAFT NOTICE
UHHHHHH?

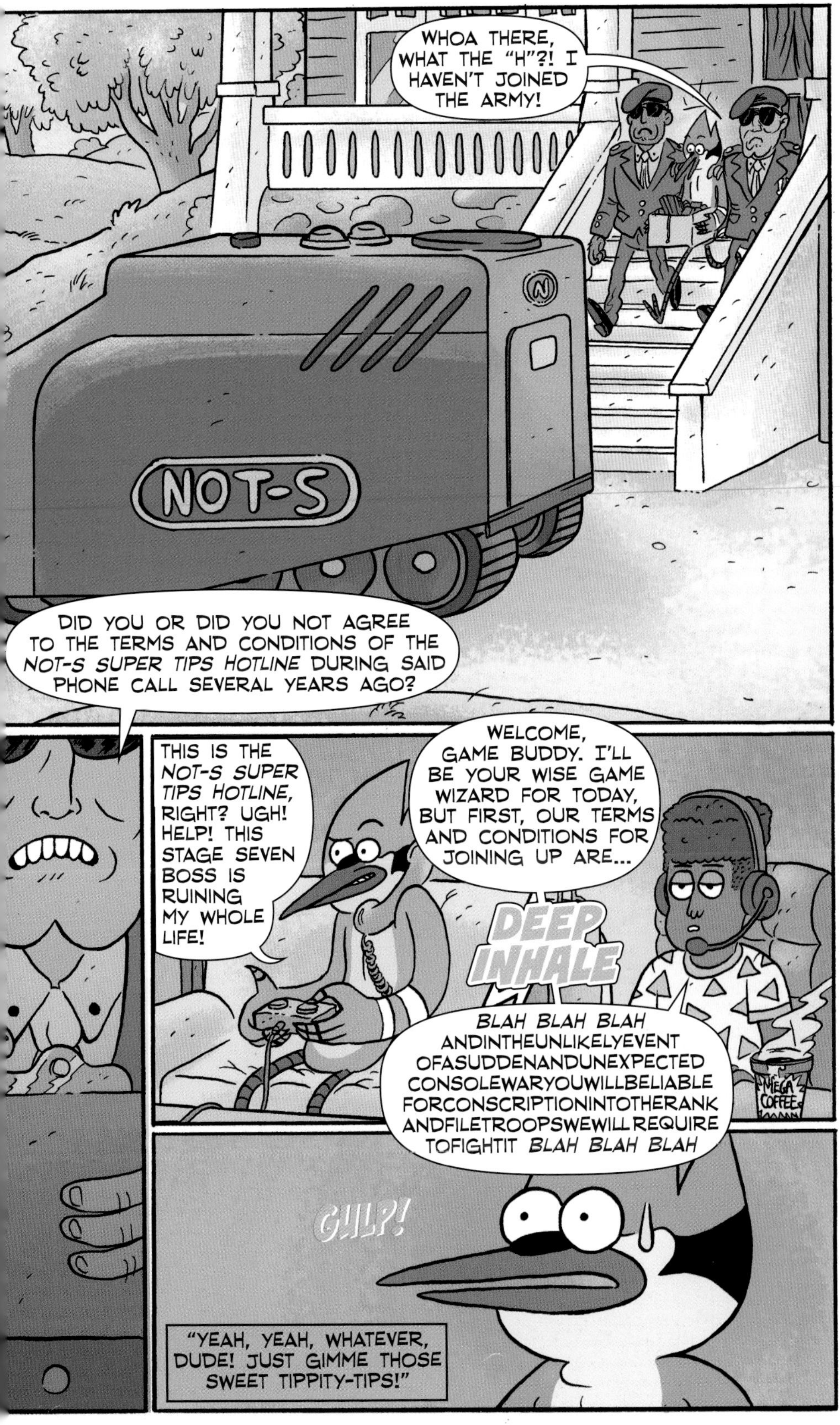
WHOA THERE, WHAT THE "H"?! I HAVEN'T JOINED THE ARMY!
NOT-S
DID YOU OR DID YOU NOT AGREE TO THE TERMS AND CONDITIONS OF THE *NOT-S SUPER TIPS HOTLINE* DURING SAID PHONE CALL SEVERAL YEARS AGO?
THIS IS THE *NOT-S SUPER TIPS HOTLINE*, RIGHT? UGH! HELP! THIS STAGE SEVEN BOSS IS RUINING MY WHOLE LIFE!
WELCOME, GAME BUDDY. I'LL BE YOUR WISE GAME WIZARD FOR TODAY, BUT FIRST, OUR TERMS AND CONDITIONS FOR JOINING UP ARE...
DEEP INHALE
BLAH BLAH BLAH ANDINTHEUNLIKELYEVENT OFASUDDENANDUNEXPECTED CONSOLEWARYOUWILLBELIABLE FORCONSCRIPTIONINTOTHERANK ANDFILETROOPSWEWILLREQUIRE TOFIGHTIT *BLAH BLAH BLAH*
MEGA COFFEE
GULP!
"YEAH, YEAH, WHATEVER, DUDE! JUST GIMME THOSE SWEET TIPPITY-TIPS!"

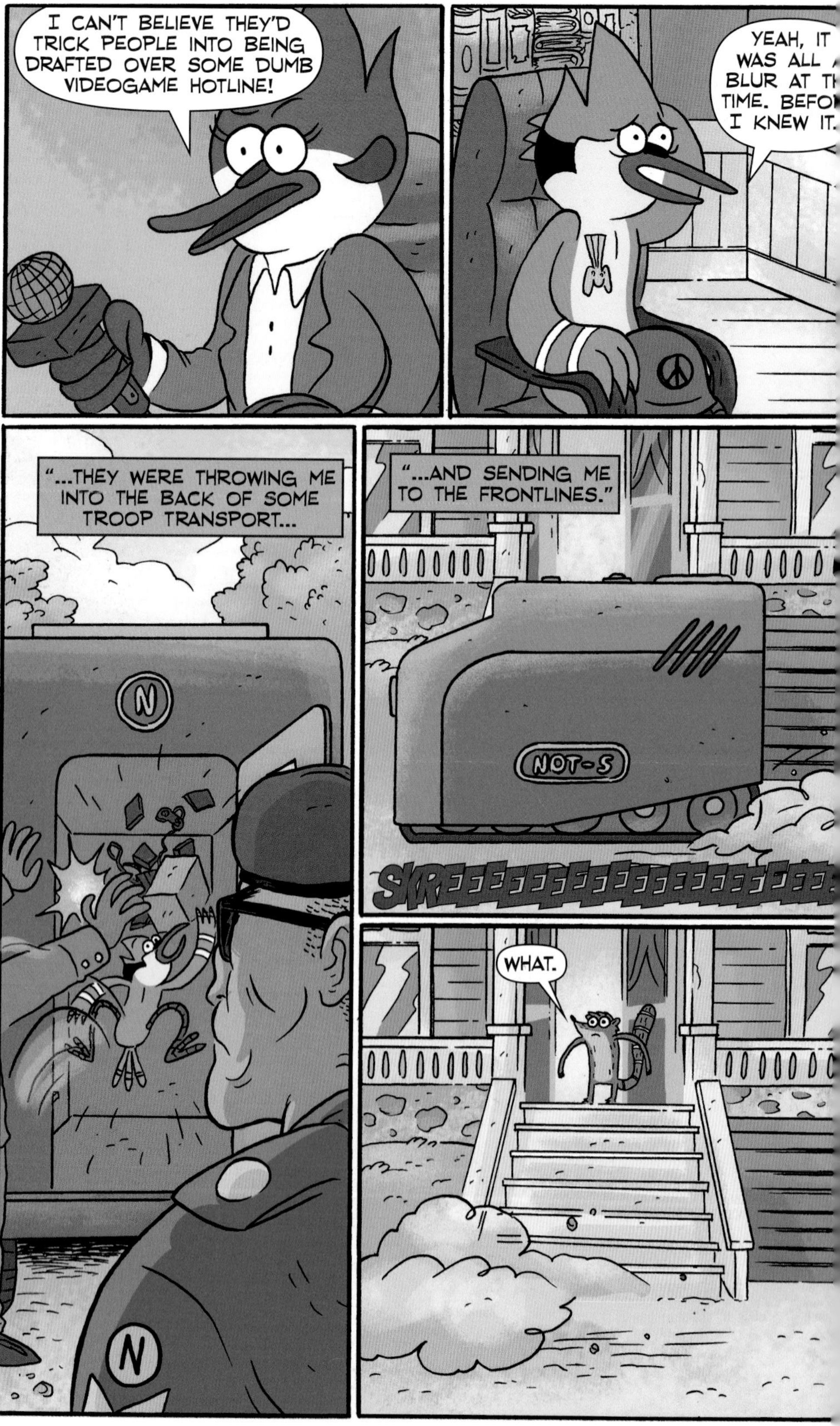
I CAN'T BELIEVE THEY'D TRICK PEOPLE INTO BEING DRAFTED OVER SOME DUMB VIDEOGAME HOTLINE!
YEAH, IT WAS ALL BLUR AT TIME. I KNEW IT.
"...THEY WERE THROWING ME INTO THE BACK OF SOME TROOP TRANSPORT...
"...AND SENDING ME TO THE FRONTLINES."
N
NOT-S
SKREEEEEEEEEEEEEEEEEE
WHAT.
N

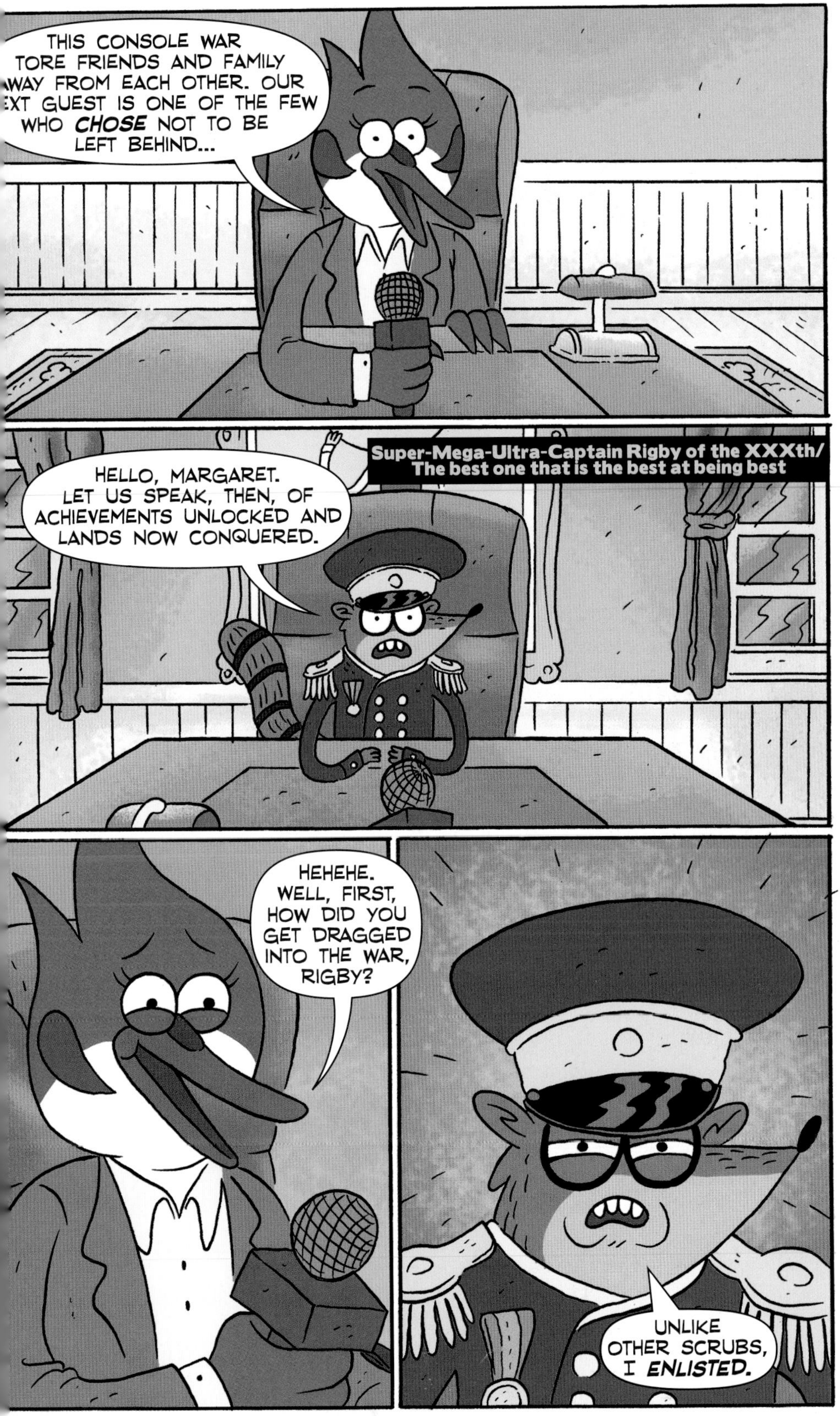
THIS CONSOLE WAR TORE FRIENDS AND FAMILY WAY FROM EACH OTHER. OUR XT GUEST IS ONE OF THE FEW WHO *CHOSE* NOT TO BE LEFT BEHIND...
Super-Mega-Ultra-Captain Rigby of the XXXth/ The best one that is the best at being best
HELLO, MARGARET. LET US SPEAK, THEN, OF ACHIEVEMENTS UNLOCKED AND LANDS NOW CONQUERED.
HEHEHE. WELL, FIRST, HOW DID YOU GET DRAGGED INTO THE WAR, RIGBY?
UNLIKE OTHER SCRUBS, I *ENLISTED.*

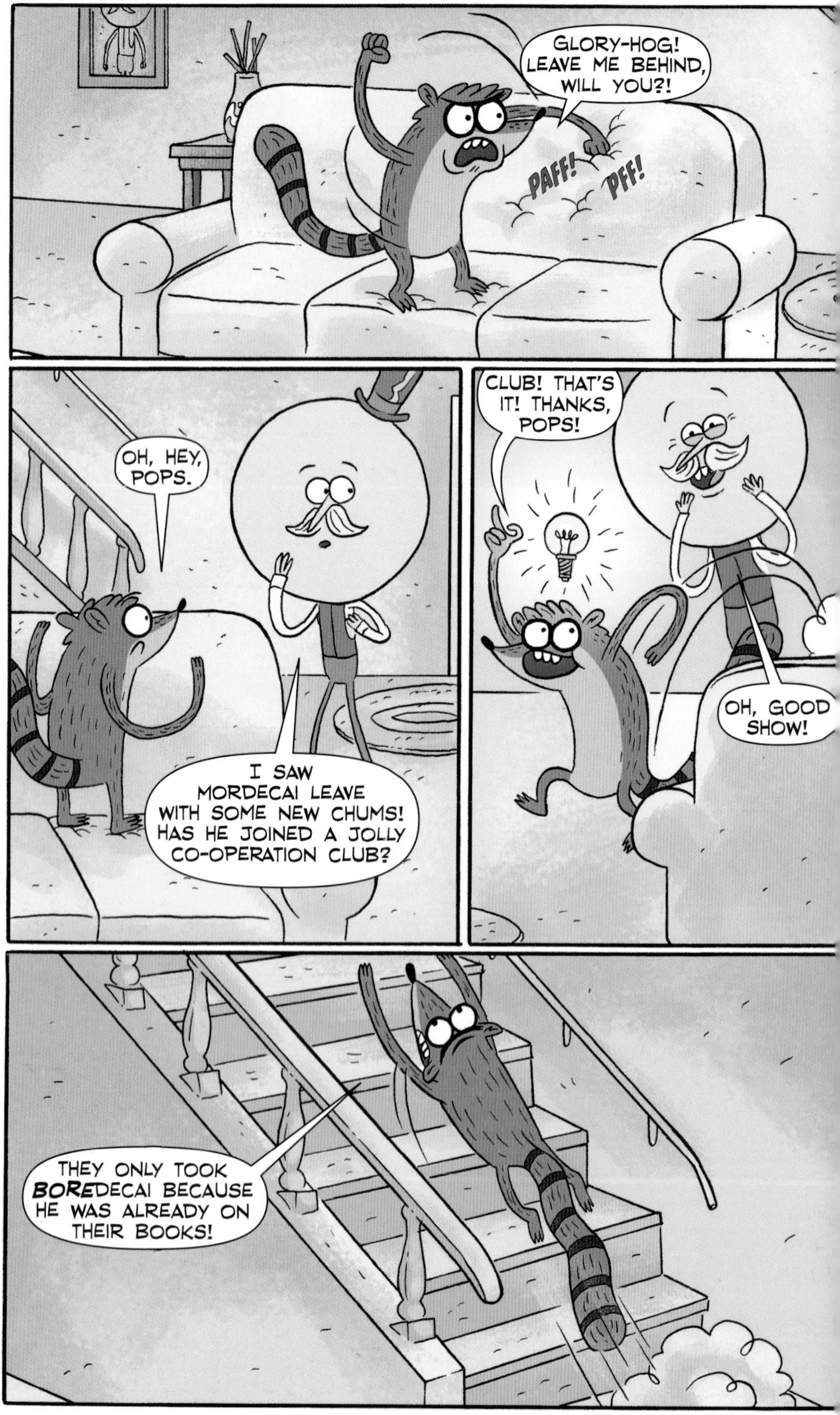
GLORY-HOG! LEAVE ME BEHIND, WILL YOU?!
PAFF!
PFF!
OH, HEY, POPS.
I SAW MORDECAI LEAVE WITH SOME NEW CHUMS! HAS HE JOINED A JOLLY CO-OPERATION CLUB?
CLUB! THAT'S IT! THANKS, POPS!
OH, GOOD SHOW!
THEY ONLY TOOK BOREDECAI BECAUSE HE WAS ALREADY ON THEIR BOOKS!

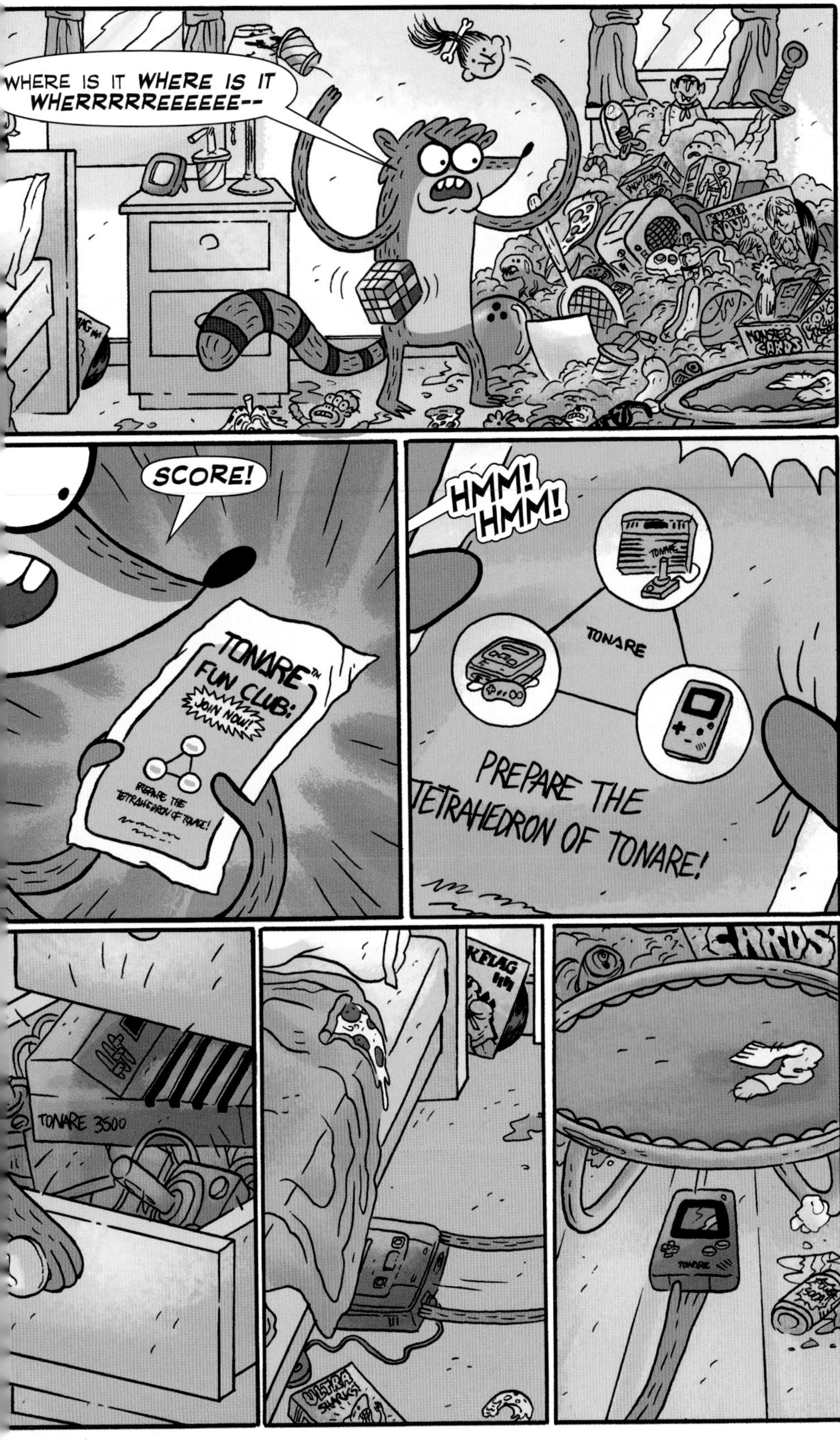
WHERE IS IT WHERE IS IT WHERRRRREEEEEE--
SCORE!
TONARE™ FUN CLUB: JOIN NOW!
PREPARE THE TETRAHEDRON OF TONARE!
HMM! HMM!
TONARE
PREPARE THE TETRAHEDRON OF TONARE!
TONARE 3500
ULTRA SHARKS!
TONARE

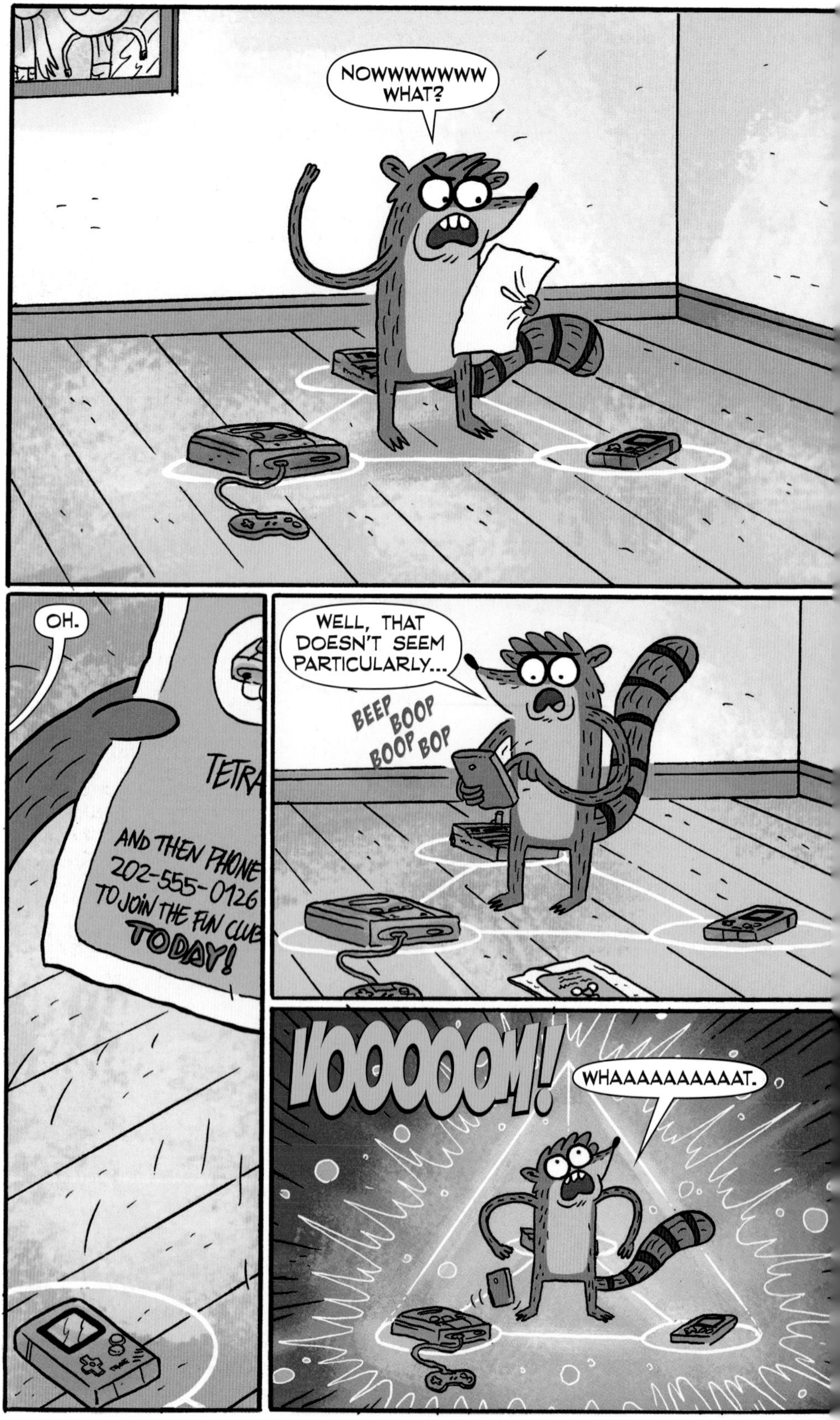
NOWWWWWWW WHAT?
OH.
TETRA
AND THEN PHONE 202-555-0126 TO JOIN THE FUN CLUB TODAY!
WELL, THAT DOESN'T SEEM PARTICULARLY...
BEEP BOOP BOOP BOP
VOOOOOM!
WHAAAAAAAAAAT.

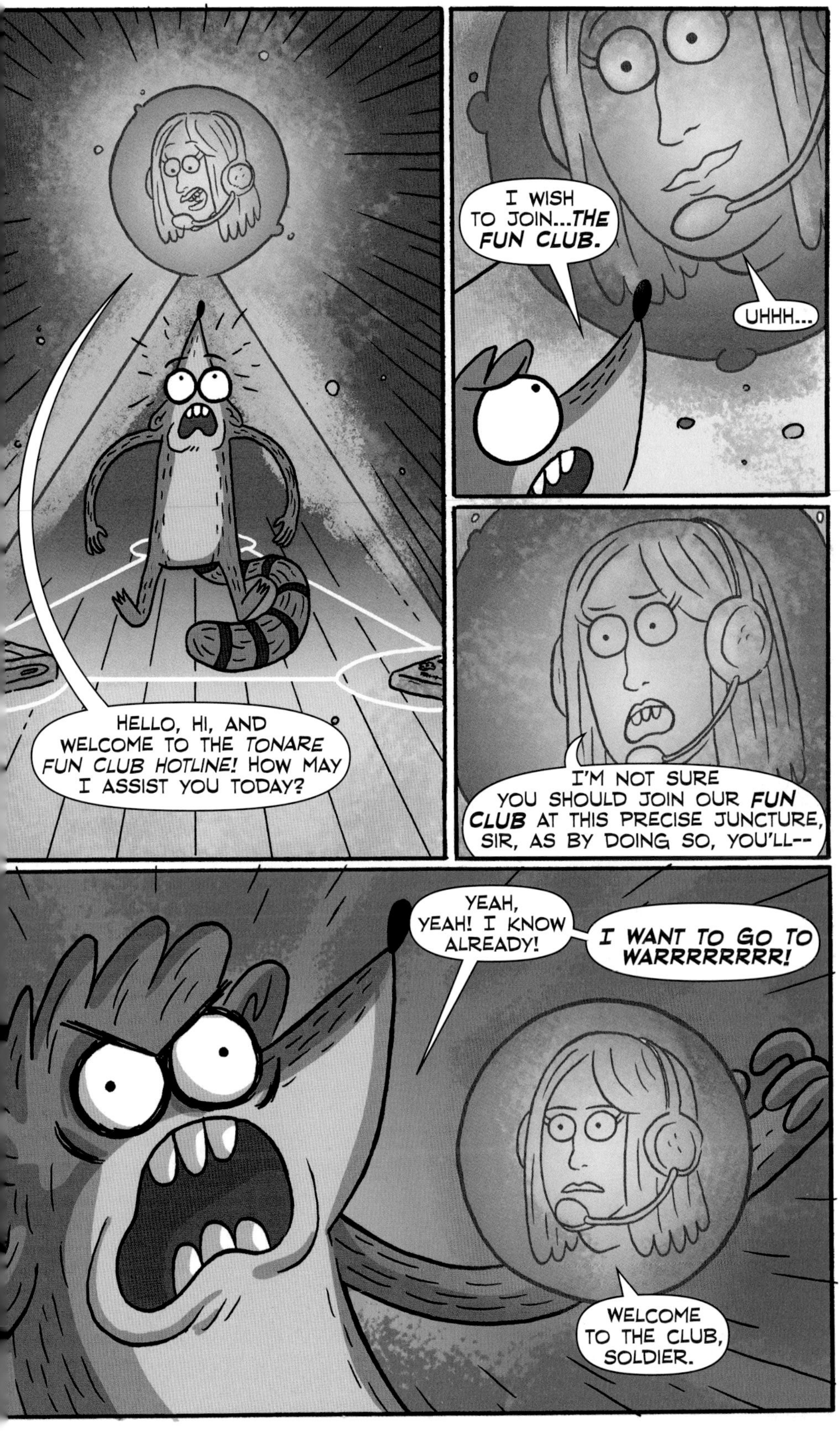
HELLO, HI, AND WELCOME TO THE TONARE FUN CLUB HOTLINE! HOW MAY I ASSIST YOU TODAY?
I WISH TO JOIN...THE FUN CLUB.
UHHH...
I'M NOT SURE YOU SHOULD JOIN OUR FUN CLUB AT THIS PRECISE JUNCTURE, SIR, AS BY DOING SO, YOU'LL--
YEAH, YEAH! I KNOW ALREADY!
I WANT TO GO TO WARRRRRRR!
WELCOME TO THE CLUB, SOLDIER.

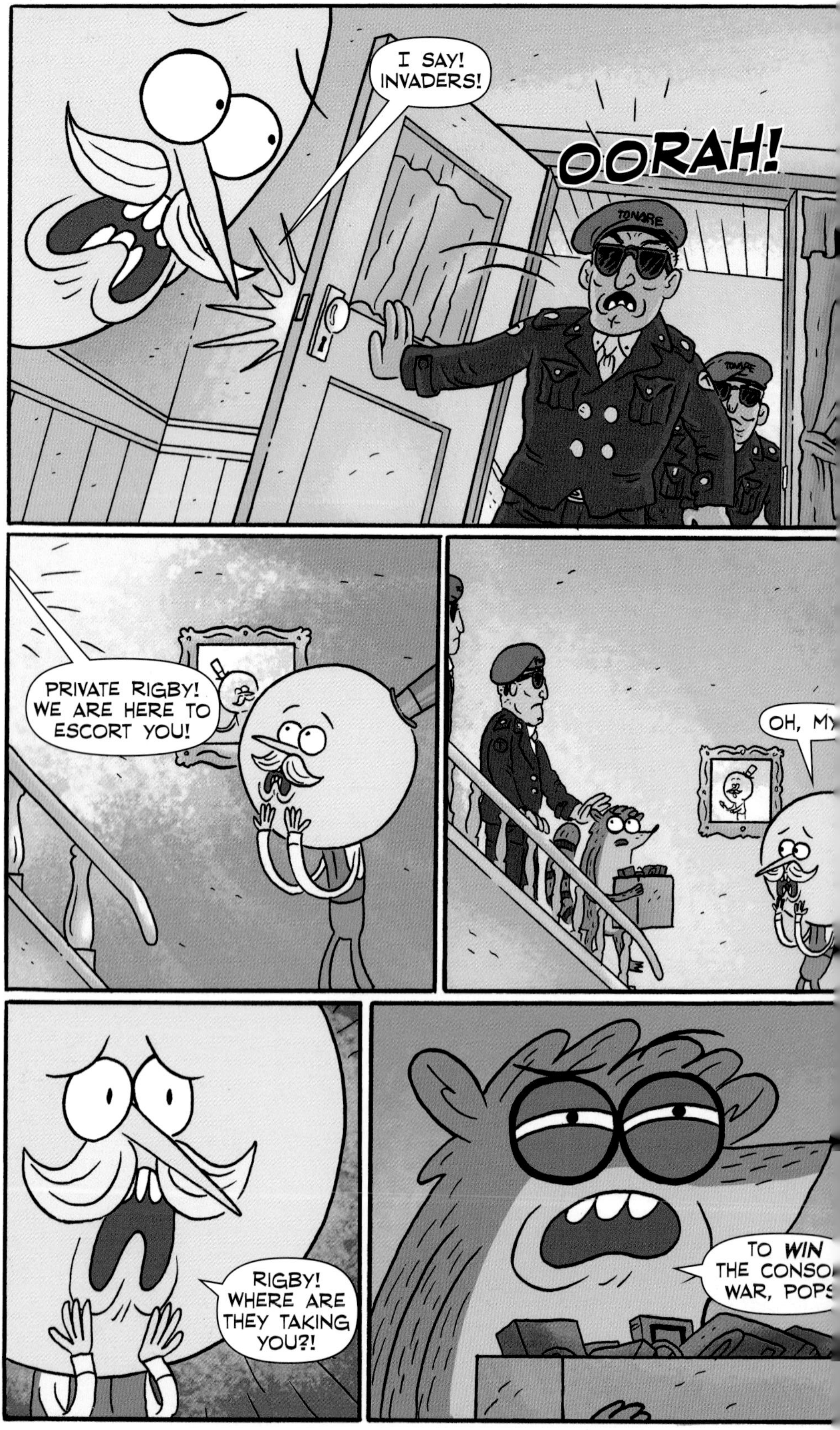
I SAY! INVADERS!
OORAH!
PRIVATE RIGBY! WE ARE HERE TO ESCORT YOU!
RIGBY! WHERE ARE THEY TAKING YOU?!

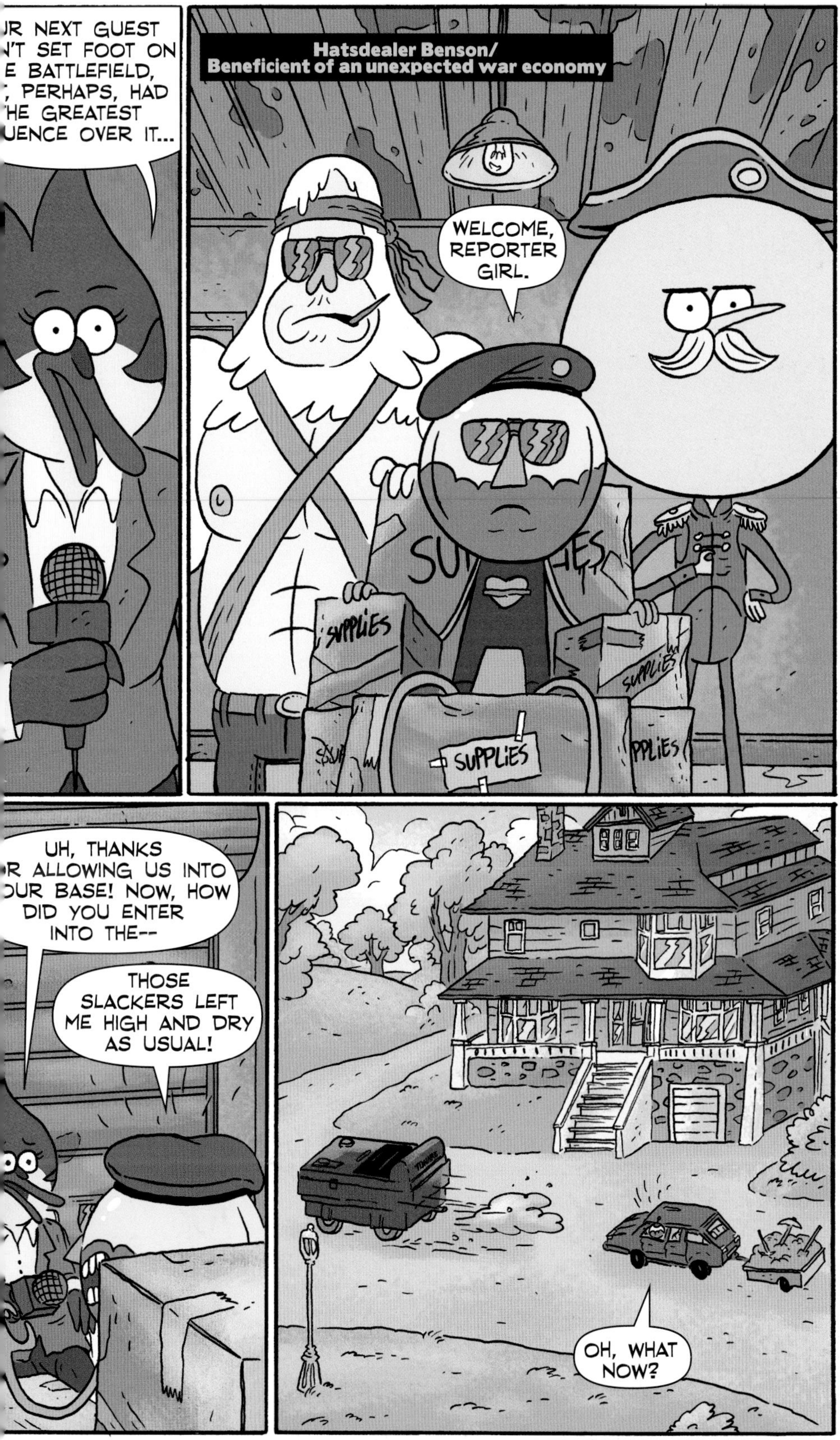

IR NEXT GUEST
N'T SET FOOT ON
E BATTLEFIELD,
, PERHAPS, HAD
HE GREATEST
UENCE OVER IT...
Hatsdealer Benson/
Beneficient of an unexpected war economy
WELCOME, REPORTER GIRL.
SUPPLIES
SUPPLIES
SUPPLIES
SUPPLIES
UH, THANKS
R ALLOWING US INTO
OUR BASE! NOW, HOW
DID YOU ENTER
INTO THE--
THOSE SLACKERS LEFT ME HIGH AND DRY AS USUAL!
OH, WHAT NOW?

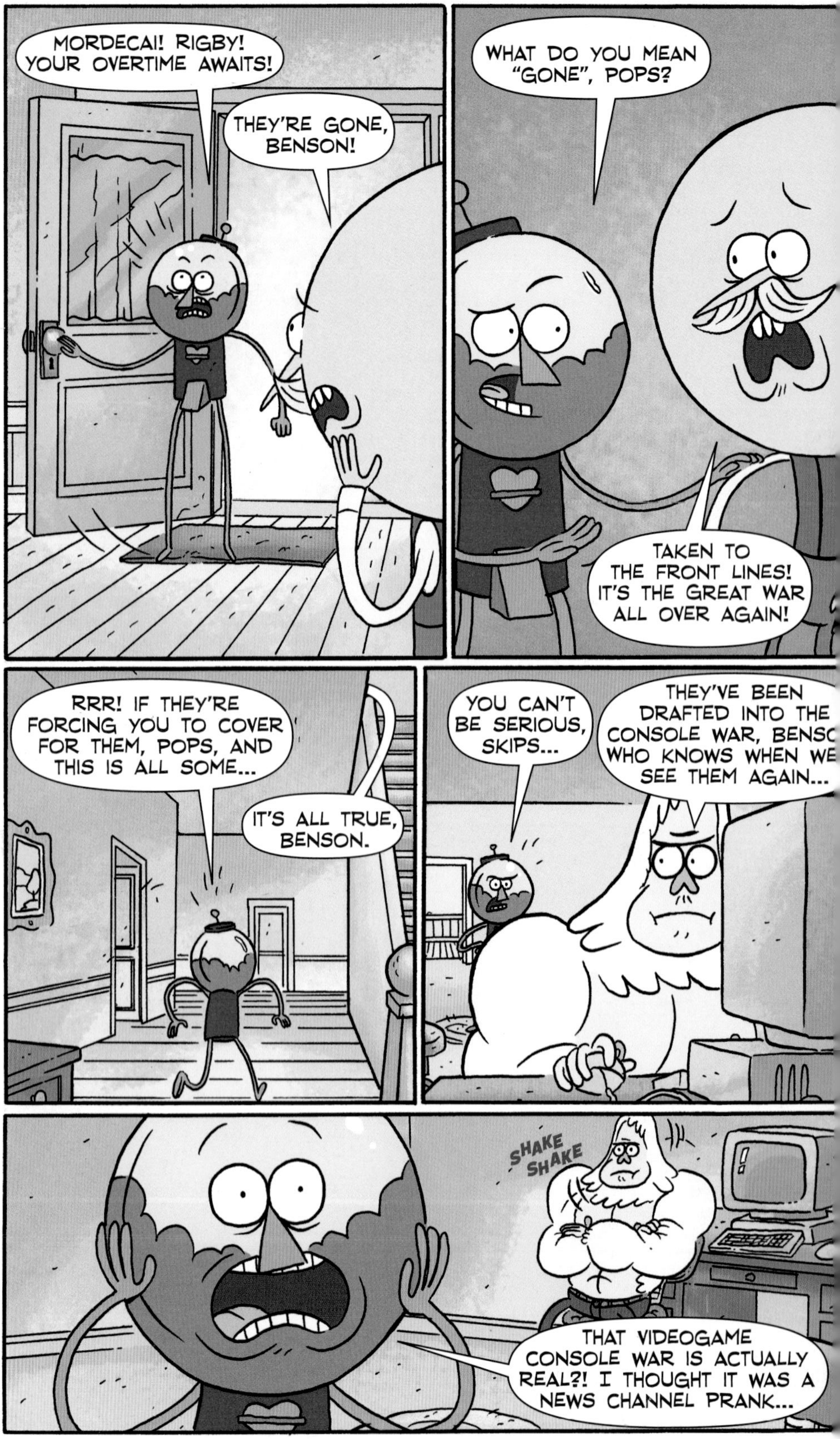
MORDECAI! RIGBY! YOUR OVERTIME AWAITS!
THEY'RE GONE, BENSON!
WHAT DO YOU MEAN "GONE", POPS?
TAKEN TO THE FRONT LINES! IT'S THE GREAT WAR ALL OVER AGAIN!
RRR! IF THEY'RE FORCING YOU TO COVER FOR THEM, POPS, AND THIS IS ALL SOME...
IT'S ALL TRUE, BENSON.
YOU CAN'T BE SERIOUS, SKIPS...
THEY'VE BEEN DRAFTED INTO THE CONSOLE WAR, BENSO WHO KNOWS WHEN WE SEE THEM AGAIN...
SHAKE SHAKE
THAT VIDEOGAME CONSOLE WAR IS ACTUALLY REAL?! I THOUGHT IT WAS A NEWS CHANNEL PRANK...

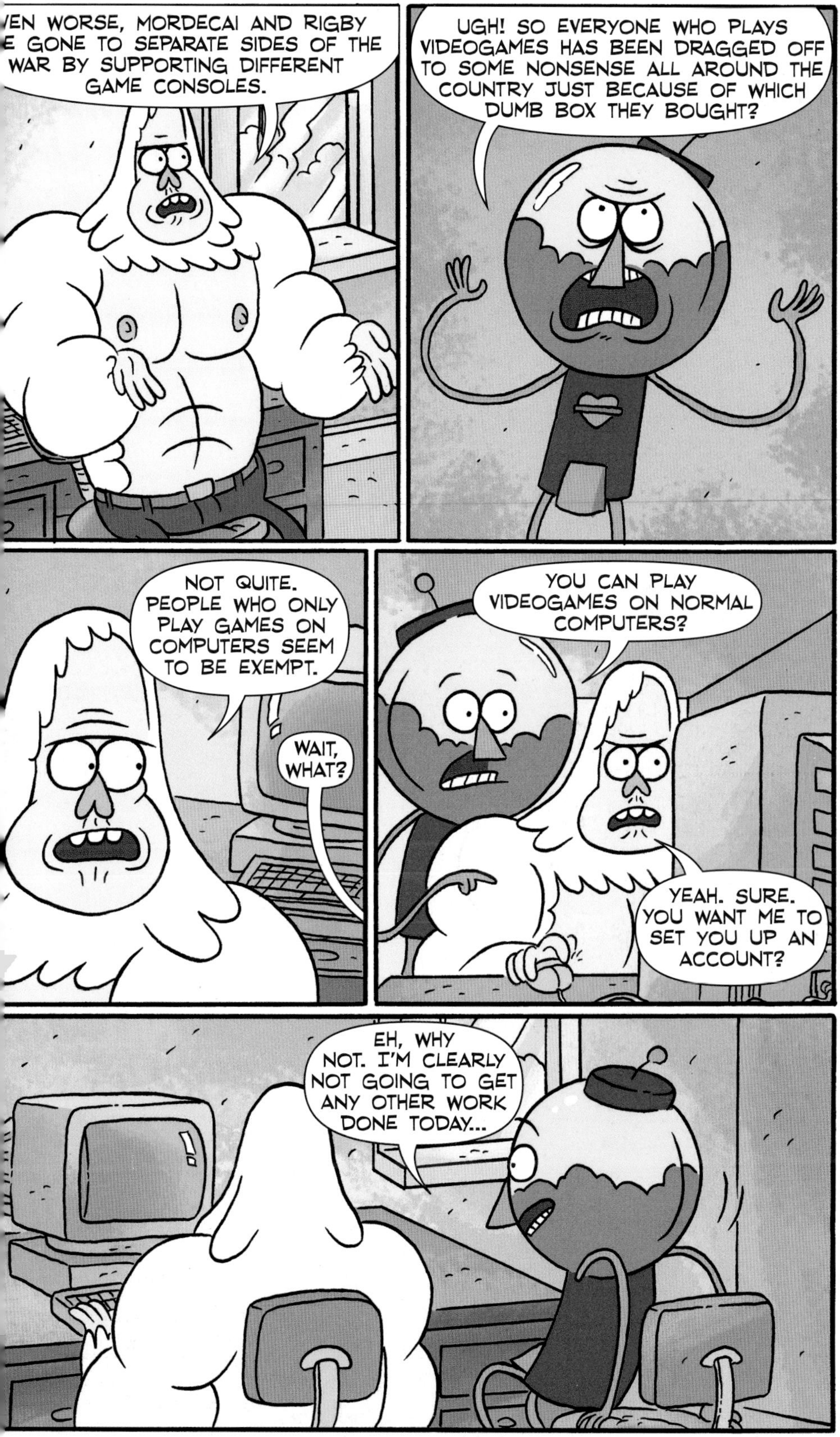

/EN WORSE, MORDECAI AND RIGBY
E GONE TO SEPARATE SIDES OF THE
WAR BY SUPPORTING DIFFERENT
GAME CONSOLES.
UGH! SO EVERYONE WHO PLAYS VIDEOGAMES HAS BEEN DRAGGED OFF TO SOME NONSENSE ALL AROUND THE COUNTRY JUST BECAUSE OF WHICH DUMB BOX THEY BOUGHT?
NOT QUITE. PEOPLE WHO ONLY PLAY GAMES ON COMPUTERS SEEM TO BE EXEMPT.
WAIT, WHAT?
YOU CAN PLAY VIDEOGAMES ON NORMAL COMPUTERS?
YEAH. SURE. YOU WANT ME TO SET YOU UP AN ACCOUNT?
EH, WHY NOT. I'M CLEARLY NOT GOING TO GET ANY OTHER WORK DONE TODAY...

FIRST YOU GOTTA RUN VAPOR...

VAPOR™

...THEN SET UP YER ACCOUNT, AND FINALLY...

POR LOGIN

V™

CREATE A NEW ACCOUNT.

USERNAME BOSSMAN BENSON_

PASSWORD ***********

LOGIN   CANCEL

PAYMENT PLAN   X

METHOD

PAY BUDDY   TIZA   MEGA CARD

$ BUY

...SET UP A PAYMENT PLAN.

IF I HAVE TO. THESE SILLY GAM AREN'T GOING TO COST ME AN AND A LEG, ARE THEY?

NAH. GAMES ARE ALWAYS CHEAPER ON P.C., ACTUALLY. GREAT TIP FROM TECHMO. THERE, YOU'RE ALL SET UP.

WOW. THIS CATEGORY OF GAMES SAYS THEY'RE **FREE?**

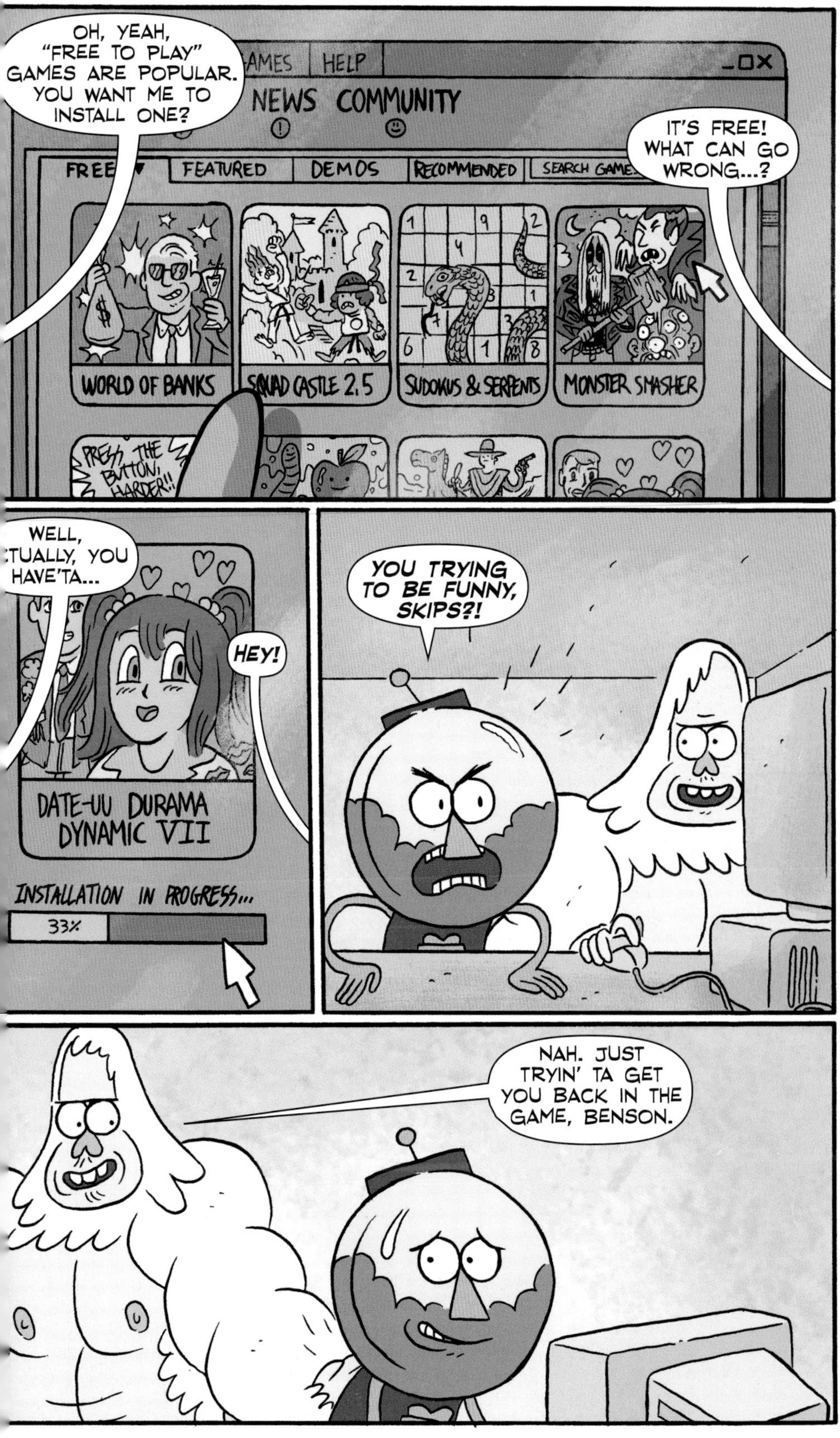
OH, YEAH, "FREE TO PLAY" GAMES ARE POPULAR. YOU WANT ME TO INSTALL ONE?
GAMES
HELP
NEWS
COMMUNITY
FREE
FEATURED
DEMOS
RECOMMENDED
SEARCH GAMES
IT'S FREE! WHAT CAN GO WRONG...?
WORLD OF BANKS
SQUAD CASTLE 2.5
SUDOKUS & SERPENTS
MONSTER SMASHER
PRESS THE BUTTON, HARDER!!
WELL, ...TUALLY, YOU HAVE'TA...
DATE-UU DURAMA DYNAMIC VII
HEY!
INSTALLATION IN PROGRESS...
33%
YOU TRYING TO BE FUNNY, SKIPS?!
NAH. JUST TRYIN' TA GET YOU BACK IN THE GAME, BENSON.

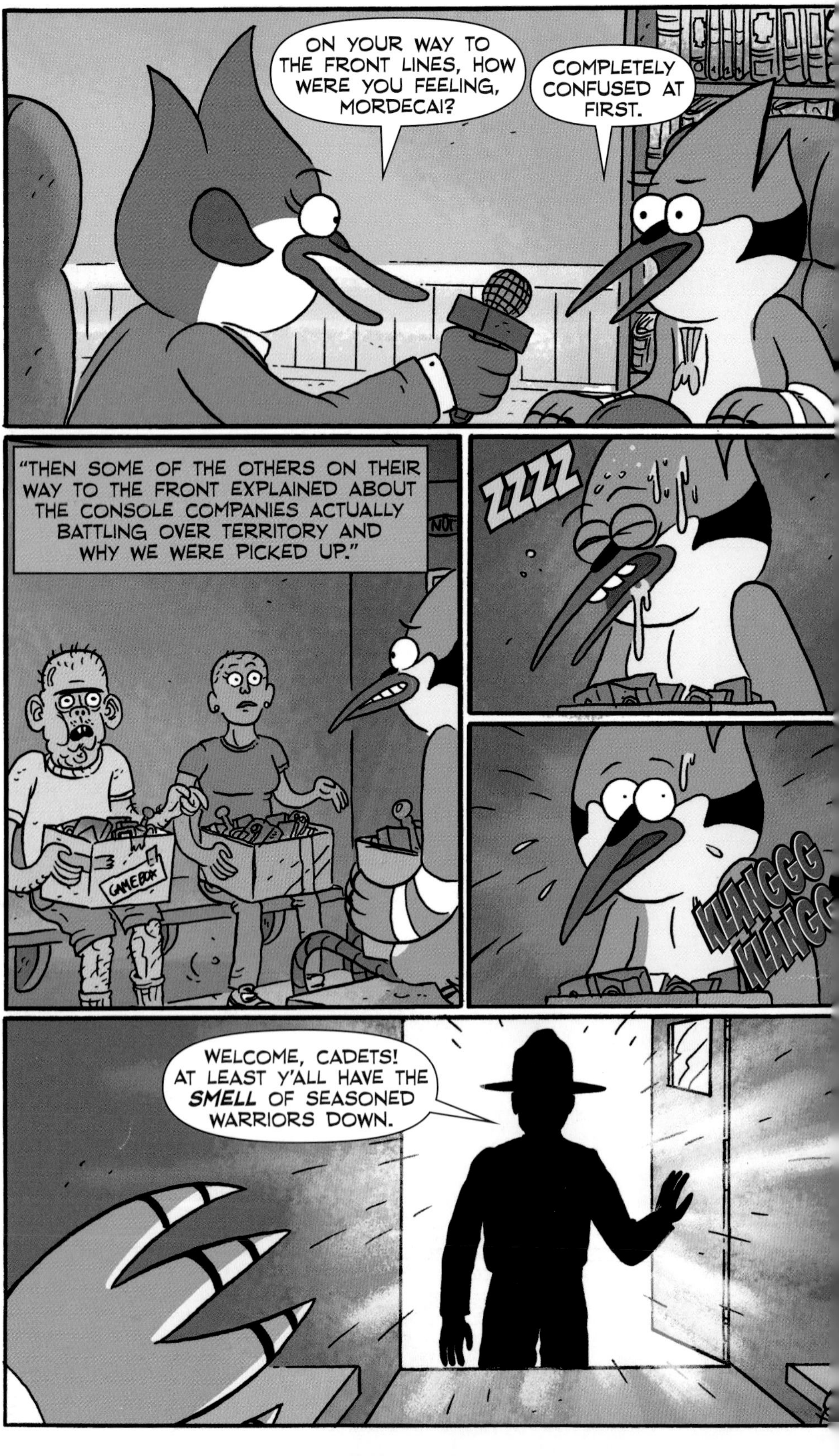
ON YOUR WAY TO THE FRONT LINES, HOW WERE YOU FEELING, MORDECAI?
COMPLETELY CONFUSED AT FIRST.
"THEN SOME OF THE OTHERS ON THEIR WAY TO THE FRONT EXPLAINED ABOUT THE CONSOLE COMPANIES ACTUALLY BATTLING OVER TERRITORY AND WHY WE WERE PICKED UP."
GAMEBOX
ZZZZ
KLANGGG
KLANGG
WELCOME, CADETS! AT LEAST Y'ALL HAVE THE *SMELL* OF SEASONED WARRIORS DOWN.

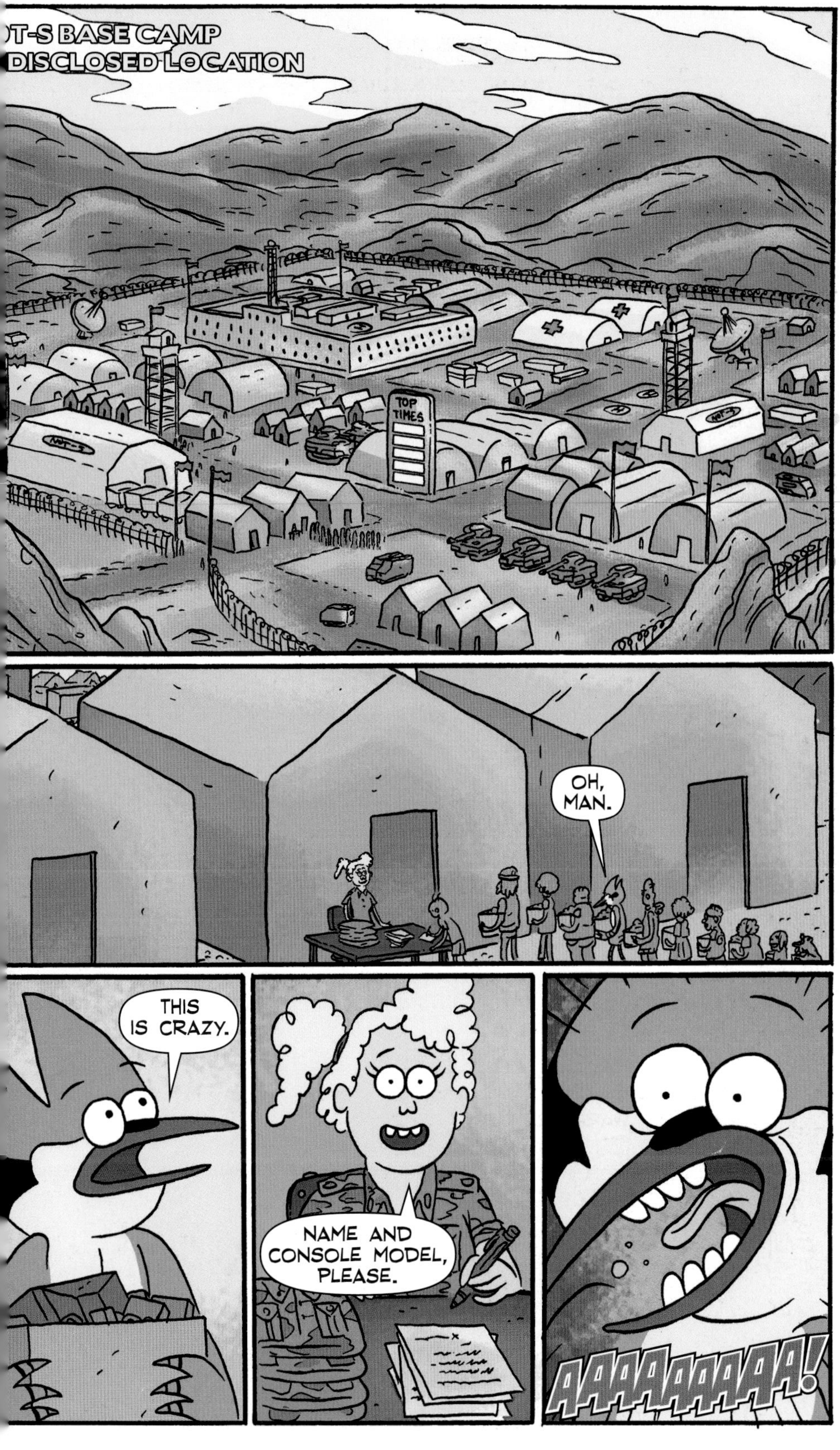
T-S BASE CAMP
DISCLOSED LOCATION
TOP TIMES
OH, MAN.
THIS IS CRAZY.
NAME AND CONSOLE MODEL, PLEASE.
AAAAAAAAA!

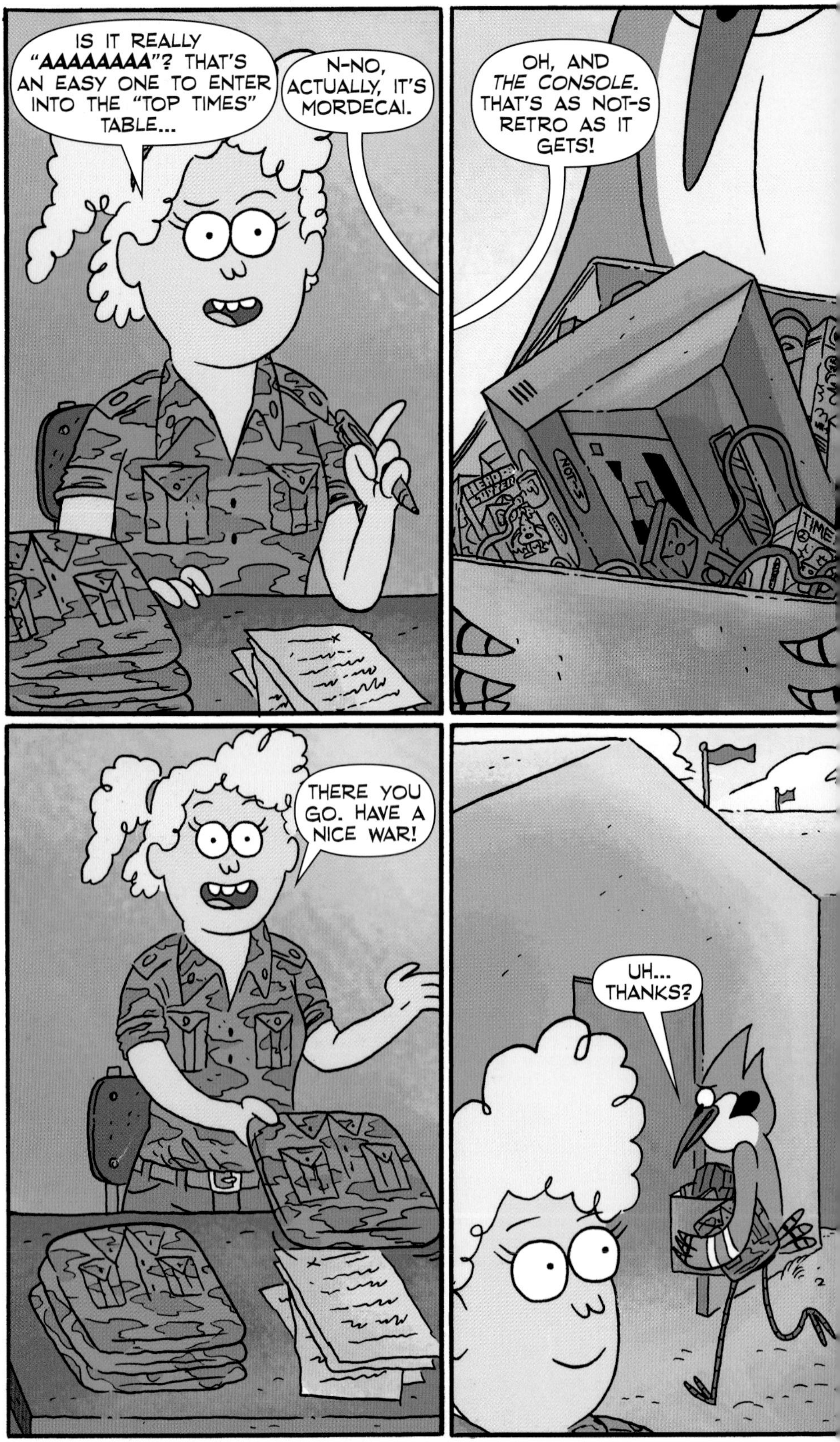
IS IT REALLY "AAAAAAAA"? THAT'S AN EASY ONE TO ENTER INTO THE "TOP TIMES" TABLE...
N-NO, ACTUALLY, IT'S MORDECAI.
OH, AND *THE CONSOLE.* THAT'S AS NOT-S RETRO AS IT GETS!
NOT-S
THERE YOU GO. HAVE A NICE WAR!
UH... THANKS?

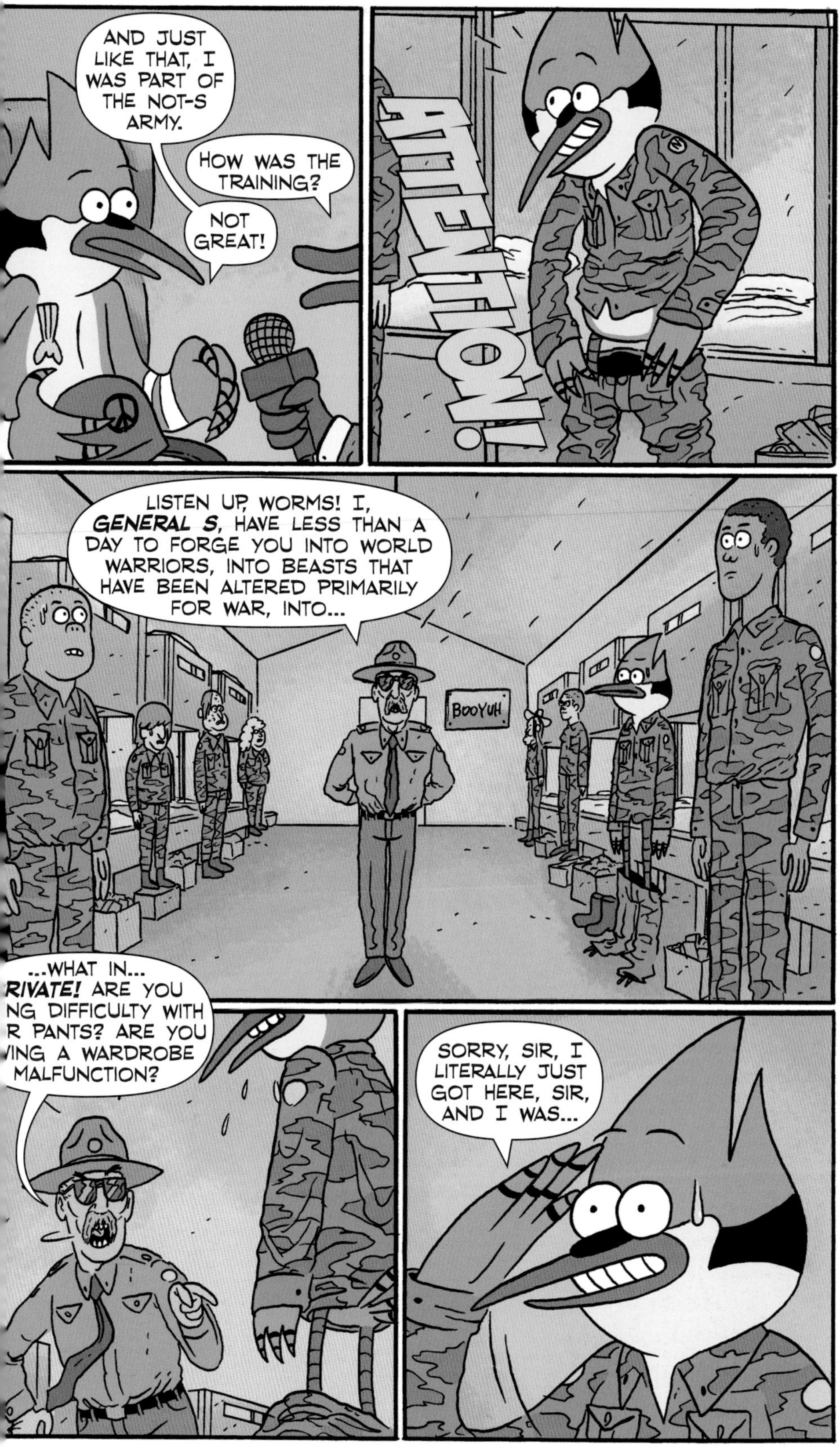
AND JUST LIKE THAT, I WAS PART OF THE NOT-S ARMY.
HOW WAS THE TRAINING?
NOT GREAT!
ATTENTION!
LISTEN UP, WORMS! I, GENERAL S, HAVE LESS THAN A DAY TO FORGE YOU INTO WORLD WARRIORS, INTO BEASTS THAT HAVE BEEN ALTERED PRIMARILY FOR WAR, INTO...
BOOYUH
...WHAT IN... RIVATE! ARE YOU NG DIFFICULTY WITH R PANTS? ARE YOU ING A WARDROBE MALFUNCTION?
SORRY, SIR, I LITERALLY JUST GOT HERE, SIR, AND I WAS...

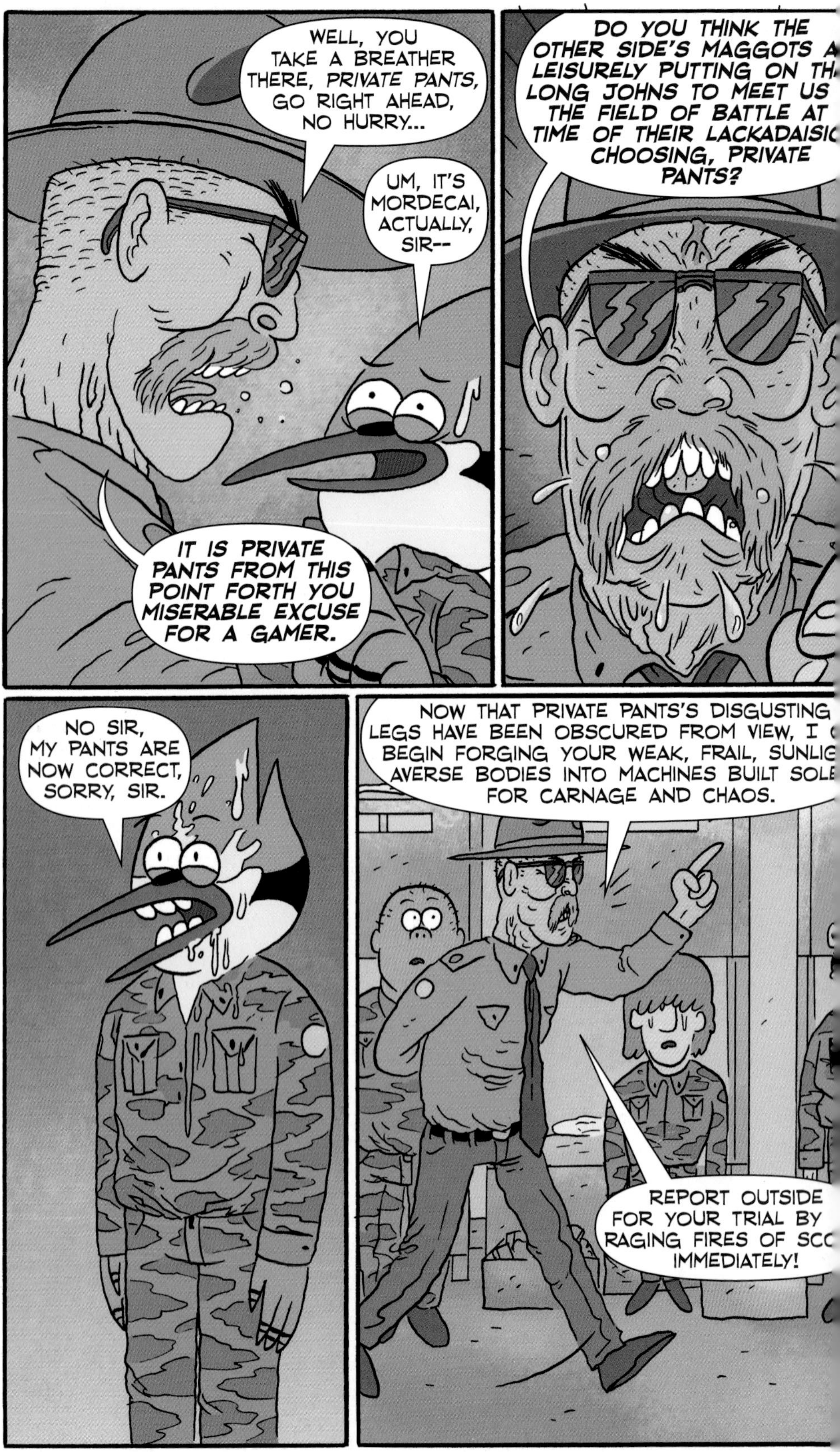
WELL, YOU TAKE A BREATHER THERE, *PRIVATE PANTS,* GO RIGHT AHEAD, NO HURRY...
UM, IT'S MORDECAI, ACTUALLY, SIR--
IT IS PRIVATE PANTS FROM THIS POINT FORTH YOU MISERABLE EXCUSE FOR A GAMER.
DO YOU THINK THE OTHER SIDE'S MAGGOTS A LEISURELY PUTTING ON TH LONG JOHNS TO MEET US THE FIELD OF BATTLE AT TIME OF THEIR LACKADAISIC CHOOSING, PRIVATE PANTS?
NO SIR, MY PANTS ARE NOW CORRECT, SORRY, SIR.
NOW THAT PRIVATE PANTS'S DISGUSTING LEGS HAVE BEEN OBSCURED FROM VIEW, I C BEGIN FORGING YOUR WEAK, FRAIL, SUNLIG AVERSE BODIES INTO MACHINES BUILT SOLE FOR CARNAGE AND CHAOS.
REPORT OUTSIDE FOR YOUR TRIAL BY RAGING FIRES OF SCO IMMEDIATELY!

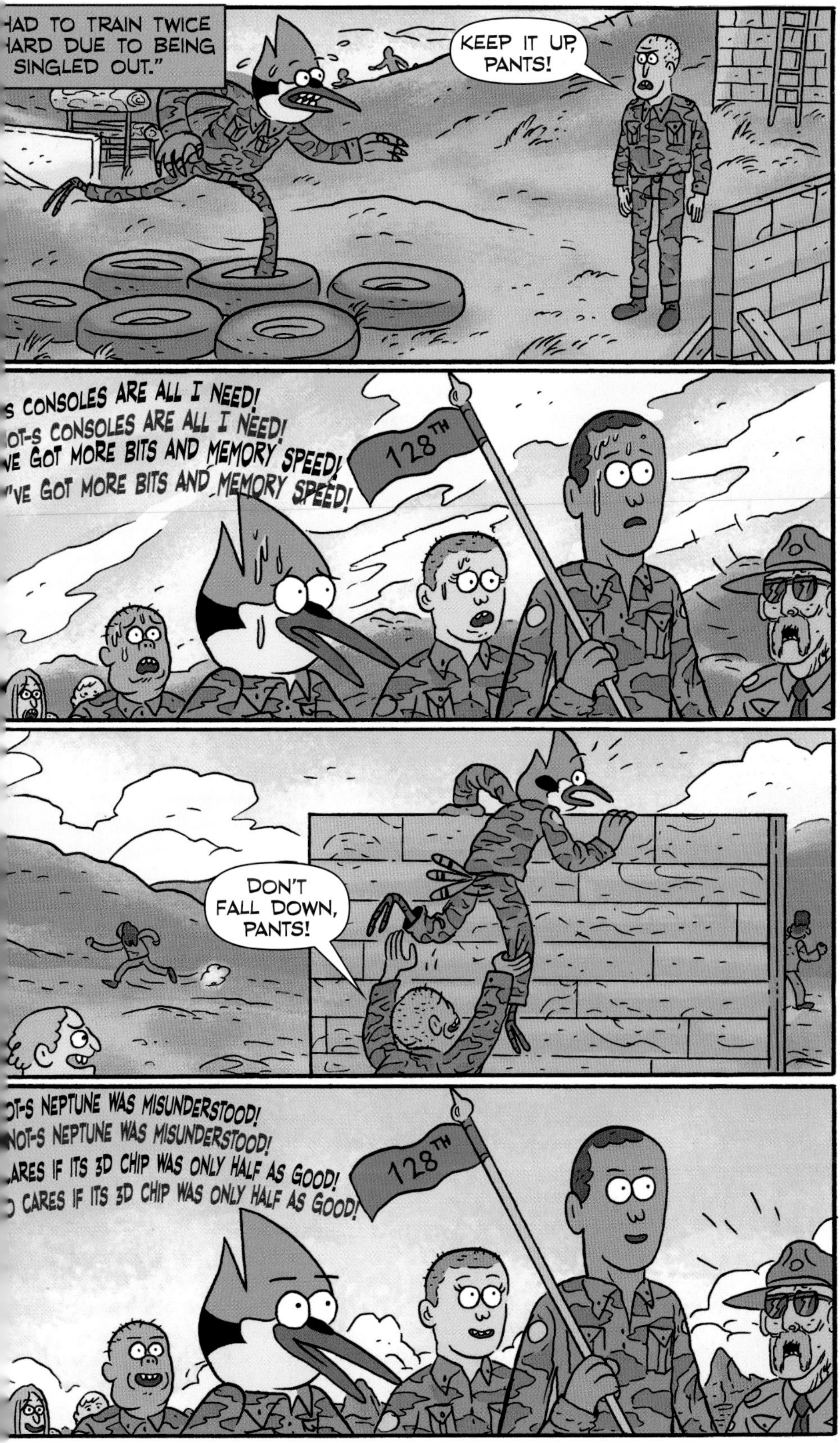

HAD TO TRAIN TWICE HARD DUE TO BEING SINGLED OUT."
KEEP IT UP, PANTS!
S CONSOLES ARE ALL I NEED!
OT-S CONSOLES ARE ALL I NEED!
VE GOT MORE BITS AND MEMORY SPEED!
'VE GOT MORE BITS AND MEMORY SPEED!
128TH
DON'T FALL DOWN, PANTS!
OT-S NEPTUNE WAS MISUNDERSTOOD!
NOT-S NEPTUNE WAS MISUNDERSTOOD!
ARES IF ITS 3D CHIP WAS ONLY HALF AS GOOD!
O CARES IF ITS 3D CHIP WAS ONLY HALF AS GOOD!
128TH

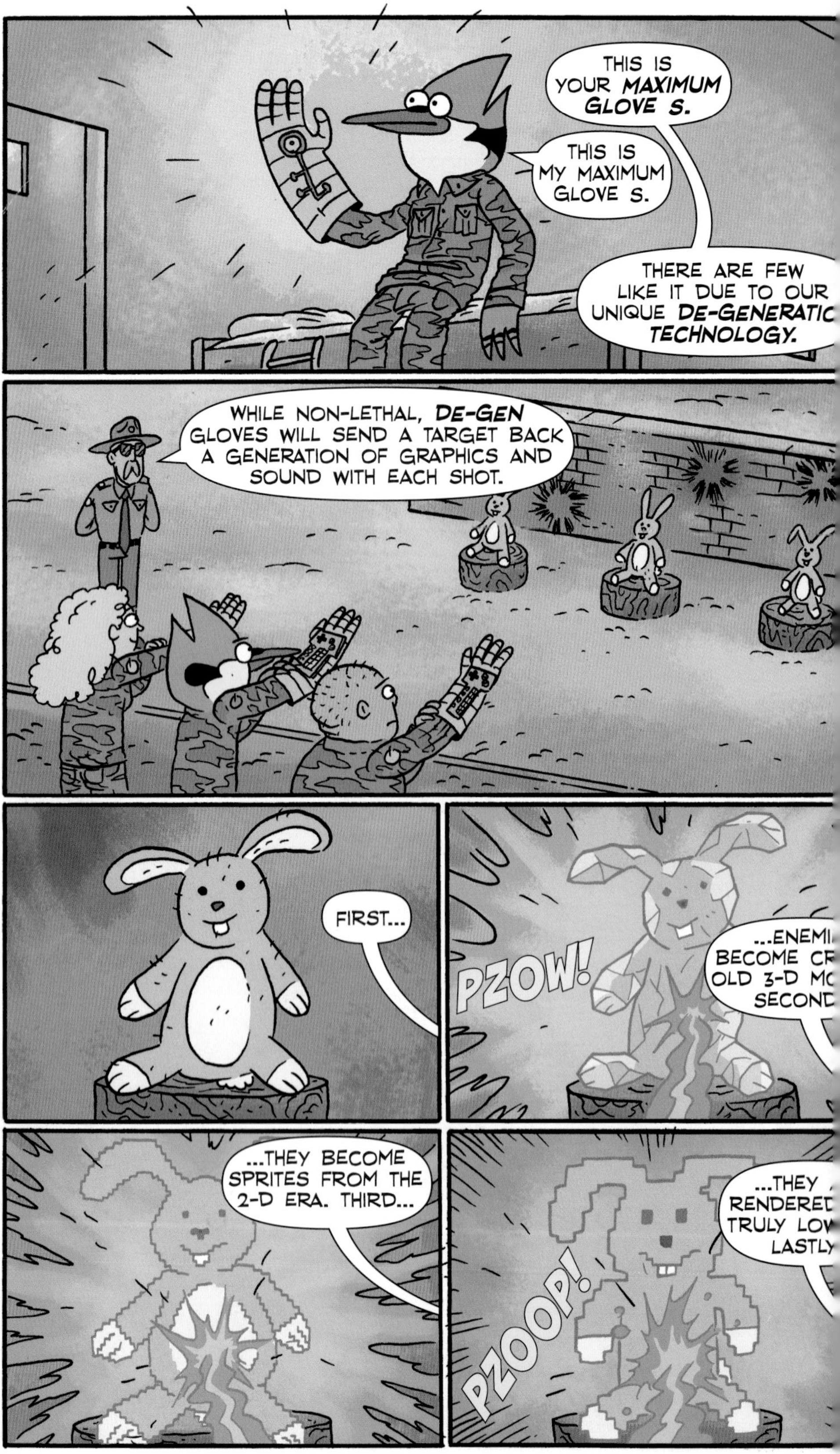
THIS IS YOUR MAXIMUM GLOVE S.
THIS IS MY MAXIMUM GLOVE S.
THERE ARE FEW LIKE IT DUE TO OUR UNIQUE DE-GENERATIC TECHNOLOGY.
WHILE NON-LETHAL, DE-GEN GLOVES WILL SEND A TARGET BACK A GENERATION OF GRAPHICS AND SOUND WITH EACH SHOT.
FIRST...
PZOW!
...ENEMI BECOME CR OLD 3-D MO SECOND
...THEY BECOME SPRITES FROM THE 2-D ERA. THIRD...
PZOOP!
...THEY RENDERED TRULY LOW LASTLY

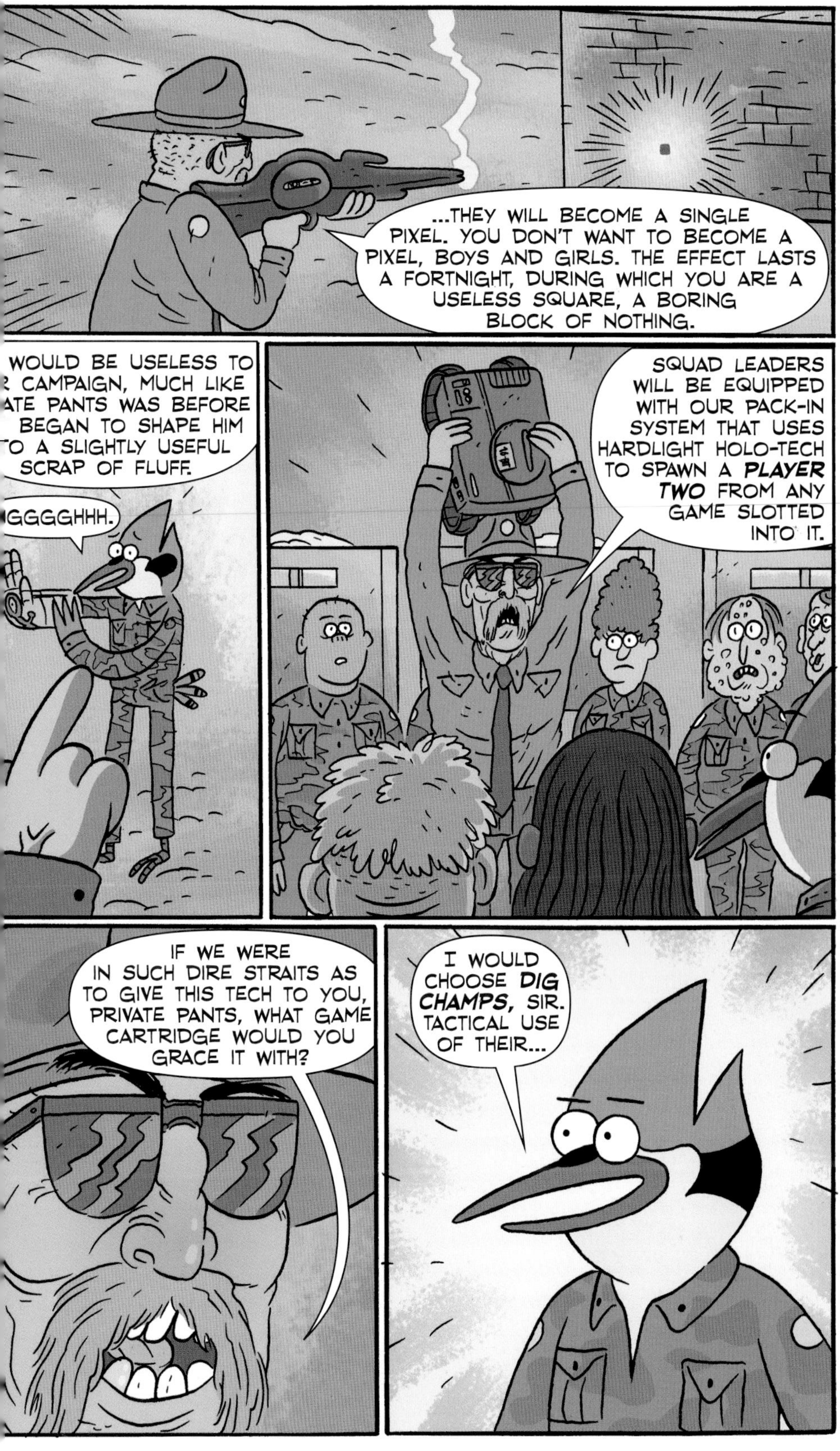
...THEY WILL BECOME A SINGLE PIXEL. YOU DON'T WANT TO BECOME A PIXEL, BOYS AND GIRLS. THE EFFECT LASTS A FORTNIGHT, DURING WHICH YOU ARE A USELESS SQUARE, A BORING BLOCK OF NOTHING.
WOULD BE USELESS TO
CAMPAIGN, MUCH LIKE
ATE PANTS WAS BEFORE
BEGAN TO SHAPE HIM
O A SLIGHTLY USEFUL
SCRAP OF FLUFF.
GGGGHHH.
SQUAD LEADERS WILL BE EQUIPPED WITH OUR PACK-IN SYSTEM THAT USES HARDLIGHT HOLO-TECH TO SPAWN A ***PLAYER TWO*** FROM ANY GAME SLOTTED INTO IT.
IF WE WERE IN SUCH DIRE STRAITS AS TO GIVE THIS TECH TO YOU, PRIVATE PANTS, WHAT GAME CARTRIDGE WOULD YOU GRACE IT WITH?
I WOULD CHOOSE ***DIG CHAMPS,*** SIR. TACTICAL USE OF THEIR...

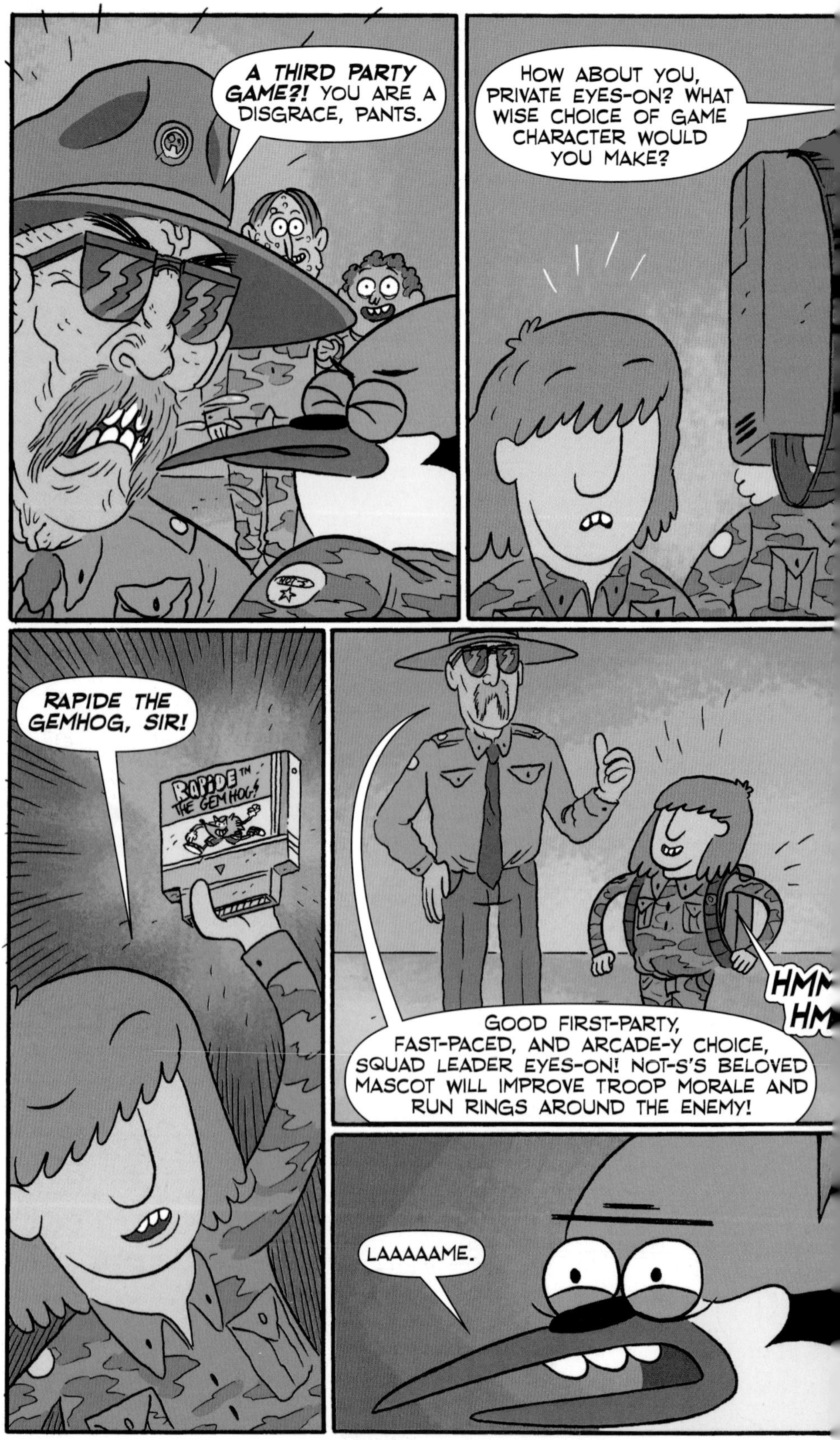
A THIRD PARTY GAME?! YOU ARE A DISGRACE, PANTS.
HOW ABOUT YOU, PRIVATE EYES-ON? WHAT WISE CHOICE OF GAME CHARACTER WOULD YOU MAKE?
RAPIDE THE GEMHOG, SIR!
RAPIDE™ THE GEM HOG!
GOOD FIRST-PARTY, FAST-PACED, AND ARCADE-Y CHOICE, SQUAD LEADER EYES-ON! NOT-S'S BELOVED MASCOT WILL IMPROVE TROOP MORALE AND RUN RINGS AROUND THE ENEMY!
LAAAAAME.

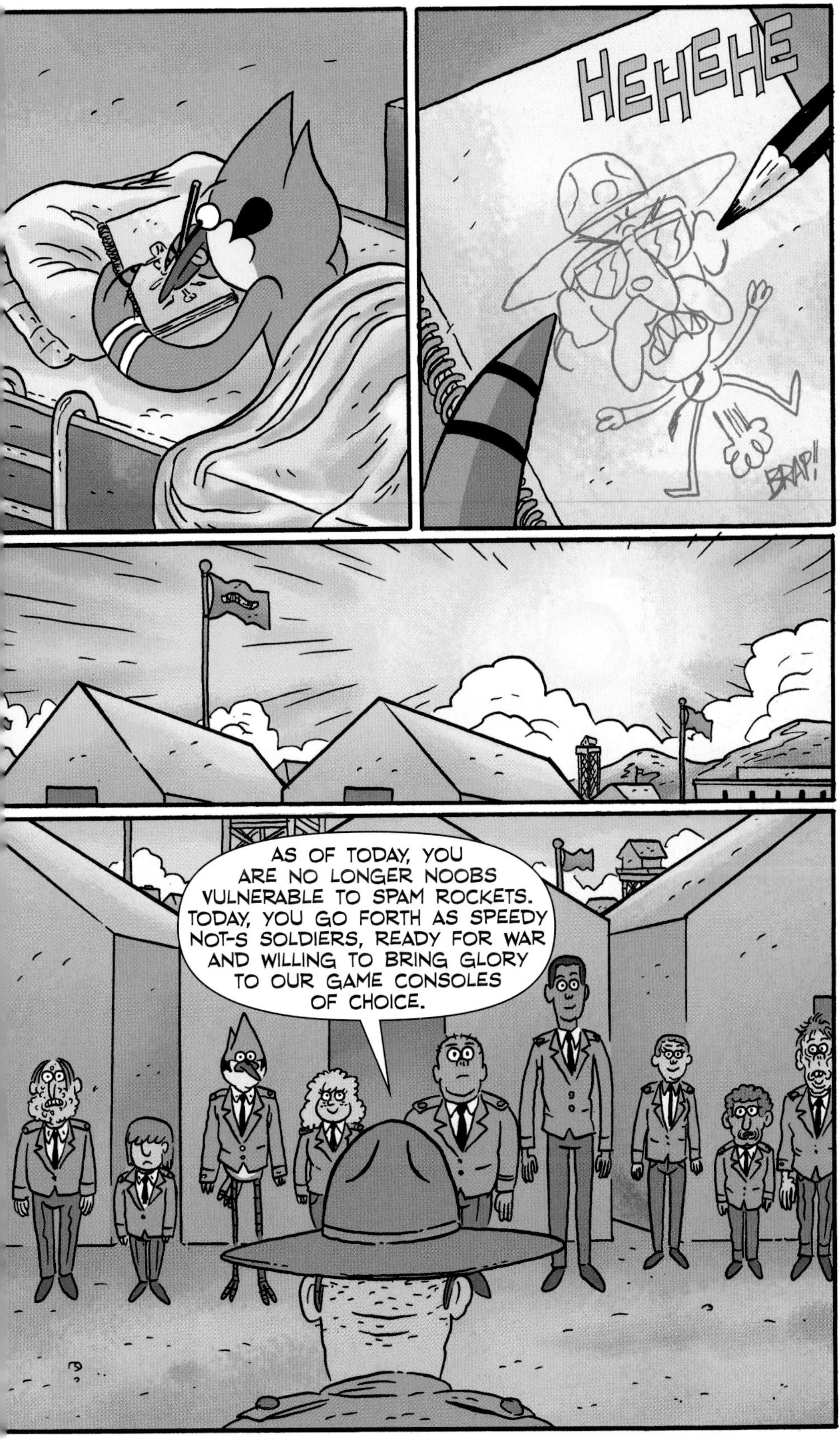
HEHEHE
BRAP!!
AS OF TODAY, YOU ARE NO LONGER NOOBS VULNERABLE TO SPAM ROCKETS. TODAY, YOU GO FORTH AS SPEEDY NOT-S SOLDIERS, READY FOR WAR AND WILLING TO BRING GLORY TO OUR GAME CONSOLES OF CHOICE.

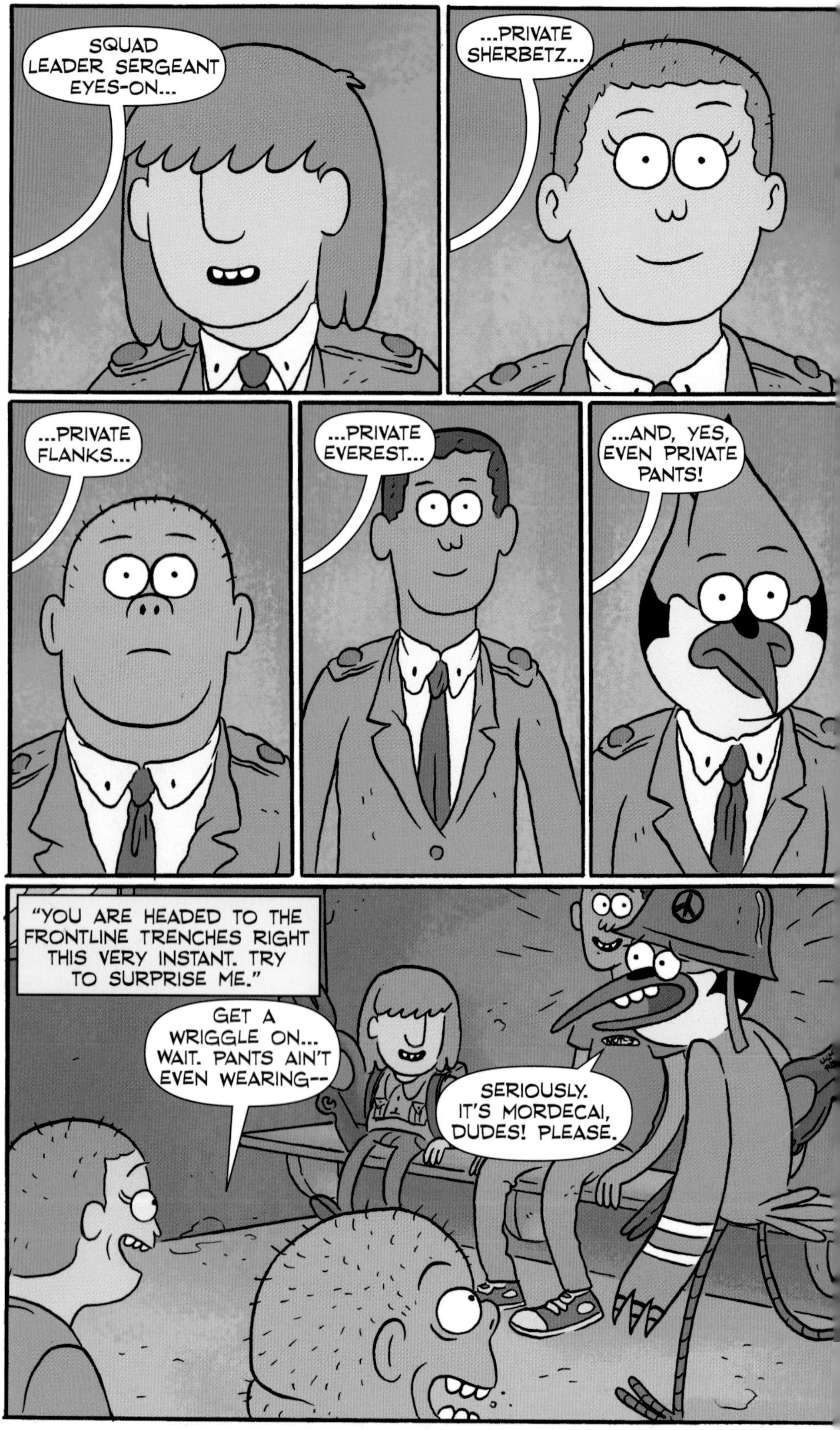
SQUAD LEADER SERGEANT EYES-ON...
...PRIVATE SHERBETZ...
...PRIVATE FLANKS...
...PRIVATE EVEREST...
...AND, YES, EVEN PRIVATE PANTS!
"YOU ARE HEADED TO THE FRONTLINE TRENCHES RIGHT THIS VERY INSTANT. TRY TO SURPRISE ME."
GET A WRIGGLE ON... WAIT. PANTS AIN'T EVEN WEARING--
SERIOUSLY. IT'S MORDECAI, DUDES! PLEASE.

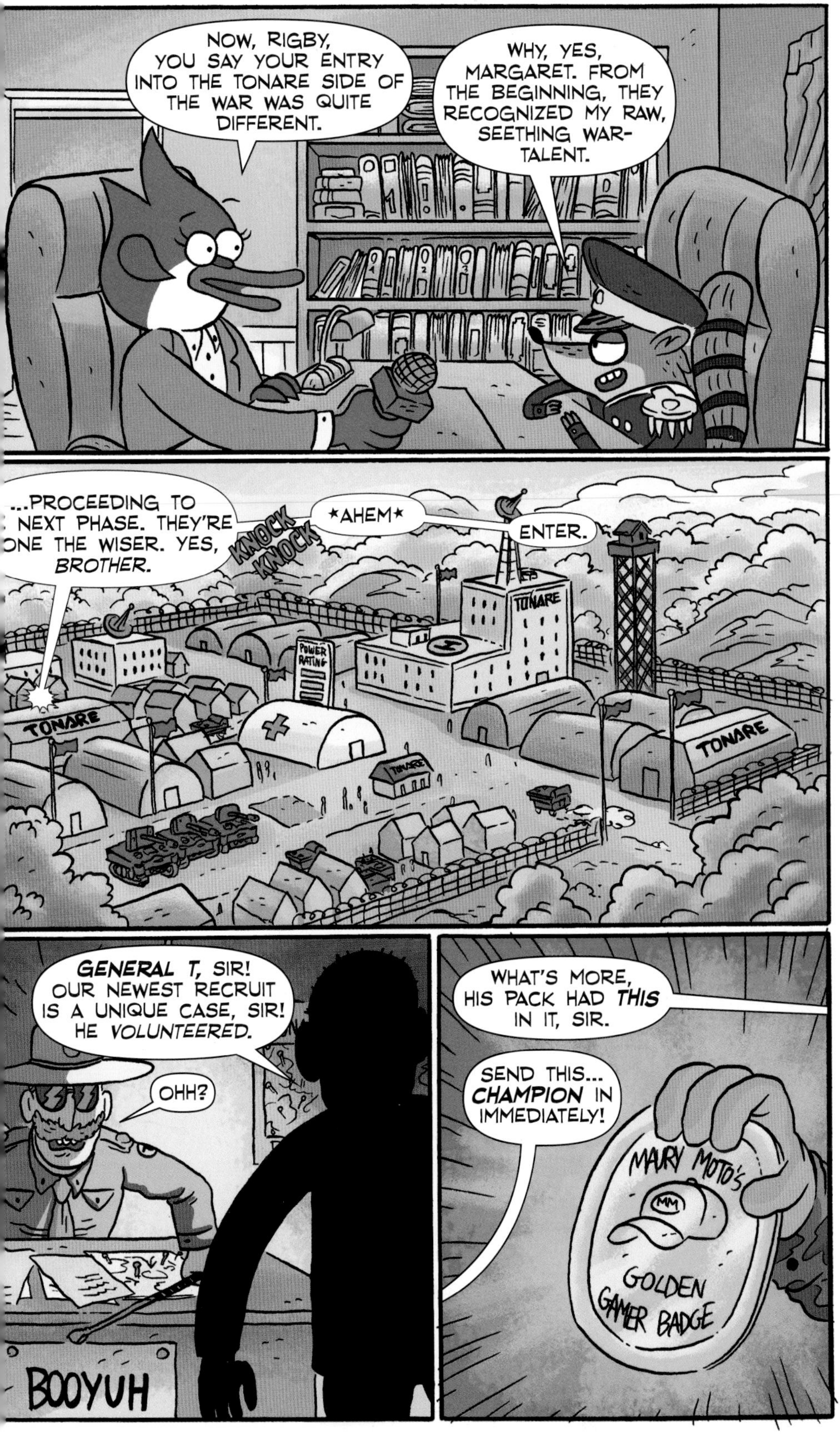
NOW, RIGBY, YOU SAY YOUR ENTRY INTO THE TONARE SIDE OF THE WAR WAS QUITE DIFFERENT.
WHY, YES, MARGARET. FROM THE BEGINNING, THEY RECOGNIZED MY RAW, SEETHING WAR-TALENT.
...PROCEEDING TO NEXT PHASE. THEY'RE NONE THE WISER. YES, BROTHER.
KNOCK KNOCK
AHEM
ENTER.
TONARE
POWER RATING
TONARE
TONARE
TONARE
GENERAL T, SIR! OUR NEWEST RECRUIT IS A UNIQUE CASE, SIR! HE VOLUNTEERED.
OHH?
BOOYUH
WHAT'S MORE, HIS PACK HAD THIS IN IT, SIR.
SEND THIS... CHAMPION IN IMMEDIATELY!
MAURY MOTO'S
MM
GOLDEN GAMER BADGE

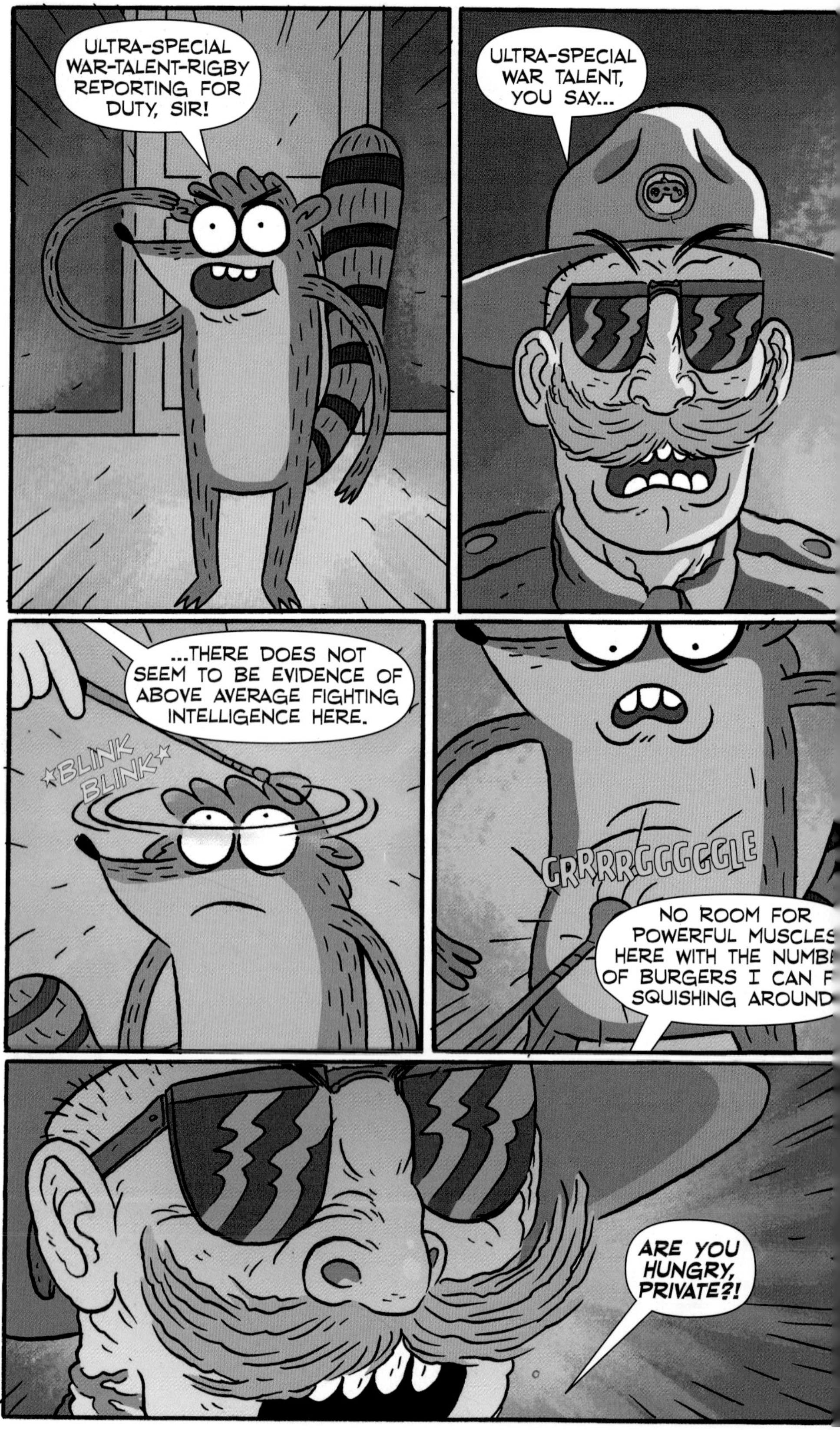
ULTRA-SPECIAL WAR-TALENT-RIGBY REPORTING FOR DUTY, SIR!
ULTRA-SPECIAL WAR TALENT, YOU SAY...
...THERE DOES NOT SEEM TO BE EVIDENCE OF ABOVE AVERAGE FIGHTING INTELLIGENCE HERE.
BLINK BLINK
GRRRRGGGGGLE
NO ROOM FOR POWERFUL MUSCLES HERE WITH THE NUMB OF BURGERS I CAN F SQUISHING AROUND
ARE YOU HUNGRY, PRIVATE?!

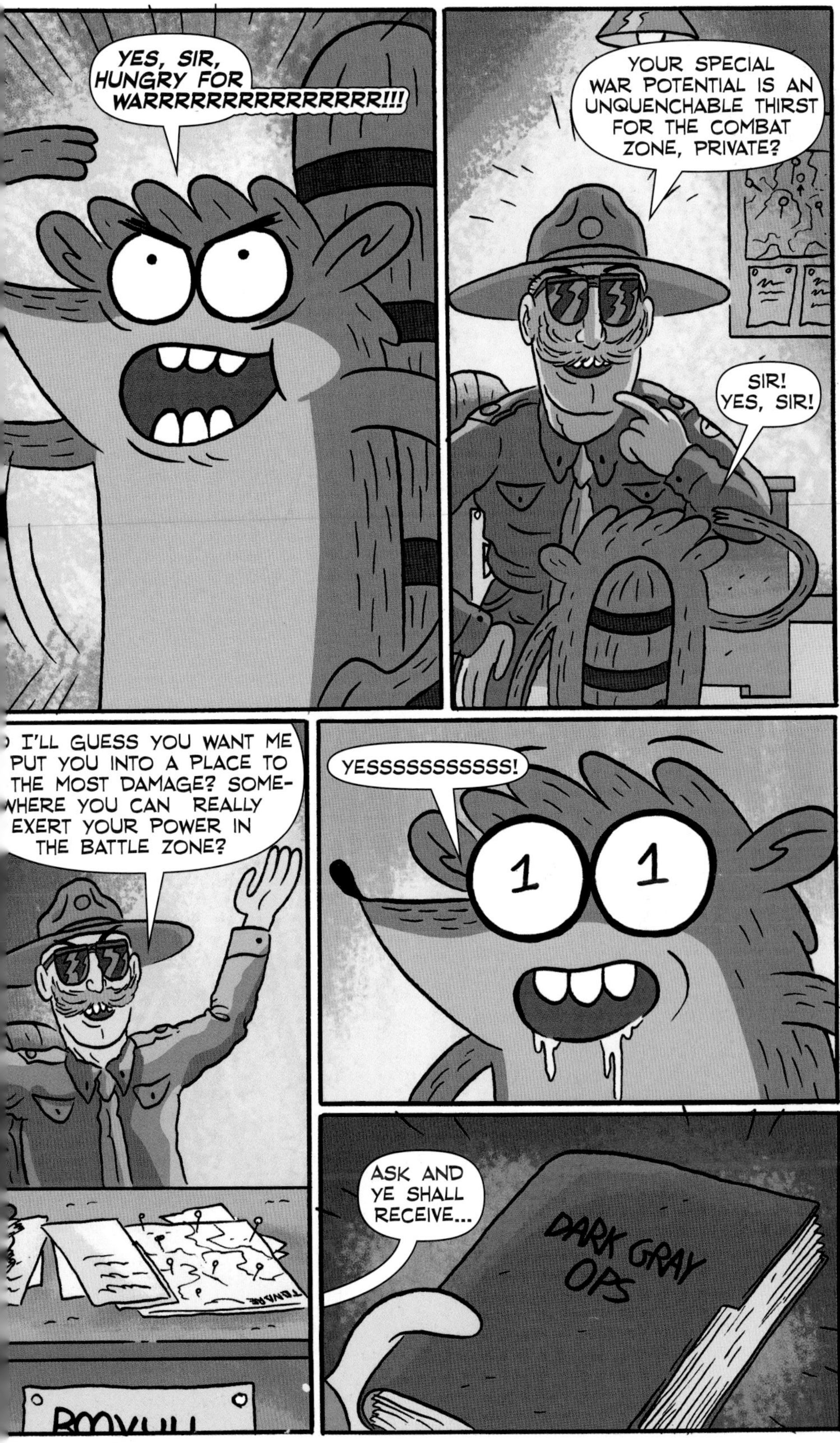
YES, SIR, HUNGRY FOR WARRRRRRRRRRRRRRR!!!
YOUR SPECIAL WAR POTENTIAL IS AN UNQUENCHABLE THIRST FOR THE COMBAT ZONE, PRIVATE?
SIR! YES, SIR!
I'LL GUESS YOU WANT ME PUT YOU INTO A PLACE TO THE MOST DAMAGE? SOME-WHERE YOU CAN REALLY EXERT YOUR POWER IN THE BATTLE ZONE?
YESSSSSSSSSSS!
ASK AND YE SHALL RECEIVE...
DARK GRAY OPS

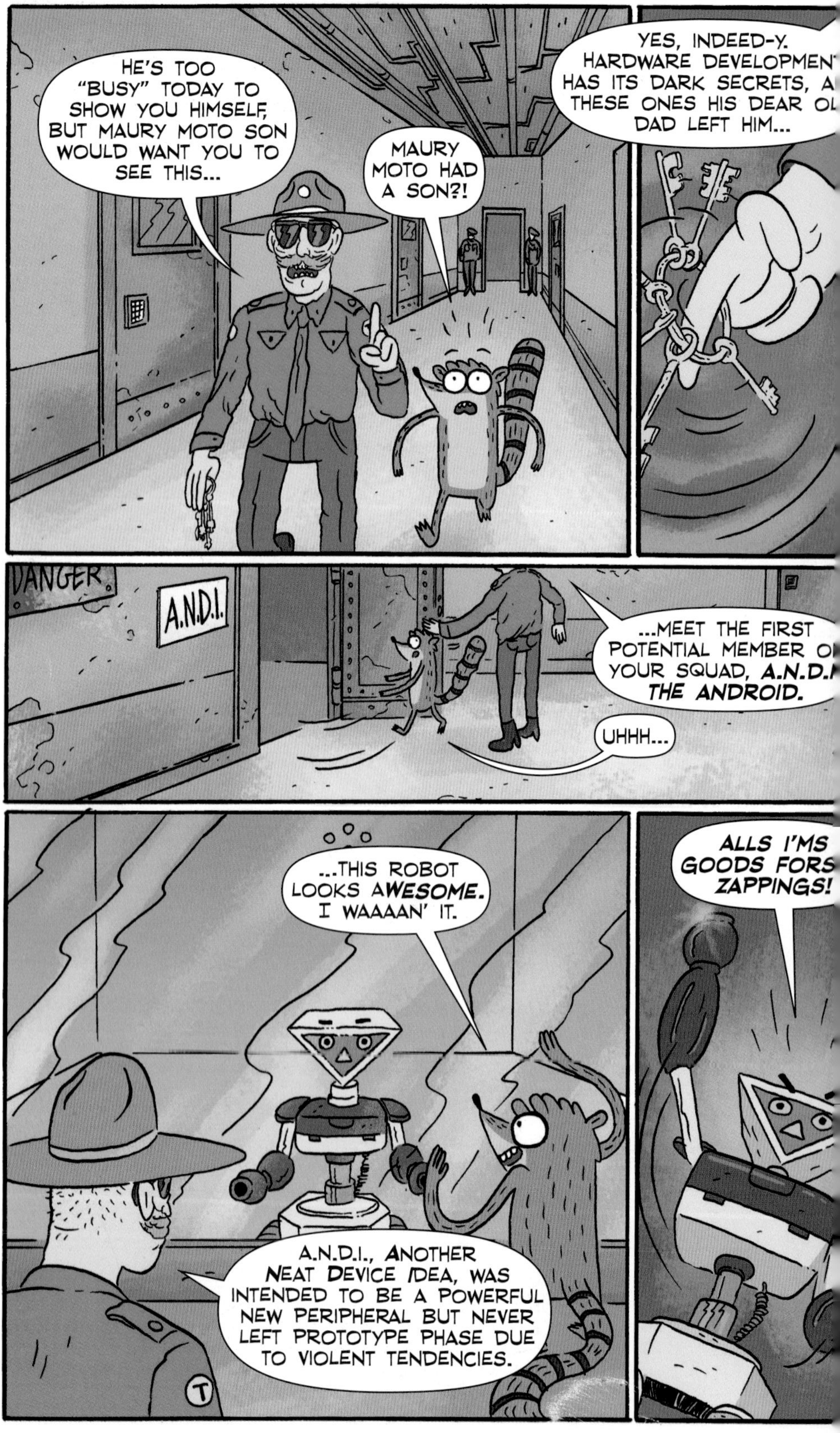
HE'S TOO "BUSY" TODAY TO SHOW YOU HIMSELF, BUT MAURY MOTO SON WOULD WANT YOU TO SEE THIS...
MAURY MOTO HAD A SON?!
YES, INDEED-Y. HARDWARE DEVELOPMEN HAS ITS DARK SECRETS, A THESE ONES HIS DEAR OL DAD LEFT HIM...
DANGER
A.N.D.I.
...MEET THE FIRST POTENTIAL MEMBER O YOUR SQUAD, A.N.D.I THE ANDROID.
UHHH...
...THIS ROBOT LOOKS AWESOME. I WAAAAN' IT.
A.N.D.I., ANOTHER NEAT DEVICE IDEA, WAS INTENDED TO BE A POWERFUL NEW PERIPHERAL BUT NEVER LEFT PROTOTYPE PHASE DUE TO VIOLENT TENDENCIES.
ALLS I'MS GOODS FORS ZAPPINGS!

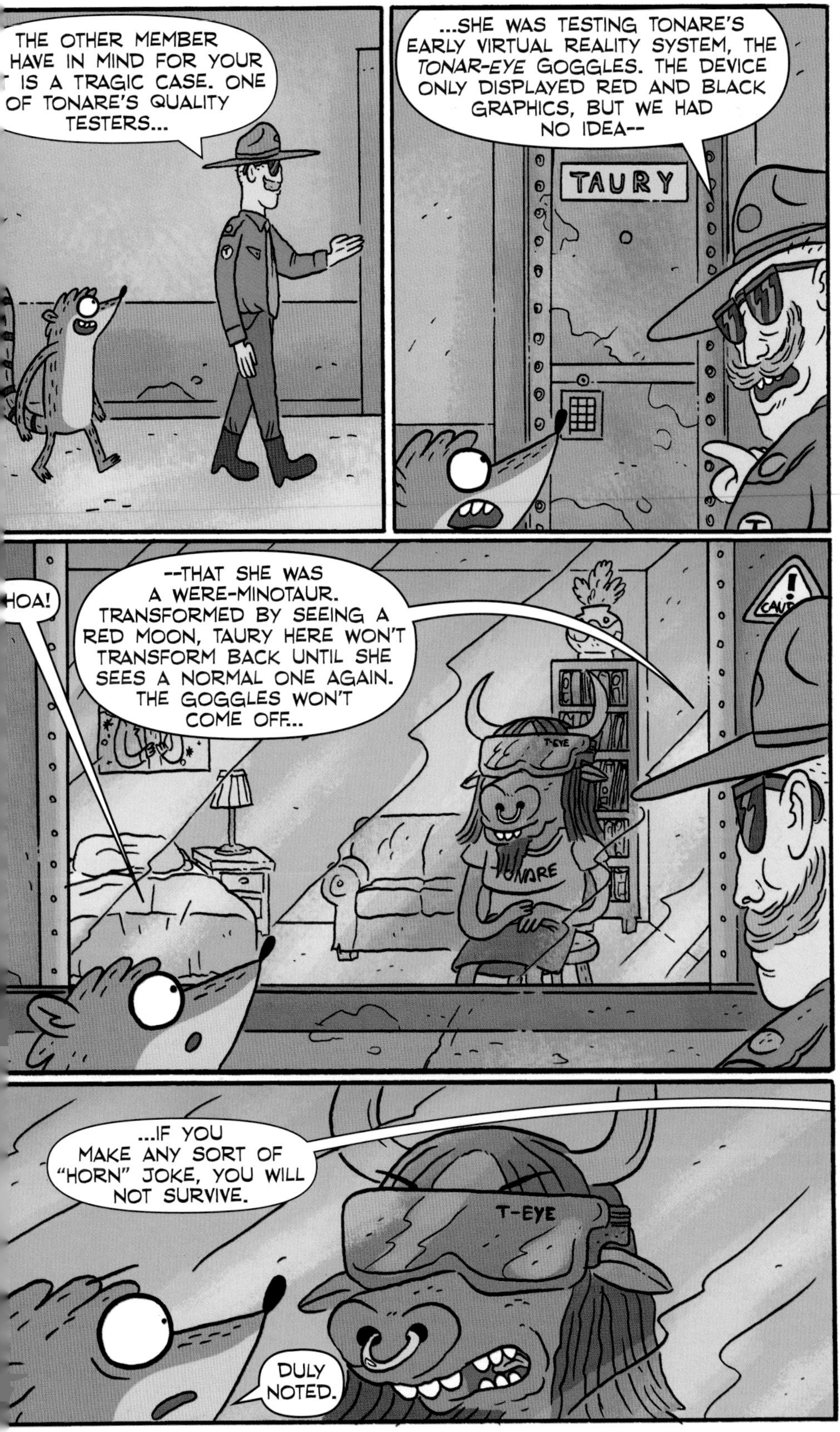
THE OTHER MEMBER
HAVE IN MIND FOR YOUR
IS A TRAGIC CASE. ONE
OF TONARE'S QUALITY
TESTERS...
...SHE WAS TESTING TONARE'S EARLY VIRTUAL REALITY SYSTEM, THE *TONAR-EYE* GOGGLES. THE DEVICE ONLY DISPLAYED RED AND BLACK GRAPHICS, BUT WE HAD NO IDEA--
TAURY
HOA!
--THAT SHE WAS A WERE-MINOTAUR. TRANSFORMED BY SEEING A RED MOON, TAURY HERE WON'T TRANSFORM BACK UNTIL SHE SEES A NORMAL ONE AGAIN. THE GOGGLES WON'T COME OFF...
T-EYE
TONARE
...IF YOU MAKE ANY SORT OF "HORN" JOKE, YOU WILL NOT SURVIVE.
T-EYE
DULY NOTED.

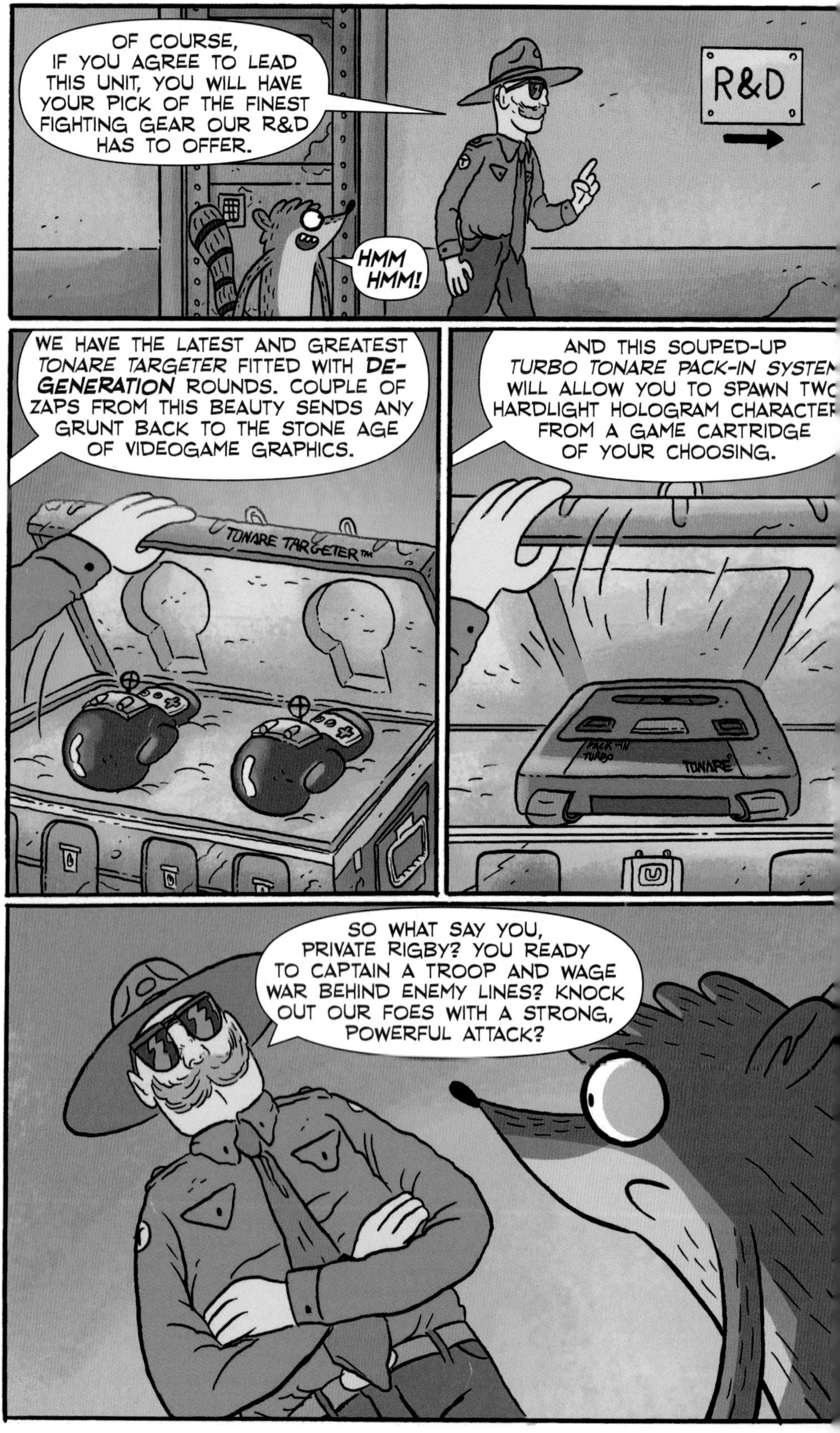
R&D
OF COURSE, IF YOU AGREE TO LEAD THIS UNIT, YOU WILL HAVE YOUR PICK OF THE FINEST FIGHTING GEAR OUR R&D HAS TO OFFER.
HMM HMM!
WE HAVE THE LATEST AND GREATEST TONARE TARGETER FITTED WITH DE-GENERATION ROUNDS. COUPLE OF ZAPS FROM THIS BEAUTY SENDS ANY GRUNT BACK TO THE STONE AGE OF VIDEOGAME GRAPHICS.
TONARE TARGETER™
AND THIS SOUPED-UP TURBO TONARE PACK-IN SYSTE
WILL ALLOW YOU TO SPAWN TW
HARDLIGHT HOLOGRAM CHARACTE
FROM A GAME CARTRIDGE OF YOUR CHOOSING.
TONARE
SO WHAT SAY YOU, PRIVATE RIGBY? YOU READY TO CAPTAIN A TROOP AND WAGE WAR BEHIND ENEMY LINES? KNOCK OUT OUR FOES WITH A STRONG, POWERFUL ATTACK?

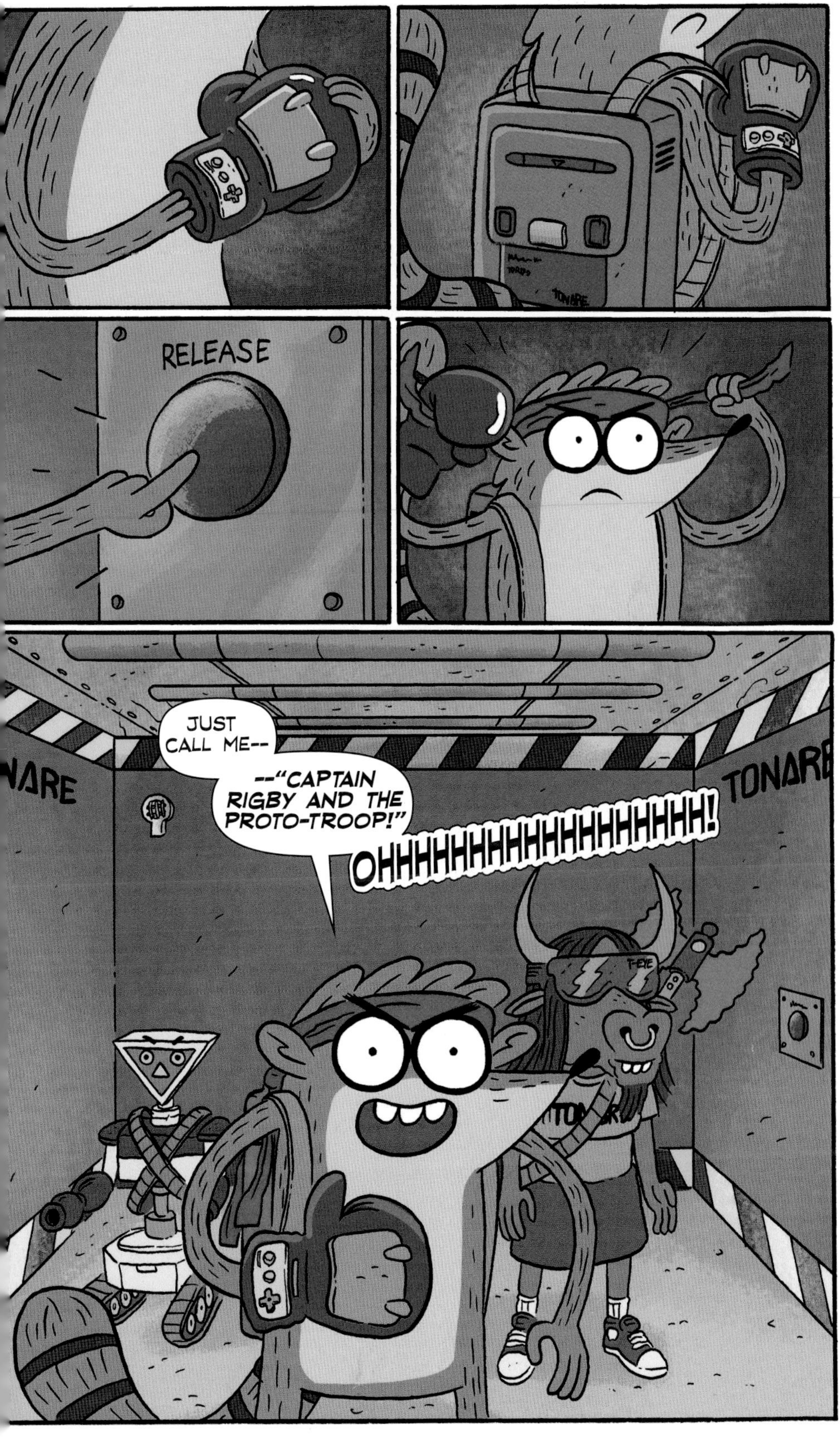
RELEASE
TONARE
TONARE
JUST CALL ME--
--"CAPTAIN RIGBY AND THE PROTO-TROOP!"
OHHHHHHHHHHHHHHHHHHH!
T-EYE

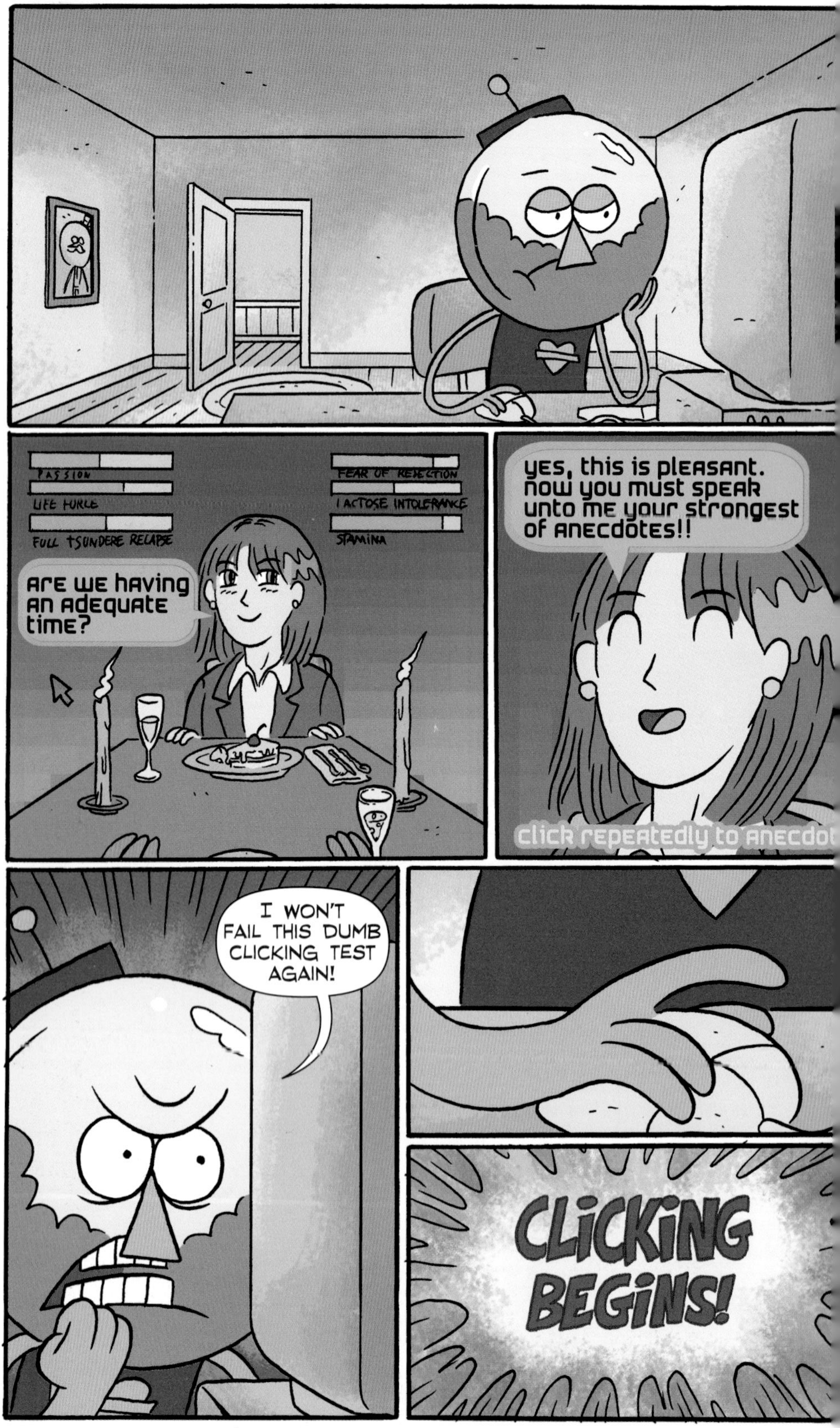

PASSION
LIFE FORCE
FULL TSUNDERE RELAPSE
FEAR OF REJECTION
LACTOSE INTOLERANCE
STAMINA
are we having an adequate time?
yes, this is pleasant. now you must speak unto me your strongest of anecdotes!!
click repeatedly to anecdot
I WON'T FAIL THIS DUMB CLICKING TEST AGAIN!
CLICKING BEGINS!

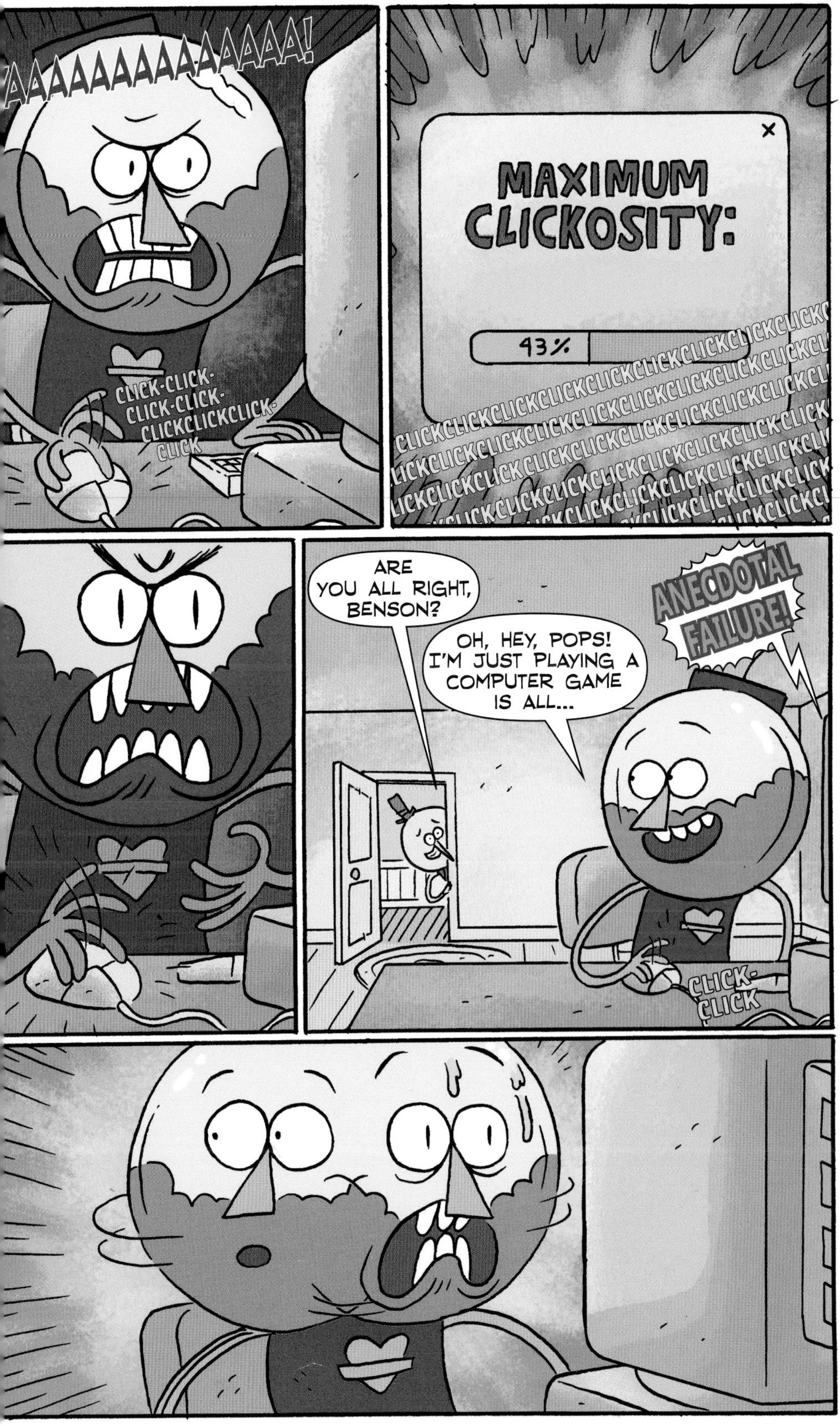
AAAAAAAAAAAAAAAA!
CLICK-CLICK-
CLICK-CLICK-
CLICKCLICKCLICK-
CLICK
MAXIMUM
CLICKOSITY:
43%
CLICKCLICKCLICKCLICKCLICKCLICKCLICKCLICK
ARE YOU ALL RIGHT, BENSON?
OH, HEY, POPS! I'M JUST PLAYING A COMPUTER GAME IS ALL...
ANECDOTAL FAILURE!
CLICK-CLICK

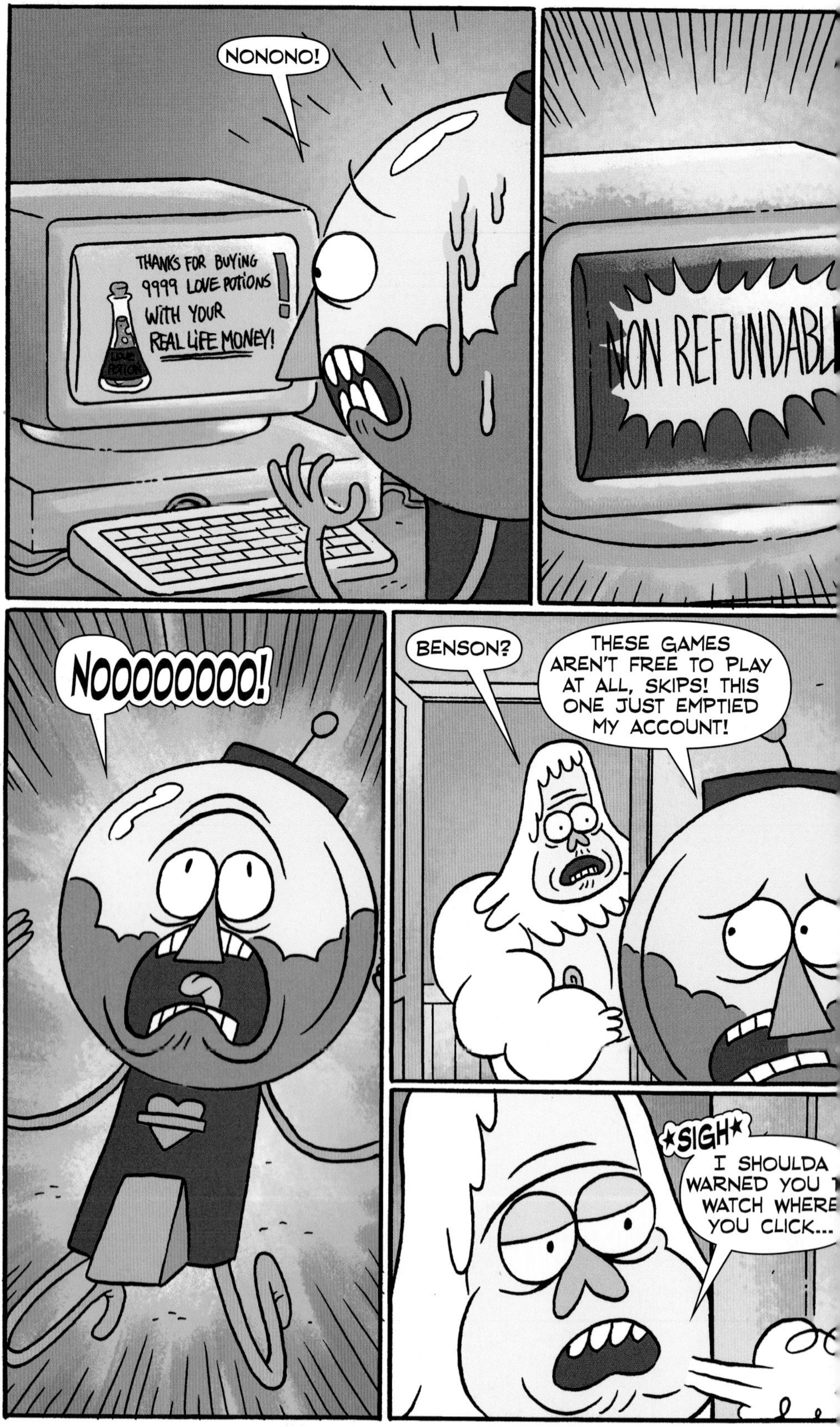
NONONO!
THANKS FOR BUYING 9999 LOVE POTIONS WITH YOUR REAL LIFE MONEY!
NON REFUNDABL
NOOOOOOOO!
BENSON?
THESE GAMES AREN'T FREE TO PLAY AT ALL, SKIPS! THIS ONE JUST EMPTIED MY ACCOUNT!
SIGH
I SHOULDA WARNED YOU WATCH WHERE YOU CLICK...

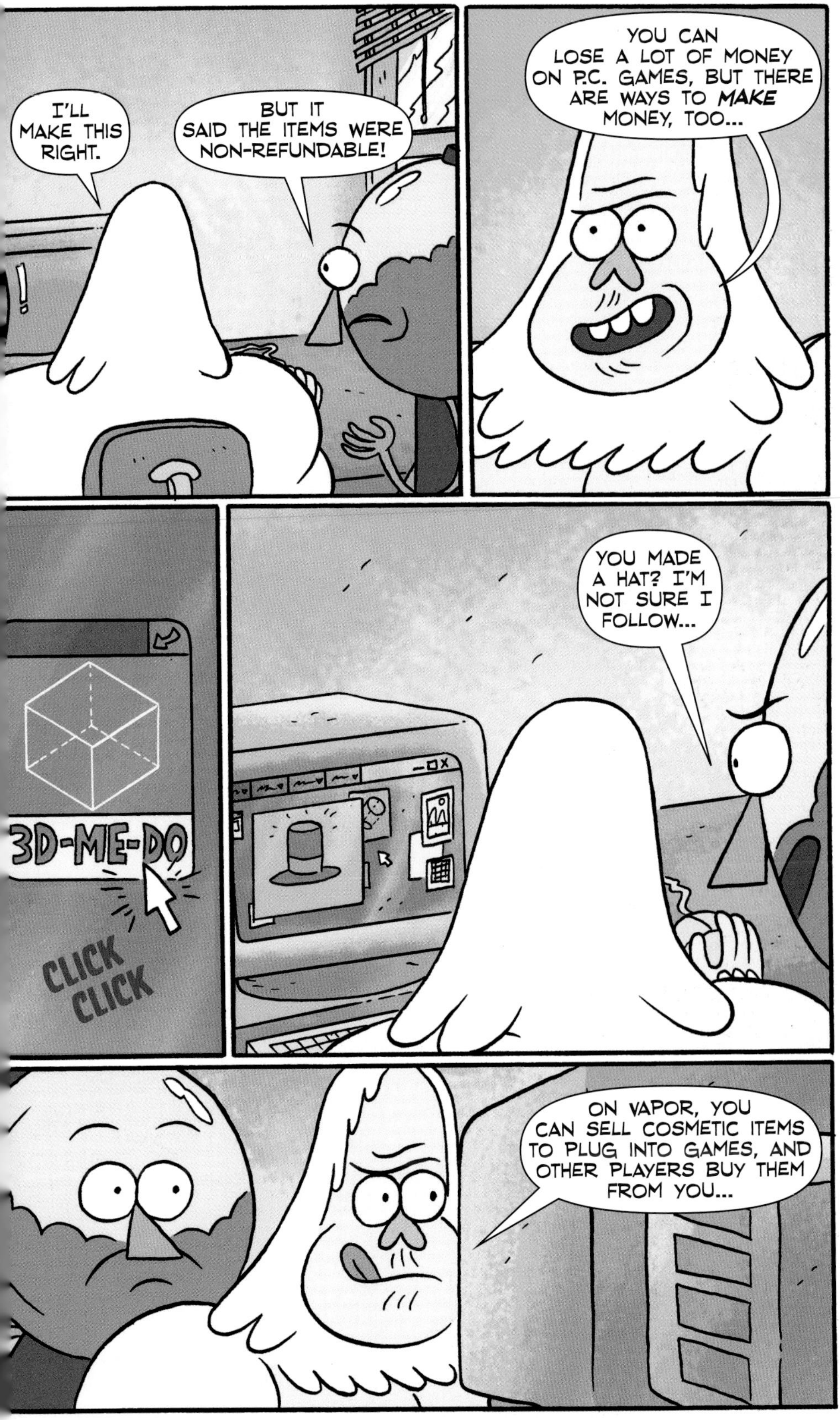

I'LL MAKE THIS RIGHT.
BUT IT SAID THE ITEMS WERE NON-REFUNDABLE!
YOU CAN LOSE A LOT OF MONEY ON P.C. GAMES, BUT THERE ARE WAYS TO *MAKE* MONEY, TOO...
3D-ME-DO
CLICK CLICK
YOU MADE A HAT? I'M NOT SURE I FOLLOW...
ON VAPOR, YOU CAN SELL COSMETIC ITEMS TO PLUG INTO GAMES, AND OTHER PLAYERS BUY THEM FROM YOU...

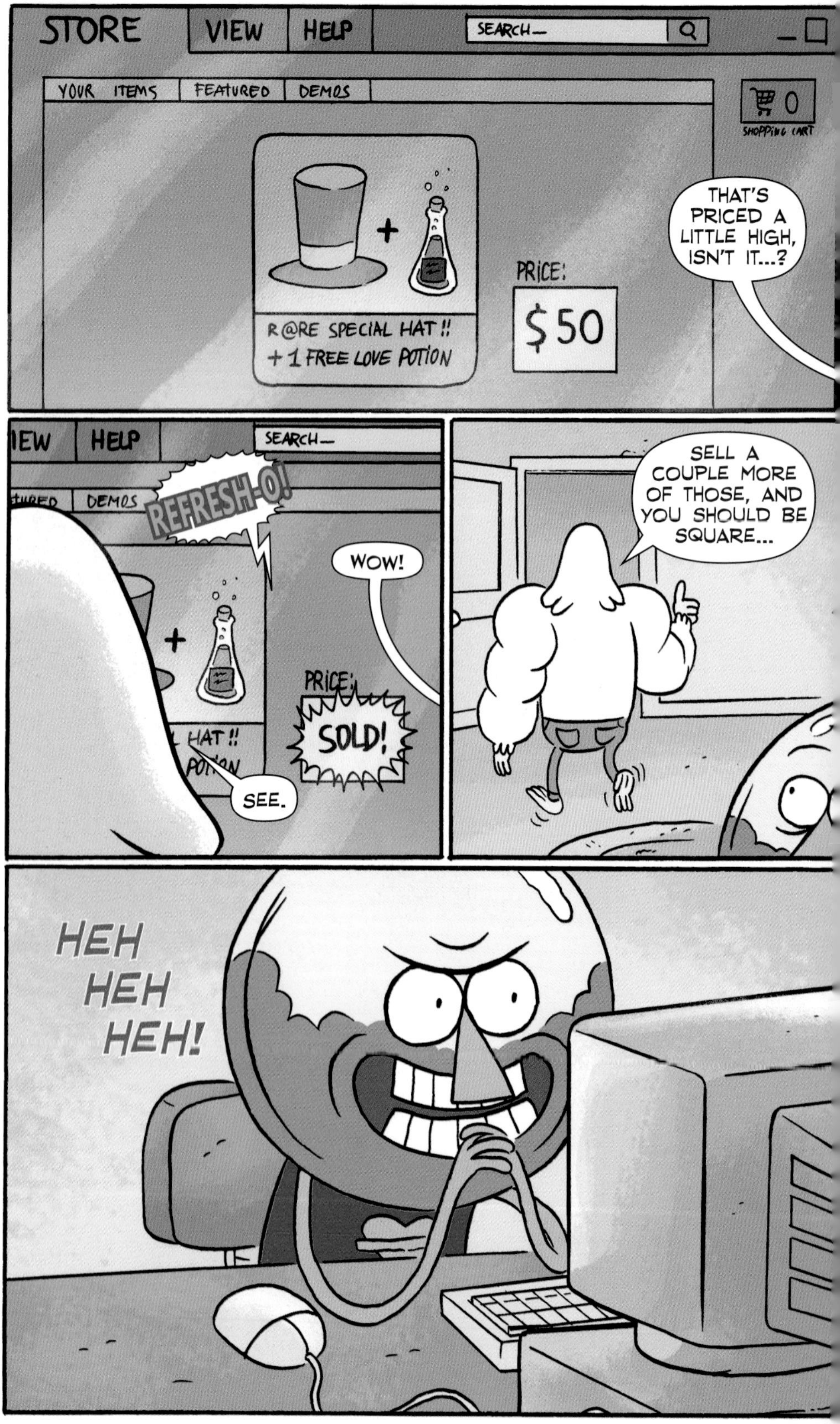
STORE
VIEW
HELP
SEARCH
YOUR ITEMS
FEATURED
DEMOS
SHOPPING CART
0
R@RE SPECIAL HAT !!
+ 1 FREE LOVE POTION
PRICE:
$50
THAT'S PRICED A LITTLE HIGH, ISN'T IT...?
REFRESH-O!
WOW!
PRICE:
SOLD!
SEE.
SELL A COUPLE MORE OF THOSE, AND YOU SHOULD BE SQUARE...
HEH HEH HEH!

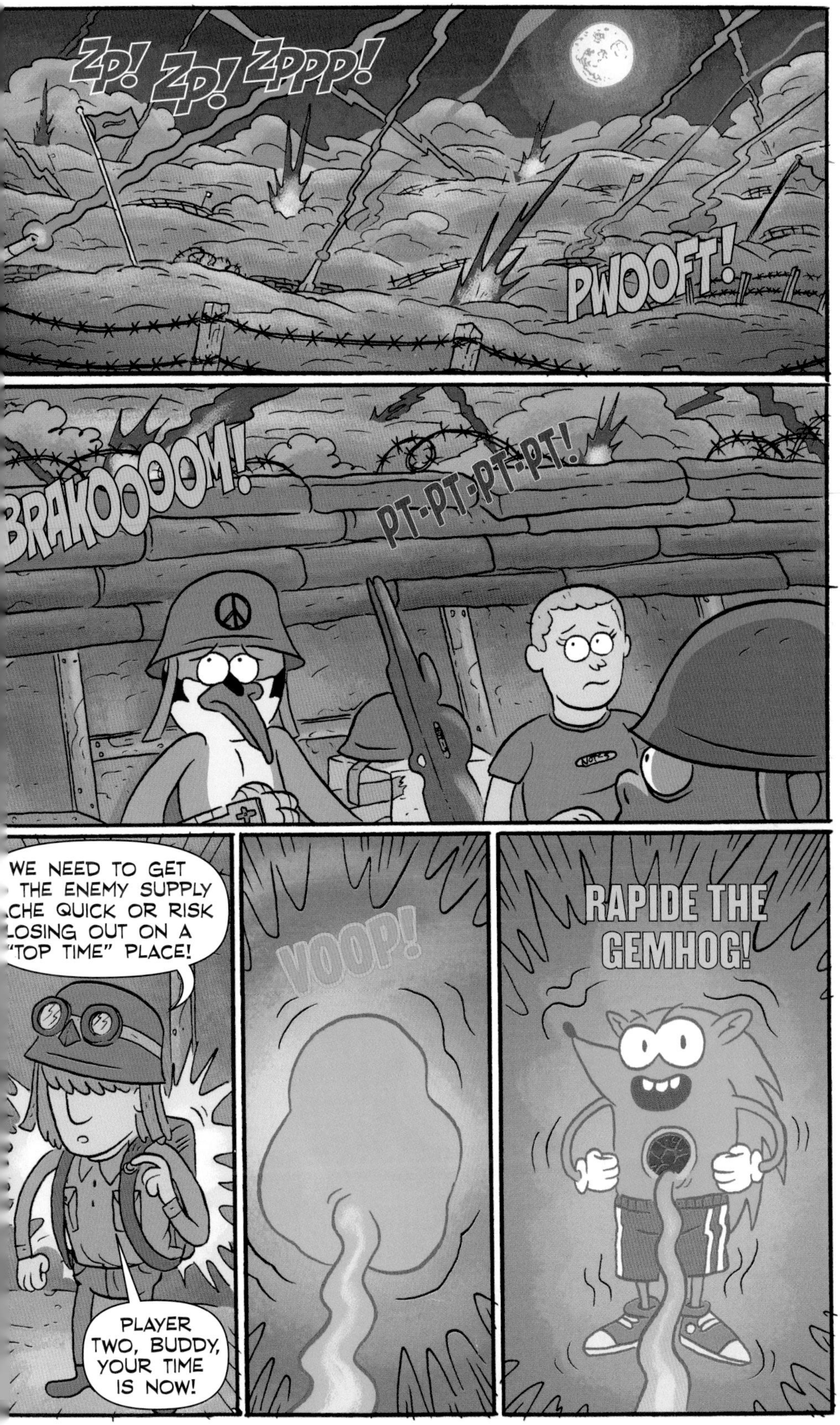
ZP! ZP! ZPPP!
PWOOFT!
BRAKOOOOOM!
PT-PT-PT-PT!
WE NEED TO GET THE ENEMY SUPPLY CHE QUICK OR RISK LOSING OUT ON A "TOP TIME" PLACE!
PLAYER TWO, BUDDY, YOUR TIME IS NOW!
VOOP!
RAPIDE THE GEMHOG!

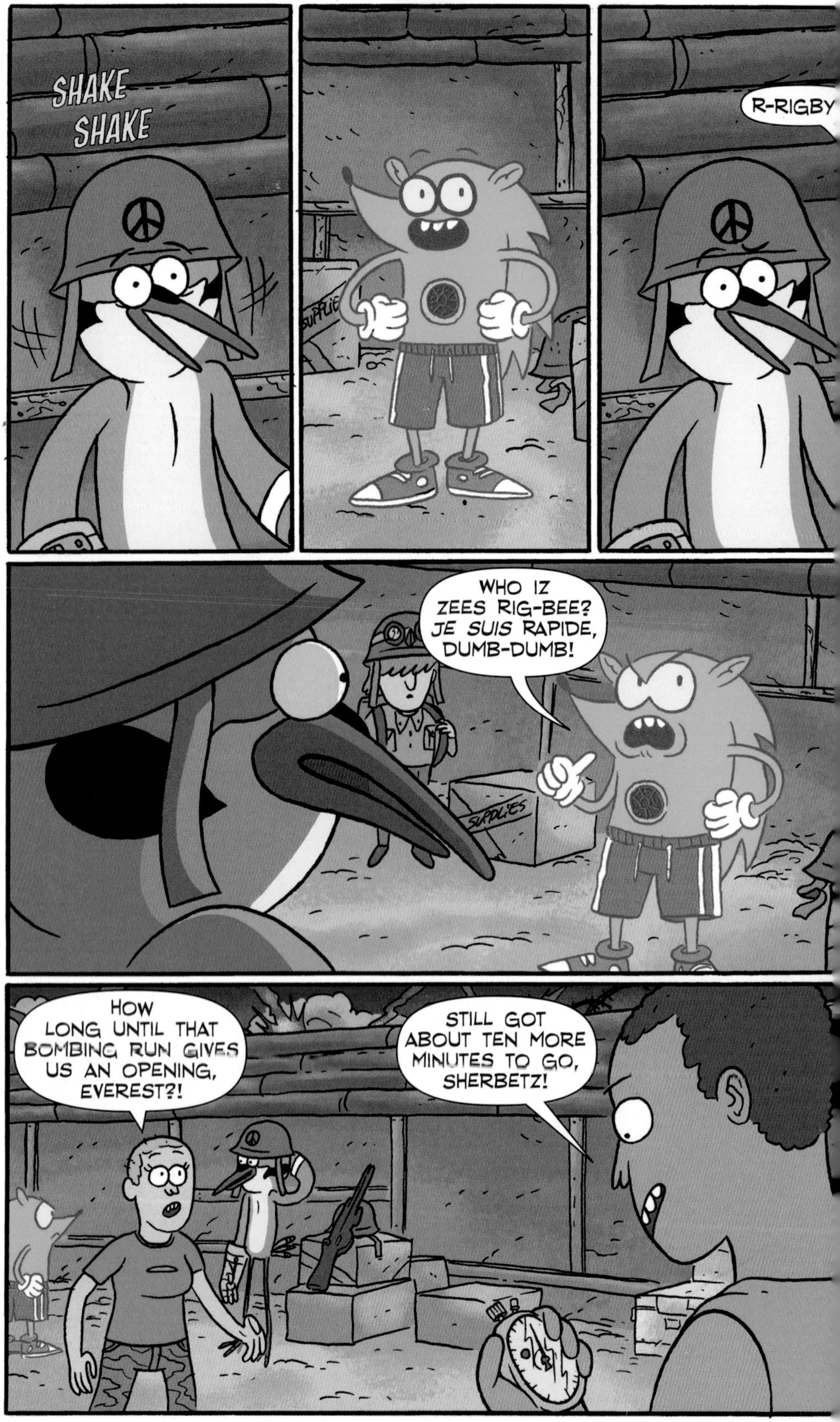
SHAKE
SHAKE
R-RIGBY
WHO IZ ZEES RIG-BEE? JE SUIS RAPIDE, DUMB-DUMB!
SUPPLIES
HOW LONG UNTIL THAT BOMBING RUN GIVES US AN OPENING, EVEREST?!
STILL GOT ABOUT TEN MORE MINUTES TO GO, SHERBETZ!

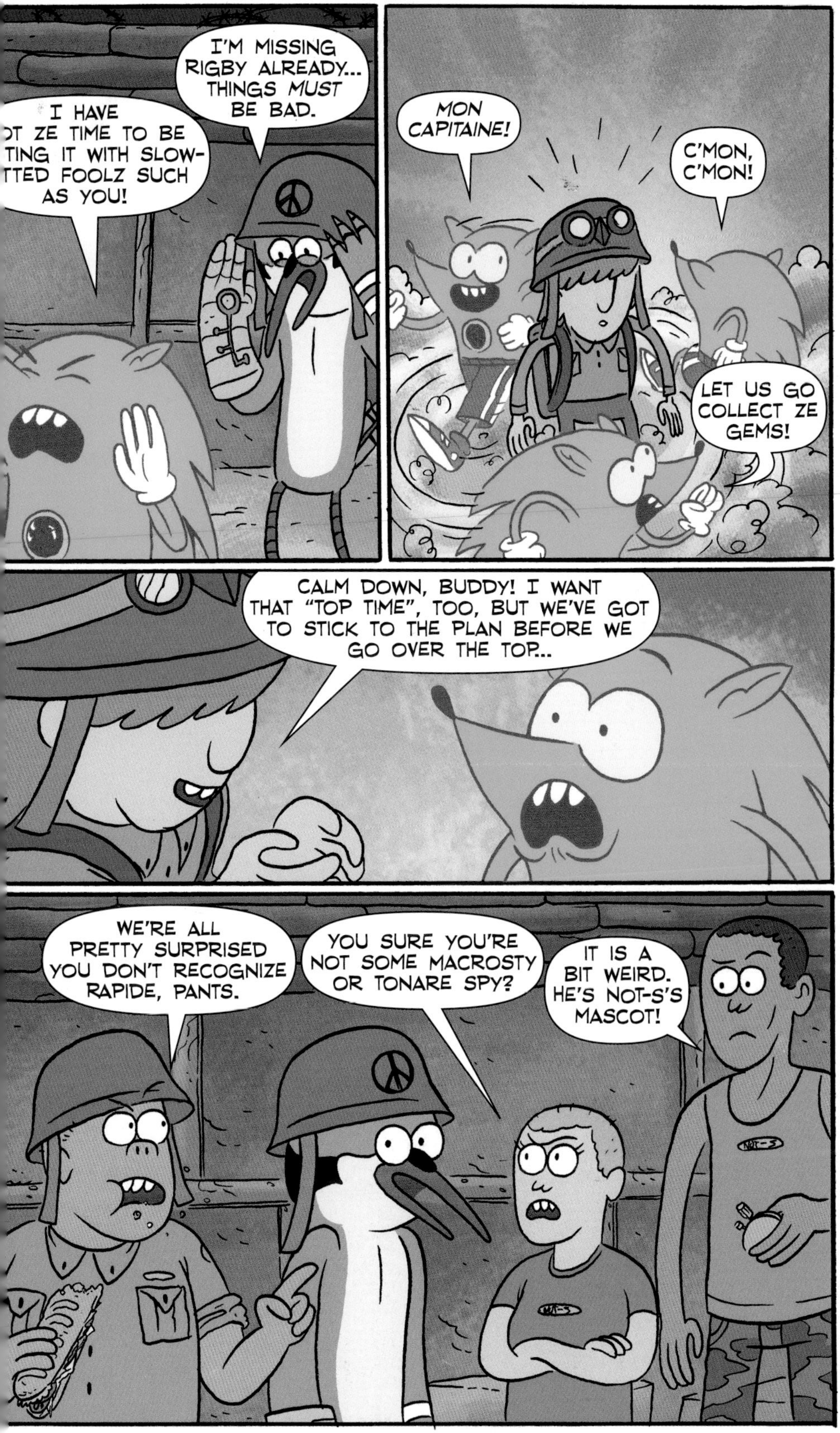
I'M MISSING RIGBY ALREADY... THINGS MUST BE BAD.
I HAVE OT ZE TIME TO BE TING IT WITH SLOW-TTED FOOLZ SUCH AS YOU!
MON CAPITAINE!
C'MON, C'MON!
LET US GO COLLECT ZE GEMS!
CALM DOWN, BUDDY! I WANT THAT "TOP TIME", TOO, BUT WE'VE GOT TO STICK TO THE PLAN BEFORE WE GO OVER THE TOP...
WE'RE ALL PRETTY SURPRISED YOU DON'T RECOGNIZE RAPIDE, PANTS.
YOU SURE YOU'RE NOT SOME MACROSTY OR TONARE SPY?
IT IS A BIT WEIRD. HE'S NOT-S'S MASCOT!

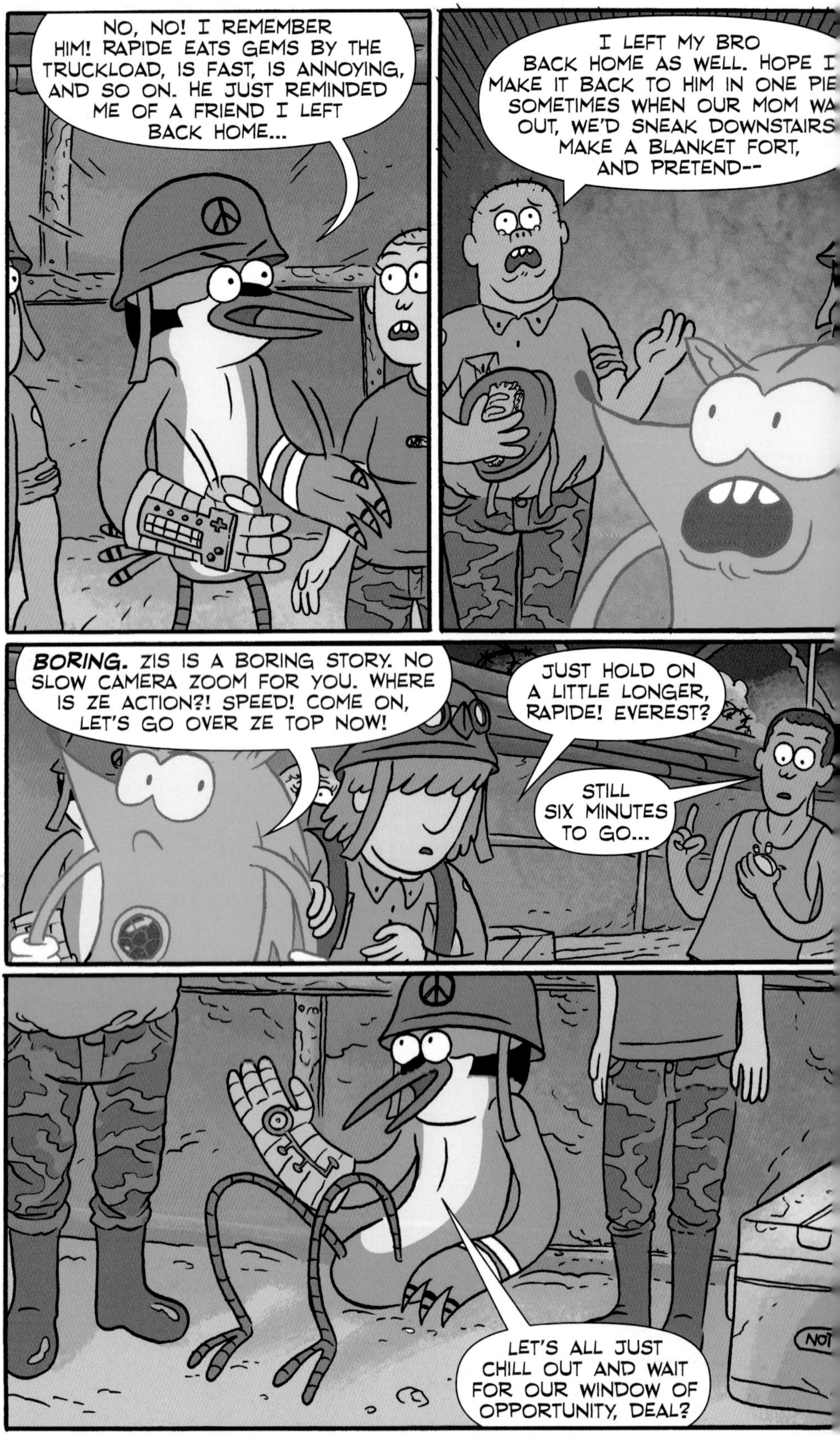

NO, NO! I REMEMBER HIM! RAPIDE EATS GEMS BY THE TRUCKLOAD, IS FAST, IS ANNOYING, AND SO ON. HE JUST REMINDED ME OF A FRIEND I LEFT BACK HOME...
I LEFT MY BRO BACK HOME AS WELL. HOPE I MAKE IT BACK TO HIM IN ONE PIE SOMETIMES WHEN OUR MOM WA OUT, WE'D SNEAK DOWNSTAIRS MAKE A BLANKET FORT, AND PRETEND--
BORING. ZIS IS A BORING STORY. NO SLOW CAMERA ZOOM FOR YOU. WHERE IS ZE ACTION?! SPEED! COME ON, LET'S GO OVER ZE TOP NOW!
JUST HOLD ON A LITTLE LONGER, RAPIDE! EVEREST?
STILL SIX MINUTES TO GO...
LET'S ALL JUST CHILL OUT AND WAIT FOR OUR WINDOW OF OPPORTUNITY, DEAL?

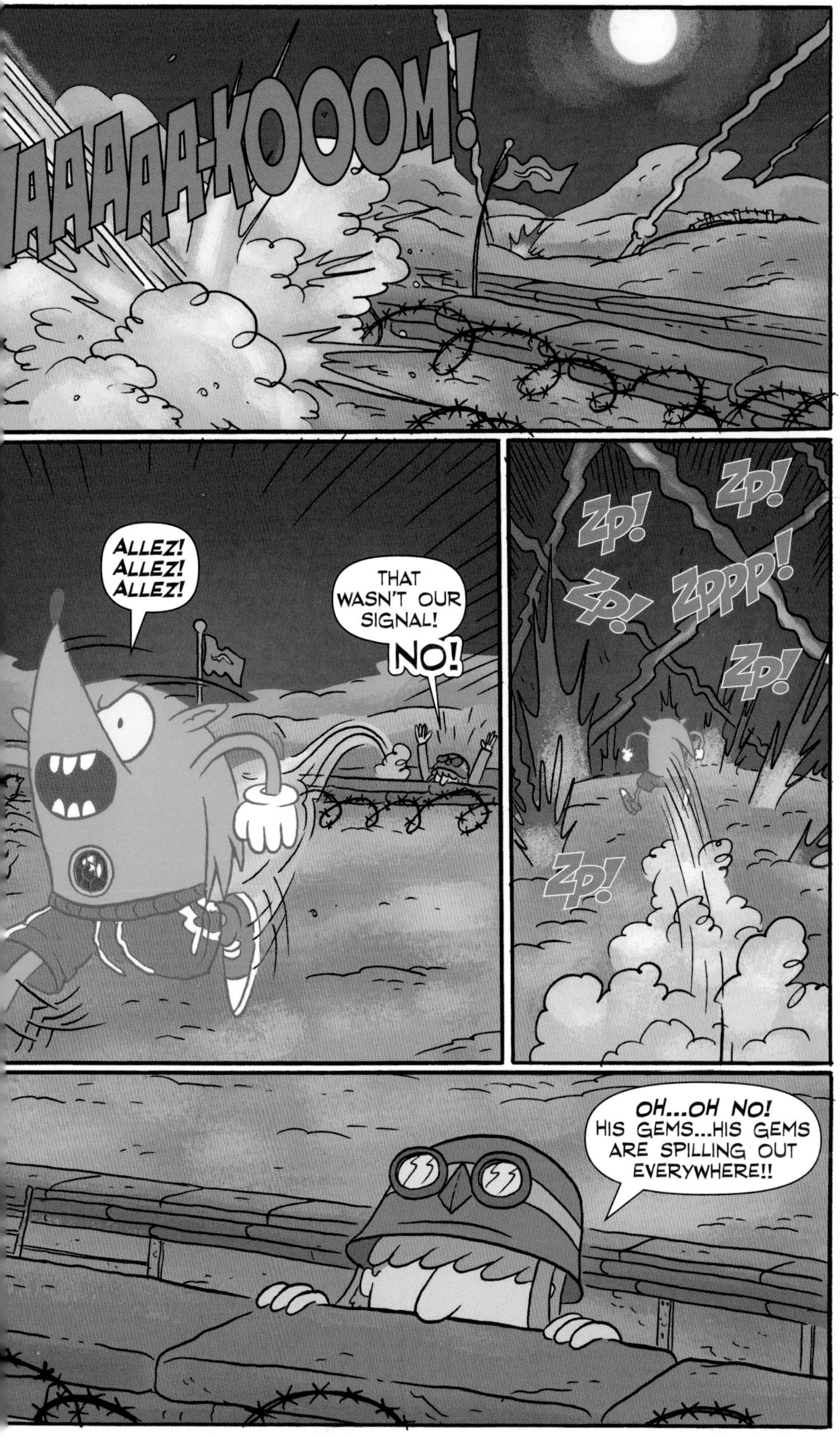
AAAAA-KOOOM!
ALLEZ! ALLEZ! ALLEZ!
THAT WASN'T OUR SIGNAL!
NO!
ZP!
ZP!
ZP!
ZPPP!
ZP!
ZP!
OH...OH NO! HIS GEMS...HIS GEMS ARE SPILLING OUT EVERYWHERE!!

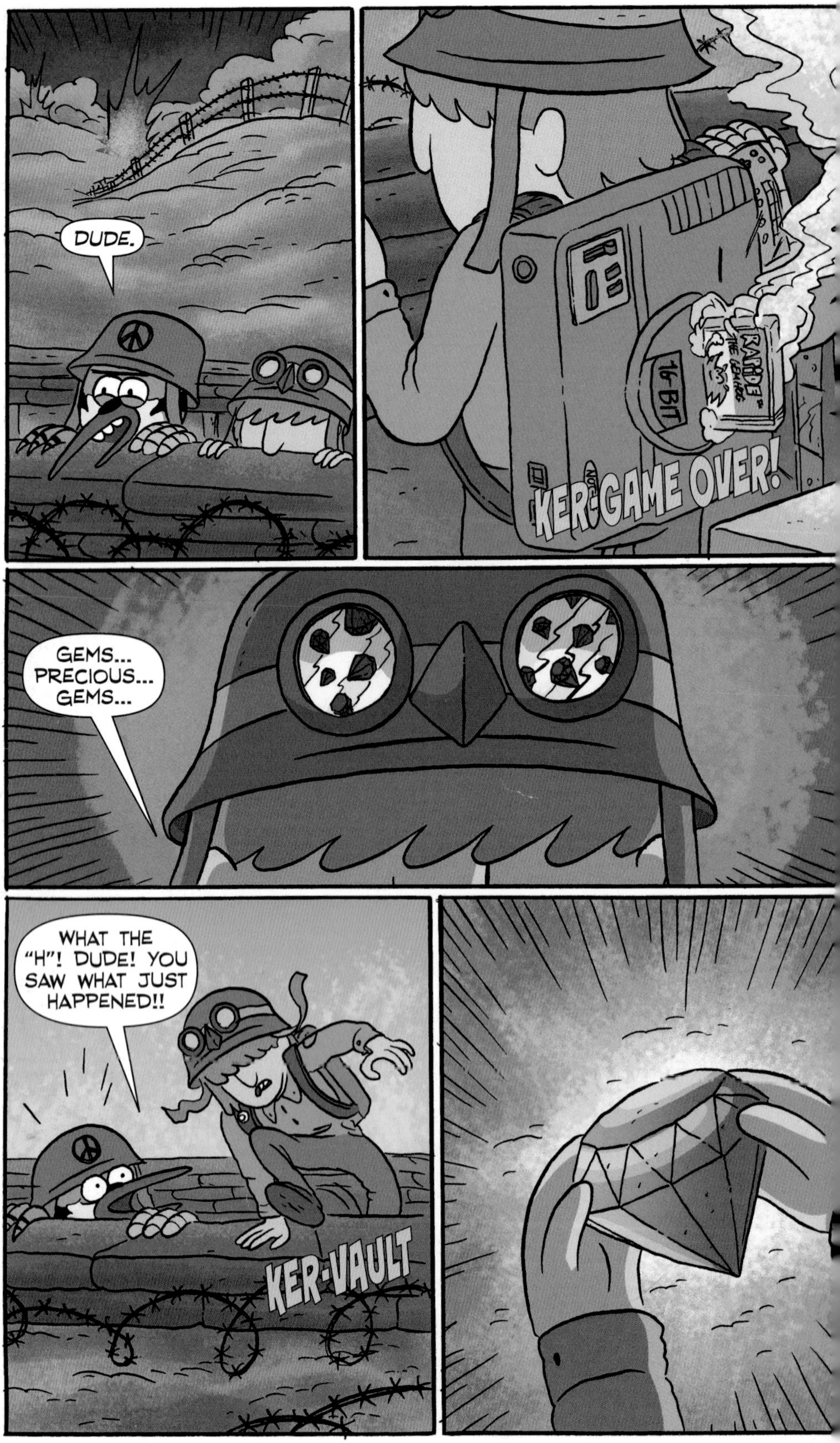
DUDE.
KER-GAME OVER!
GEMS... PRECIOUS... GEMS...
WHAT THE "H"! DUDE! YOU SAW WHAT JUST HAPPENED!!
KER-VAULT

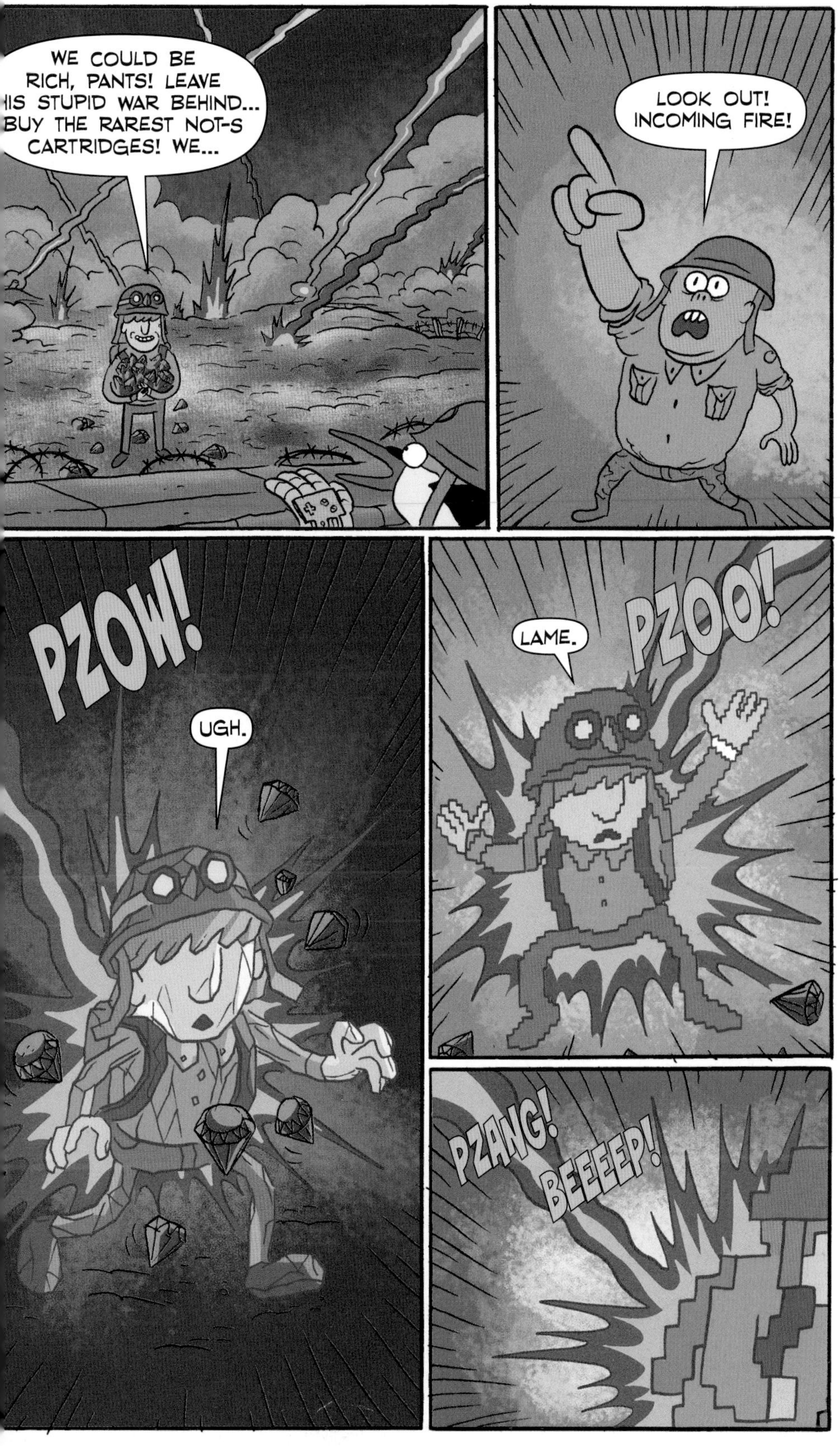
WE COULD BE RICH, PANTS! LEAVE HIS STUPID WAR BEHIND... BUY THE RAREST NOT-S CARTRIDGES! WE...
LOOK OUT! INCOMING FIRE!
PZOW!
UGH.
LAME.
PZOO!
PZANG!
BEEEEP!

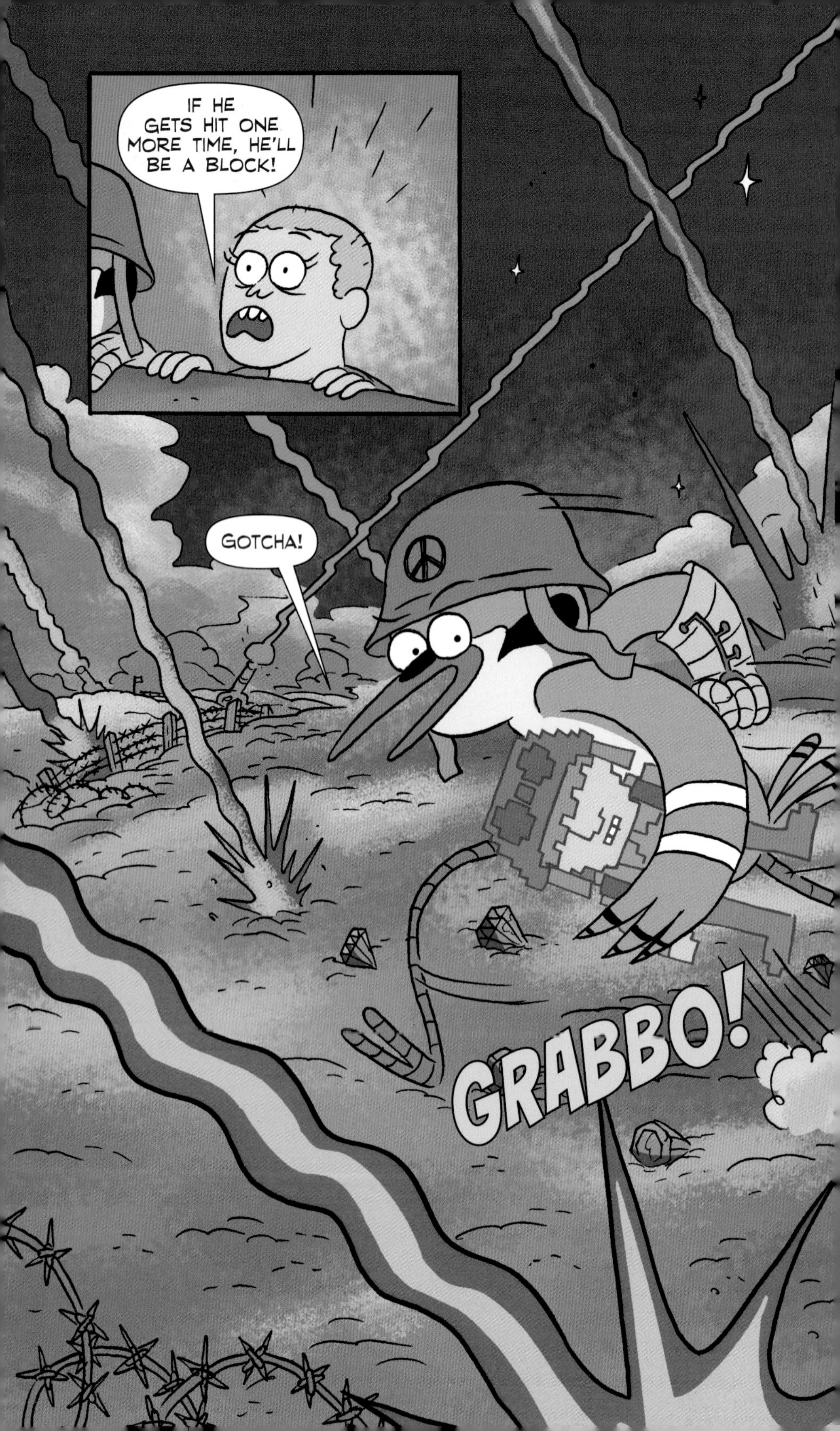

IF HE GETS HIT ONE MORE TIME, HE'LL BE A BLOCK!
GOTCHA!
GRABBO!

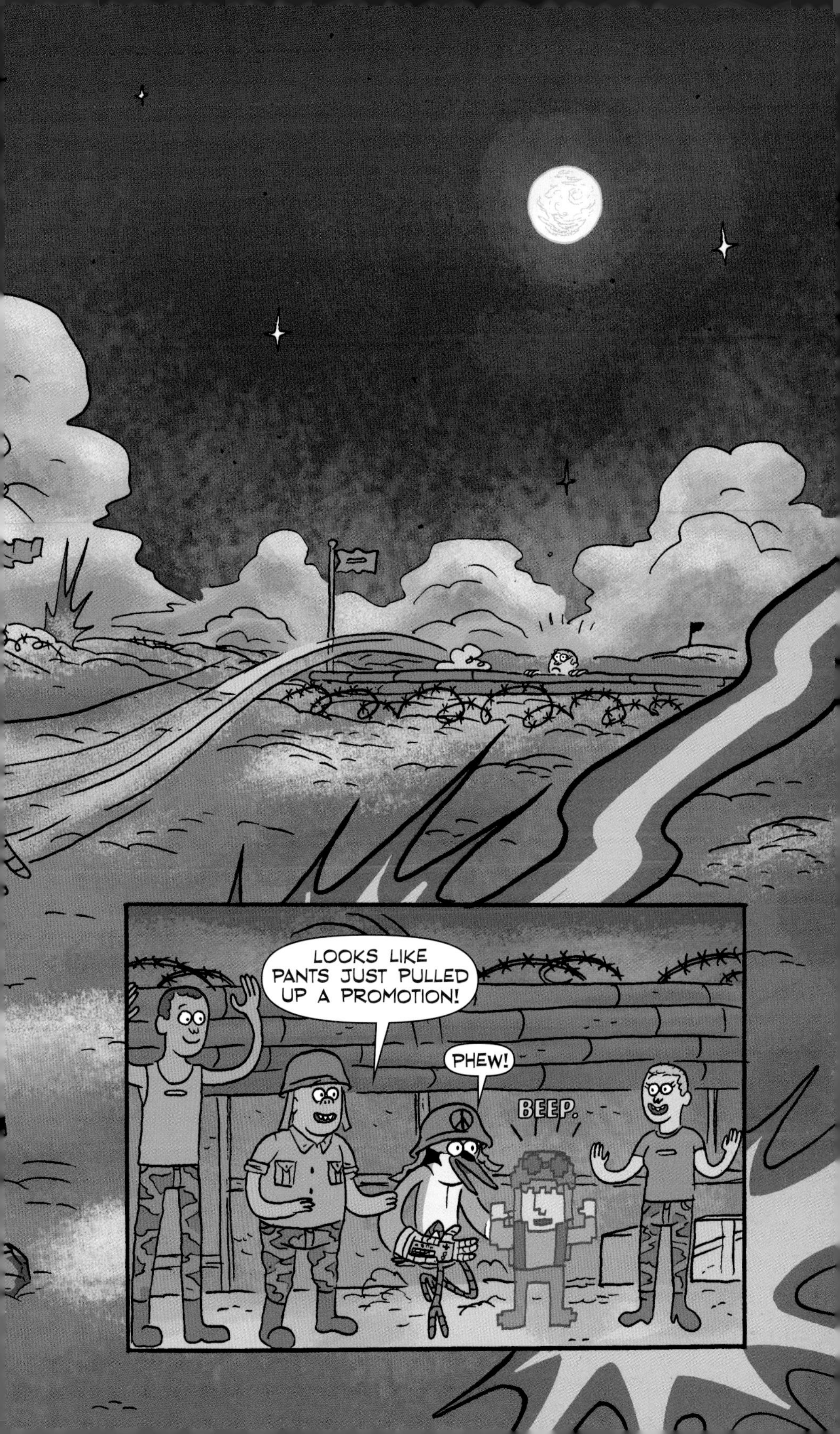
LOOKS LIKE PANTS JUST PULLED UP A PROMOTION!
PHEW!
BEEP.

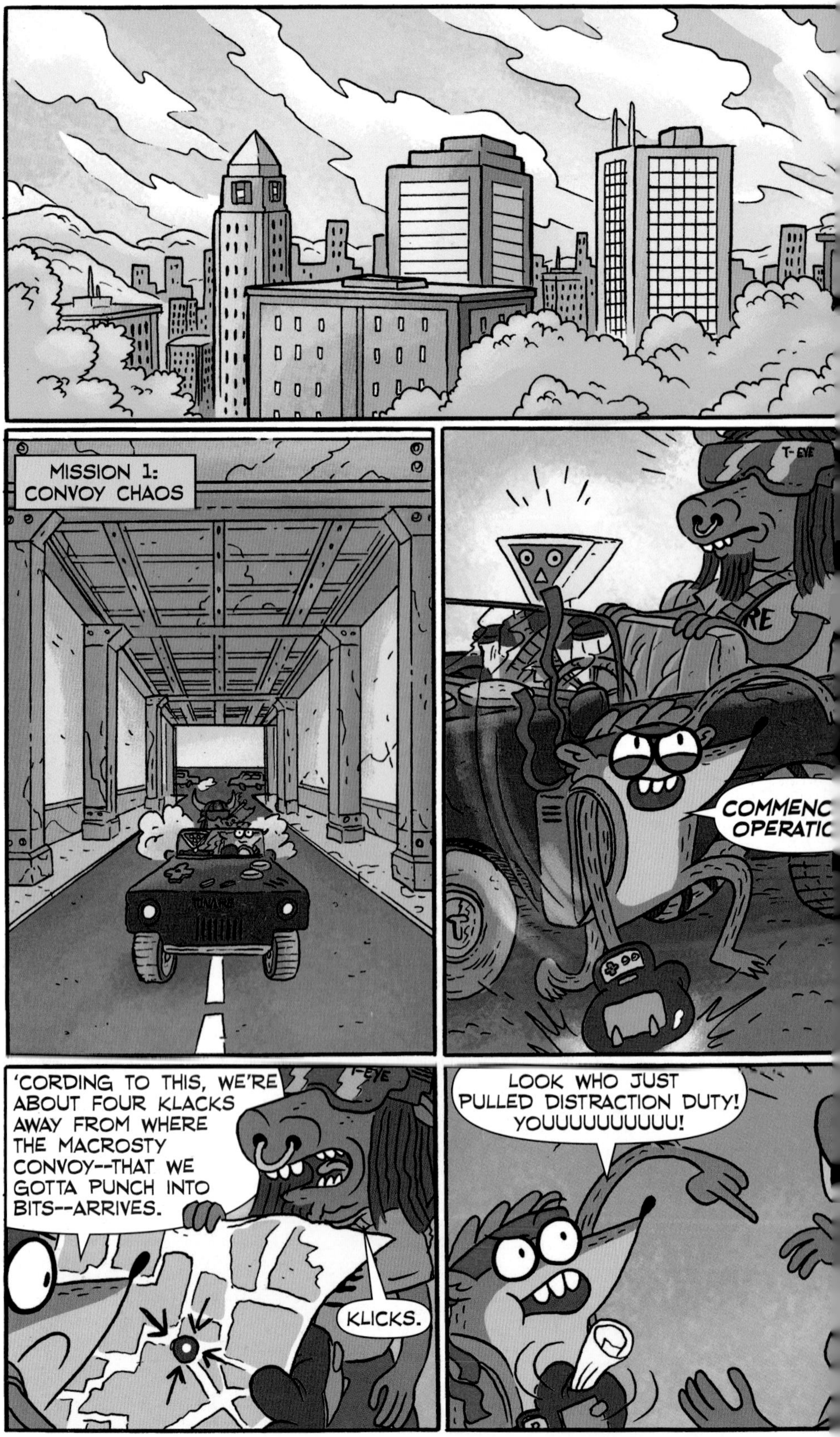
MISSION 1:
CONVOY CHAOS
COMMENC
OPERATIC
'CORDING TO THIS, WE'RE ABOUT FOUR KLACKS AWAY FROM WHERE THE MACROSTY CONVOY--THAT WE GOTTA PUNCH INTO BITS--ARRIVES.
KLICKS.
LOOK WHO JUST PULLED DISTRACTION DUTY! YOUUUUUUUUUU!

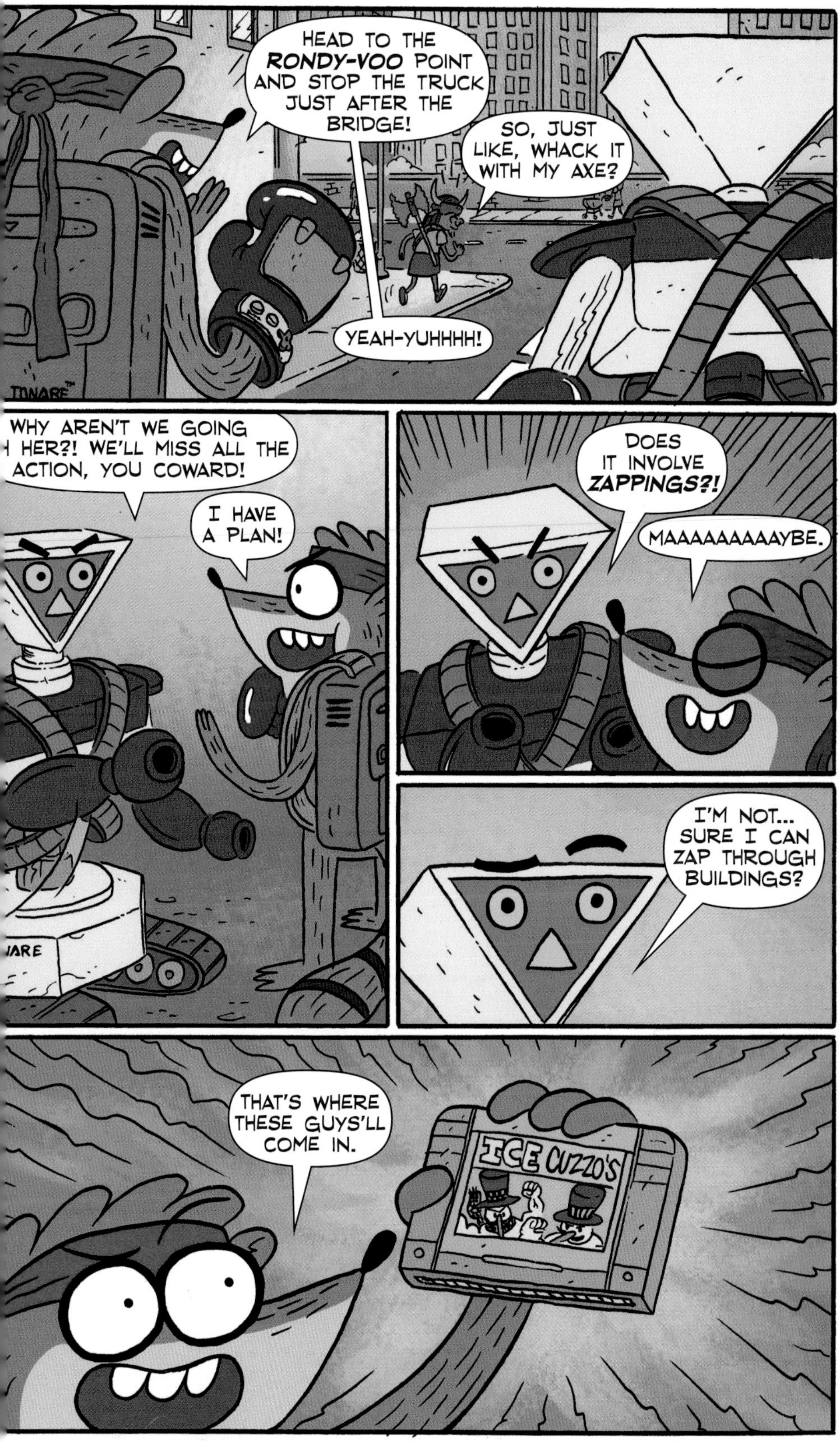
HEAD TO THE RONDY-VOO POINT AND STOP THE TRUCK JUST AFTER THE BRIDGE!
SO, JUST LIKE, WHACK IT WITH MY AXE?
YEAH-YUHHHH!
WHY AREN'T WE GOING
HER?! WE'LL MISS ALL THE ACTION, YOU COWARD!
I HAVE A PLAN!
DOES IT INVOLVE ZAPPINGS?!
MAAAAAAAAAYBE.
I'M NOT... SURE I CAN ZAP THROUGH BUILDINGS?
THAT'S WHERE THESE GUYS'LL COME IN.
ICE CUZZO'S

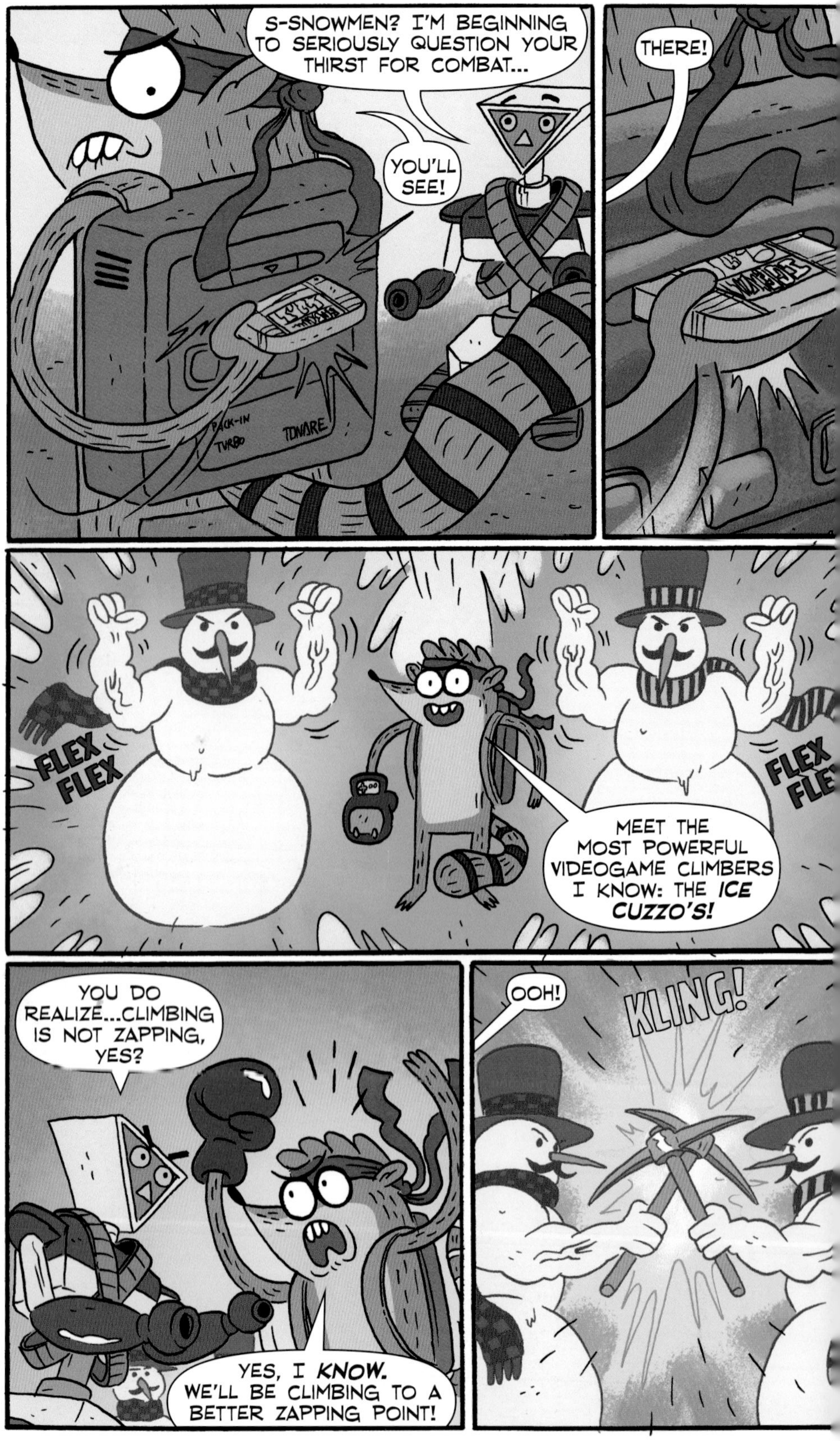
S-SNOWMEN? I'M BEGINNING TO SERIOUSLY QUESTION YOUR THIRST FOR COMBAT...
YOU'LL SEE!
PACK-IN
TURBO
THERE!
FLEX FLEX
MEET THE MOST POWERFUL VIDEOGAME CLIMBERS I KNOW: THE *ICE CUZZO'S!*
FLEX FLEX
YOU DO REALIZE...CLIMBING IS NOT ZAPPING, YES?
YES, I *KNOW.* WE'LL BE CLIMBING TO A BETTER ZAPPING POINT!
OOH!
KLING!

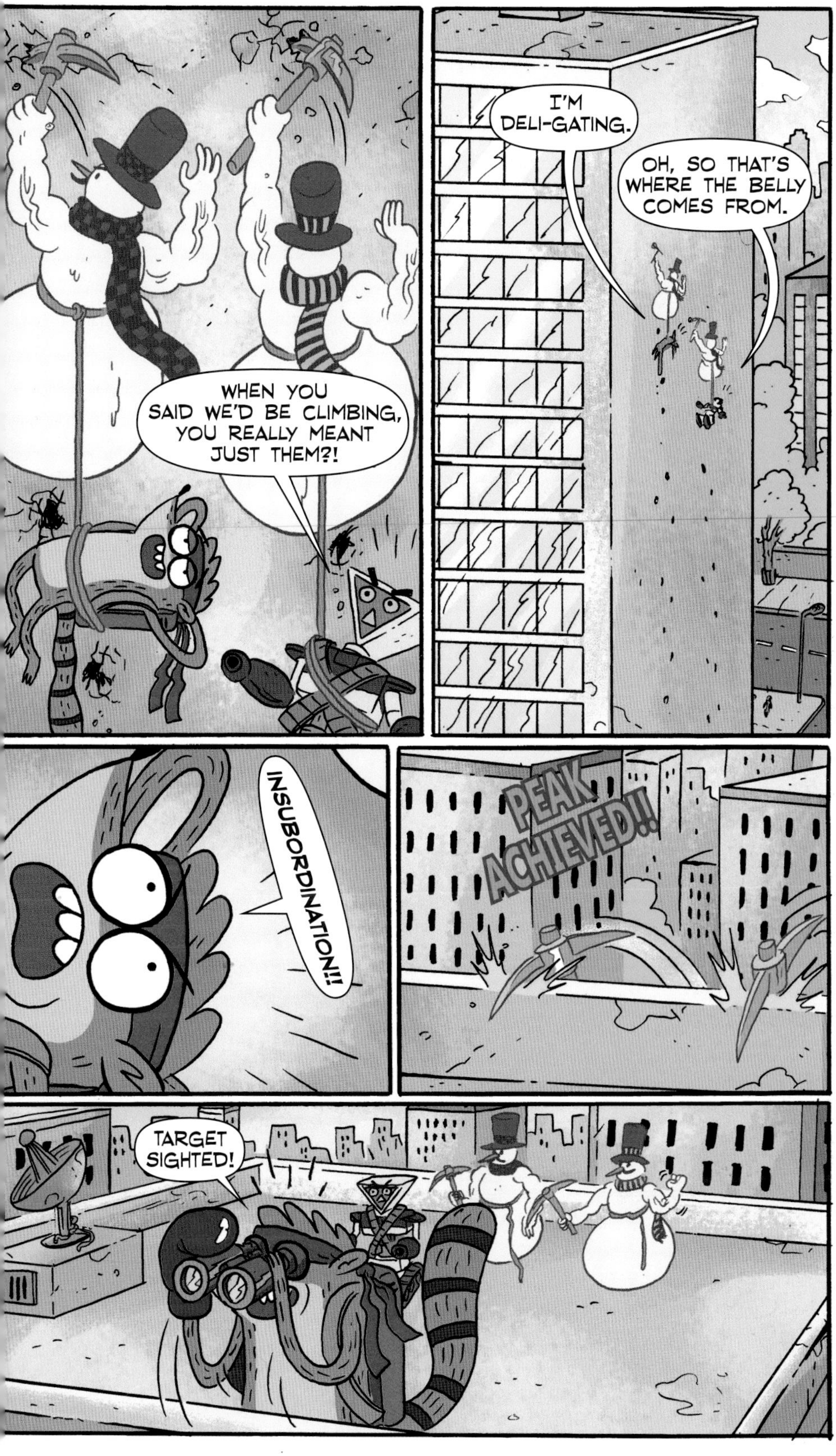
WHEN YOU SAID WE'D BE CLIMBING, YOU REALLY MEANT JUST THEM?!
I'M DELI-GATING.
OH, SO THAT'S WHERE THE BELLY COMES FROM.
INSUBORDINATION!!
PEAK ACHIEVED!!
TARGET SIGHTED!

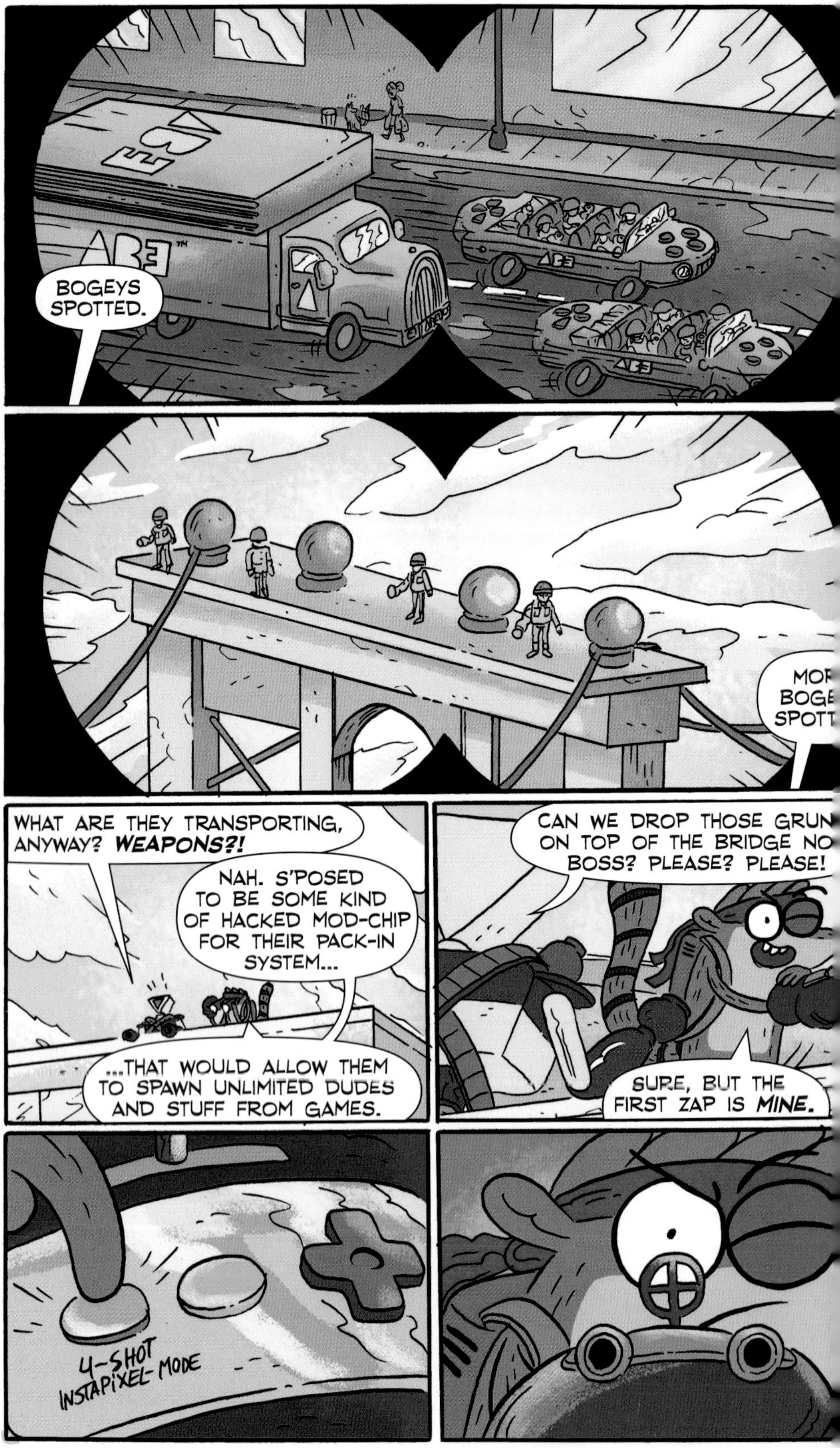
BOGEYS SPOTTED.
MOR BOGE SPOTT
WHAT ARE THEY TRANSPORTING, ANYWAY? **WEAPONS?!**
NAH. S'POSED TO BE SOME KIND OF HACKED MOD-CHIP FOR THEIR PACK-IN SYSTEM...
...THAT WOULD ALLOW THEM TO SPAWN UNLIMITED DUDES AND STUFF FROM GAMES.
CAN WE DROP THOSE GRUN ON TOP OF THE BRIDGE NO BOSS? PLEASE? PLEASE!
SURE, BUT THE FIRST ZAP IS **MINE.**
4-SHOT INSTAPIXEL-MODE

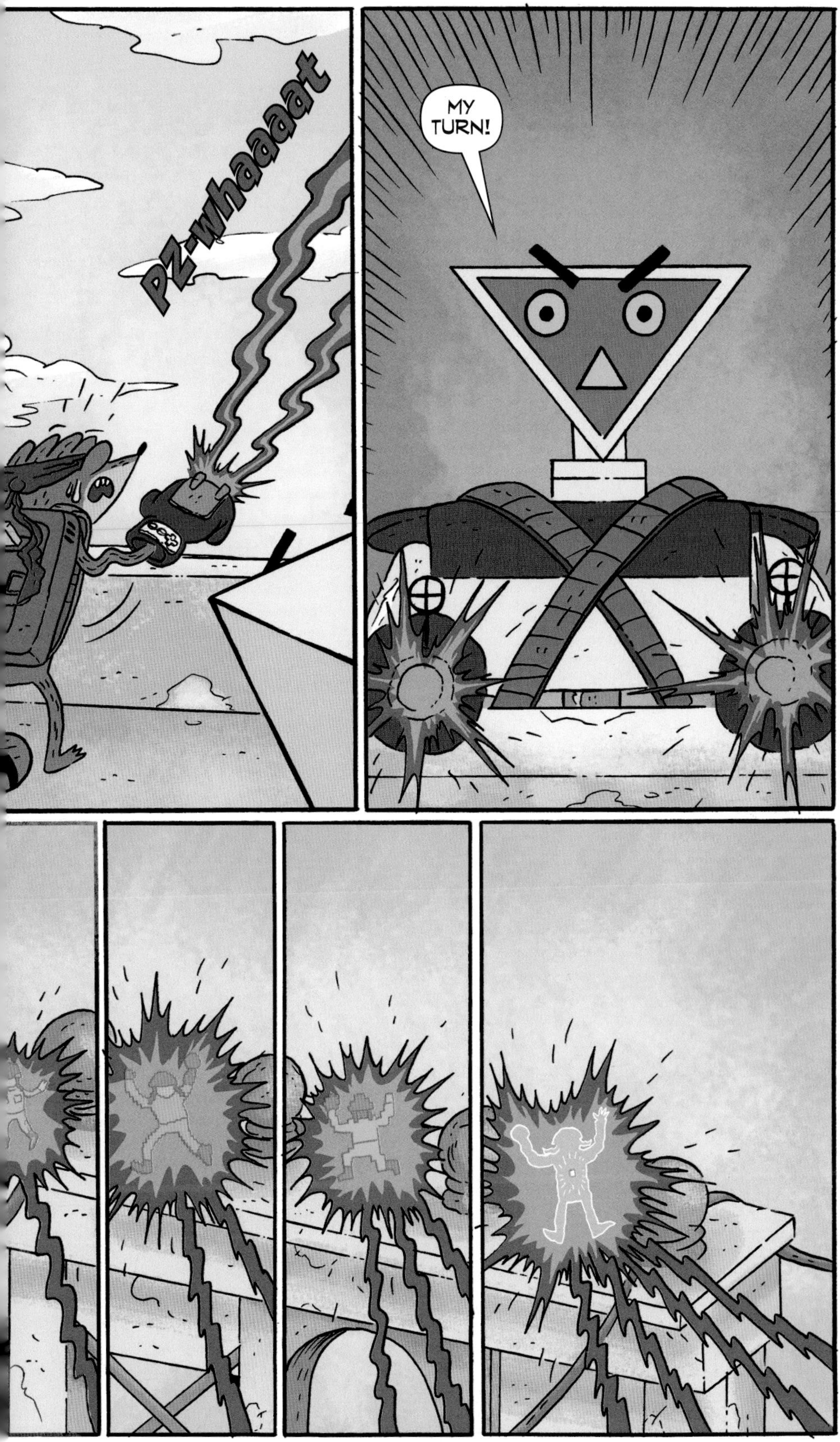
PZ-whaaaat
MY TURN!

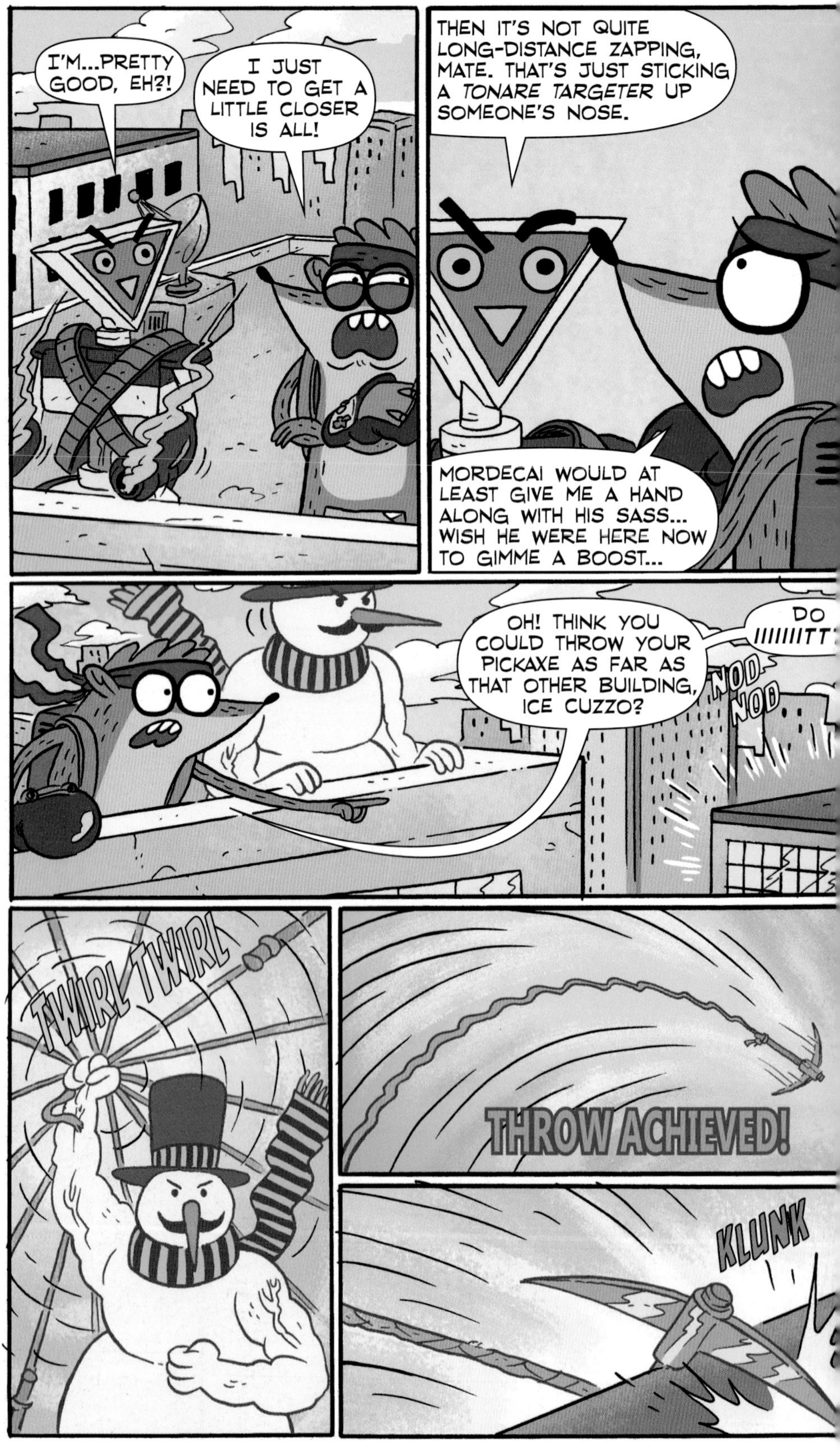
I'M...PRETTY GOOD, EH?!
I JUST NEED TO GET A LITTLE CLOSER IS ALL!
THEN IT'S NOT QUITE LONG-DISTANCE ZAPPING, MATE. THAT'S JUST STICKING A *TONARE TARGETER* UP SOMEONE'S NOSE.
MORDECAI WOULD AT LEAST GIVE ME A HAND ALONG WITH HIS SASS... WISH HE WERE HERE NOW TO GIMME A BOOST...
OH! THINK YOU COULD THROW YOUR PICKAXE AS FAR AS THAT OTHER BUILDING, ICE CUZZO?
NOD NOD
TWIRL TWIRL
THROW ACHIEVED!
KLUNK

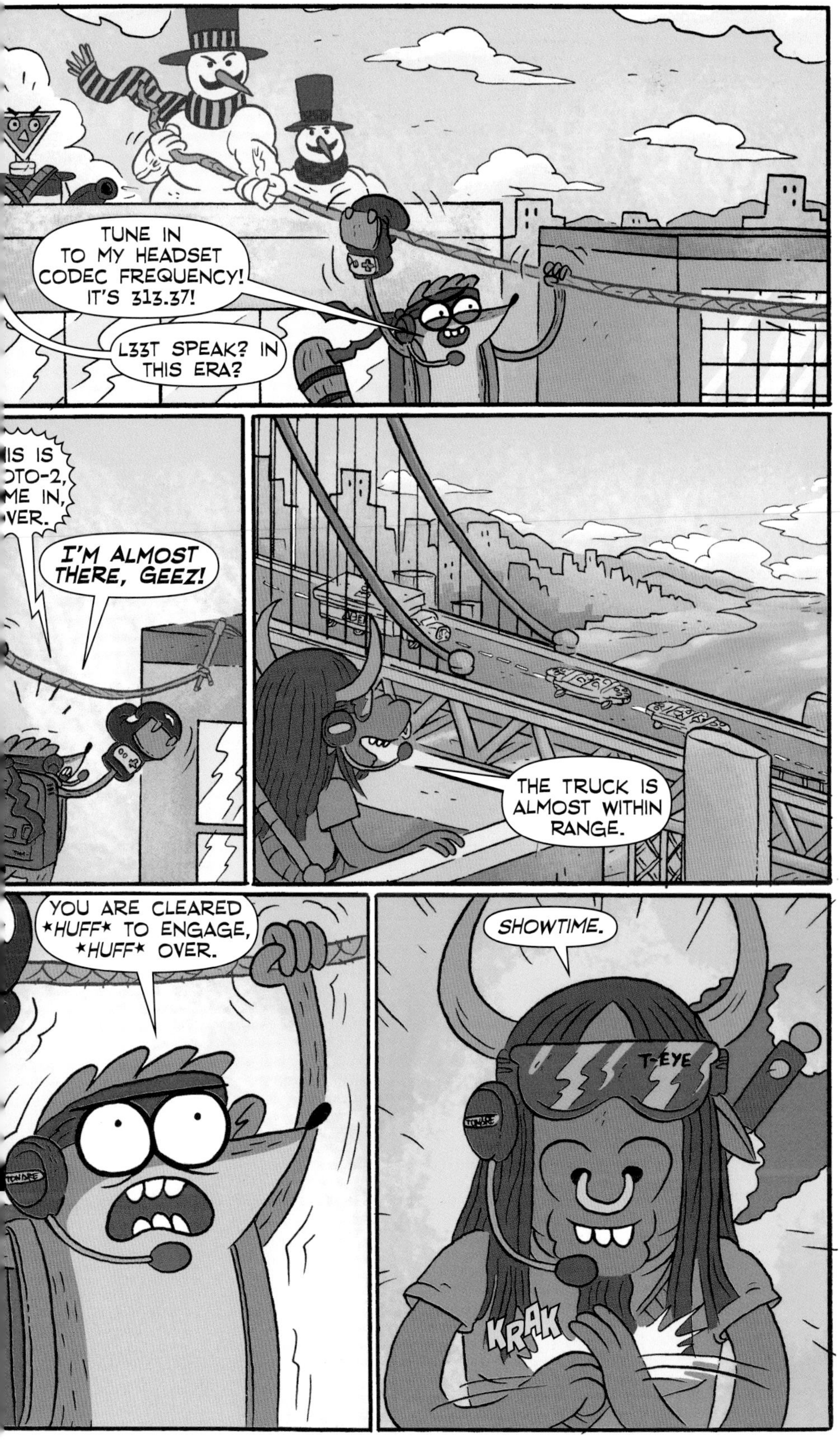
TUNE IN TO MY HEADSET CODEC FREQUENCY! IT'S 313.37!
L33T SPEAK? IN THIS ERA?
IS IS OTO-2, ME IN, VER.
I'M ALMOST THERE, GEEZ!
THE TRUCK IS ALMOST WITHIN RANGE.
YOU ARE CLEARED *HUFF* TO ENGAGE, *HUFF* OVER.
SHOWTIME.
T-EYE
KRAK

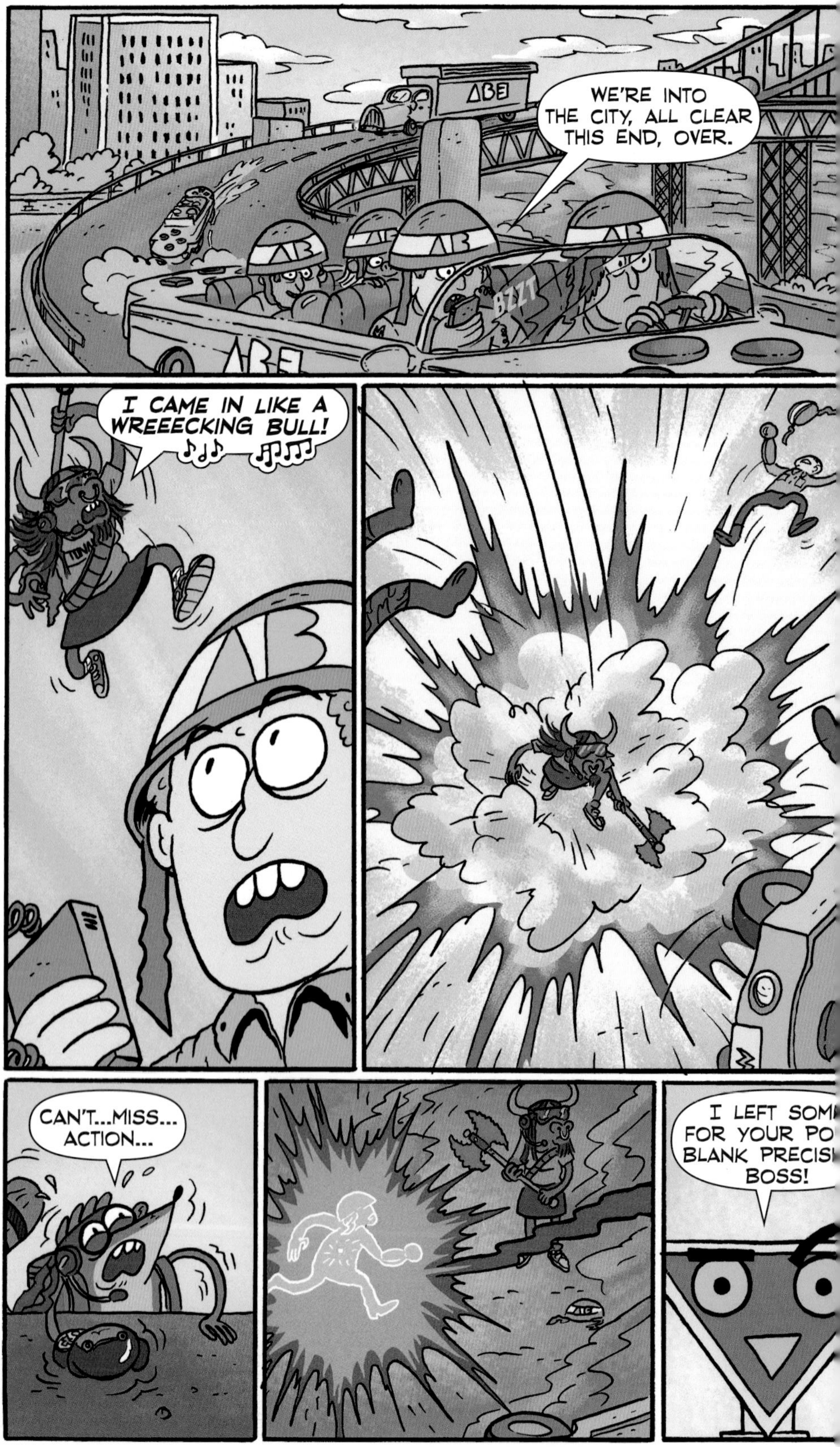
WE'RE INTO THE CITY, ALL CLEAR THIS END, OVER.
BZZT
I CAME IN LIKE A WREEECKING BULL!
CAN'T...MISS... ACTION...
I LEFT SOM
FOR YOUR PO
BLANK PRECIS
BOSS!

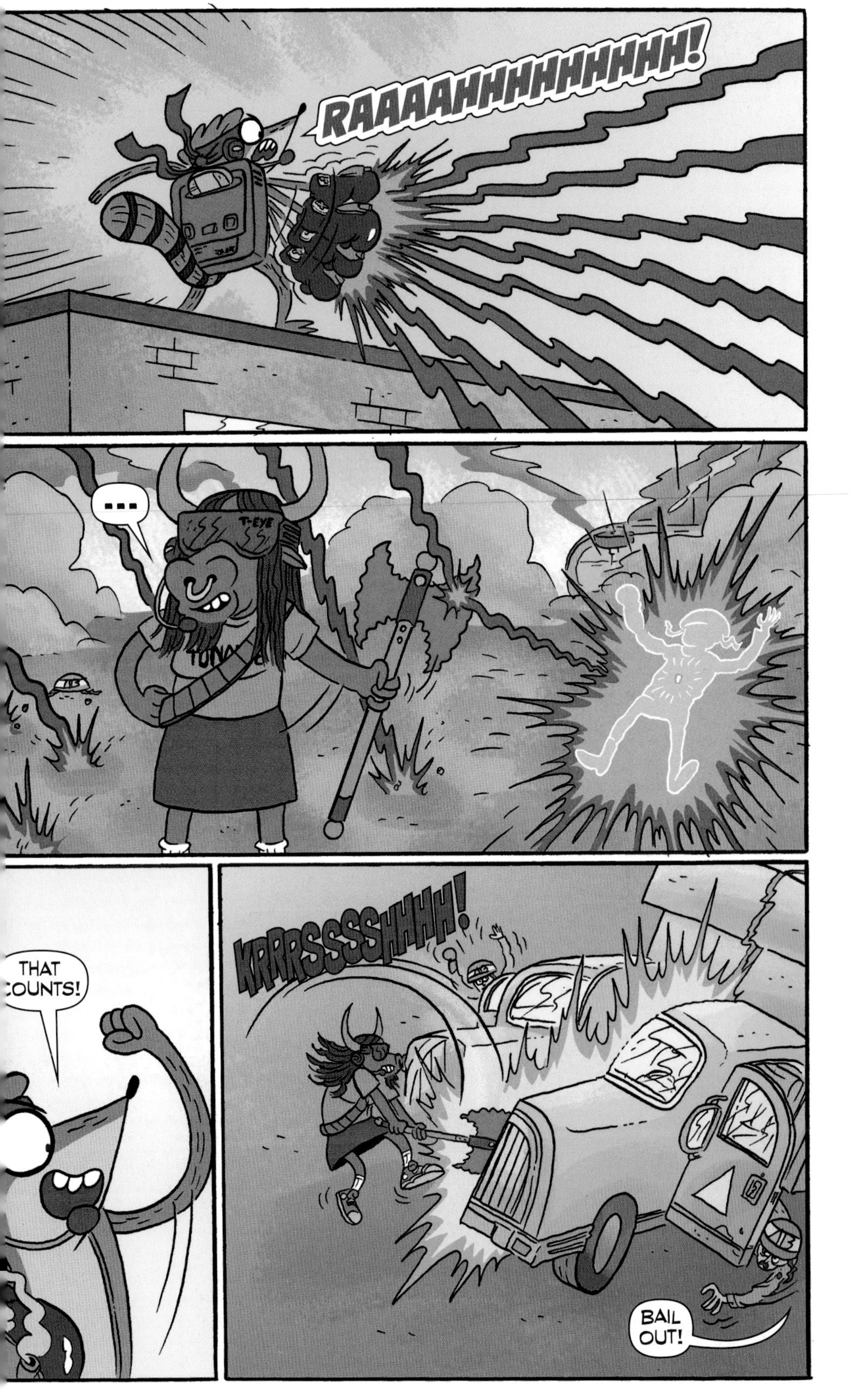
RAAAAHHHHHHHHH!
...
T-EYE
THAT COUNTS!
KRRRSSSSHHHH!
BAIL OUT!

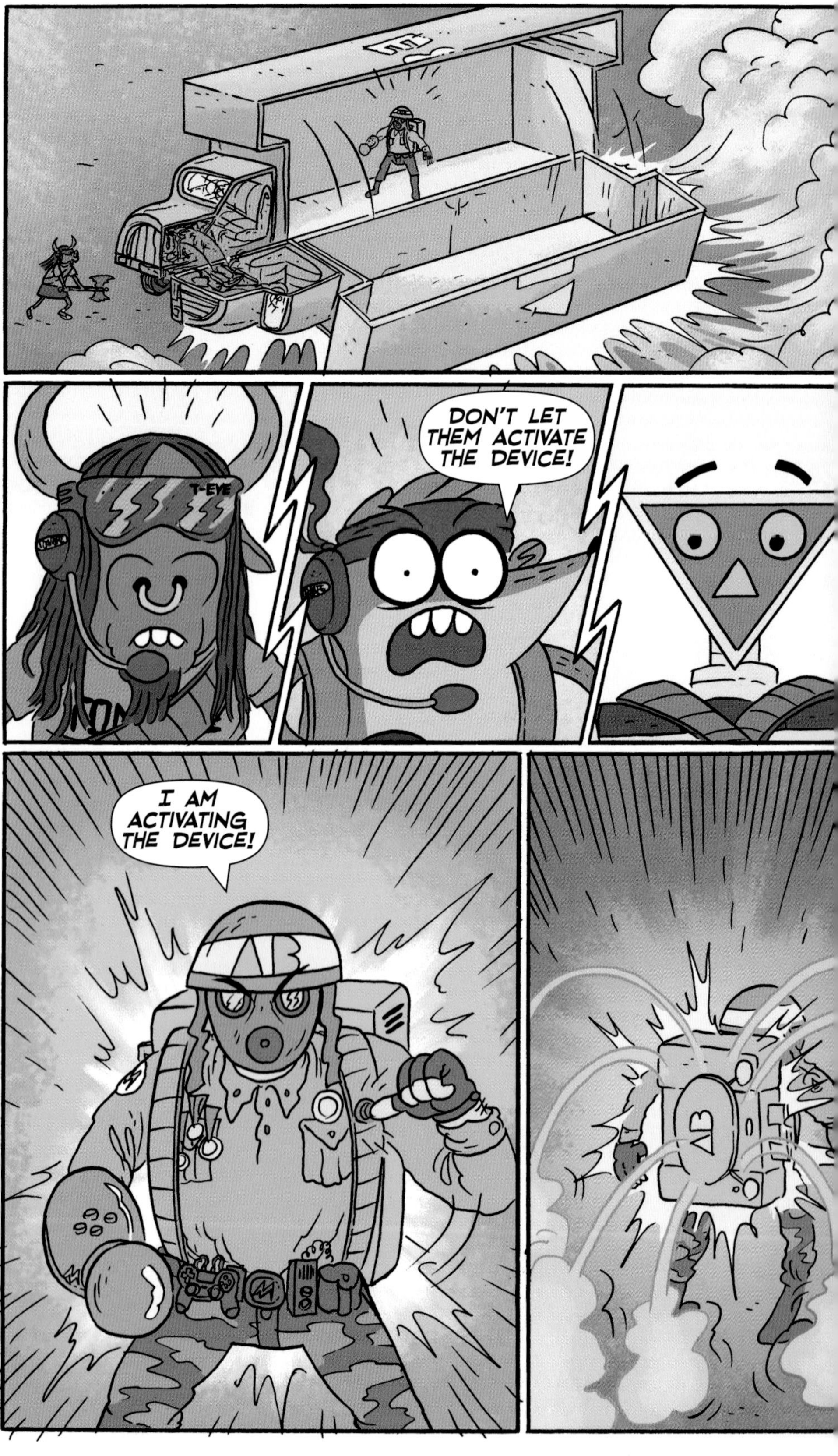

T-EYE
DON'T LET THEM ACTIVATE THE DEVICE!
I AM ACTIVATING THE DEVICE!
AB
AB

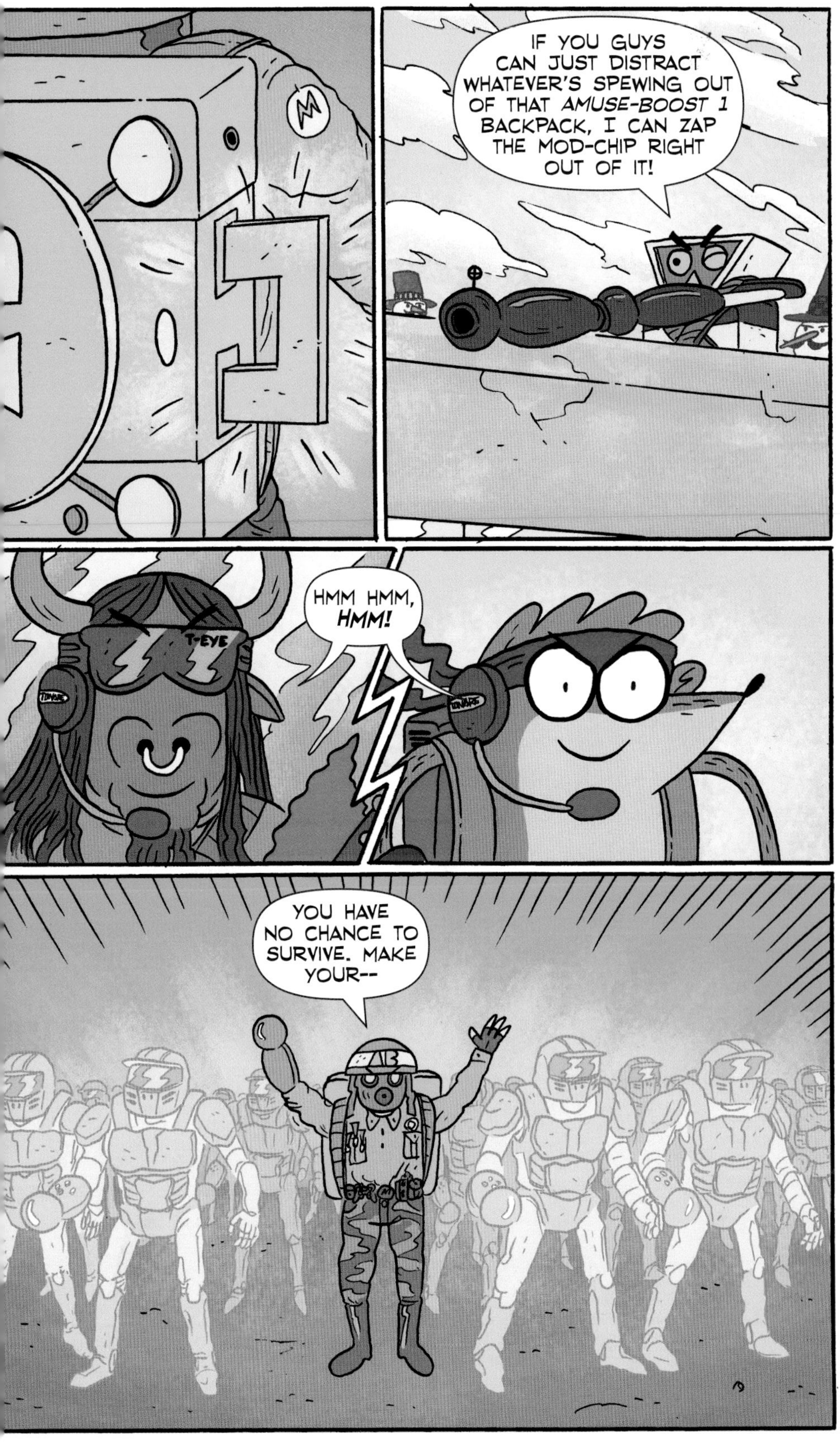
IF YOU GUYS CAN JUST DISTRACT WHATEVER'S SPEWING OUT OF THAT *AMUSE-BOOST 1* BACKPACK, I CAN ZAP THE MOD-CHIP RIGHT OUT OF IT!
T-EYE
HMM HMM, ***HMM!***
YOU HAVE NO CHANCE TO SURVIVE. MAKE YOUR--

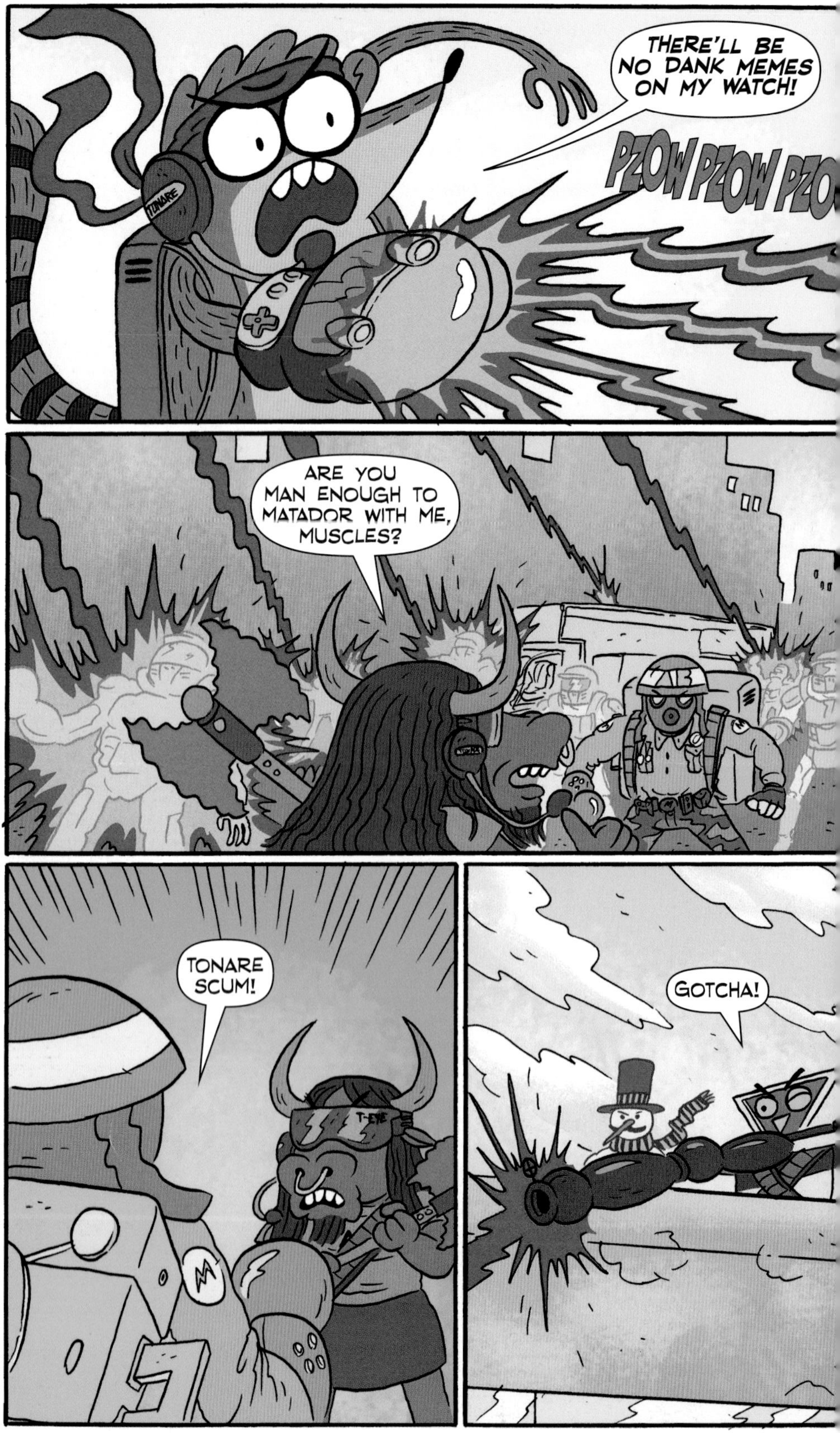

THERE'LL BE NO DANK MEMES ON MY WATCH!
PZOW PZOW PZO
ARE YOU MAN ENOUGH TO MATADOR WITH ME, MUSCLES?
TONARE SCUM!
GOTCHA!

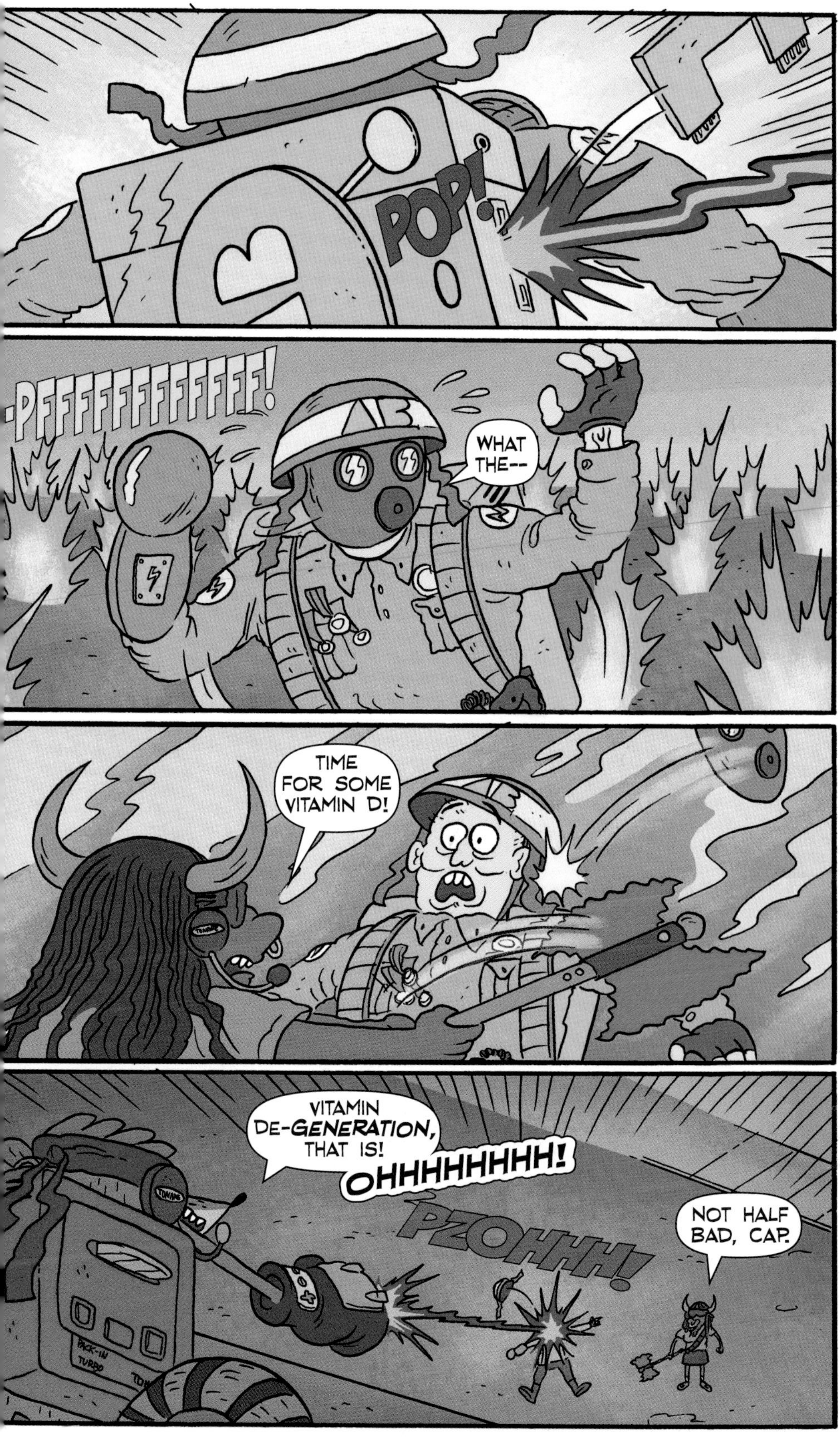
POP!
PFFFFFFFFFFFFF!
WHAT THE--
TIME FOR SOME VITAMIN D!
VITAMIN DE-GENERATION, THAT IS!
OHHHHHHHH!
PZOHHH!
NOT HALF BAD, CAP.

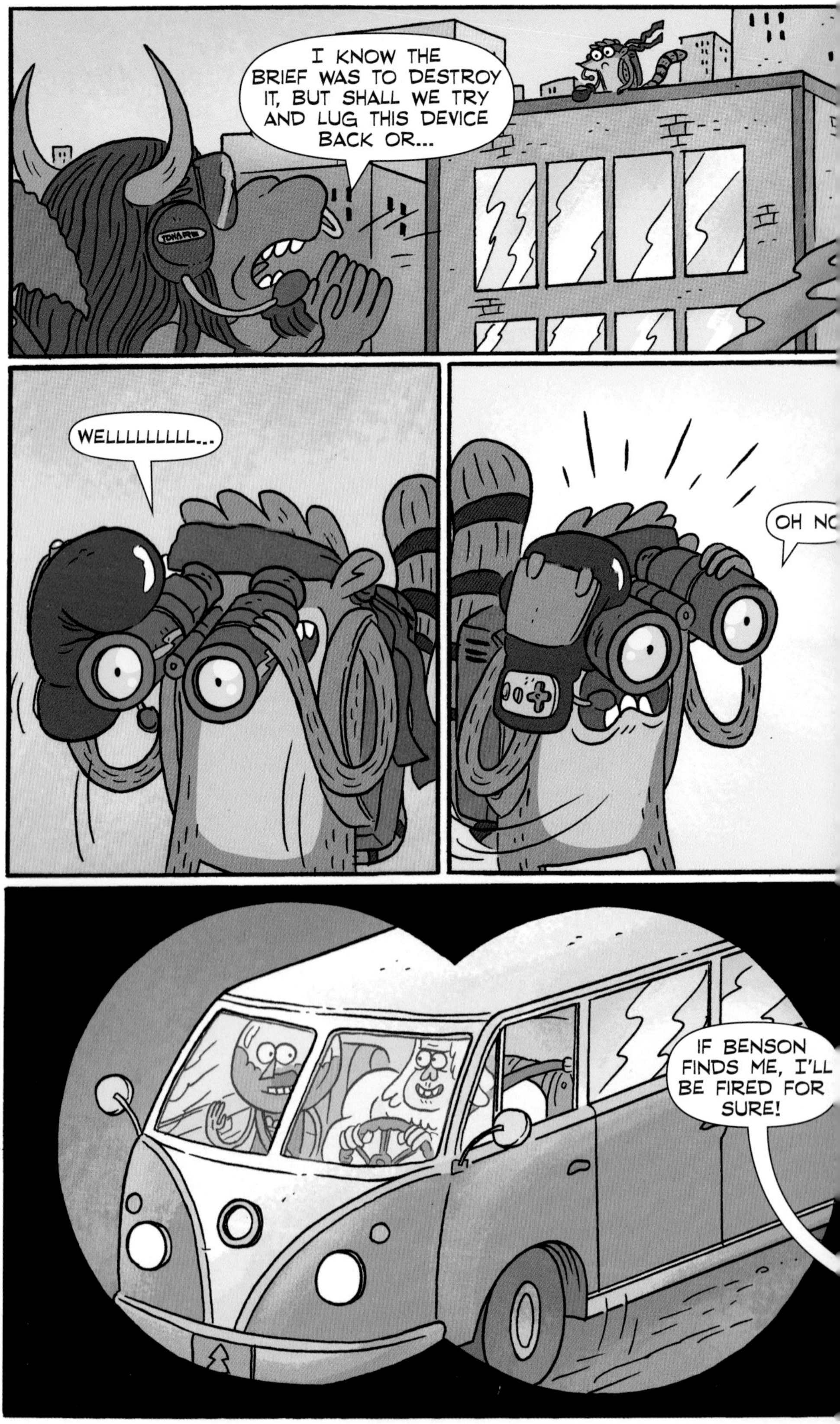
I KNOW THE BRIEF WAS TO DESTROY IT, BUT SHALL WE TRY AND LUG THIS DEVICE BACK OR...
WELLLLLLLLLL...
IF BENSON FINDS ME, I'LL BE FIRED FOR SURE!

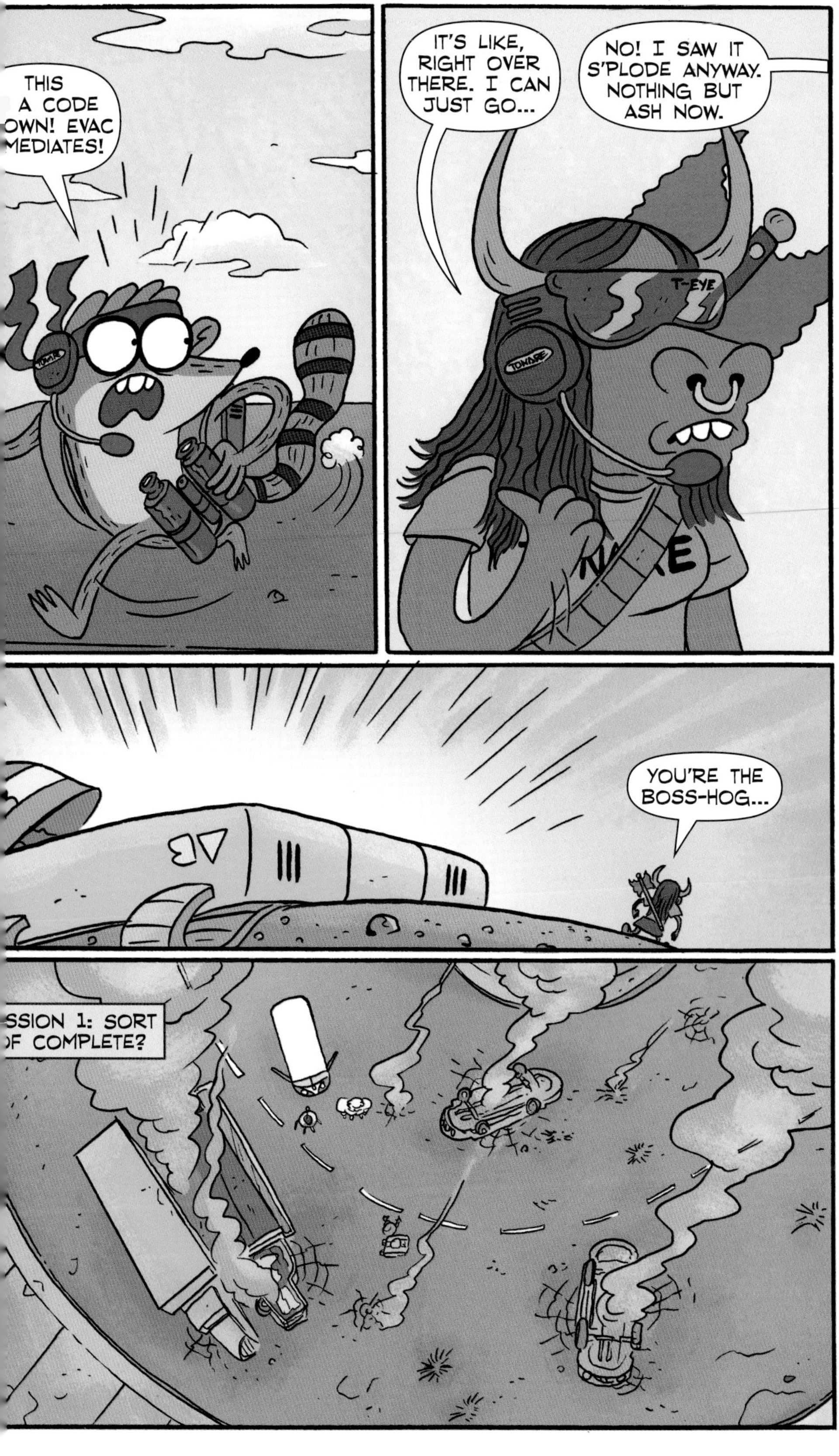
THIS
A CODE
OWN! EVAC
MEDIATES!
TOWARE
IT'S LIKE, RIGHT OVER THERE. I CAN JUST GO...
NO! I SAW IT S'PLODE ANYWAY. NOTHING BUT ASH NOW.
T-EYE
TOWARE
YOU'RE THE BOSS-HOG...
SSION 1: SORT
OF COMPLETE?

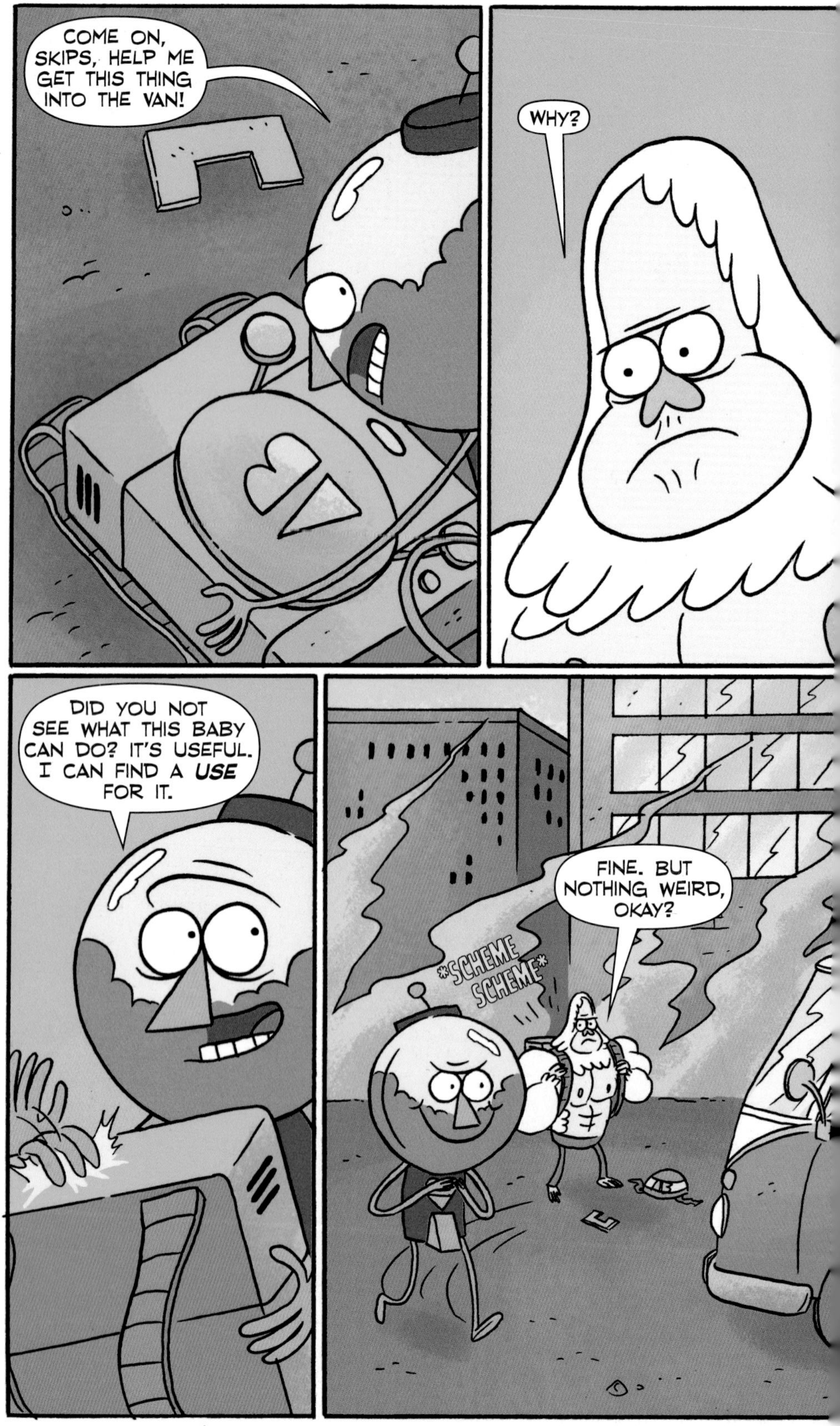
COME ON, SKIPS, HELP ME GET THIS THING INTO THE VAN!
WHY?
DID YOU NOT SEE WHAT THIS BABY CAN DO? IT'S USEFUL. I CAN FIND A *USE* FOR IT.
SCHEME SCHEME
FINE. BUT NOTHING WEIRD, OKAY?

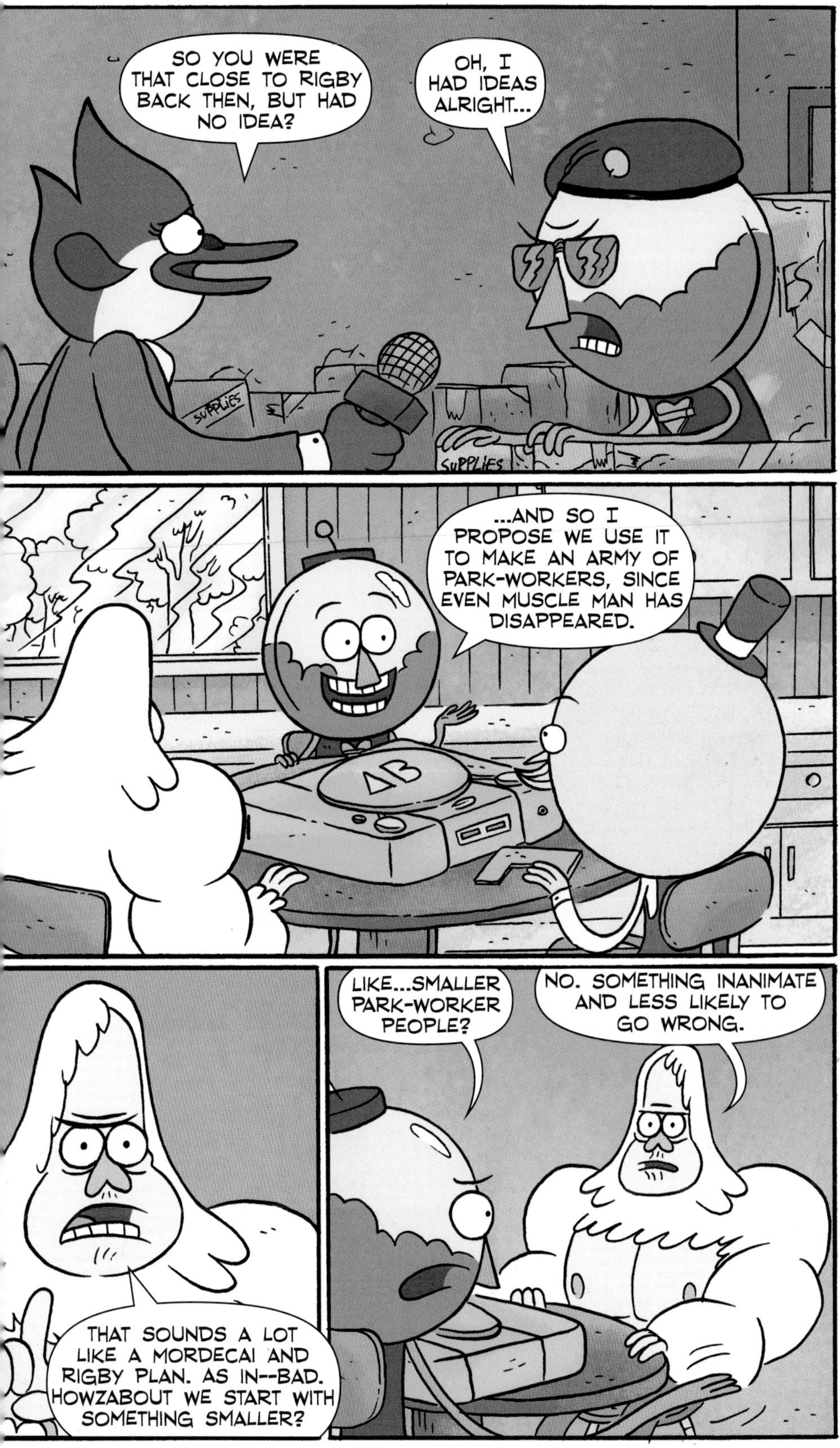

SO YOU WERE THAT CLOSE TO RIGBY BACK THEN, BUT HAD NO IDEA?
OH, I HAD IDEAS ALRIGHT...
SUPPLIES
SUPPLIES
...AND SO I PROPOSE WE USE IT TO MAKE AN ARMY OF PARK-WORKERS, SINCE EVEN MUSCLE MAN HAS DISAPPEARED.
THAT SOUNDS A LOT LIKE A MORDECAI AND RIGBY PLAN. AS IN--BAD. HOWZABOUT WE START WITH SOMETHING SMALLER?
LIKE...SMALLER PARK-WORKER PEOPLE?
NO. SOMETHING INANIMATE AND LESS LIKELY TO GO WRONG.

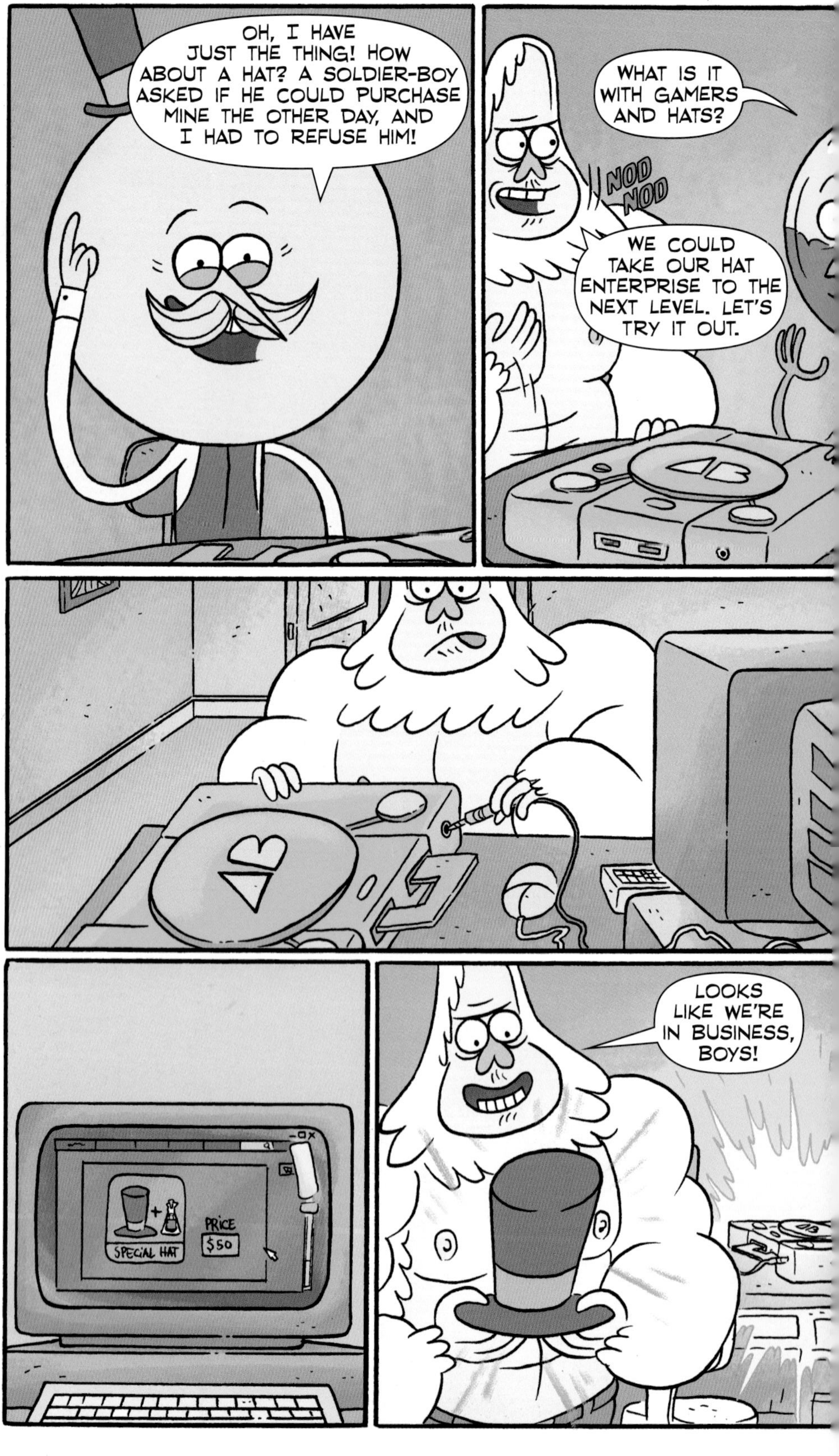
OH, I HAVE JUST THE THING! HOW ABOUT A HAT? A SOLDIER-BOY ASKED IF HE COULD PURCHASE MINE THE OTHER DAY, AND I HAD TO REFUSE HIM!
WHAT IS IT WITH GAMERS AND HATS?
NOD NOD
WE COULD TAKE OUR HAT ENTERPRISE TO THE NEXT LEVEL. LET'S TRY IT OUT.
SPECIAL HAT
PRICE
$50
LOOKS LIKE WE'RE IN BUSINESS, BOYS!

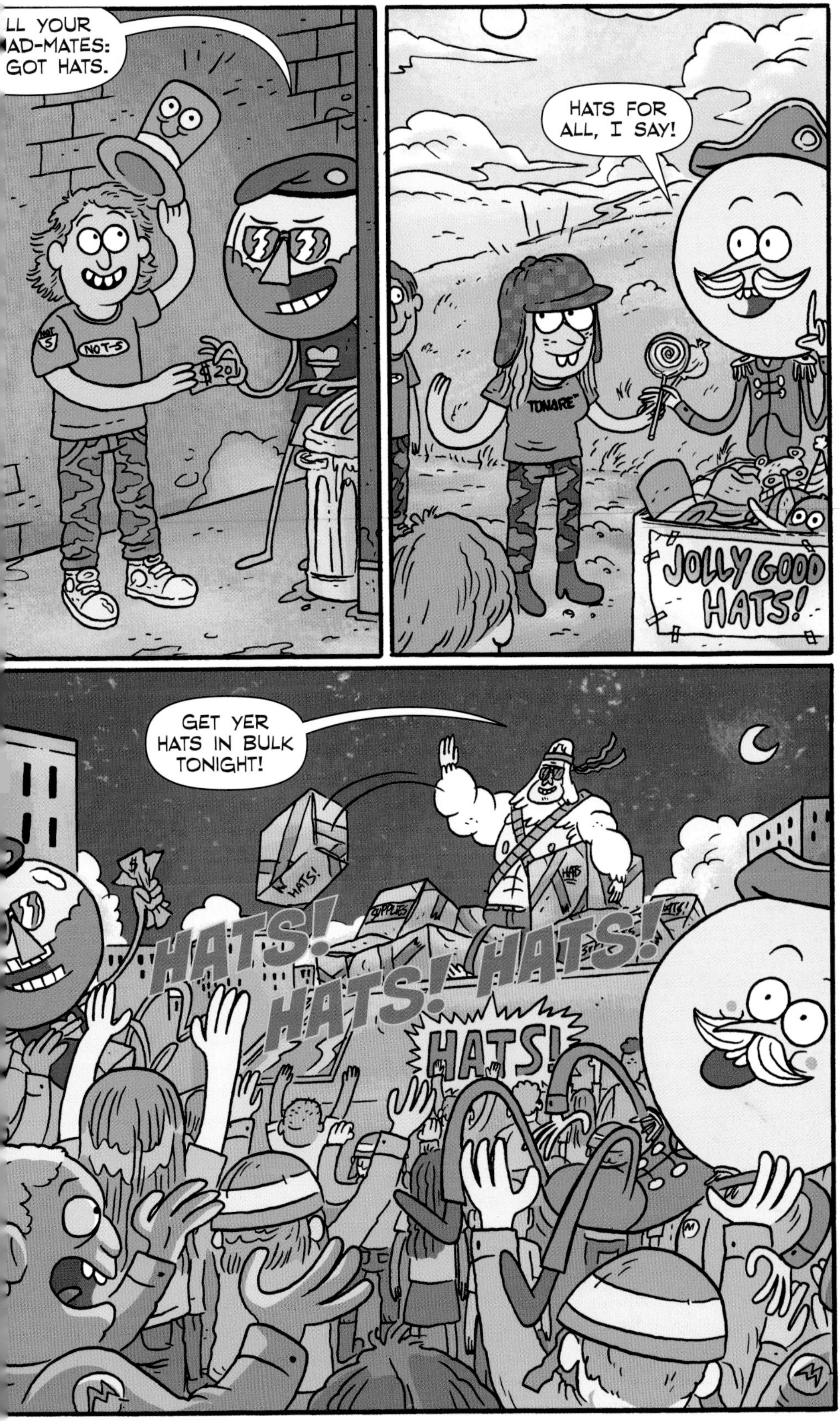
LL YOUR
AD-MATES:
GOT HATS.
NOT-5
$20
HATS FOR ALL, I SAY!
TONARE
JOLLY GOOD HATS!
GET YER HATS IN BULK TONIGHT!
HATS!
SUPPLIES
HATS! HATS! HATS!
HATS!

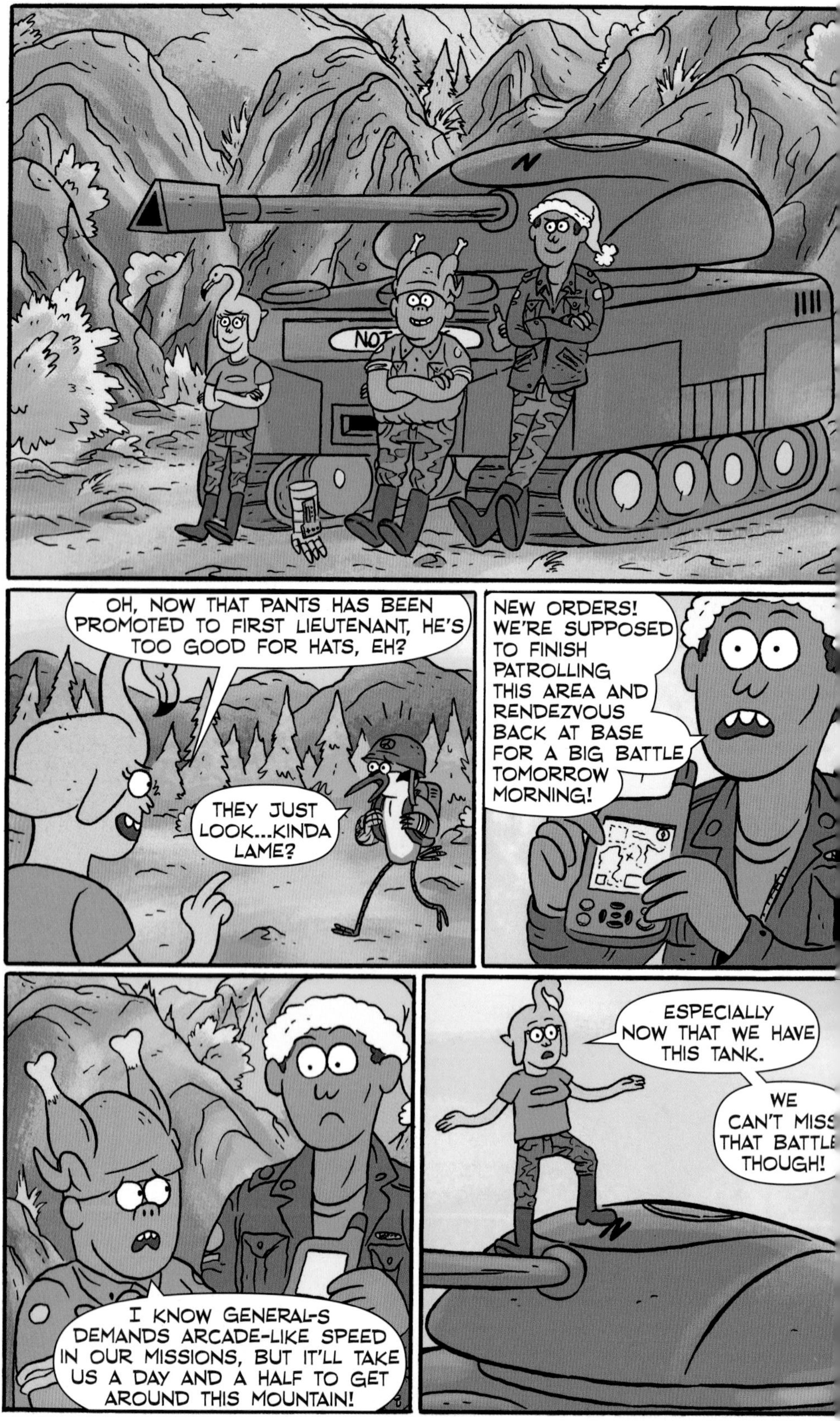
NOT
OH, NOW THAT PANTS HAS BEEN PROMOTED TO FIRST LIEUTENANT, HE'S TOO GOOD FOR HATS, EH?
THEY JUST LOOK...KINDA LAME?
NEW ORDERS! WE'RE SUPPOSED TO FINISH PATROLLING THIS AREA AND RENDEZVOUS BACK AT BASE FOR A BIG BATTLE TOMORROW MORNING!
I KNOW GENERAL-S DEMANDS ARCADE-LIKE SPEED IN OUR MISSIONS, BUT IT'LL TAKE US A DAY AND A HALF TO GET AROUND THIS MOUNTAIN!
ESPECIALLY NOW THAT WE HAVE THIS TANK.
WE CAN'T MISS THAT BATTLE THOUGH!

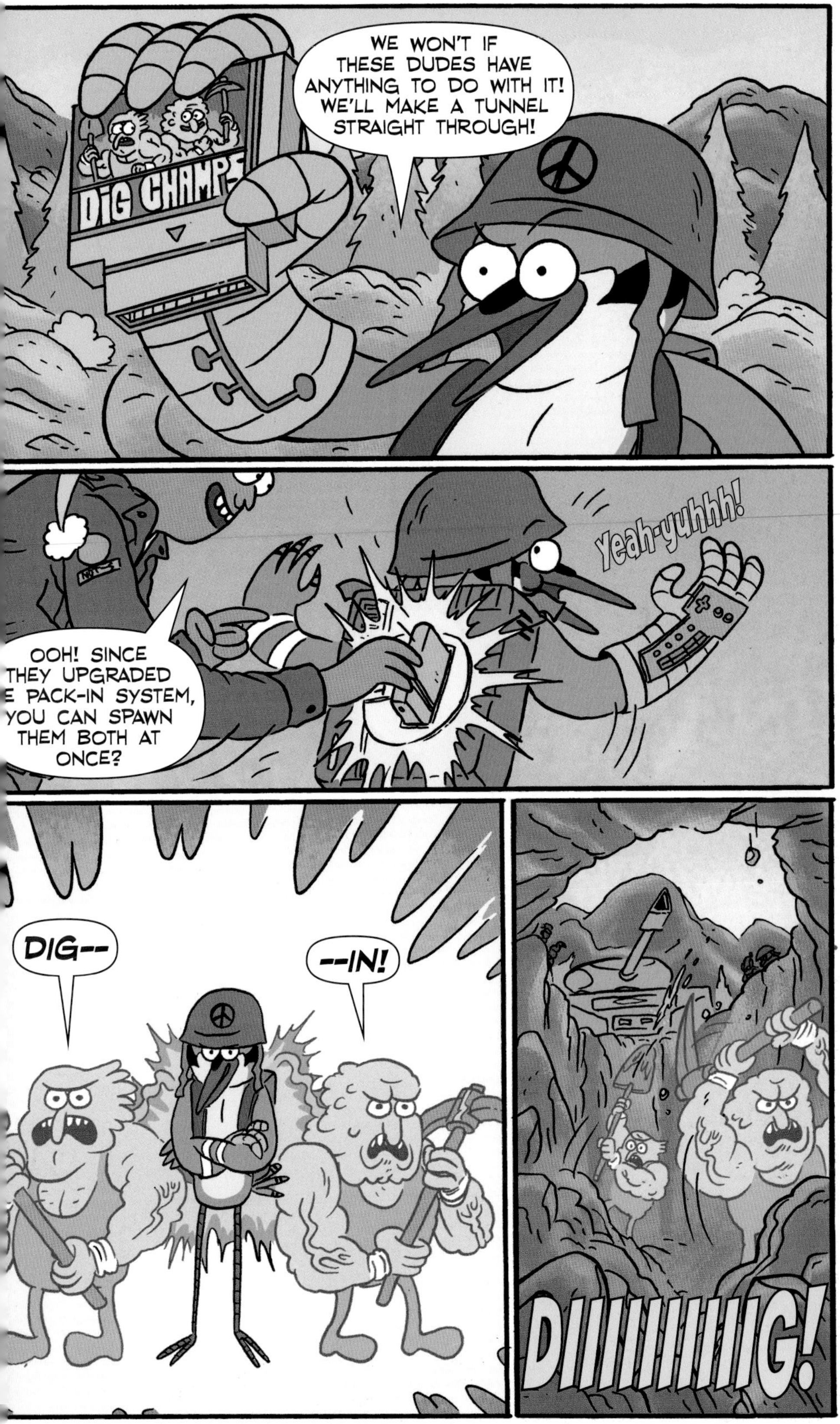
DIG CHAMPS
WE WON'T IF THESE DUDES HAVE ANYTHING TO DO WITH IT! WE'LL MAKE A TUNNEL STRAIGHT THROUGH!
Yeah-yuhhh!
OOH! SINCE THEY UPGRADED E PACK-IN SYSTEM, YOU CAN SPAWN THEM BOTH AT ONCE?
DIG--
--IN!
DIIIIIIIIIG!

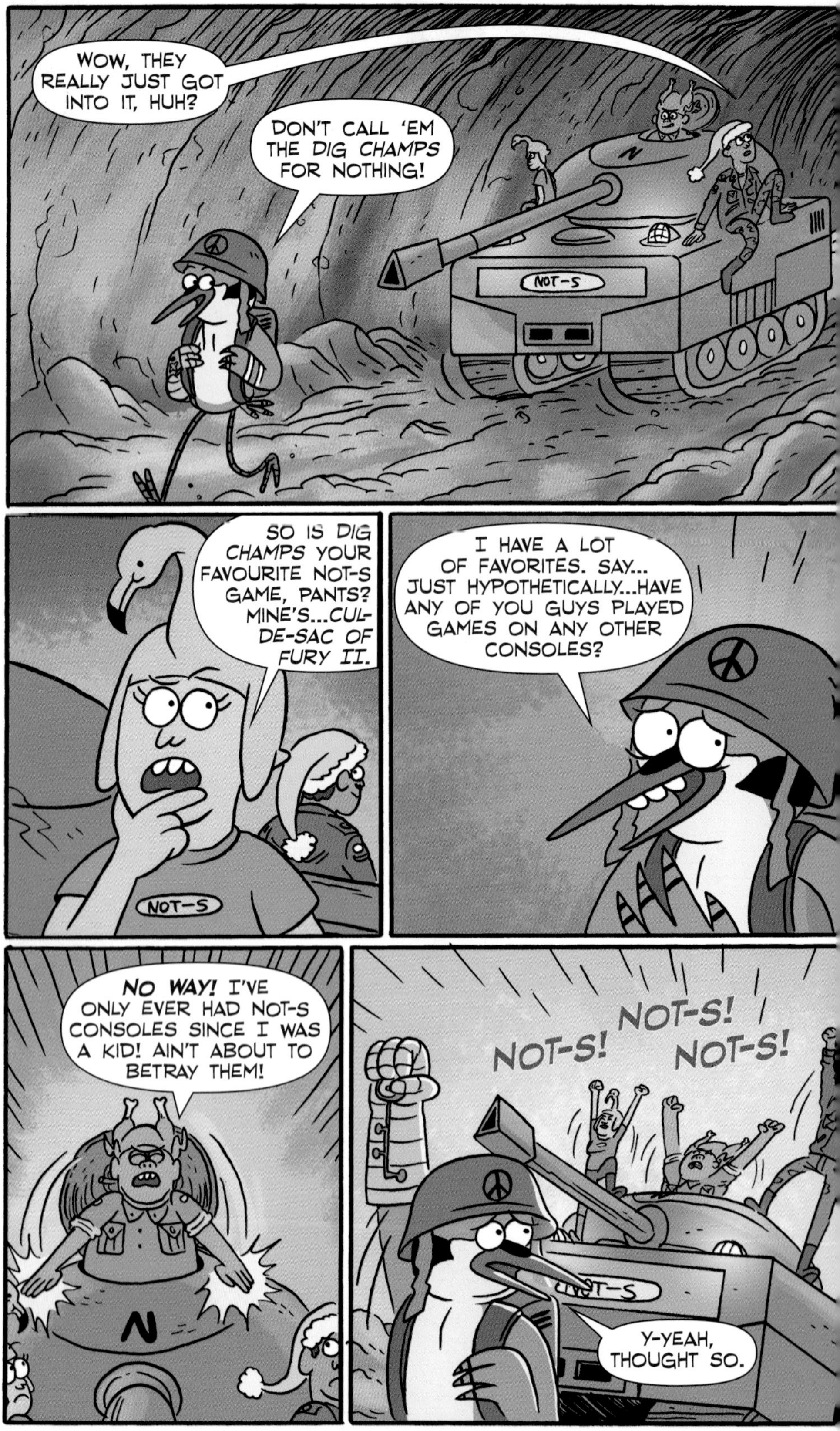
WOW, THEY REALLY JUST GOT INTO IT, HUH?
DON'T CALL 'EM THE *DIG CHAMPS* FOR NOTHING!
NOT-S
SO IS *DIG CHAMPS* YOUR FAVOURITE NOT-S GAME, PANTS? MINE'S...*CUL-DE-SAC OF FURY II.*
NOT-S
I HAVE A LOT OF FAVORITES. SAY... JUST HYPOTHETICALLY...HAVE ANY OF YOU GUYS PLAYED GAMES ON ANY OTHER CONSOLES?
NO WAY! I'VE ONLY EVER HAD NOT-S CONSOLES SINCE I WAS A KID! AIN'T ABOUT TO BETRAY THEM!
NOT-S! NOT-S! NOT-S!
Y-YEAH, THOUGHT SO.

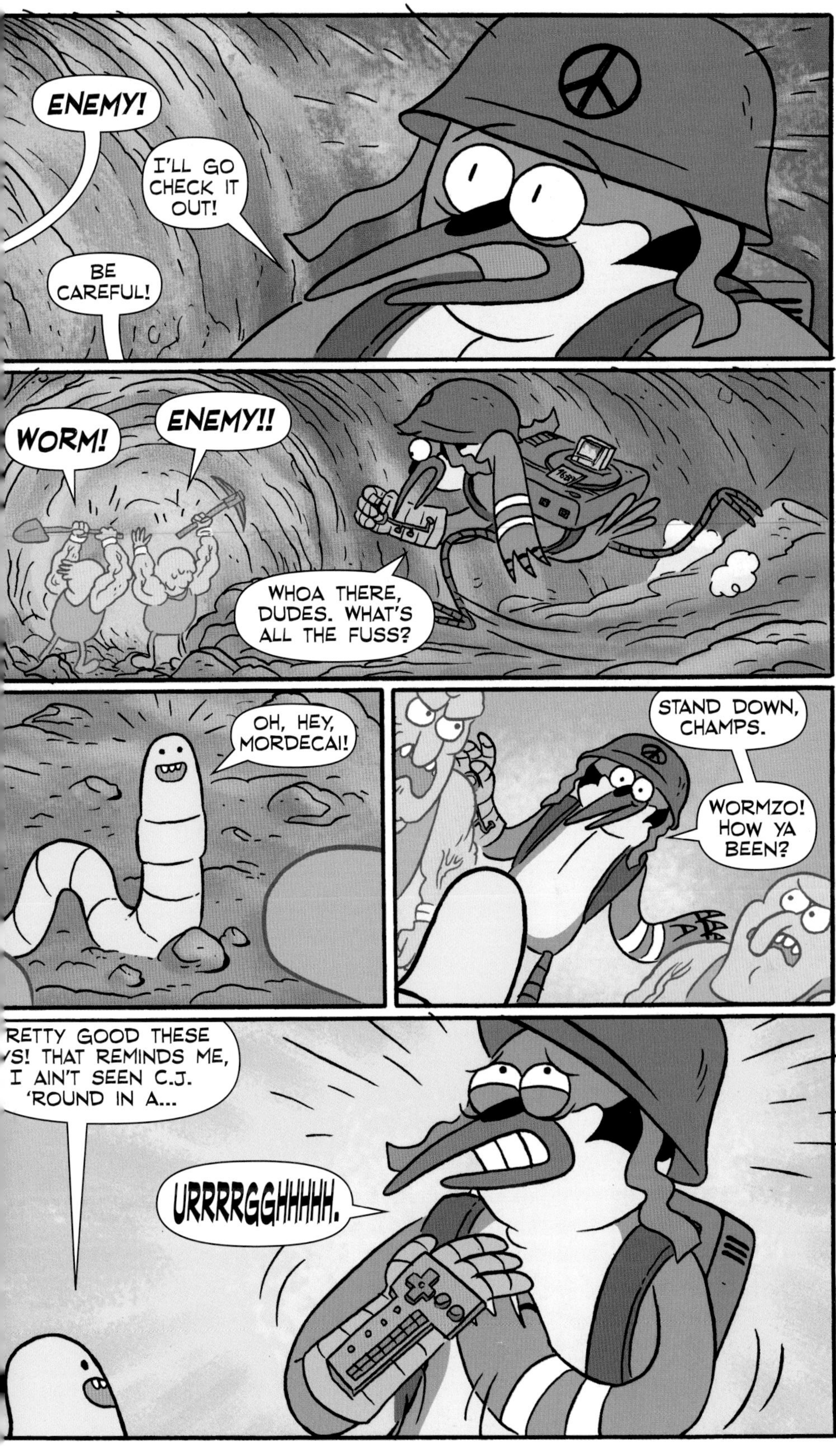
ENEMY!
I'LL GO CHECK IT OUT!
BE CAREFUL!
WORM!
ENEMY!!
WHOA THERE, DUDES. WHAT'S ALL THE FUSS?
OH, HEY, MORDECAI!
STAND DOWN, CHAMPS.
WORMZO! HOW YA BEEN?
RETTY GOOD THESE
S! THAT REMINDS ME,
I AIN'T SEEN C.J.
'ROUND IN A...
URRRRGGHHHHH.

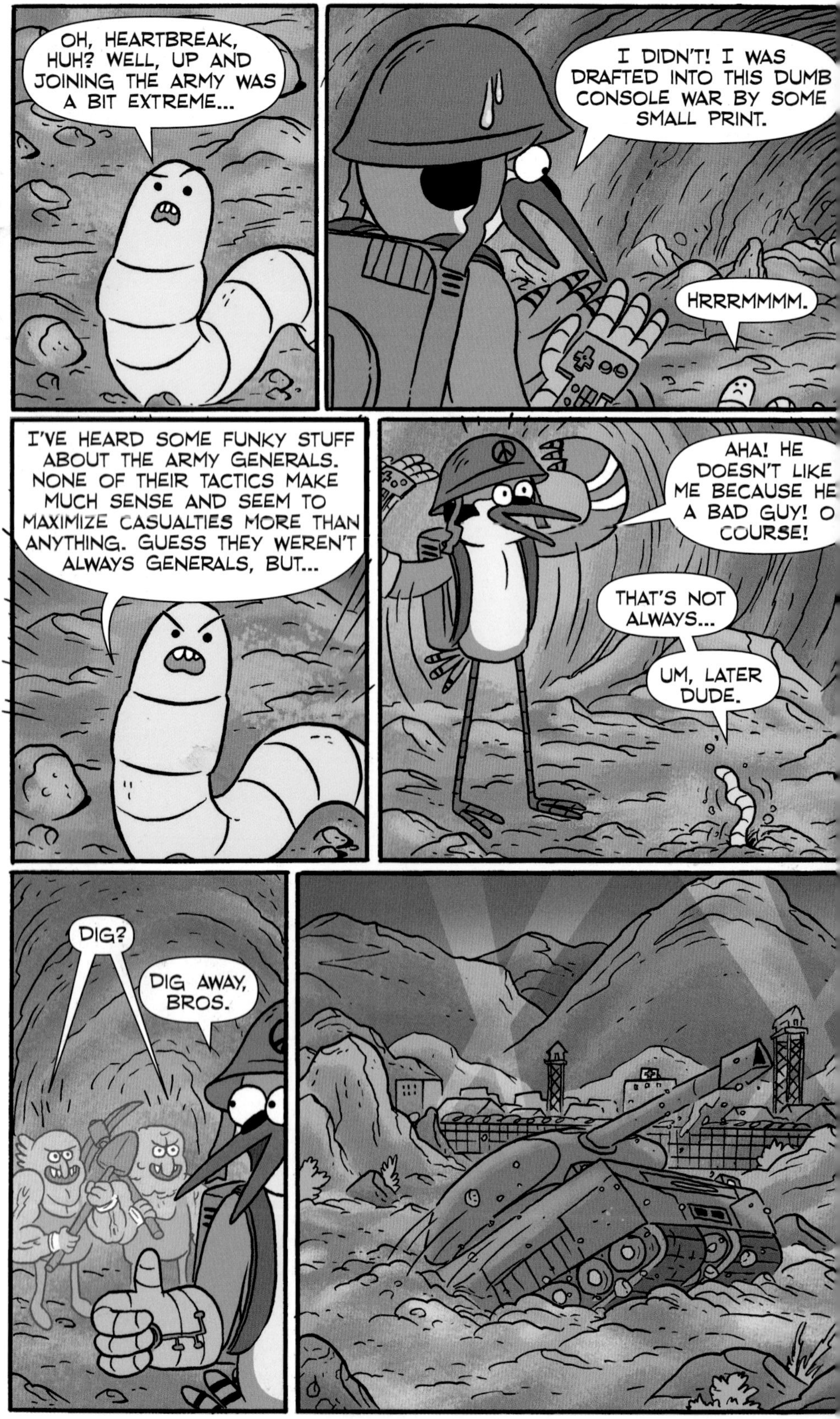
OH, HEARTBREAK, HUH? WELL, UP AND JOINING THE ARMY WAS A BIT EXTREME...
I DIDN'T! I WAS DRAFTED INTO THIS DUMB CONSOLE WAR BY SOME SMALL PRINT.
HRRRMMMM.
I'VE HEARD SOME FUNKY STUFF ABOUT THE ARMY GENERALS. NONE OF THEIR TACTICS MAKE MUCH SENSE AND SEEM TO MAXIMIZE CASUALTIES MORE THAN ANYTHING. GUESS THEY WEREN'T ALWAYS GENERALS, BUT...
AHA! HE DOESN'T LIKE ME BECAUSE HE A BAD GUY! O COURSE!
THAT'S NOT ALWAYS...
UM, LATER DUDE.
DIG?
DIG AWAY, BROS.

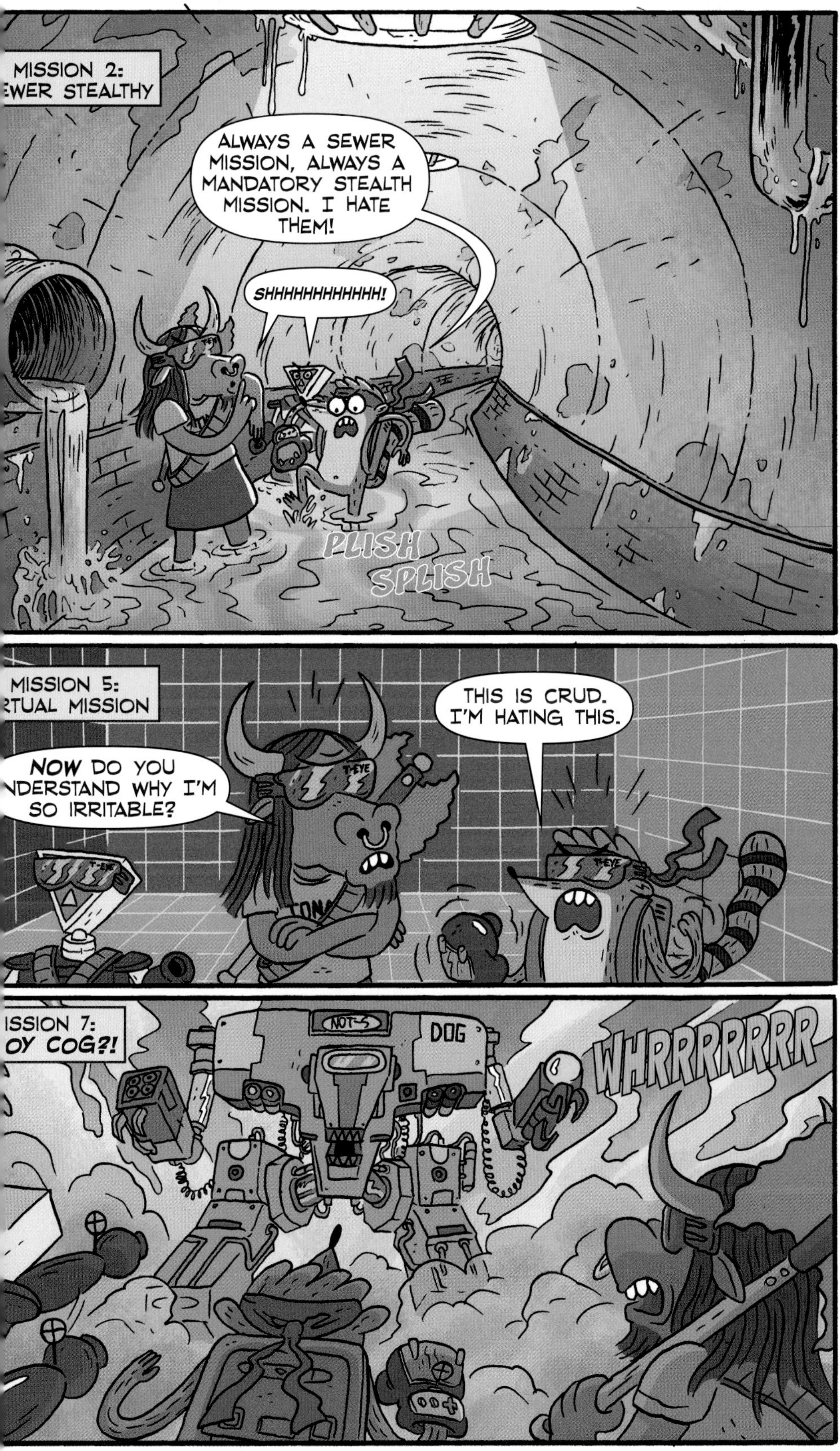
MISSION 2:
EWER STEALTHY
ALWAYS A SEWER MISSION, ALWAYS A MANDATORY STEALTH MISSION. I HATE THEM!
SHHHHHHHHHHHH!
PLISH
SPLISH
MISSION 5:
RTUAL MISSION
THIS IS CRUD. I'M HATING THIS.
NOW DO YOU
NDERSTAND WHY I'M
SO IRRITABLE?
ISSION 7:
OY COG?!
DOG
WHRRRRRRR

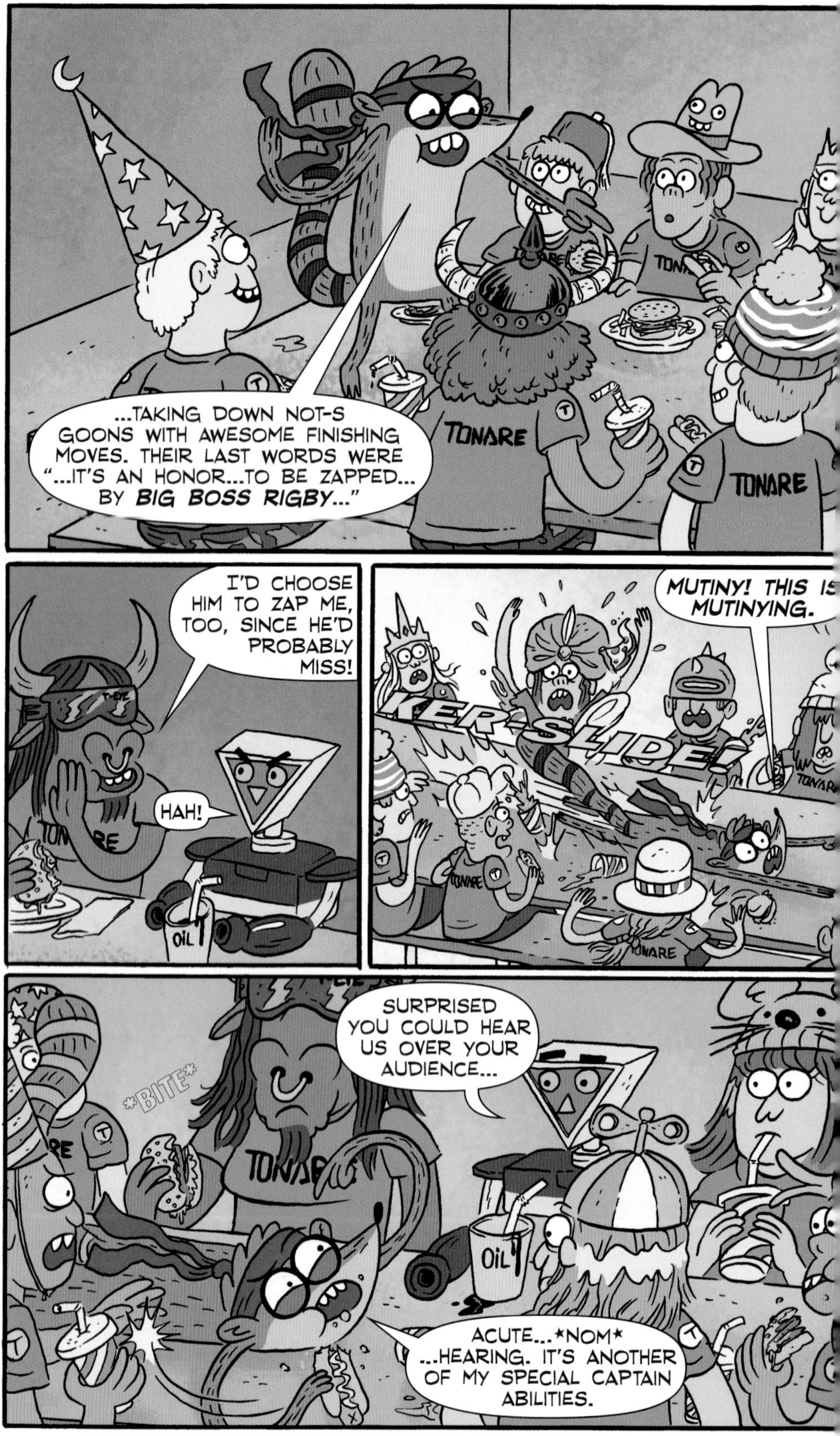
...TAKING DOWN NOT-S GOONS WITH AWESOME FINISHING MOVES. THEIR LAST WORDS WERE "...IT'S AN HONOR...TO BE ZAPPED... BY BIG BOSS RIGBY..."
I'D CHOOSE HIM TO ZAP ME, TOO, SINCE HE'D PROBABLY MISS!
HAH!
OIL
MUTINY! THIS IS MUTINYING.
KER-SLIDE!
SURPRISED YOU COULD HEAR US OVER YOUR AUDIENCE...
BITE
OIL
ACUTE...*NOM* ...HEARING. IT'S ANOTHER OF MY SPECIAL CAPTAIN ABILITIES.

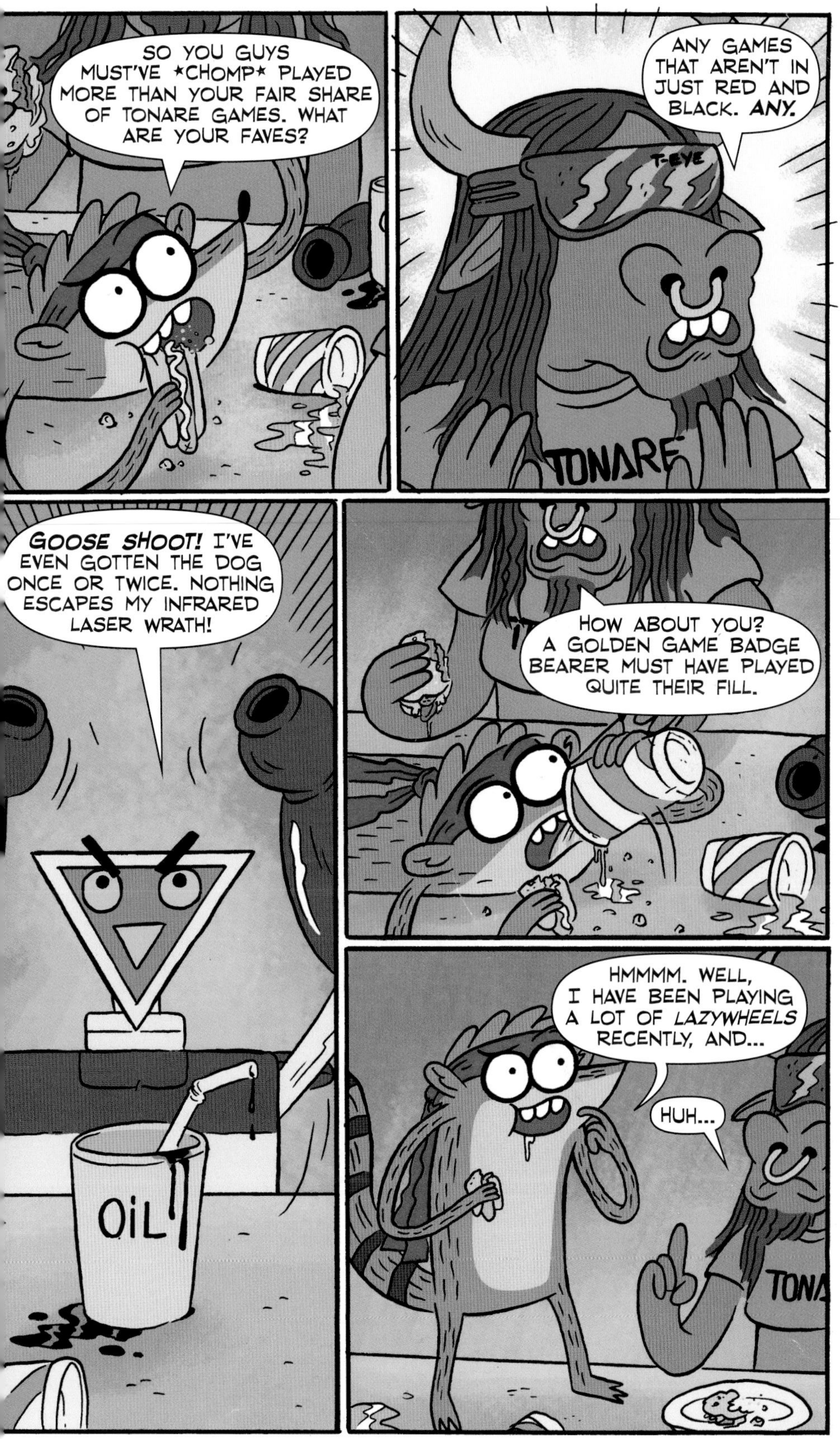
SO YOU GUYS MUST'VE *CHOMP* PLAYED MORE THAN YOUR FAIR SHARE OF TONARE GAMES. WHAT ARE YOUR FAVES?
ANY GAMES THAT AREN'T IN JUST RED AND BLACK. **ANY.**
T-EYE
TONARE
GOOSE SHOOT! I'VE EVEN GOTTEN THE DOG ONCE OR TWICE. NOTHING ESCAPES MY INFRARED LASER WRATH!
OIL
HOW ABOUT YOU? A GOLDEN GAME BADGE BEARER MUST HAVE PLAYED QUITE THEIR FILL.
HMMMM. WELL, I HAVE BEEN PLAYING A LOT OF *LAZYWHEELS* RECENTLY, AND...
HUH...

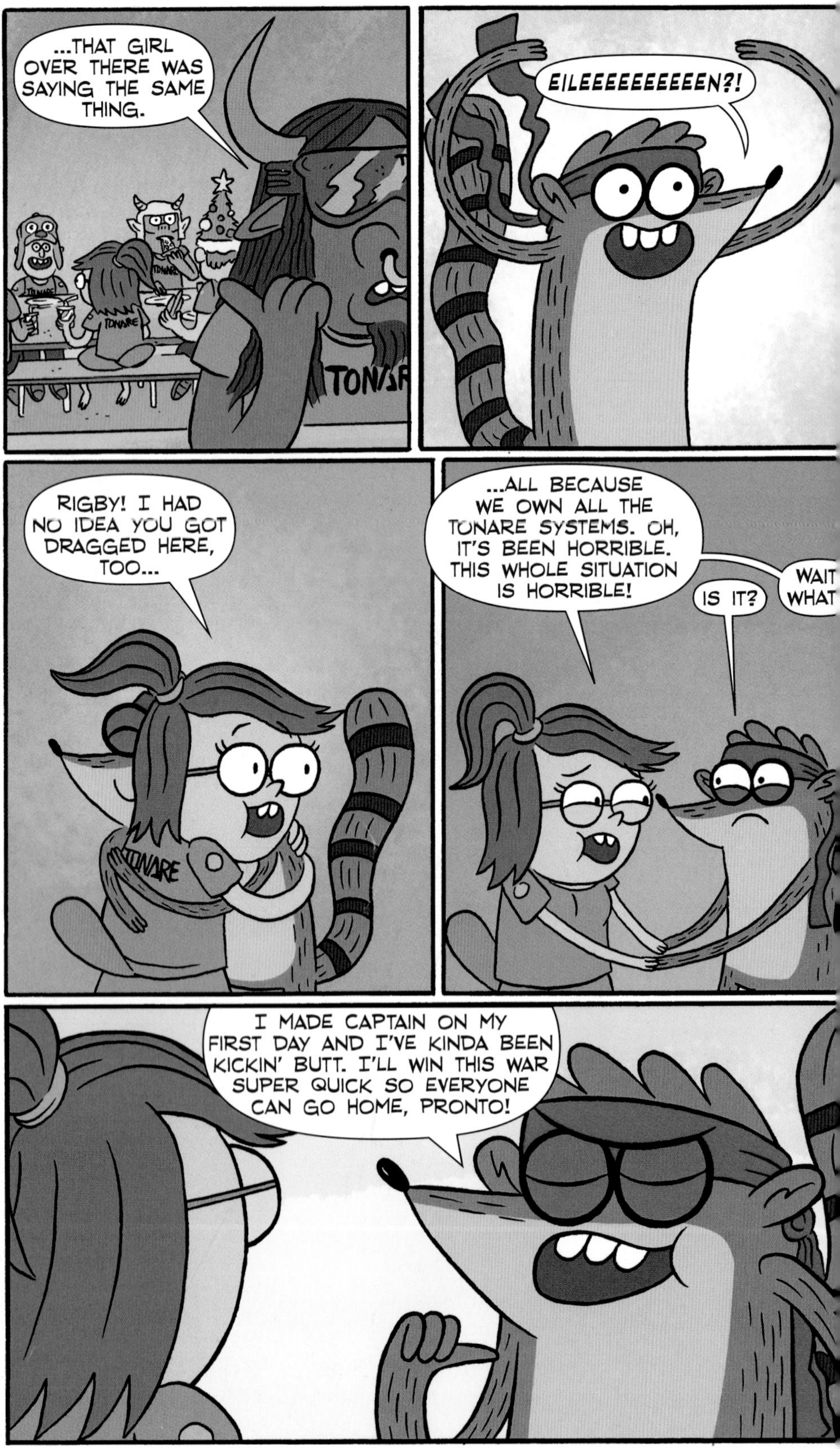

...THAT GIRL OVER THERE WAS SAYING THE SAME THING.
TONARE
EILEEEEEEEEEEN?!
RIGBY! I HAD NO IDEA YOU GOT DRAGGED HERE, TOO...
TONARE
...ALL BECAUSE WE OWN ALL THE TONARE SYSTEMS. OH, IT'S BEEN HORRIBLE. THIS WHOLE SITUATION IS HORRIBLE!
IS IT?
WAIT WHAT
I MADE CAPTAIN ON MY FIRST DAY AND I'VE KINDA BEEN KICKIN' BUTT. I'LL WIN THIS WAR SUPER QUICK SO EVERYONE CAN GO HOME, PRONTO!

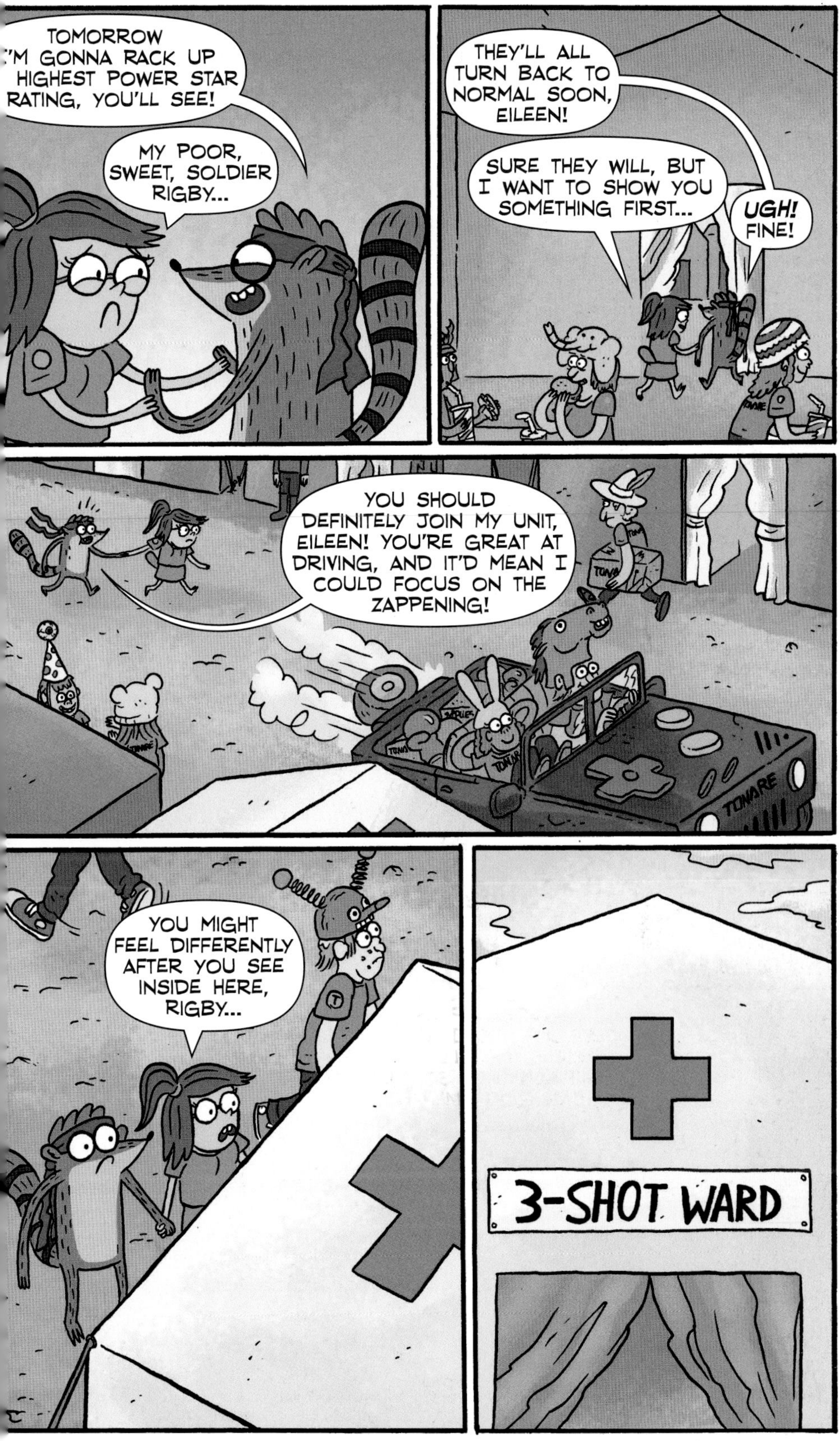
TOMORROW 'M GONNA RACK UP HIGHEST POWER STAR RATING, YOU'LL SEE!
MY POOR, SWEET, SOLDIER RIGBY...
THEY'LL ALL TURN BACK TO NORMAL SOON, EILEEN!
SURE THEY WILL, BUT I WANT TO SHOW YOU SOMETHING FIRST...
UGH! FINE!
YOU SHOULD DEFINITELY JOIN MY UNIT, EILEEN! YOU'RE GREAT AT DRIVING, AND IT'D MEAN I COULD FOCUS ON THE ZAPPENING!
TONARE
YOU MIGHT FEEL DIFFERENTLY AFTER YOU SEE INSIDE HERE, RIGBY...
3-SHOT WARD

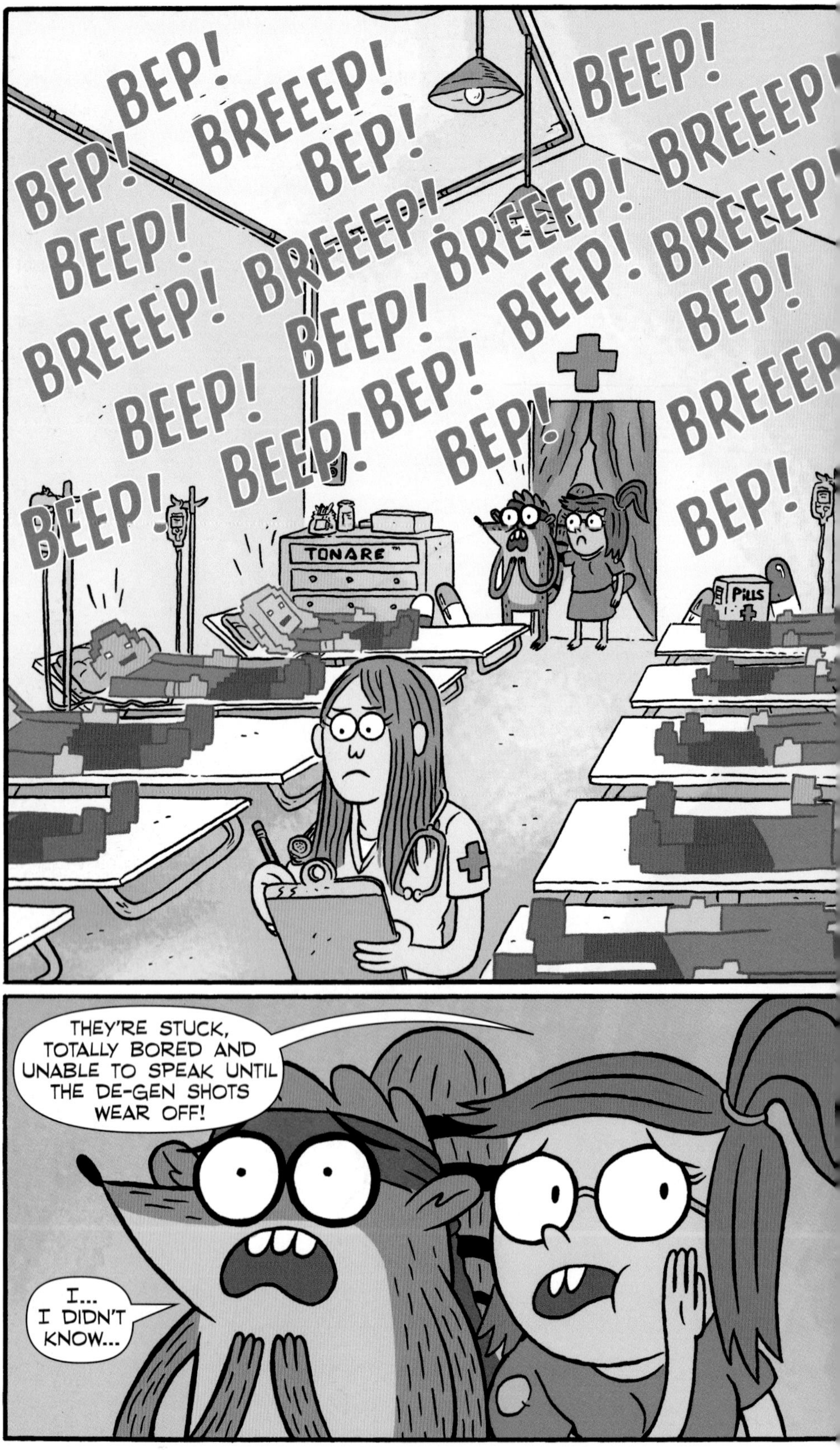
BEP!
BEP!
BREEEP!
BEP!
BEEP!
BEEP!
BREEEP!
BREEEP!
BREEEP!
BREEEP!
BREEEP!
BEEP!
BEEP!
BEEP!
BEP!
BEEP!
BEEP!
BEP!
BEP!
BEP!
BEEP!
TONARE™
PILLS
THEY'RE STUCK, TOTALLY BORED AND UNABLE TO SPEAK UNTIL THE DE-GEN SHOTS WEAR OFF!
I... I DIDN'T KNOW...

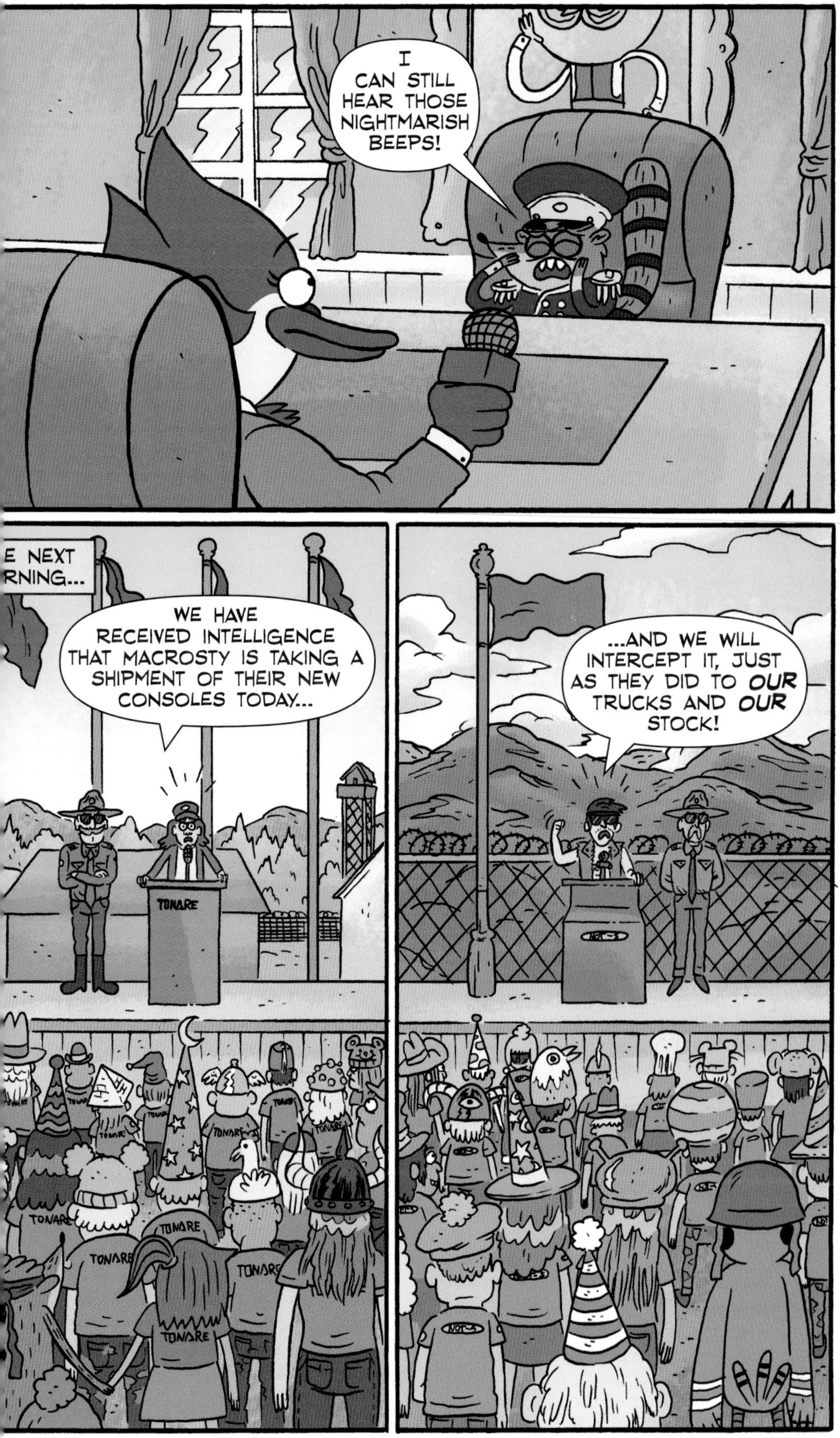
I CAN STILL HEAR THOSE NIGHTMARISH BEEPS!
E NEXT RNING...
WE HAVE RECEIVED INTELLIGENCE THAT MACROSTY IS TAKING A SHIPMENT OF THEIR NEW CONSOLES TODAY...
TONARE
...AND WE WILL INTERCEPT IT, JUST AS THEY DID TO *OUR* TRUCKS AND *OUR* STOCK!

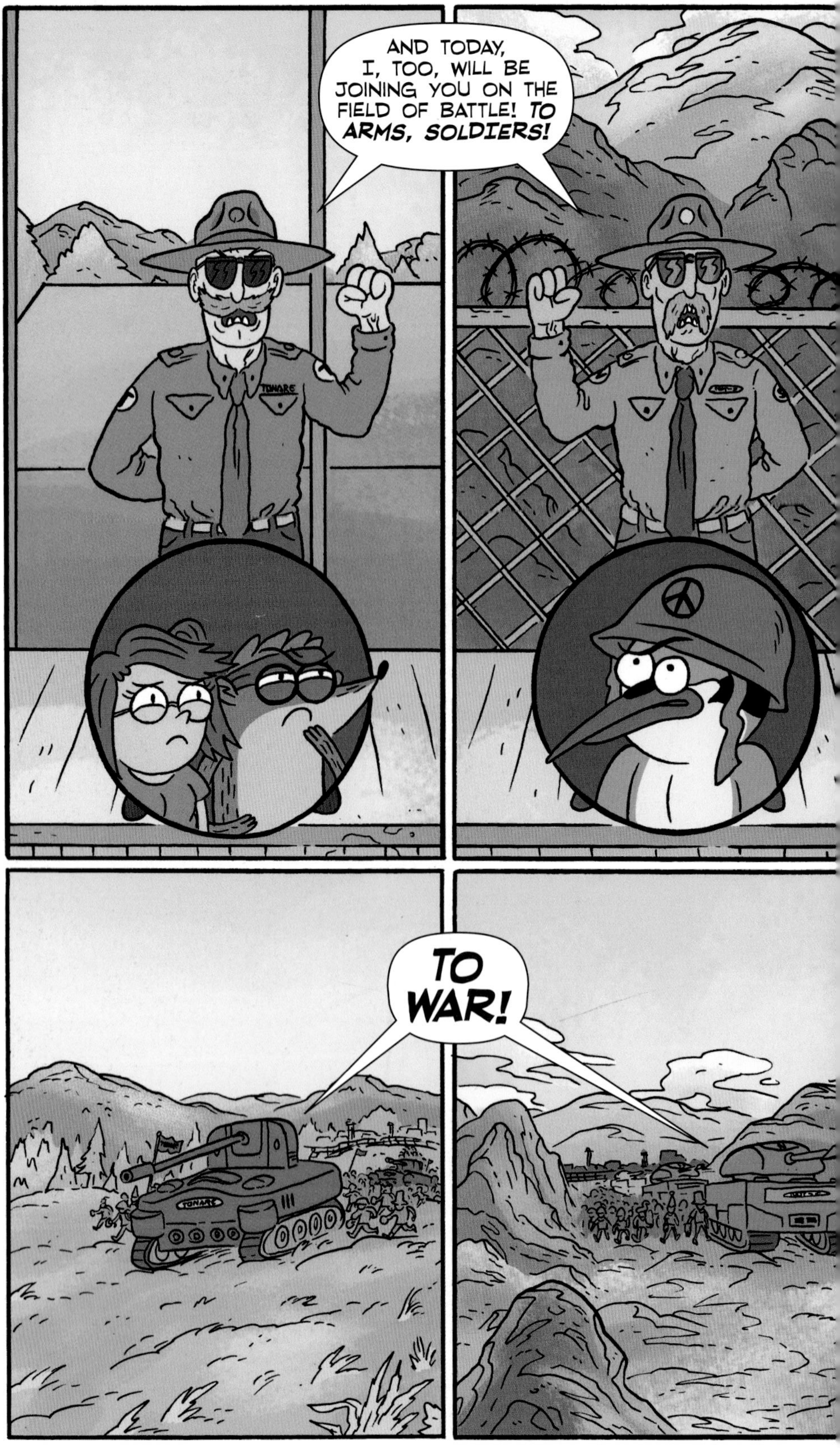
AND TODAY, I, TOO, WILL BE JOINING YOU ON THE FIELD OF BATTLE! TO ARMS, SOLDIERS!
TO WAR!

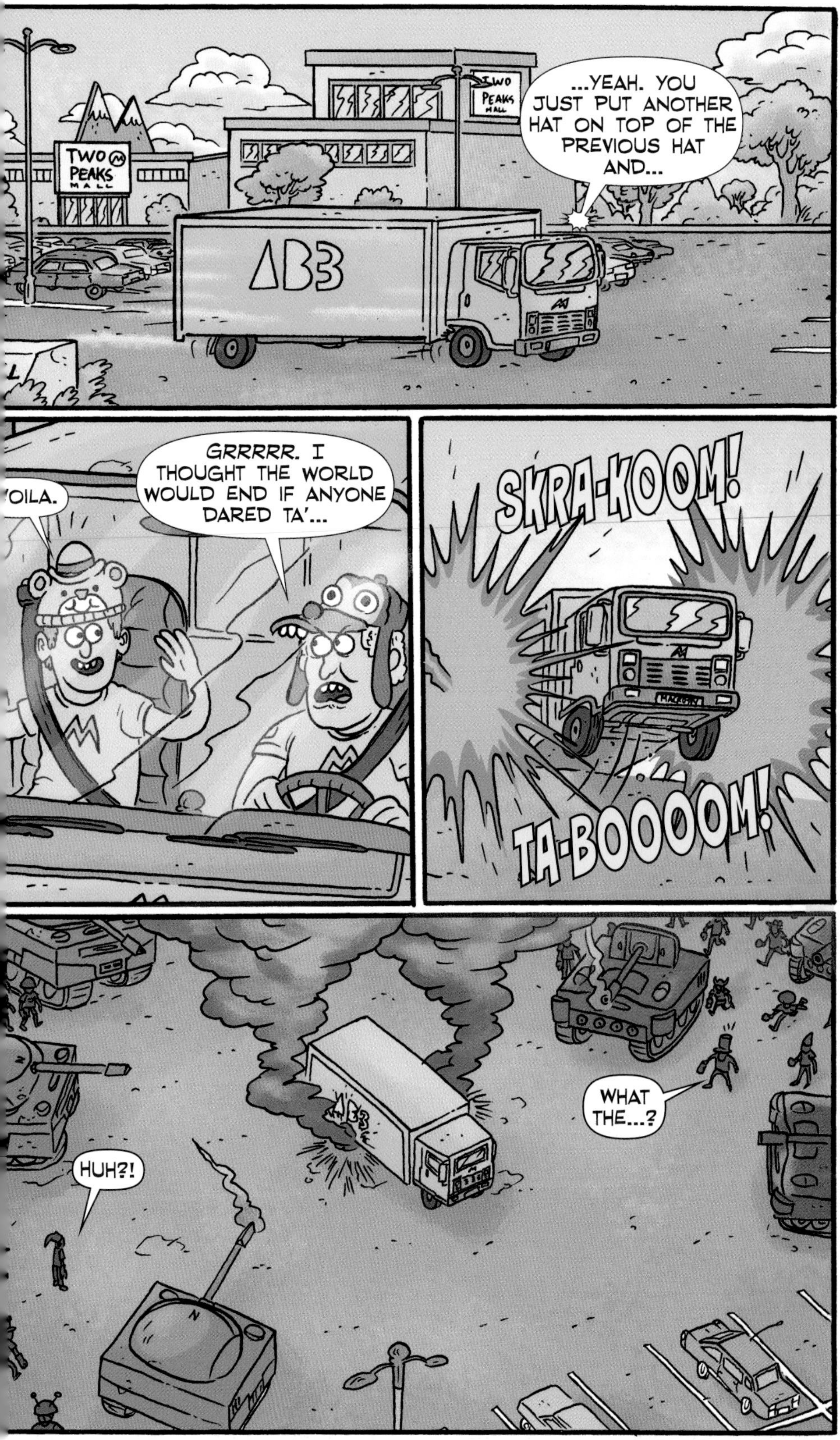
...YEAH. YOU JUST PUT ANOTHER HAT ON TOP OF THE PREVIOUS HAT AND...
TWO PEAKS MALL
ΔB3
OILA.
GRRRRR. I THOUGHT THE WORLD WOULD END IF ANYONE DARED TA'...
SKRA-KOOM!
TA-BOOOOM!
WHAT THE...?
HUH?!

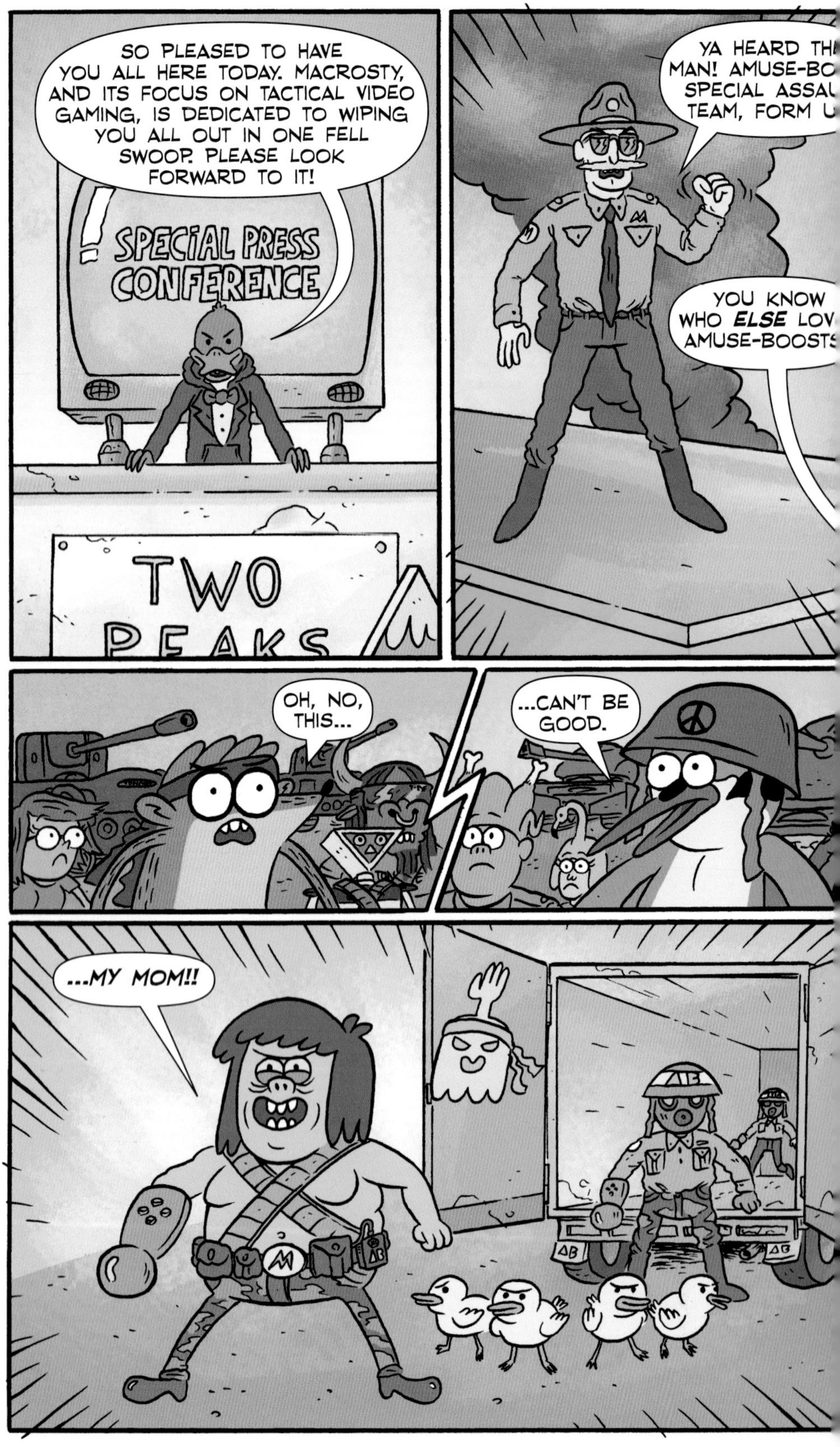
SO PLEASED TO HAVE YOU ALL HERE TODAY. MACROSTY, AND ITS FOCUS ON TACTICAL VIDEO GAMING, IS DEDICATED TO WIPING YOU ALL OUT IN ONE FELL SWOOP. PLEASE LOOK FORWARD TO IT!
SPECIAL PRESS CONFERENCE
TWO PEAKS
YA HEARD TH MAN! AMUSE-BO SPECIAL ASSAU TEAM, FORM U
YOU KNOW WHO *ELSE* LOV AMUSE-BOOSTS
OH, NO, THIS...
...CAN'T BE GOOD.
...MY MOM!!

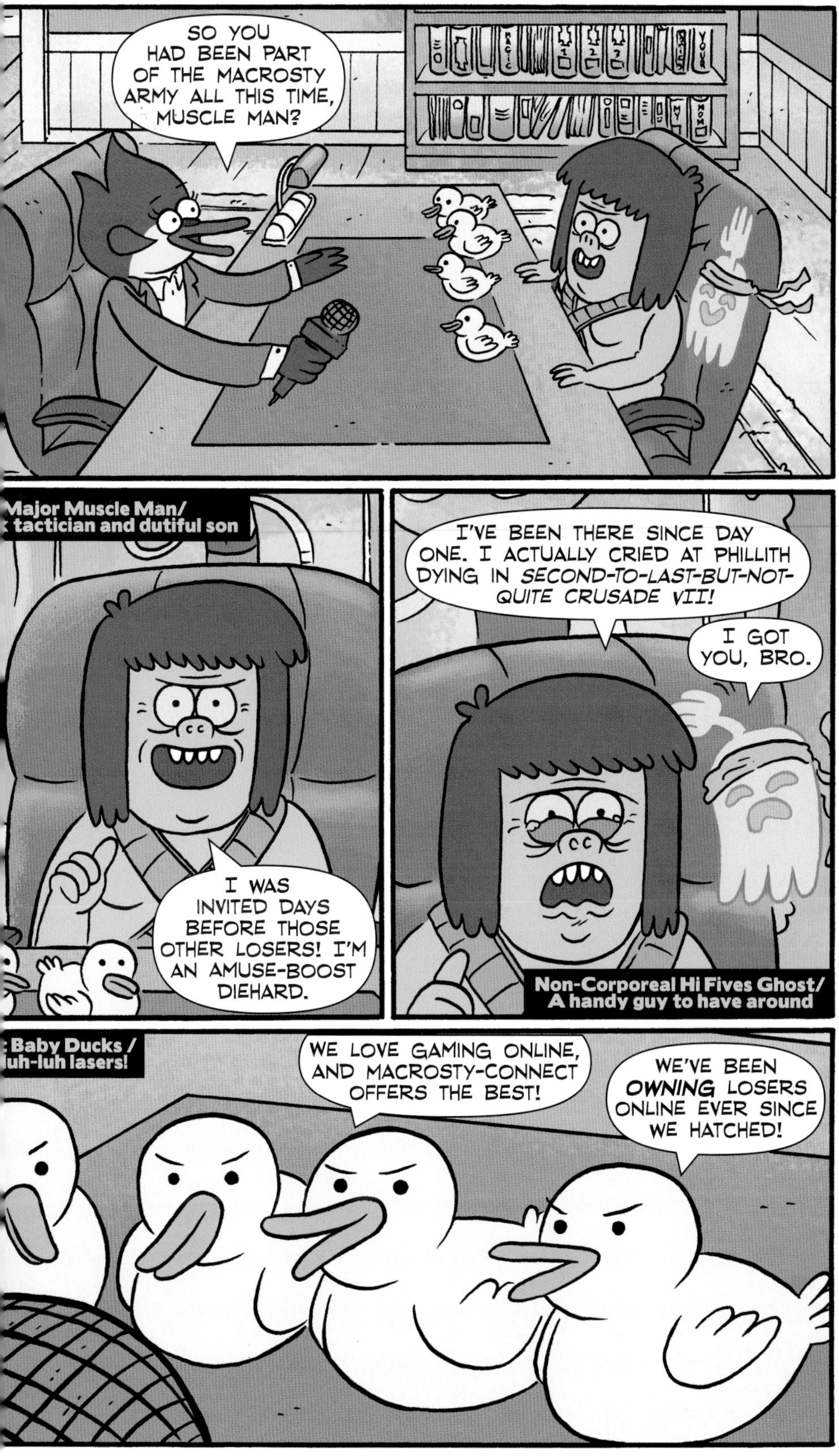
SO YOU HAD BEEN PART OF THE MACROSTY ARMY ALL THIS TIME, MUSCLE MAN?
Major Muscle Man/
tactician and dutiful son
I WAS INVITED DAYS BEFORE THOSE OTHER LOSERS! I'M AN AMUSE-BOOST DIEHARD.
I'VE BEEN THERE SINCE DAY ONE. I ACTUALLY CRIED AT PHILLITH DYING IN *SECOND-TO-LAST-BUT-NOT-QUITE CRUSADE VII!*
I GOT YOU, BRO.
Non-Corporeal Hi Fives Ghost/
A handy guy to have around
Baby Ducks /
luh-luh lasers!
WE LOVE GAMING ONLINE, AND MACROSTY-CONNECT OFFERS THE BEST!
WE'VE BEEN **OWNING** LOSERS ONLINE EVER SINCE WE HATCHED!

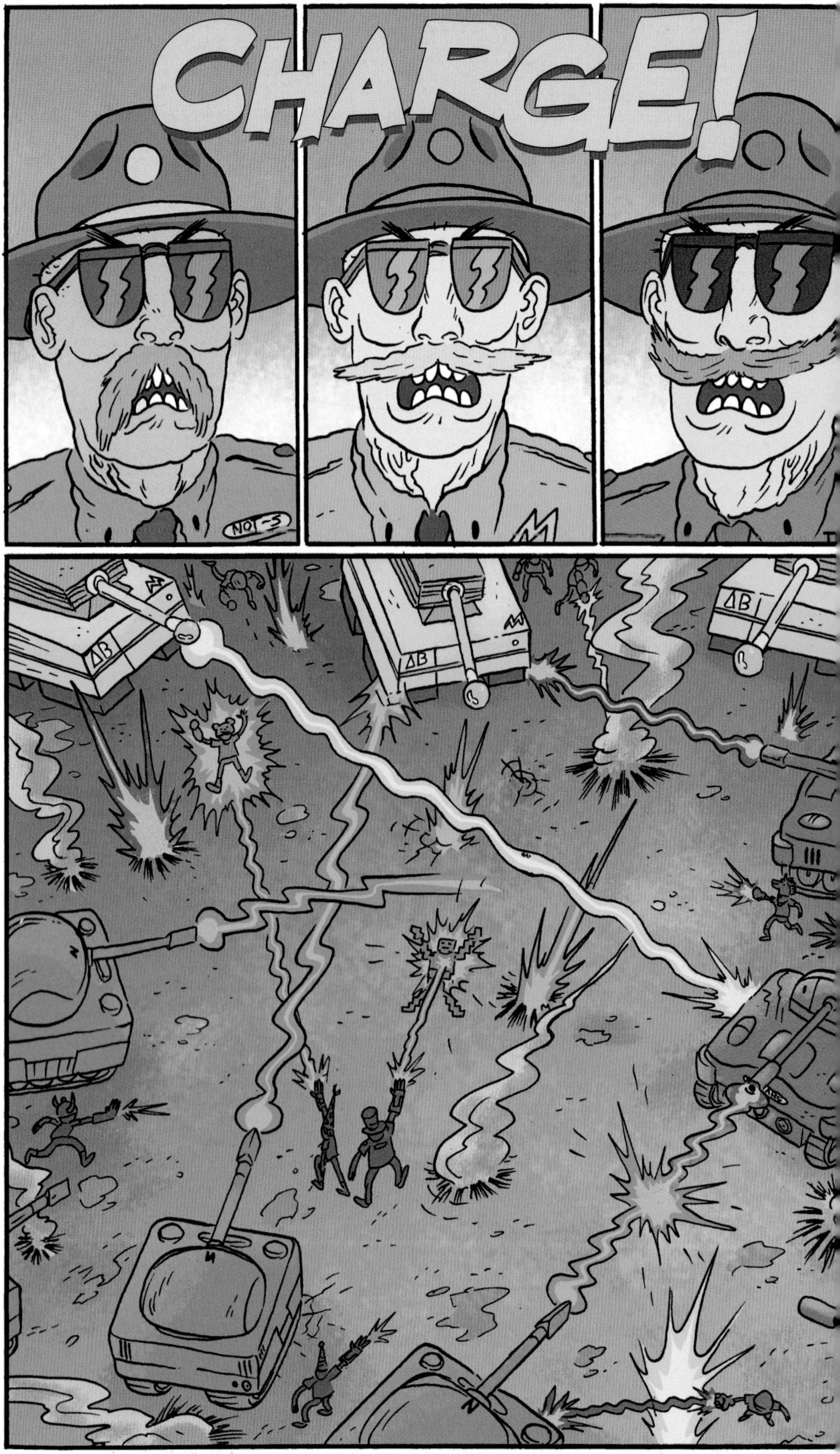
CHARGE!

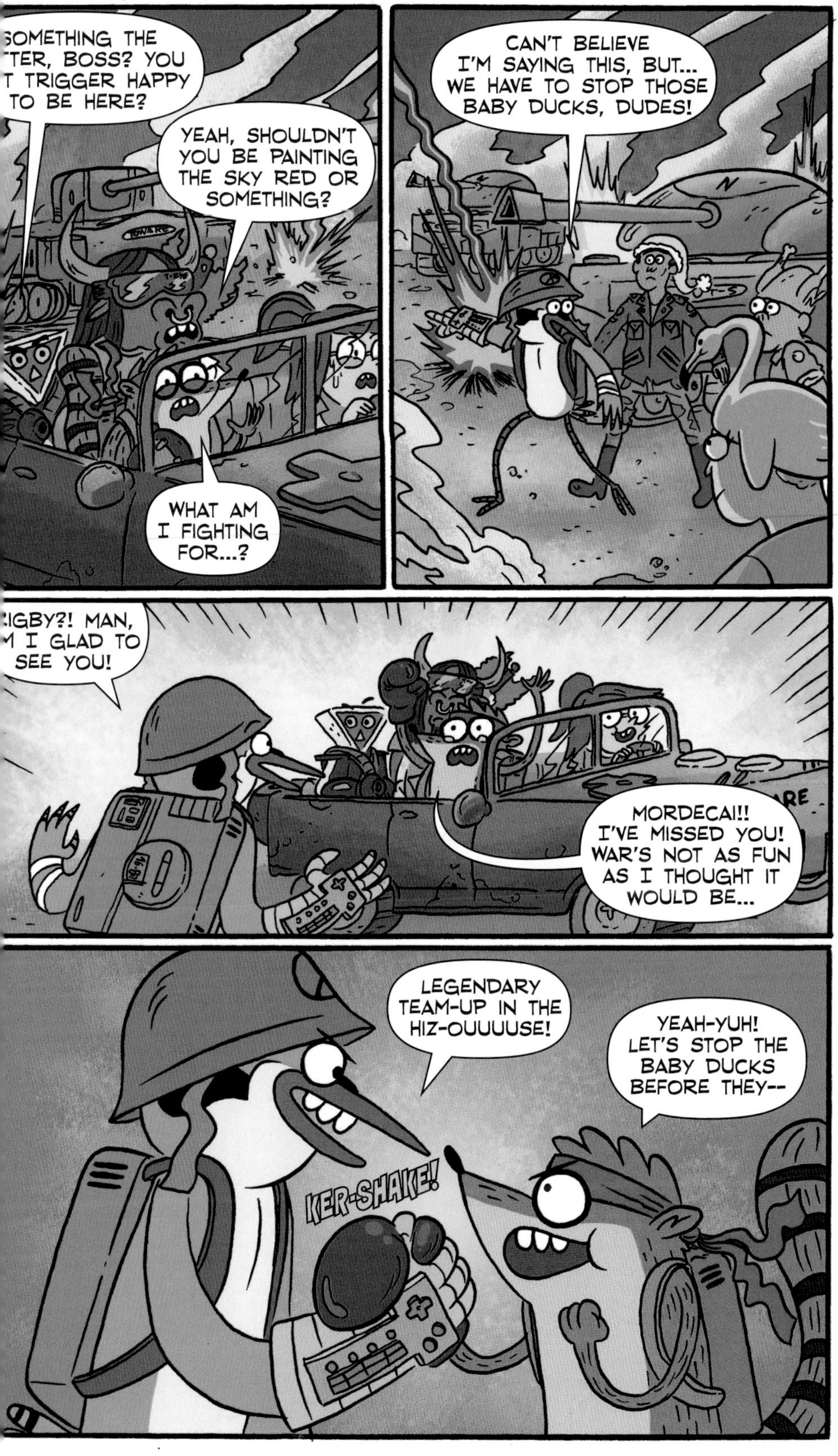
SOMETHING THE
TTER, BOSS? YOU
T TRIGGER HAPPY
TO BE HERE?
YEAH, SHOULDN'T YOU BE PAINTING THE SKY RED OR SOMETHING?
WHAT AM I FIGHTING FOR...?
CAN'T BELIEVE I'M SAYING THIS, BUT... WE HAVE TO STOP THOSE BABY DUCKS, DUDES!
IGBY?! MAN,
I GLAD TO
SEE YOU!
MORDECAI!! I'VE MISSED YOU! WAR'S NOT AS FUN AS I THOUGHT IT WOULD BE...
LEGENDARY TEAM-UP IN THE HIZ-OUUUUSE!
YEAH-YUH! LET'S STOP THE BABY DUCKS BEFORE THEY--
KER-SHAKE!

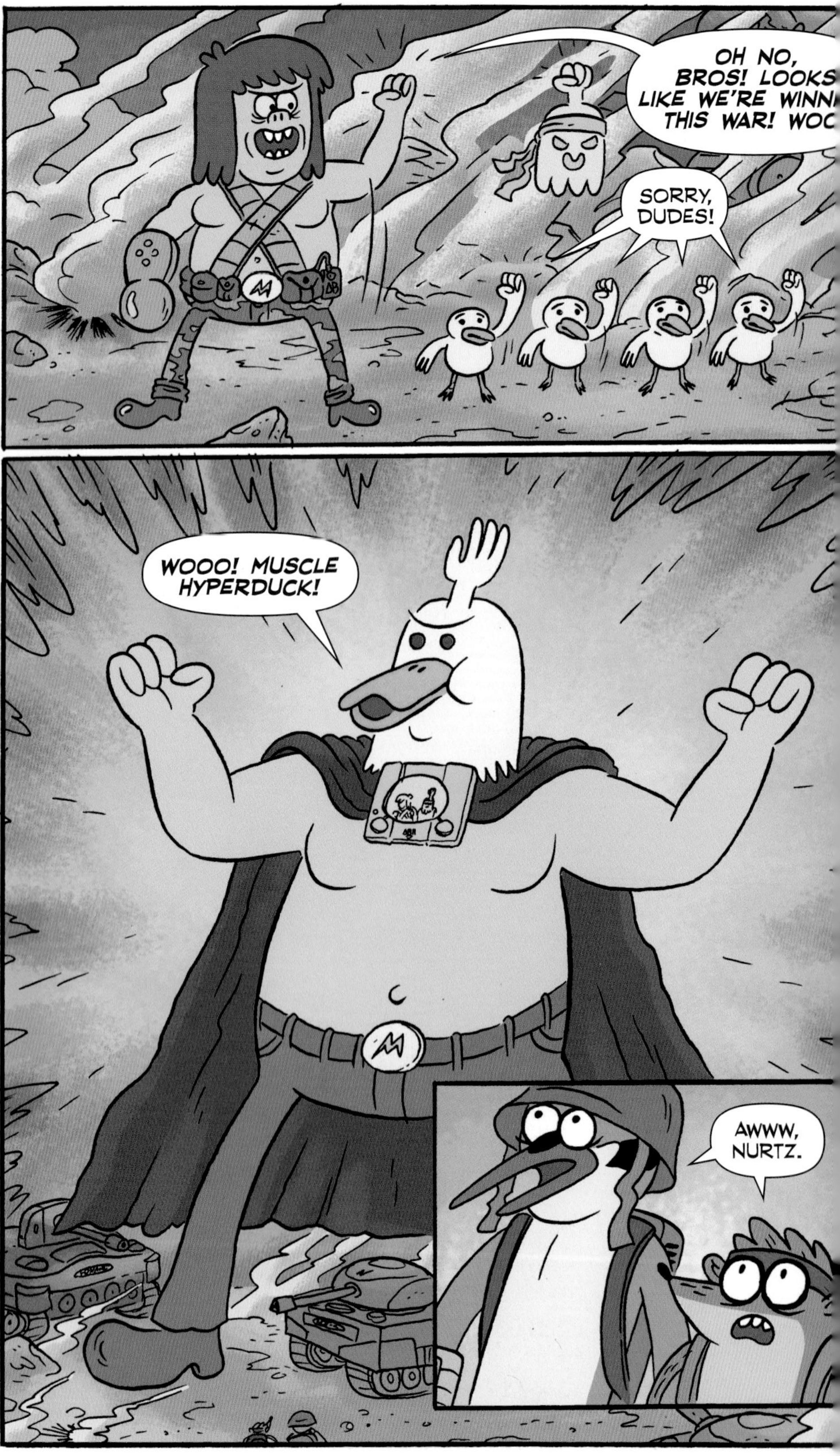
OH NO, BROS! LOOKS LIKE WE'RE WINN THIS WAR! WOO
SORRY, DUDES!
WOOO! MUSCLE HYPERDUCK!
AWWW, NURTZ.

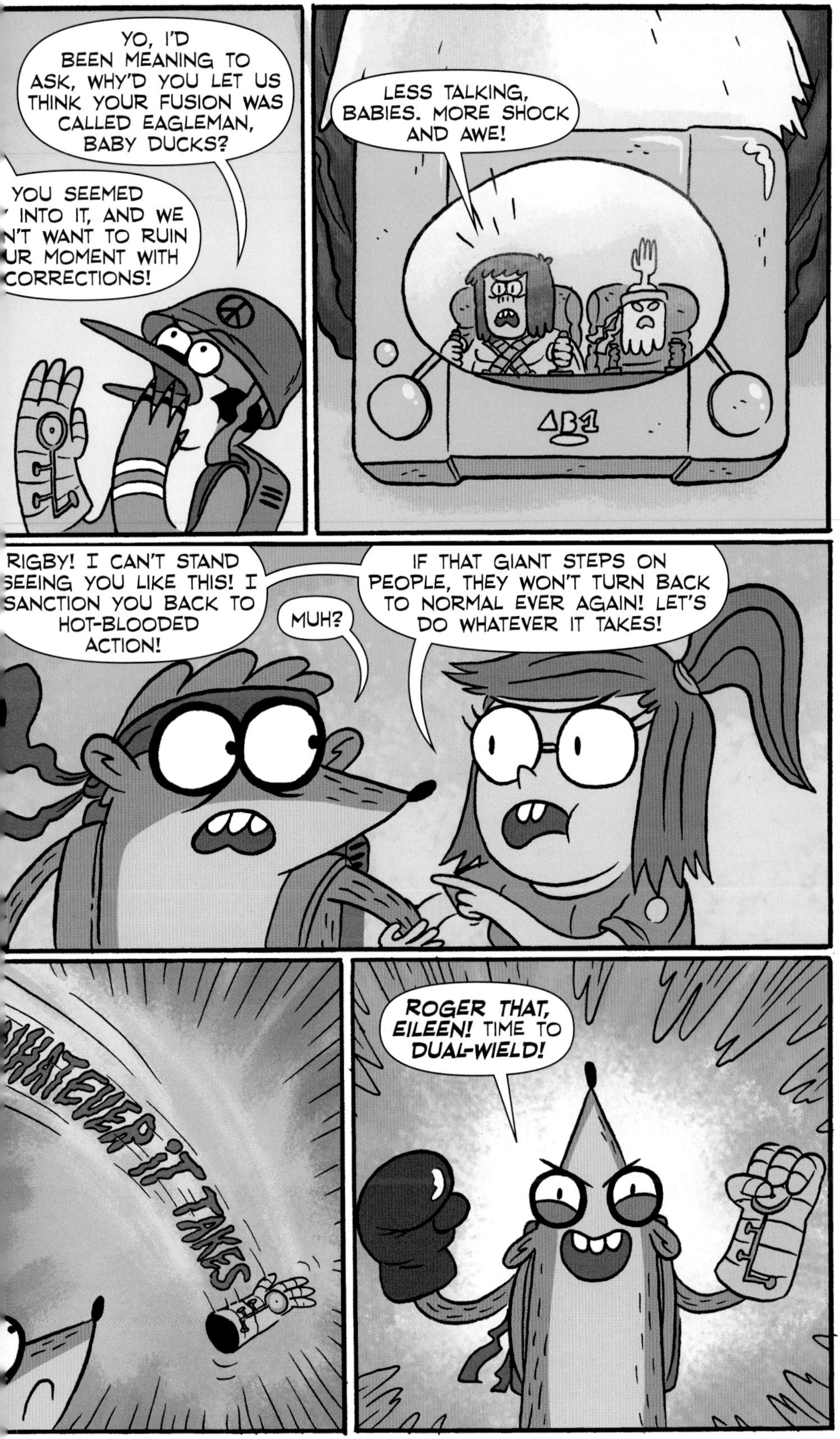

YO, I'D BEEN MEANING TO ASK, WHY'D YOU LET US THINK YOUR FUSION WAS CALLED EAGLEMAN, BABY DUCKS?
YOU SEEMED INTO IT, AND WE N'T WANT TO RUIN UR MOMENT WITH CORRECTIONS!
LESS TALKING, BABIES. MORE SHOCK AND AWE!
ΔB1
RIGBY! I CAN'T STAND SEEING YOU LIKE THIS! I SANCTION YOU BACK TO HOT-BLOODED ACTION!
MUH?
IF THAT GIANT STEPS ON PEOPLE, THEY WON'T TURN BACK TO NORMAL EVER AGAIN! LET'S DO WHATEVER IT TAKES!
HATEVER IT TAKES
ROGER THAT, EILEEN! TIME TO DUAL-WIELD!

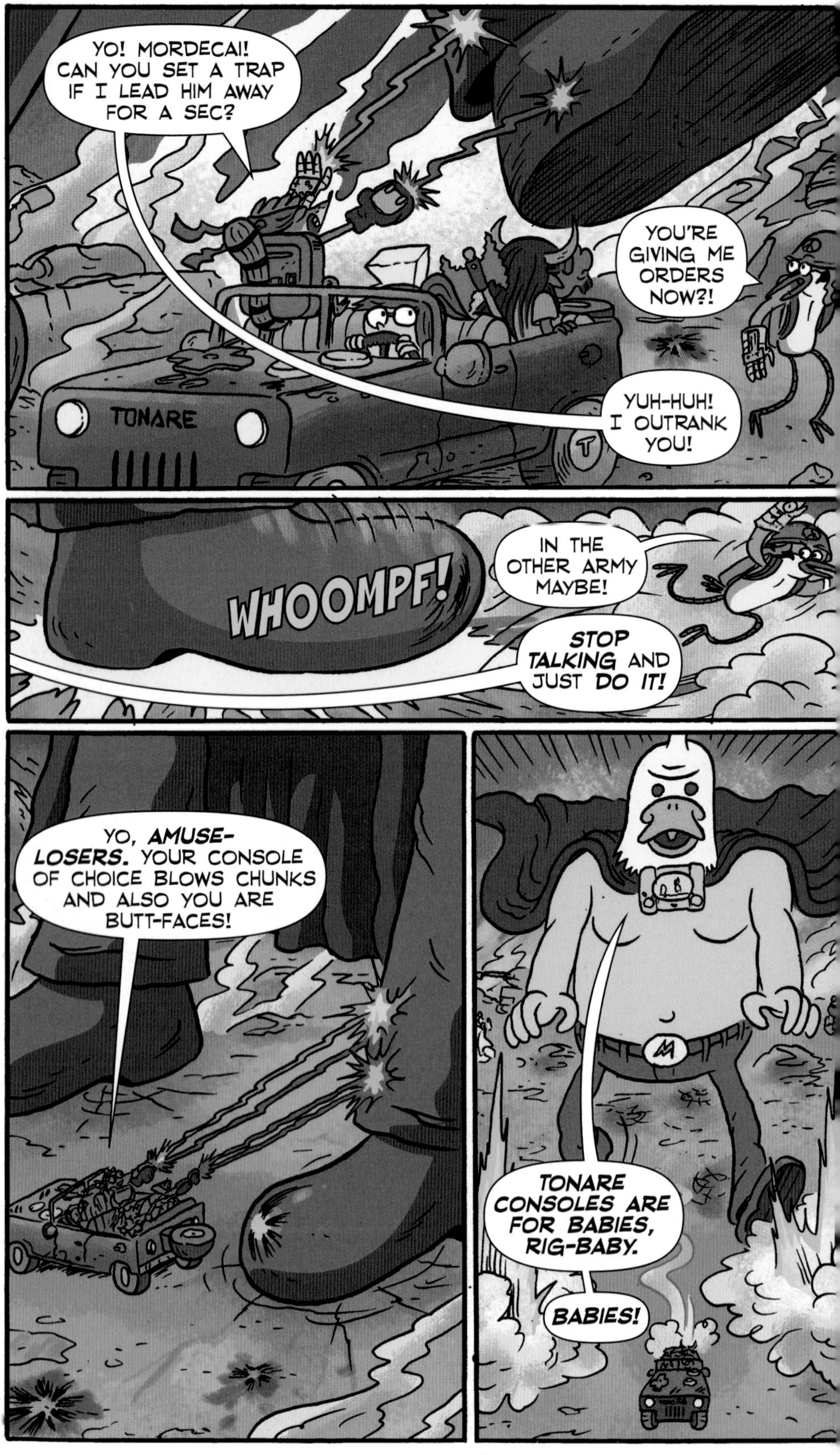
YO! MORDECAI! CAN YOU SET A TRAP IF I LEAD HIM AWAY FOR A SEC?
YOU'RE GIVING ME ORDERS NOW?!
TONARE
YUH-HUH! I OUTRANK YOU!
WHOOMPF!
IN THE OTHER ARMY MAYBE!
STOP TALKING AND JUST DO IT!
YO, AMUSE-LOSERS. YOUR CONSOLE OF CHOICE BLOWS CHUNKS AND ALSO YOU ARE BUTT-FACES!
TONARE CONSOLES ARE FOR BABIES, RIG-BABY.
BABIES!

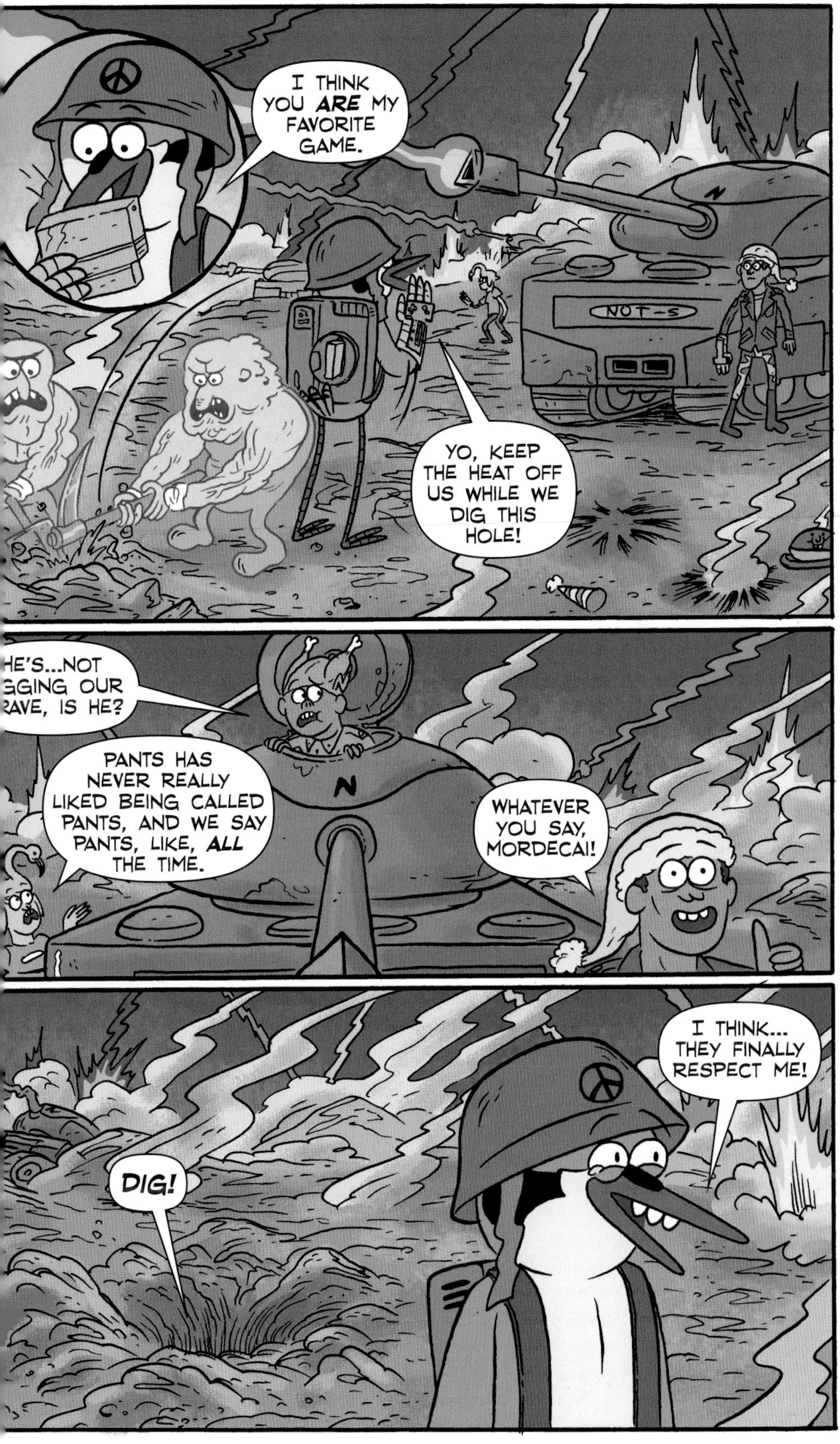
I THINK YOU ARE MY FAVORITE GAME.
NOT-S
YO, KEEP THE HEAT OFF US WHILE WE DIG THIS HOLE!
HE'S...NOT GGING OUR RAVE, IS HE?
PANTS HAS NEVER REALLY LIKED BEING CALLED PANTS, AND WE SAY PANTS, LIKE, ALL THE TIME.
WHATEVER YOU SAY, MORDECAI!
I THINK... THEY FINALLY RESPECT ME!
DIG!

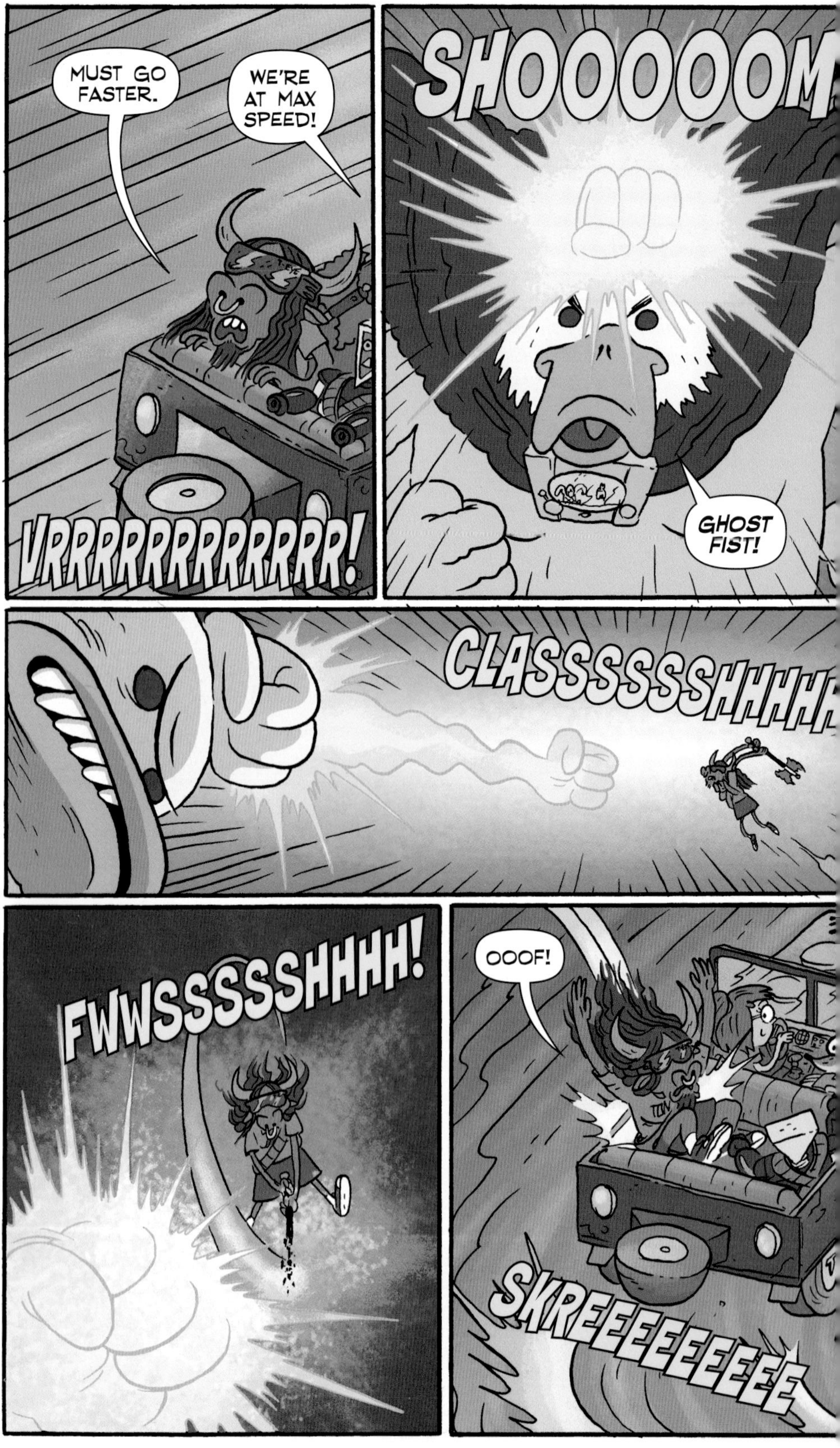

MUST GO FASTER.
WE'RE AT MAX SPEED!
VRRRRRRRRRRRRRR!
SHOOOOOM
GHOST FIST!
CLASSSSSSSHHHHH
FWWSSSSSSHHHH!
OOOF!
SKREEEEEEEEEEE

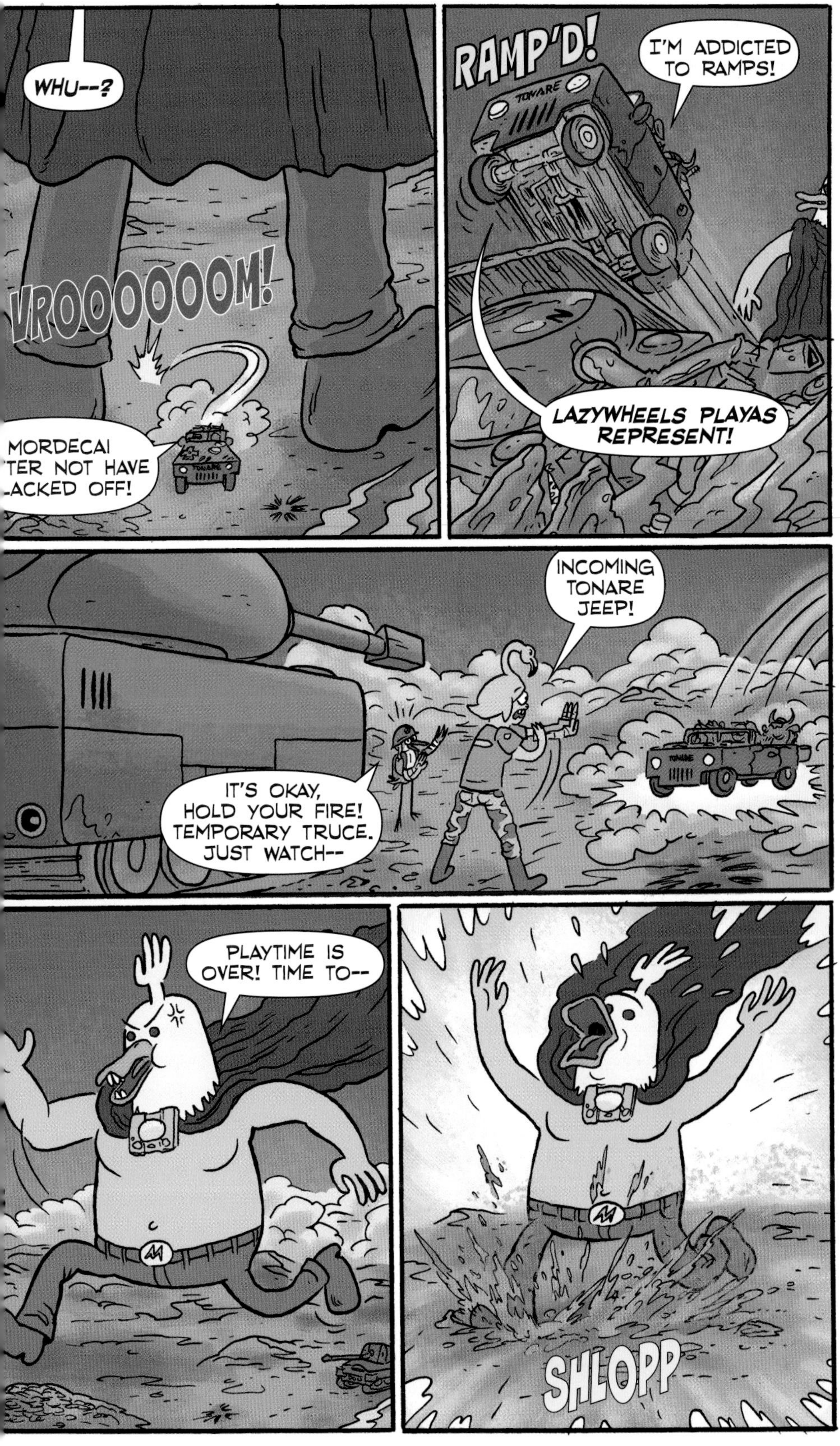
WHU--?
VROOOOOOM!
MORDECAI
TER NOT HAVE
ACKED OFF!
RAMP'D!
I'M ADDICTED TO RAMPS!
LAZYWHEELS PLAYAS REPRESENT!
INCOMING TONARE JEEP!
IT'S OKAY, HOLD YOUR FIRE! TEMPORARY TRUCE. JUST WATCH--
PLAYTIME IS OVER! TIME TO--
SHLOPP

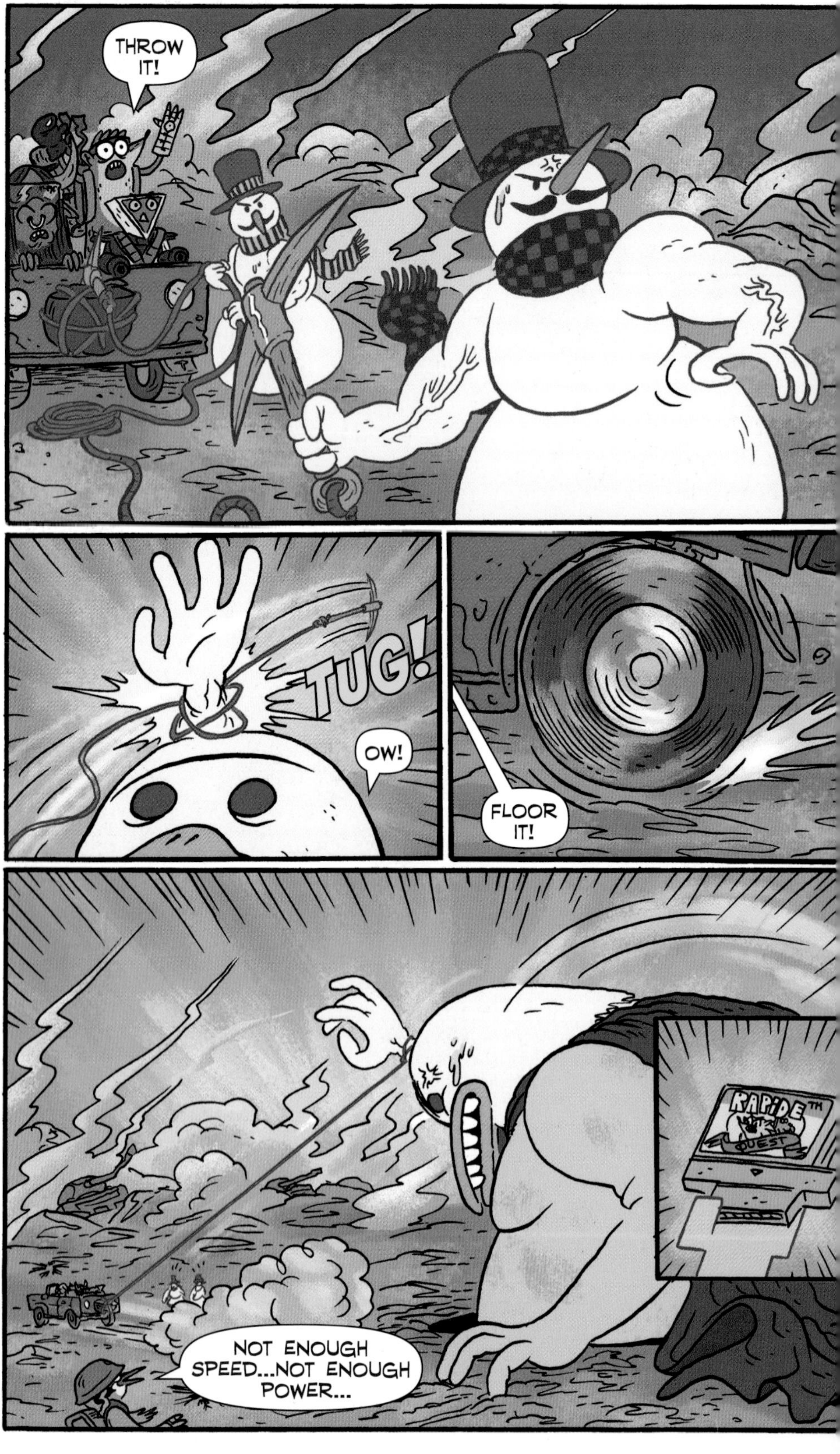
THROW IT!
TUG!
OW!
FLOOR IT!
RAPIDE™ QUEST
NOT ENOUGH SPEED...NOT ENOUGH POWER...

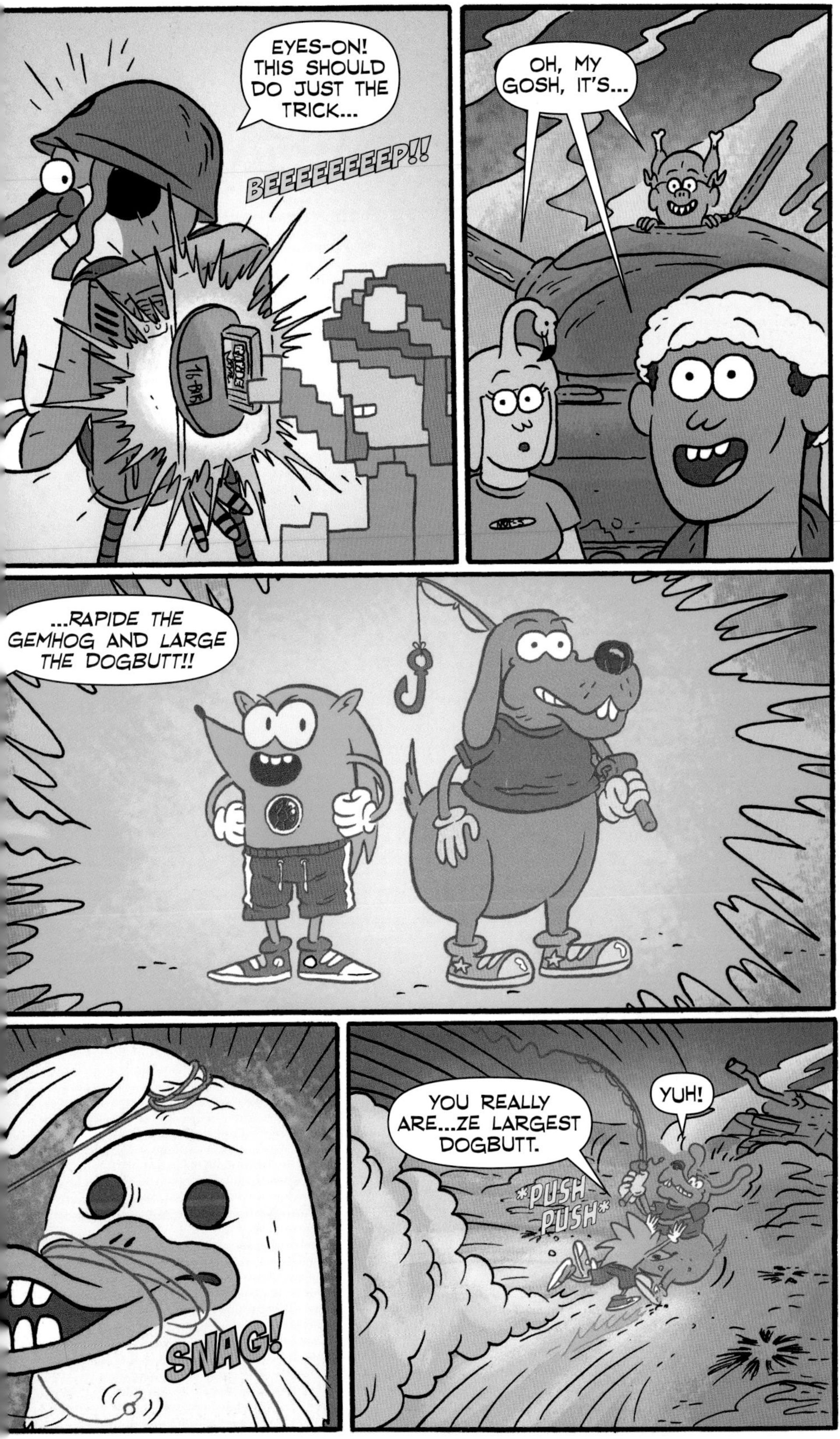
EYES-ON! THIS SHOULD DO JUST THE TRICK...
BEEEEEEEEP!!
OH, MY GOSH, IT'S...
...RAPIDE THE GEMHOG AND LARGE THE DOGBUTT!!
SNAG!
YOU REALLY ARE...ZE LARGEST DOGBUTT.
YUH!
PUSH PUSH

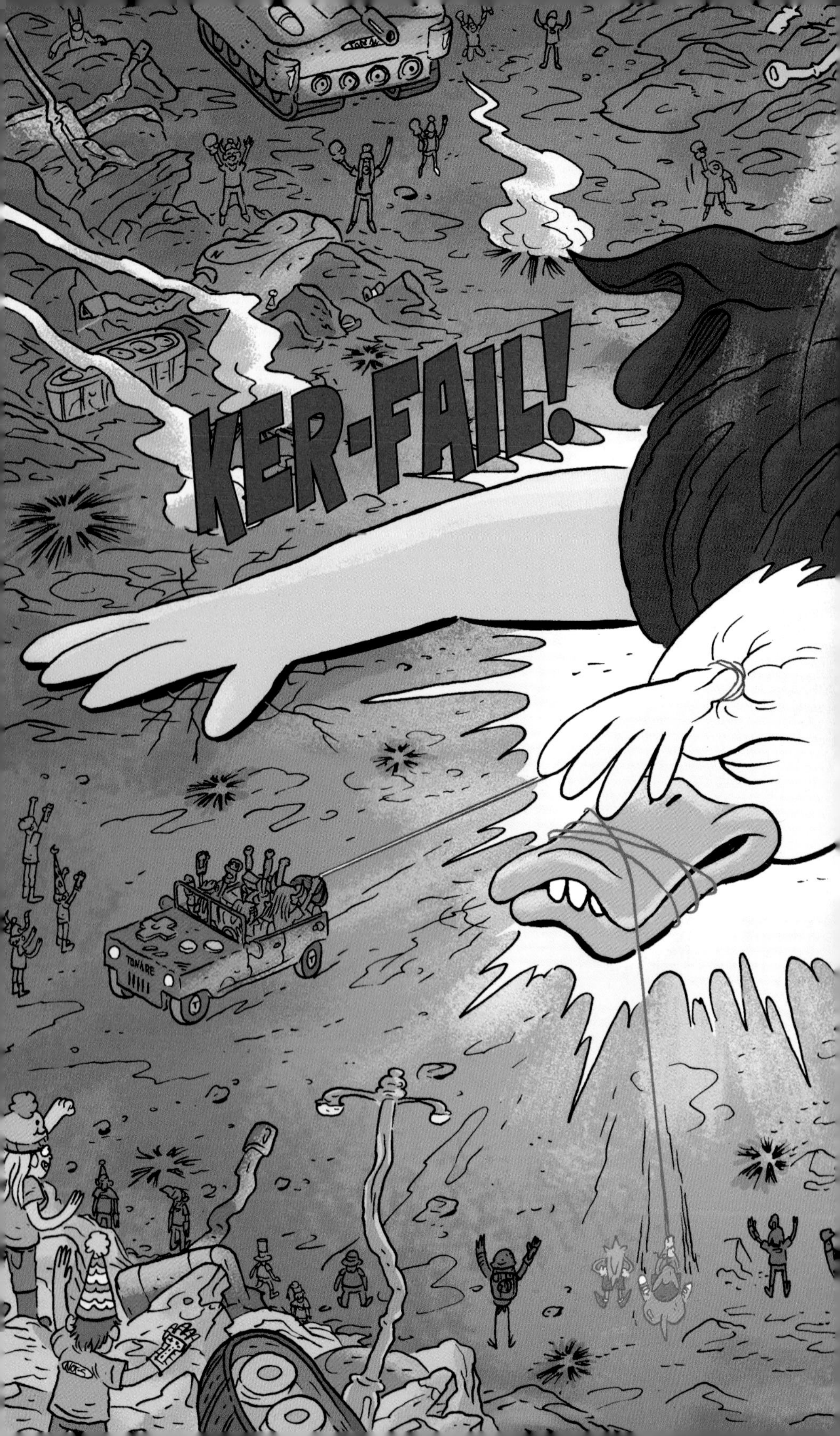
KER-FAIL!

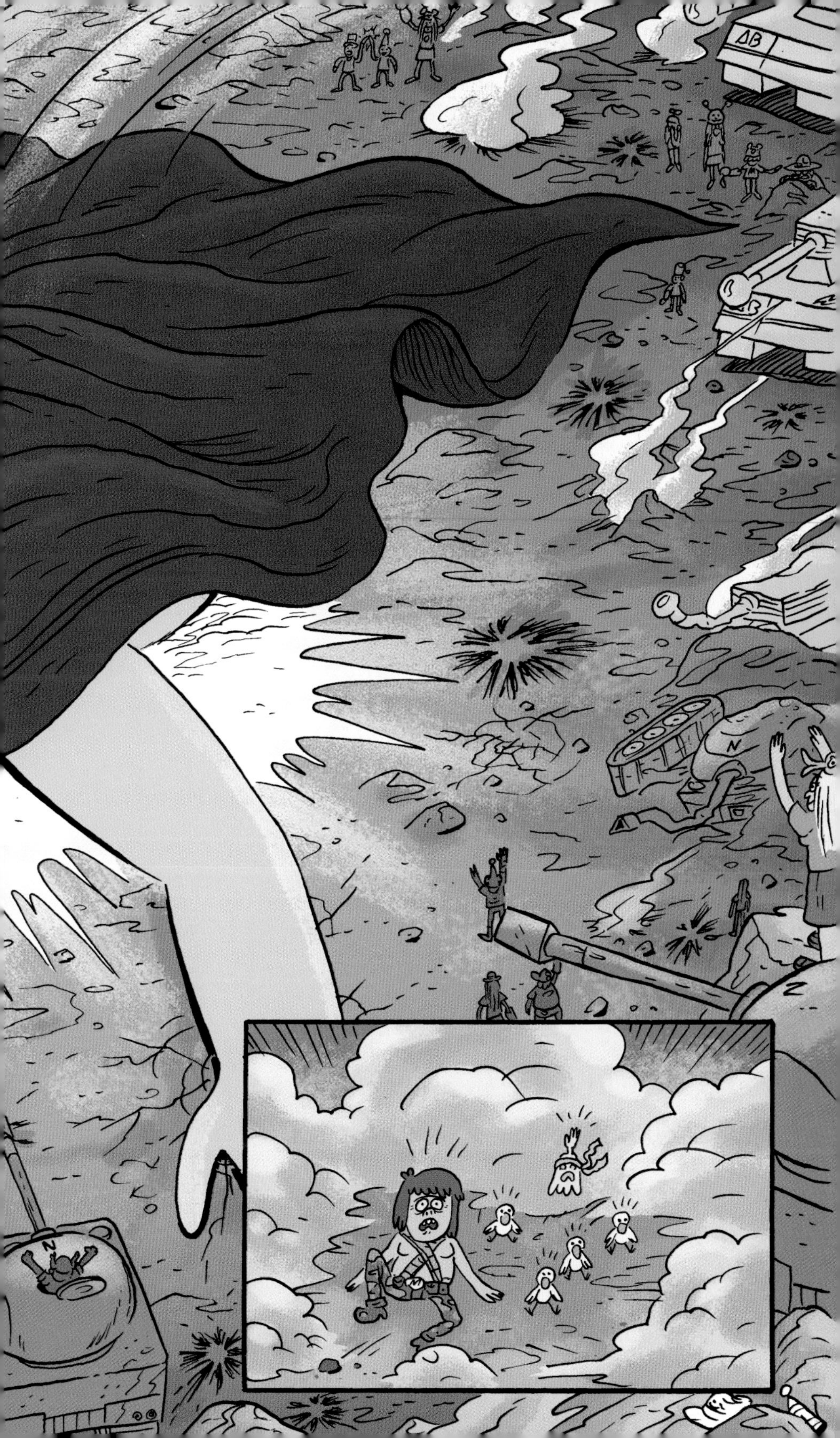

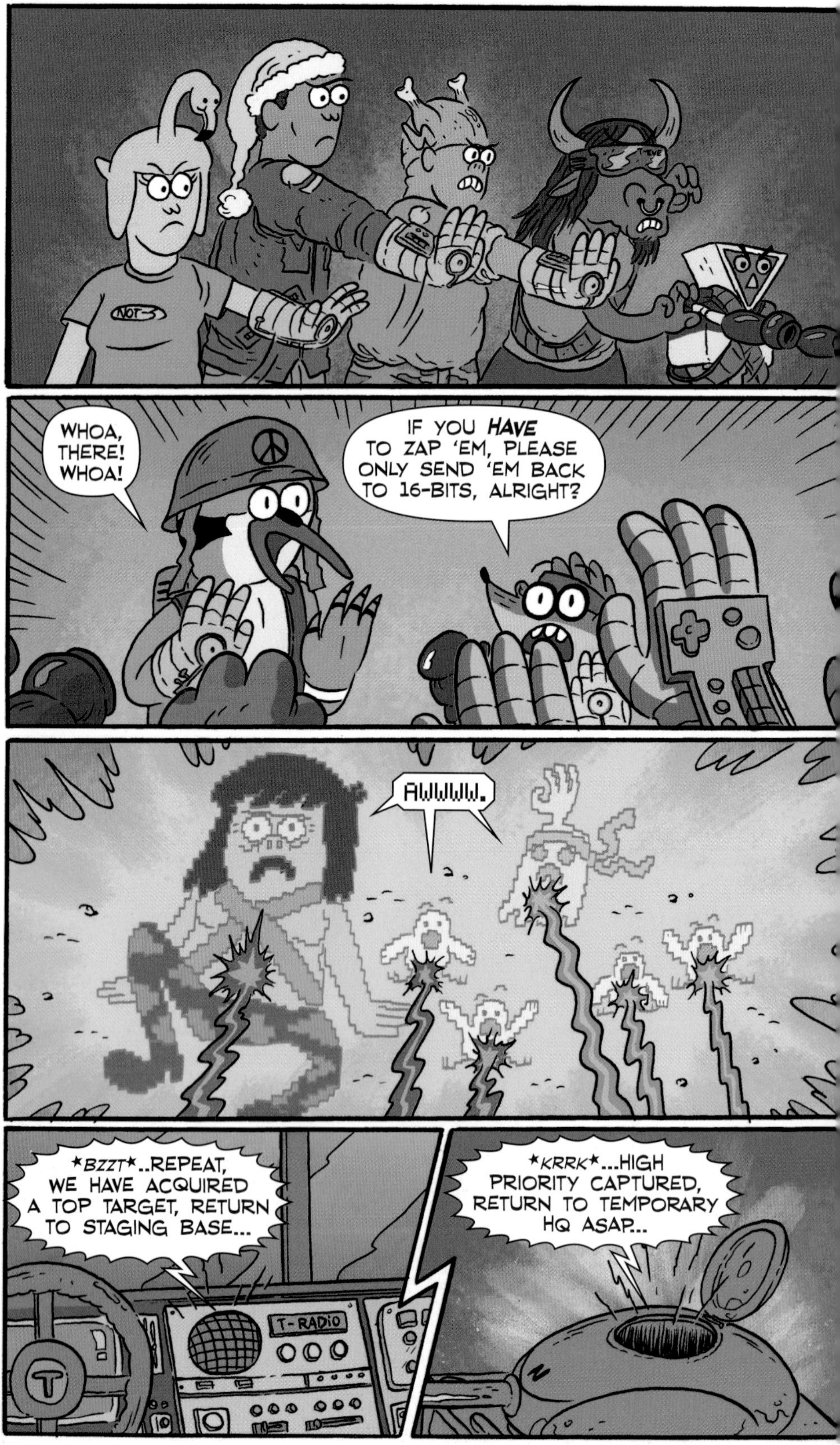
NOT-3
WHOA, THERE! WHOA!
IF YOU *HAVE* TO ZAP 'EM, PLEASE ONLY SEND 'EM BACK TO 16-BITS, ALRIGHT?
AWWWW.
BZZT..REPEAT, WE HAVE ACQUIRED A TOP TARGET, RETURN TO STAGING BASE...
T-RADIO
KRRK...HIGH PRIORITY CAPTURED, RETURN TO TEMPORARY HQ ASAP...

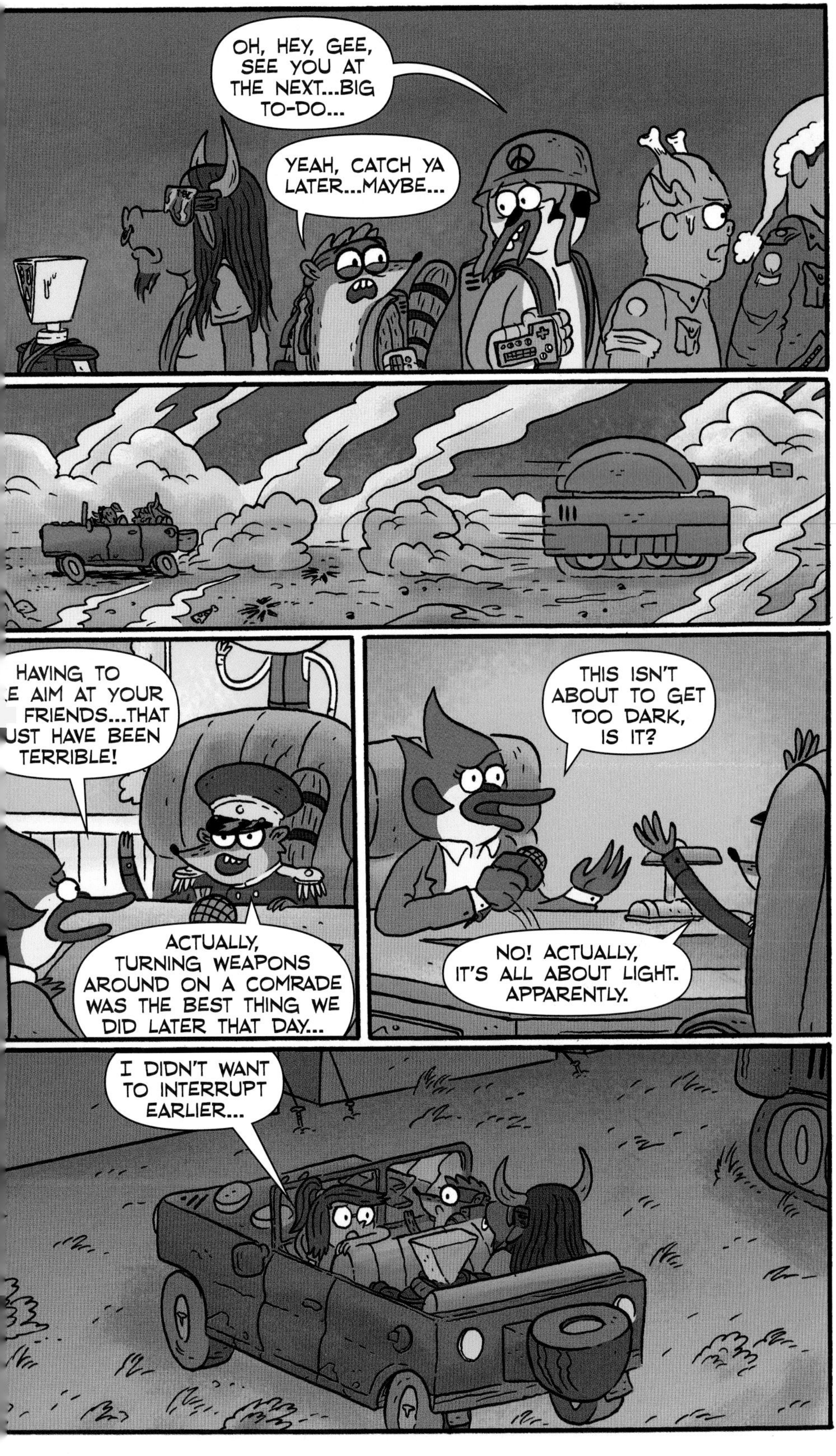
OH, HEY, GEE, SEE YOU AT THE NEXT...BIG TO-DO...
YEAH, CATCH YA LATER...MAYBE...
HAVING TO
E AIM AT YOUR
FRIENDS...THAT
UST HAVE BEEN
TERRIBLE!
ACTUALLY, TURNING WEAPONS AROUND ON A COMRADE WAS THE BEST THING WE DID LATER THAT DAY...
THIS ISN'T ABOUT TO GET TOO DARK, IS IT?
NO! ACTUALLY, IT'S ALL ABOUT LIGHT. APPARENTLY.
I DIDN'T WANT TO INTERRUPT EARLIER...

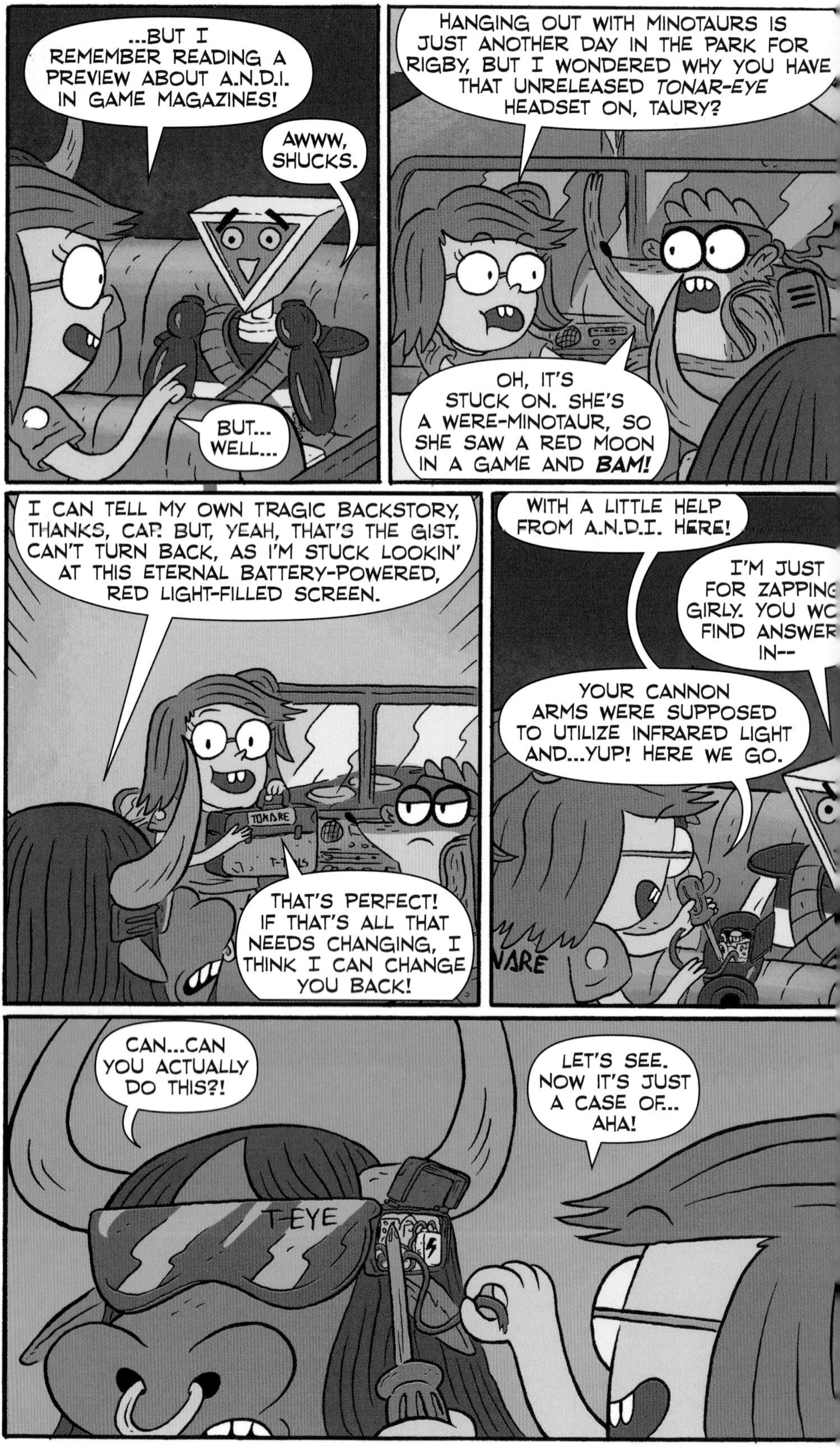
...BUT I REMEMBER READING A PREVIEW ABOUT A.N.D.I. IN GAME MAGAZINES!
AWWW, SHUCKS.
BUT... WELL...
HANGING OUT WITH MINOTAURS IS JUST ANOTHER DAY IN THE PARK FOR RIGBY, BUT I WONDERED WHY YOU HAVE THAT UNRELEASED *TONAR-EYE* HEADSET ON, TAURY?
OH, IT'S STUCK ON. SHE'S A WERE-MINOTAUR, SO SHE SAW A RED MOON IN A GAME AND ***BAM!***
I CAN TELL MY OWN TRAGIC BACKSTORY, THANKS, CAP. BUT, YEAH, THAT'S THE GIST. CAN'T TURN BACK, AS I'M STUCK LOOKIN' AT THIS ETERNAL BATTERY-POWERED, RED LIGHT-FILLED SCREEN.
TONARE
THAT'S PERFECT! IF THAT'S ALL THAT NEEDS CHANGING, I THINK I CAN CHANGE YOU BACK!
WITH A LITTLE HELP FROM A.N.D.I. HERE!
I'M JUST FOR ZAPPING GIRLY. YOU WO FIND ANSWER IN--
YOUR CANNON ARMS WERE SUPPOSED TO UTILIZE INFRARED LIGHT AND...YUP! HERE WE GO.
CAN...CAN YOU ACTUALLY DO THIS?!
LET'S SEE. NOW IT'S JUST A CASE OF... AHA!
T-EYE

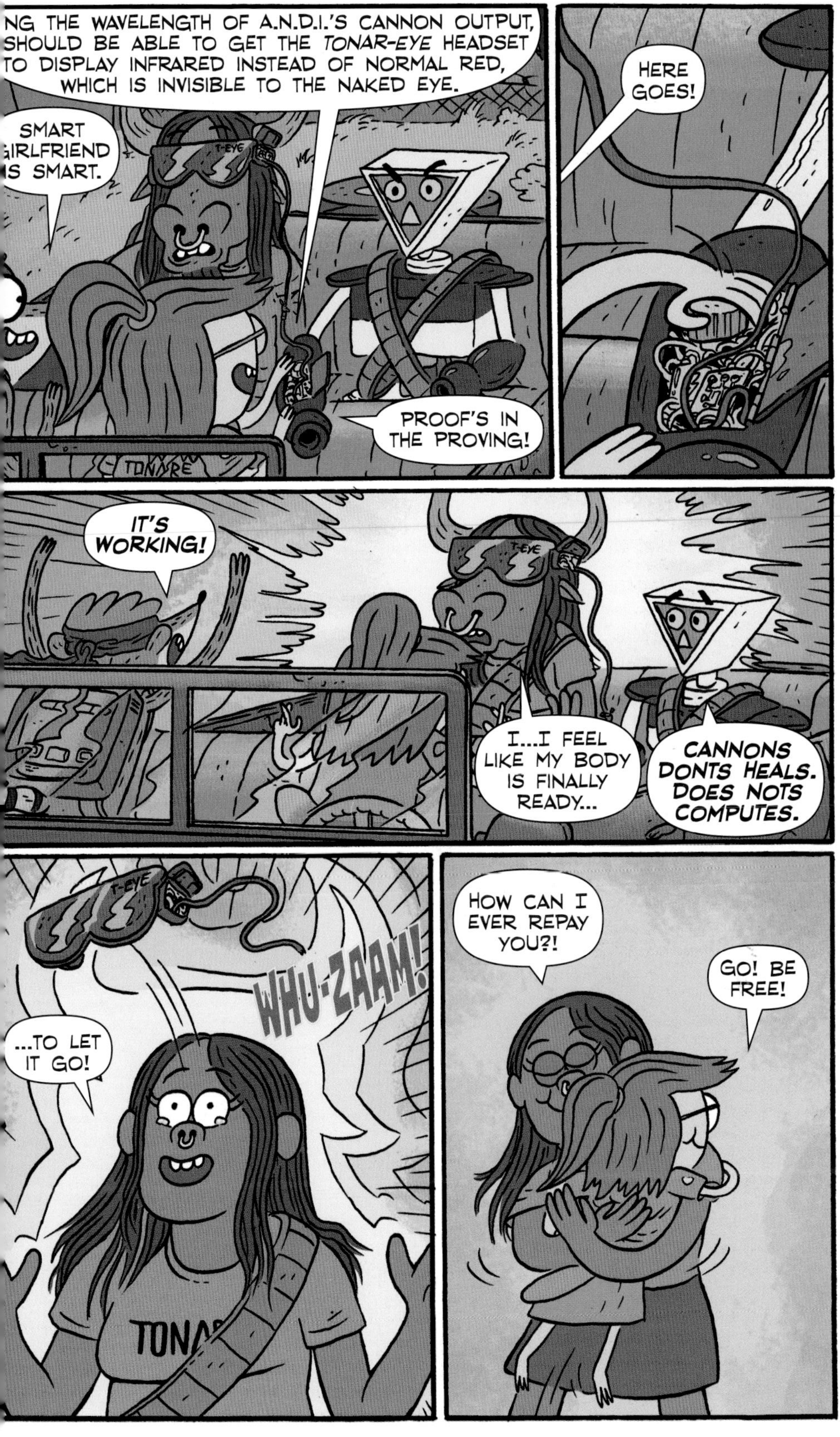
NG THE WAVELENGTH OF A.N.D.I.'S CANNON OUTPUT, SHOULD BE ABLE TO GET THE TONAR-EYE HEADSET TO DISPLAY INFRARED INSTEAD OF NORMAL RED, WHICH IS INVISIBLE TO THE NAKED EYE.
SMART GIRLFRIEND IS SMART.
T-EYE
PROOF'S IN THE PROVING!
TONARE
HERE GOES!
IT'S WORKING!
T-EYE
I...I FEEL LIKE MY BODY IS FINALLY READY...
CANNONS DONTS HEALS. DOES NOTS COMPUTES.
T-EYE
WHU-ZAAM!
...TO LET IT GO!
TONA
HOW CAN I EVER REPAY YOU?!
GO! BE FREE!

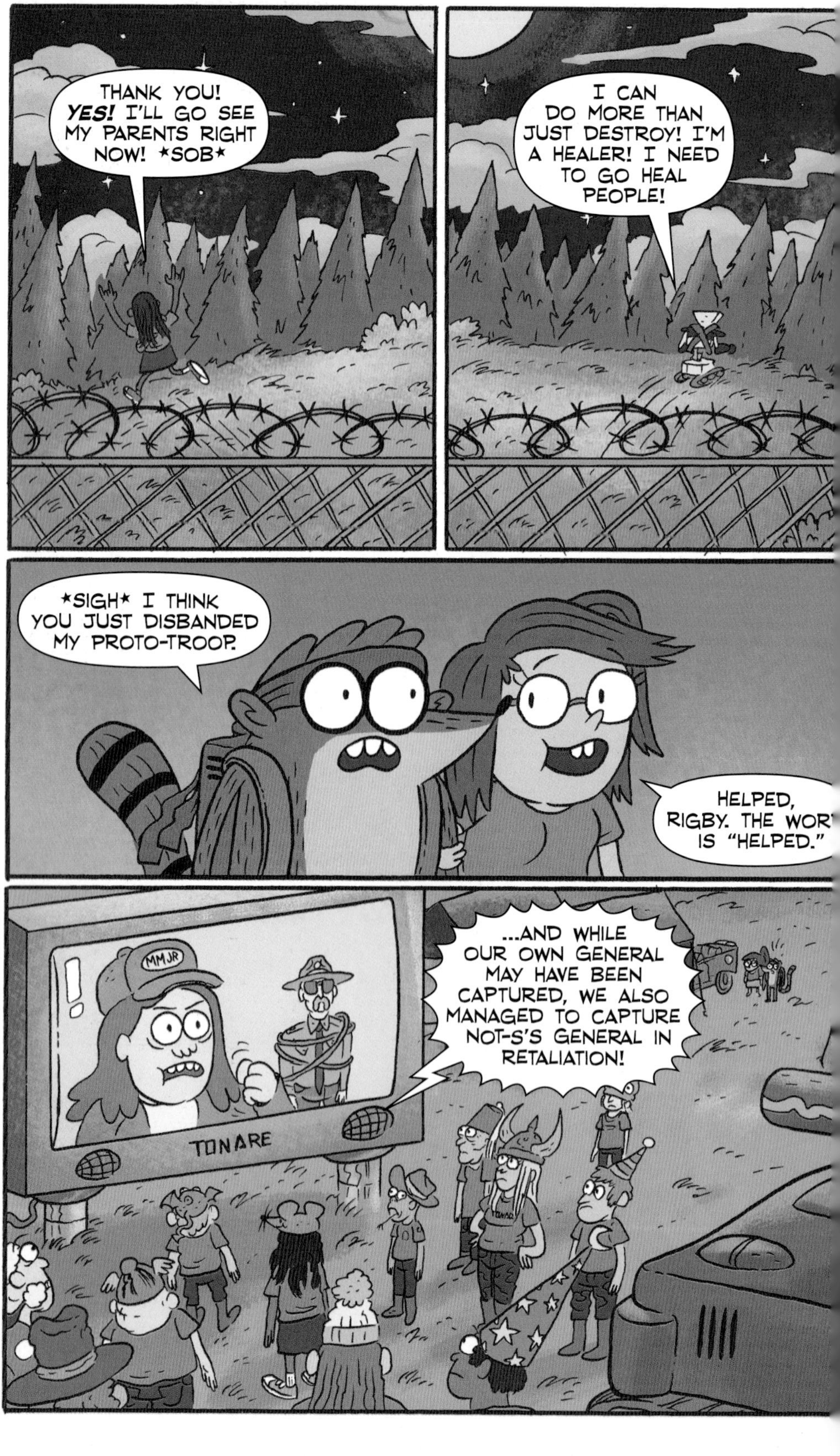
THANK YOU! *YES!* I'LL GO SEE MY PARENTS RIGHT NOW! *SOB*
I CAN DO MORE THAN JUST DESTROY! I'M A HEALER! I NEED TO GO HEAL PEOPLE!
SIGH I THINK YOU JUST DISBANDED MY PROTO-TROOP.
HELPED, RIGBY. THE WOR IS "HELPED."
MMJR
...AND WHILE OUR OWN GENERAL MAY HAVE BEEN CAPTURED, WE ALSO MANAGED TO CAPTURE NOT-S'S GENERAL IN RETALIATION!
TONARE

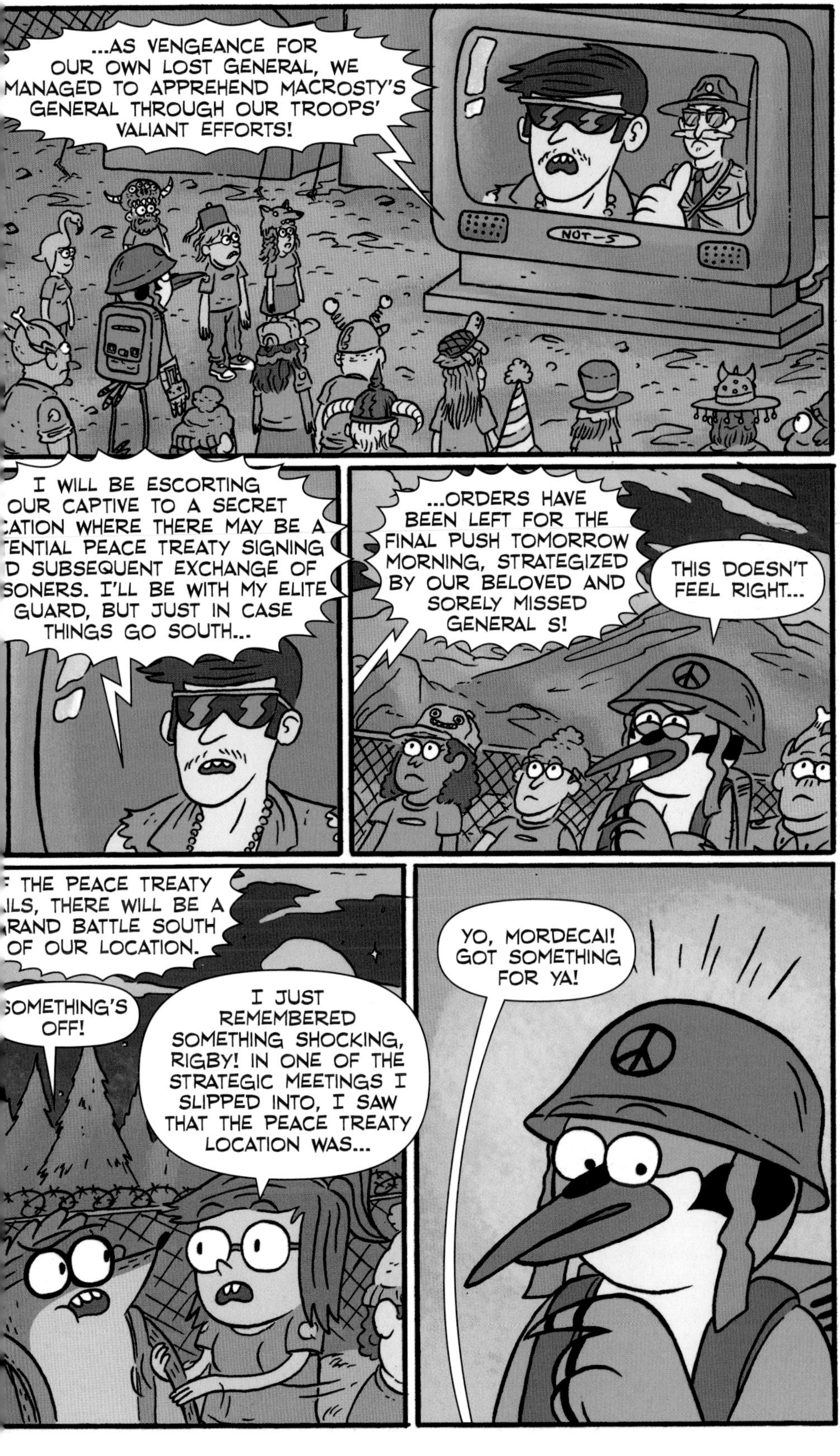
...AS VENGEANCE FOR OUR OWN LOST GENERAL, WE MANAGED TO APPREHEND MACROSTY'S GENERAL THROUGH OUR TROOPS' VALIANT EFFORTS!
NOT-S
I WILL BE ESCORTING OUR CAPTIVE TO A SECRET CATION WHERE THERE MAY BE A TENTIAL PEACE TREATY SIGNING D SUBSEQUENT EXCHANGE OF SONERS. I'LL BE WITH MY ELITE GUARD, BUT JUST IN CASE THINGS GO SOUTH...
...ORDERS HAVE BEEN LEFT FOR THE FINAL PUSH TOMORROW MORNING, STRATEGIZED BY OUR BELOVED AND SORELY MISSED GENERAL S!
THIS DOESN'T FEEL RIGHT...
THE PEACE TREATY ILS, THERE WILL BE A RAND BATTLE SOUTH OF OUR LOCATION.
OMETHING'S OFF!
I JUST REMEMBERED SOMETHING SHOCKING, RIGBY! IN ONE OF THE STRATEGIC MEETINGS I SLIPPED INTO, I SAW THAT THE PEACE TREATY LOCATION WAS...
YO, MORDECAI! GOT SOMETHING FOR YA!

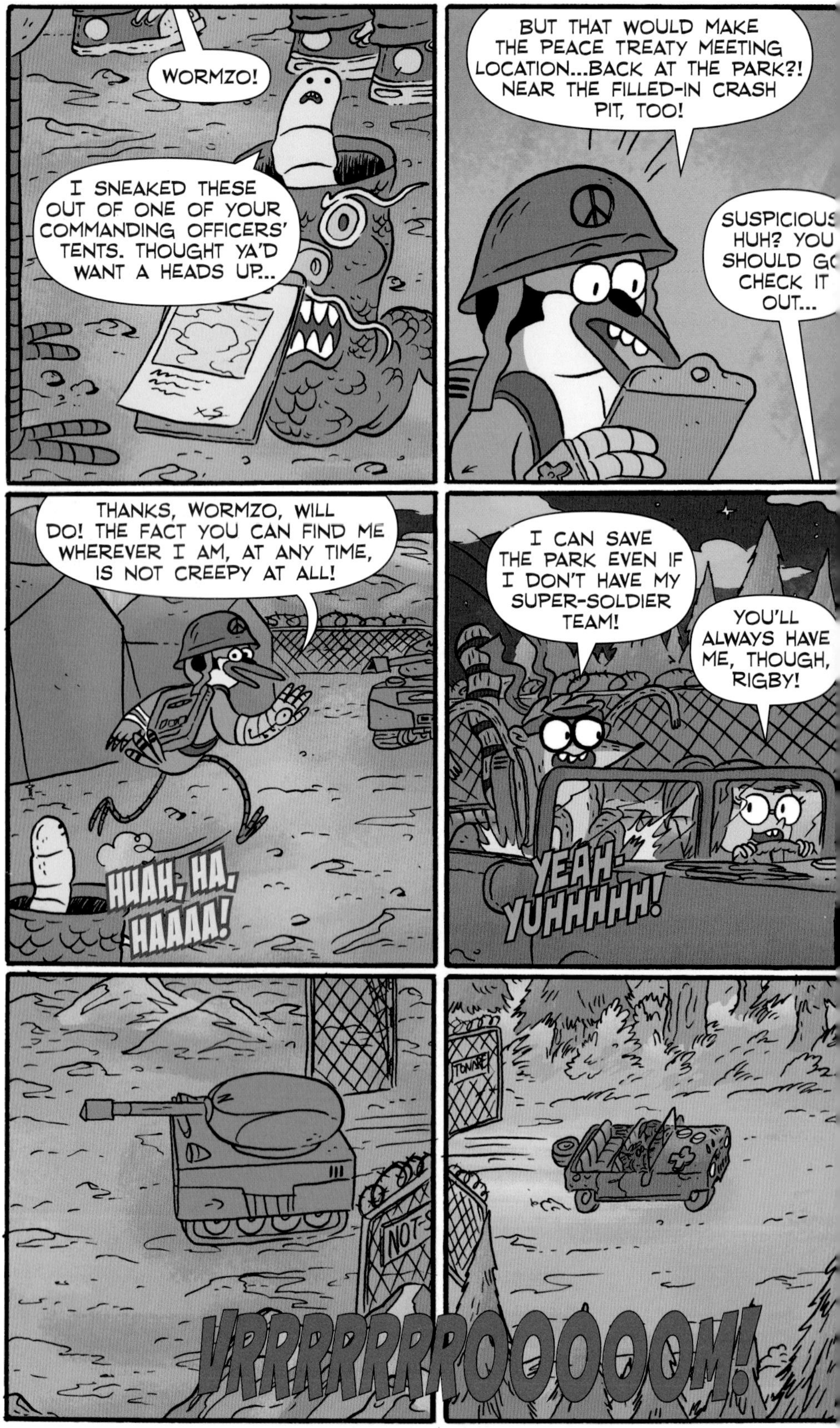
WORMZO!
I SNEAKED THESE OUT OF ONE OF YOUR COMMANDING OFFICERS' TENTS. THOUGHT YA'D WANT A HEADS UP...
BUT THAT WOULD MAKE THE PEACE TREATY MEETING LOCATION...BACK AT THE PARK?! NEAR THE FILLED-IN CRASH PIT, TOO!
SUSPICIOUS HUH? YOU SHOULD GO CHECK IT OUT...
THANKS, WORMZO, WILL DO! THE FACT YOU CAN FIND ME WHEREVER I AM, AT ANY TIME, IS NOT CREEPY AT ALL!
HUAH, HA, HAAAA!
I CAN SAVE THE PARK EVEN IF I DON'T HAVE MY SUPER-SOLDIER TEAM!
YOU'LL ALWAYS HAVE ME, THOUGH, RIGBY!
YEAH-YUHHHHH!
VRRRRRRROOOOOM!

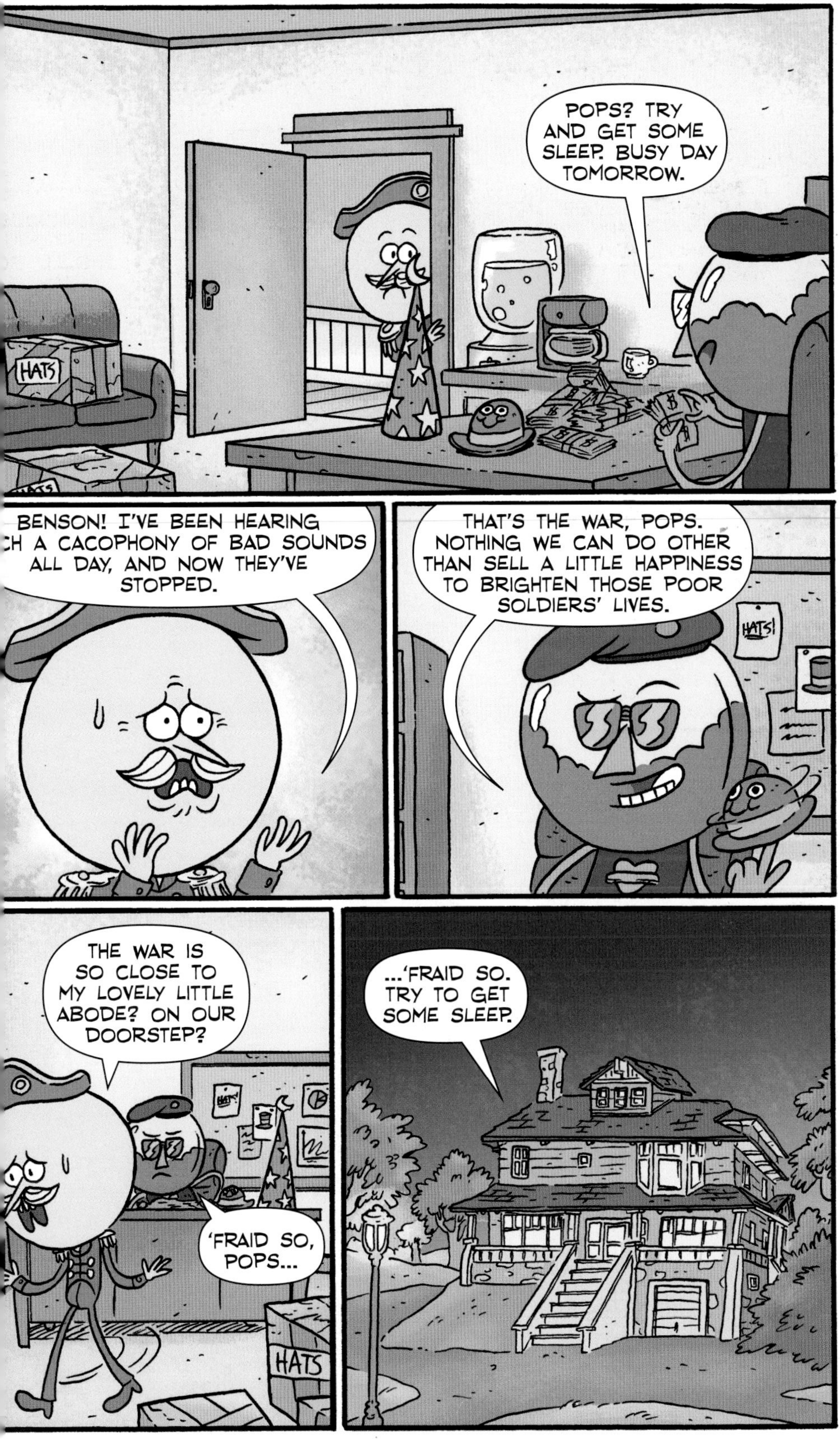
POPS? TRY AND GET SOME SLEEP. BUSY DAY TOMORROW.
HATS
BENSON! I'VE BEEN HEARING
CH A CACOPHONY OF BAD SOUNDS ALL DAY, AND NOW THEY'VE STOPPED.
THAT'S THE WAR, POPS. NOTHING WE CAN DO OTHER THAN SELL A LITTLE HAPPINESS TO BRIGHTEN THOSE POOR SOLDIERS' LIVES.
HATS!
THE WAR IS SO CLOSE TO MY LOVELY LITTLE ABODE? ON OUR DOORSTEP?
'FRAID SO, POPS...
HATS
...'FRAID SO. TRY TO GET SOME SLEEP.

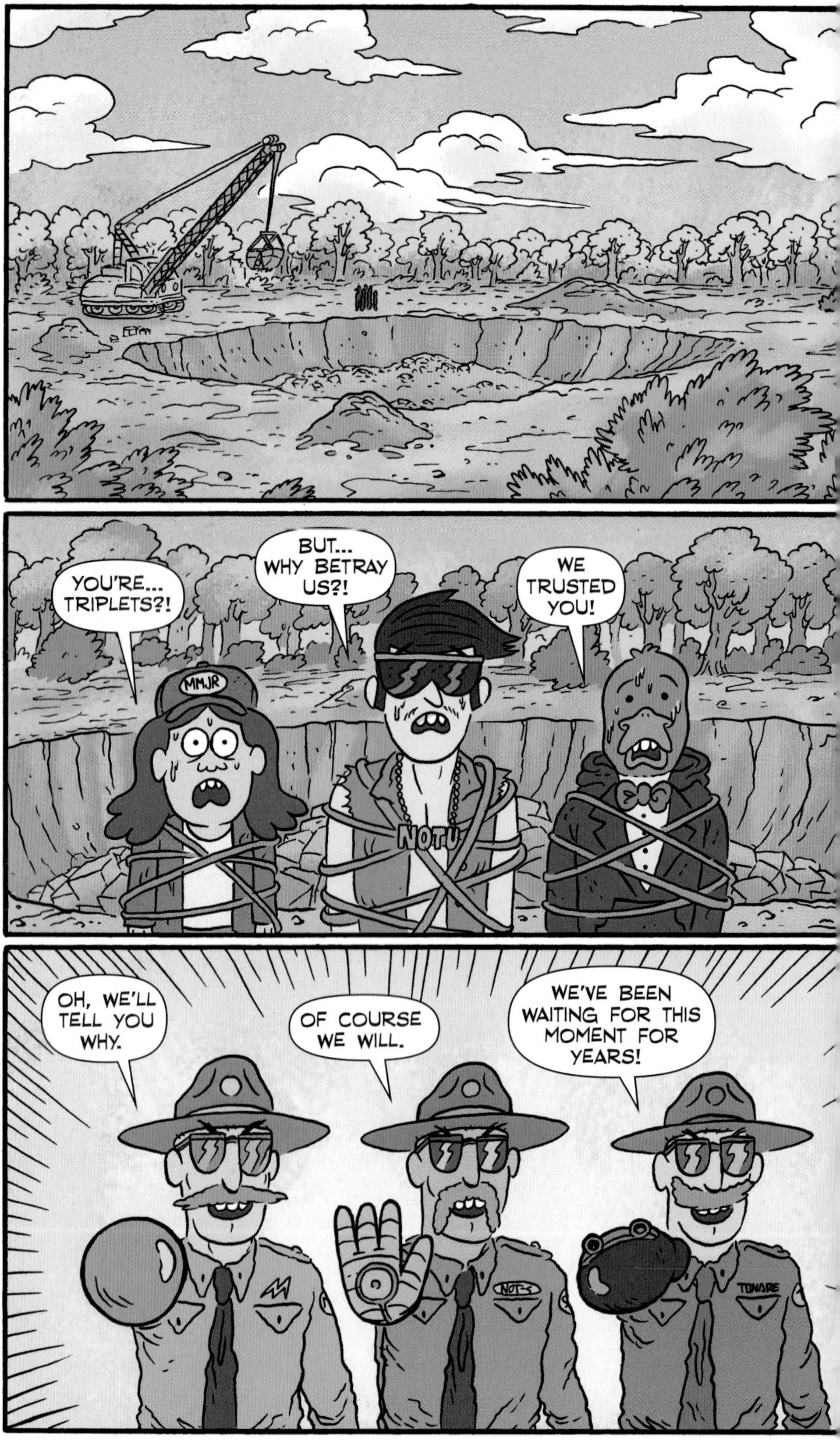
YOU'RE... TRIPLETS?!
BUT... WHY BETRAY US?!
WE TRUSTED YOU!
MMJR
NOTU
OH, WE'LL TELL YOU WHY.
OF COURSE WE WILL.
WE'VE BEEN WAITING FOR THIS MOMENT FOR YEARS!
TOWARE

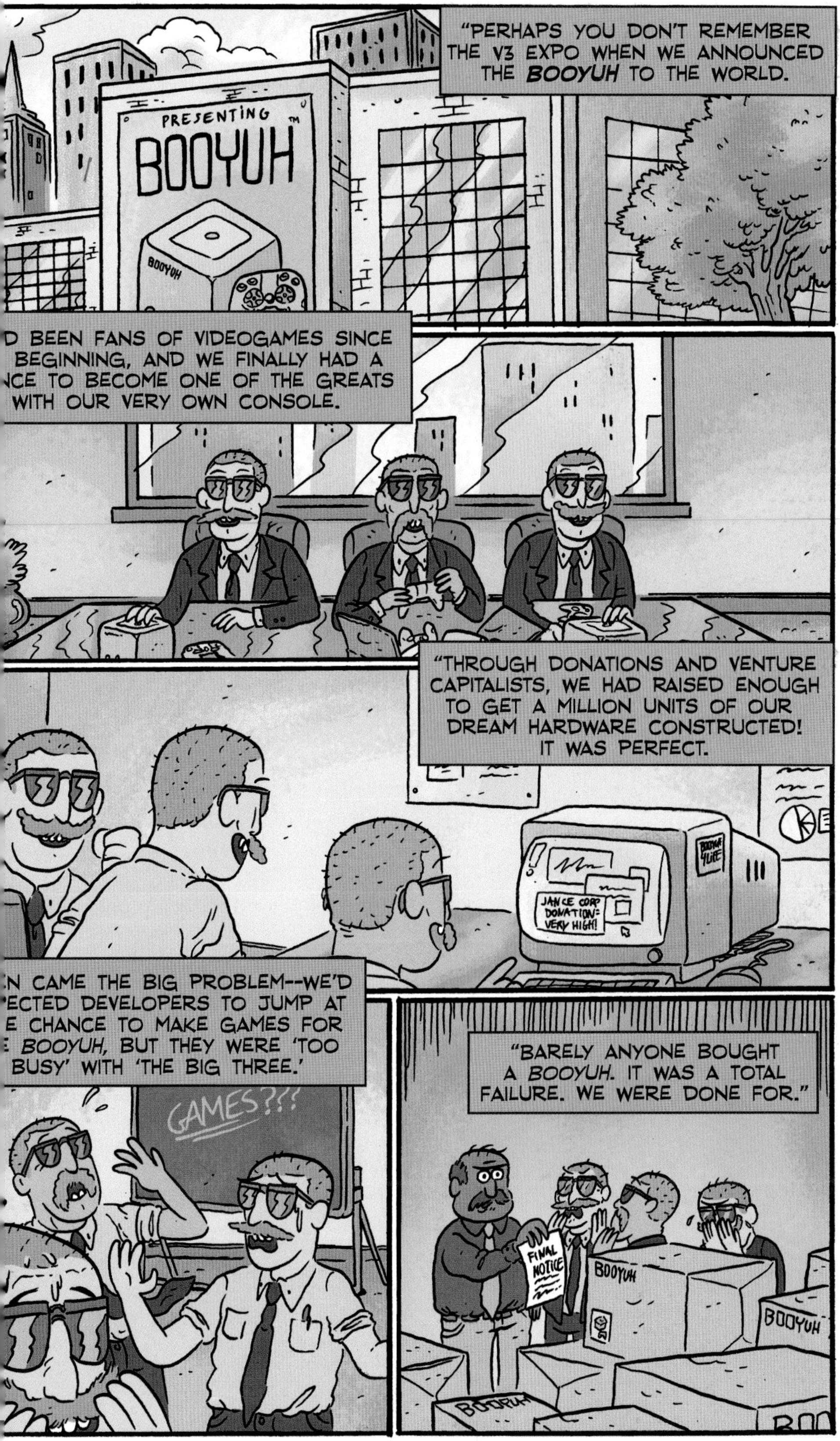

"PERHAPS YOU DON'T REMEMBER THE V3 EXPO WHEN WE ANNOUNCED THE BOOYUH TO THE WORLD.
PRESENTING
BOOYUH
TM
BOOYUH
D BEEN FANS OF VIDEOGAMES SINCE BEGINNING, AND WE FINALLY HAD A NCE TO BECOME ONE OF THE GREATS WITH OUR VERY OWN CONSOLE.
"THROUGH DONATIONS AND VENTURE CAPITALISTS, WE HAD RAISED ENOUGH TO GET A MILLION UNITS OF OUR DREAM HARDWARE CONSTRUCTED! IT WAS PERFECT.
JANCE CORP DONATION: VERY HIGH!
N CAME THE BIG PROBLEM--WE'D ECTED DEVELOPERS TO JUMP AT E CHANCE TO MAKE GAMES FOR BOOYUH, BUT THEY WERE 'TOO BUSY' WITH 'THE BIG THREE.'
GAMES???
"BARELY ANYONE BOUGHT A BOOYUH. IT WAS A TOTAL FAILURE. WE WERE DONE FOR."
FINAL NOTICE
BOOYUH
BOOYUH
BOOYUH

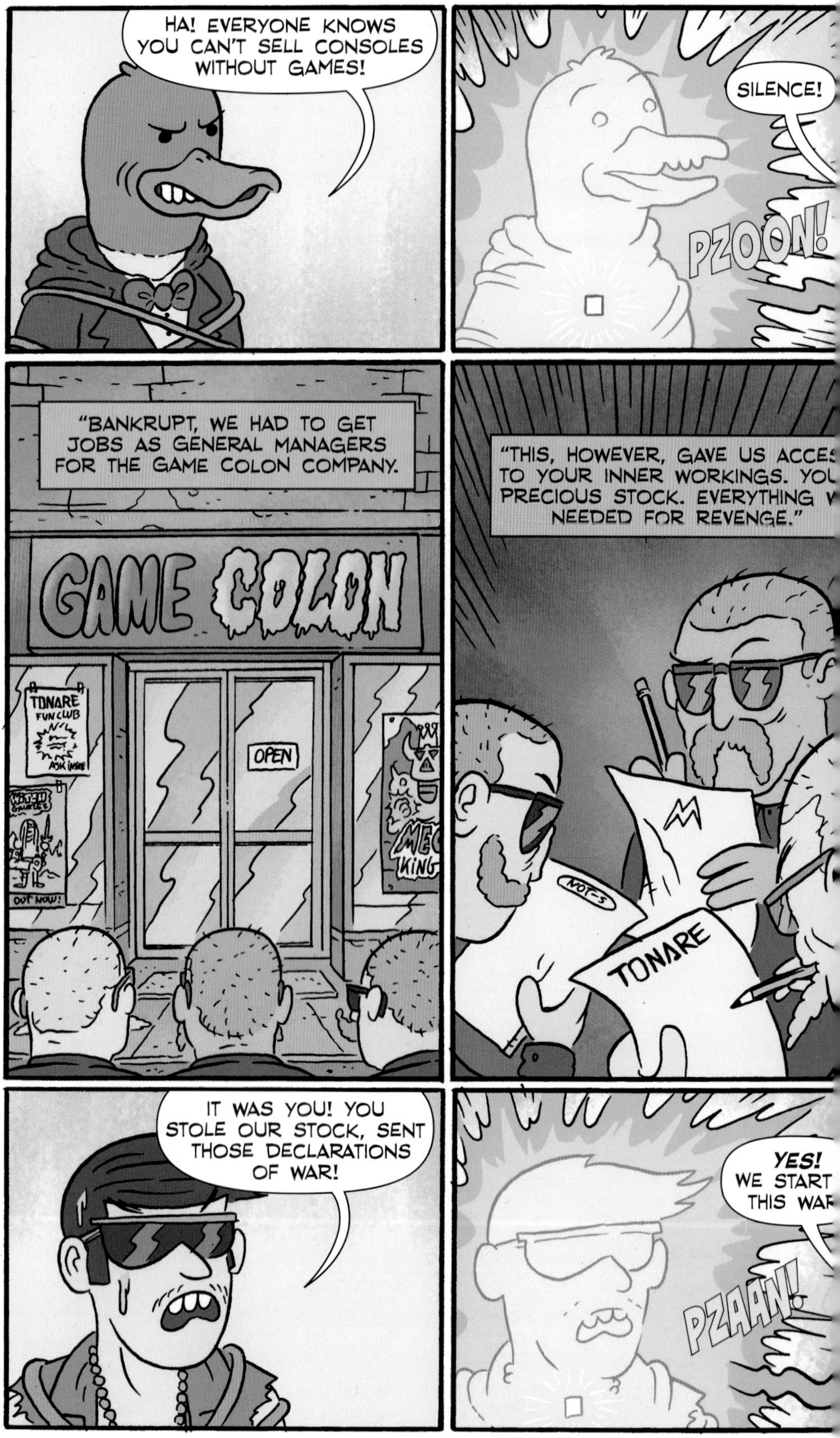
HA! EVERYONE KNOWS YOU CAN'T SELL CONSOLES WITHOUT GAMES!
SILENCE!
PZOON!
"BANKRUPT, WE HAD TO GET JOBS AS GENERAL MANAGERS FOR THE GAME COLON COMPANY.
GAME COLON
TONARE FUN CLUB
ASK INSIDE
OPEN
OUT NOW!
"THIS, HOWEVER, GAVE US ACCES TO YOUR INNER WORKINGS. YOU PRECIOUS STOCK. EVERYTHING W NEEDED FOR REVENGE."
NOT-S
TONARE
IT WAS YOU! YOU STOLE OUR STOCK, SENT THOSE DECLARATIONS OF WAR!
YES! WE START THIS WAR
PZAAN!

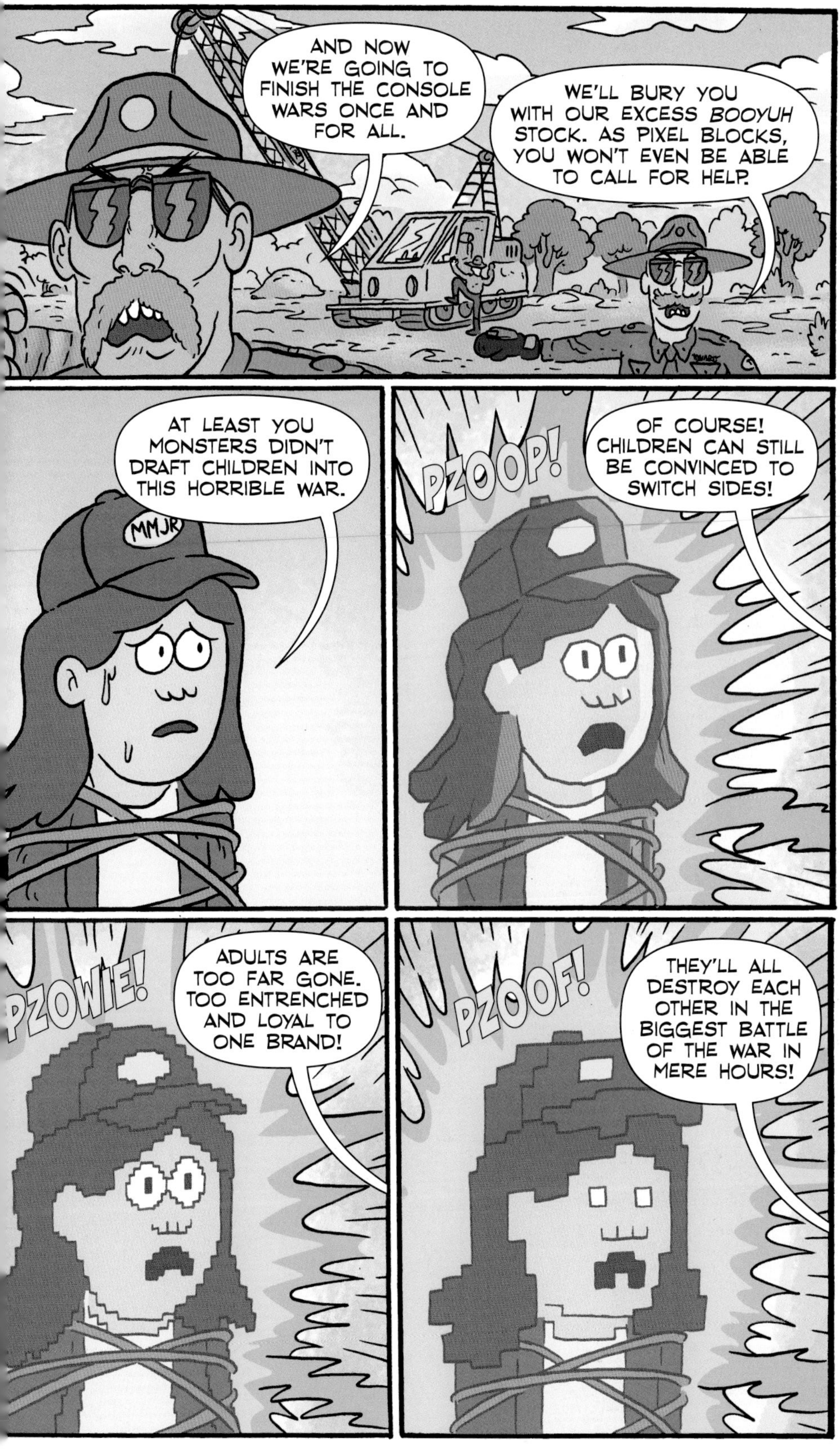
AND NOW WE'RE GOING TO FINISH THE CONSOLE WARS ONCE AND FOR ALL.
WE'LL BURY YOU WITH OUR EXCESS *BOOYUH* STOCK. AS PIXEL BLOCKS, YOU WON'T EVEN BE ABLE TO CALL FOR HELP.
AT LEAST YOU MONSTERS DIDN'T DRAFT CHILDREN INTO THIS HORRIBLE WAR.
MMJR
PZOOP!
OF COURSE! CHILDREN CAN STILL BE CONVINCED TO SWITCH SIDES!
PZOWIE!
ADULTS ARE TOO FAR GONE. TOO ENTRENCHED AND LOYAL TO ONE BRAND!
PZOOF!
THEY'LL ALL DESTROY EACH OTHER IN THE BIGGEST BATTLE OF THE WAR IN MERE HOURS!

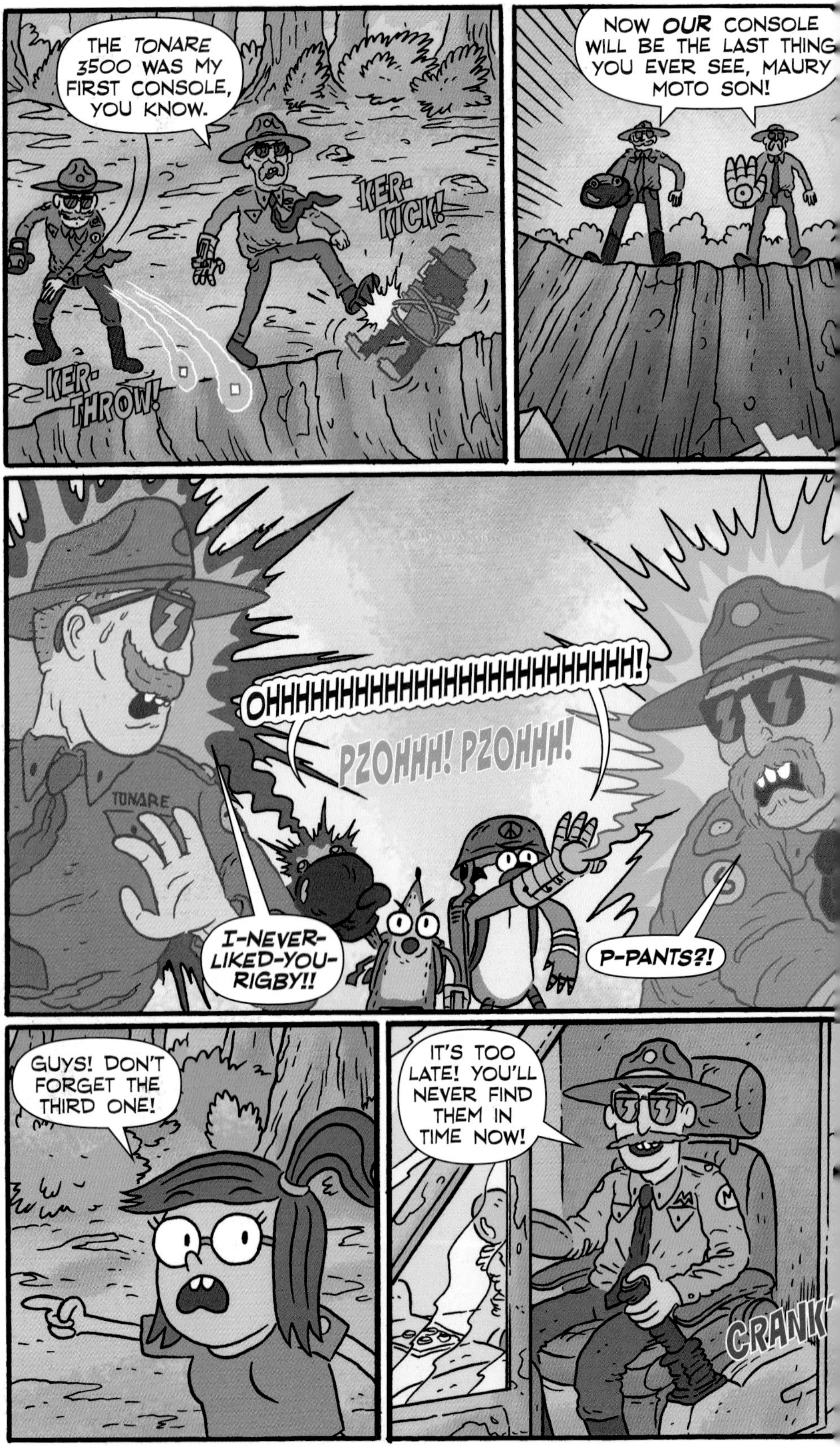
THE *TONARE* 3500 WAS MY FIRST CONSOLE, YOU KNOW.
KER-KICK!
KER-THROW!
NOW *OUR* CONSOLE WILL BE THE LAST THING YOU EVER SEE, MAURY MOTO SON!
OHHHHHHHHHHHHHHHHHHHHHHHHH!
PZOHHH! PZOHHH!
TONARE
I-NEVER-LIKED-YOU-RIGBY!!
P-PANTS?!
GUYS! DON'T FORGET THE THIRD ONE!
IT'S TOO LATE! YOU'LL NEVER FIND THEM IN TIME NOW!
CRANK

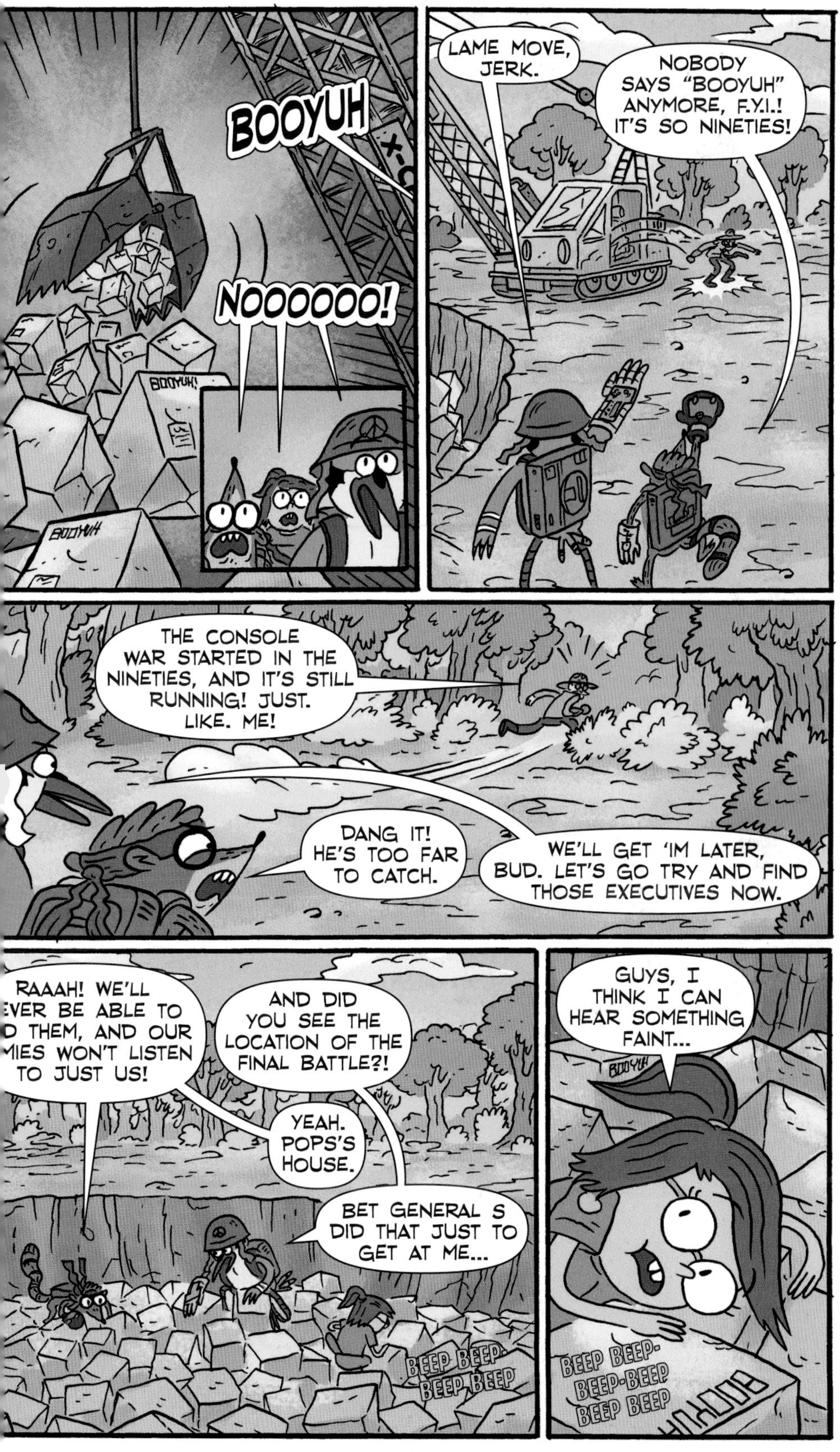
BOOYUH
NOOOOOO!
BOOYUH!
BOOYUH
LAME MOVE, JERK.
NOBODY SAYS "BOOYUH" ANYMORE, F.Y.I.! IT'S SO NINETIES!
THE CONSOLE WAR STARTED IN THE NINETIES, AND IT'S STILL RUNNING! JUST. LIKE. ME!
DANG IT! HE'S TOO FAR TO CATCH.
WE'LL GET 'IM LATER, BUD. LET'S GO TRY AND FIND THOSE EXECUTIVES NOW.
RAAAH! WE'LL EVER BE ABLE TO D THEM, AND OUR MIES WON'T LISTEN TO JUST US!
AND DID YOU SEE THE LOCATION OF THE FINAL BATTLE?!
YEAH. POPS'S HOUSE.
BET GENERAL S DID THAT JUST TO GET AT ME...
BEEP BEEP-BEEP BEEP
GUYS, I THINK I CAN HEAR SOMETHING FAINT...
BOOYUH
BEEP BEEP-BEEP-BEEP BEEP BEEP
BOOYUH

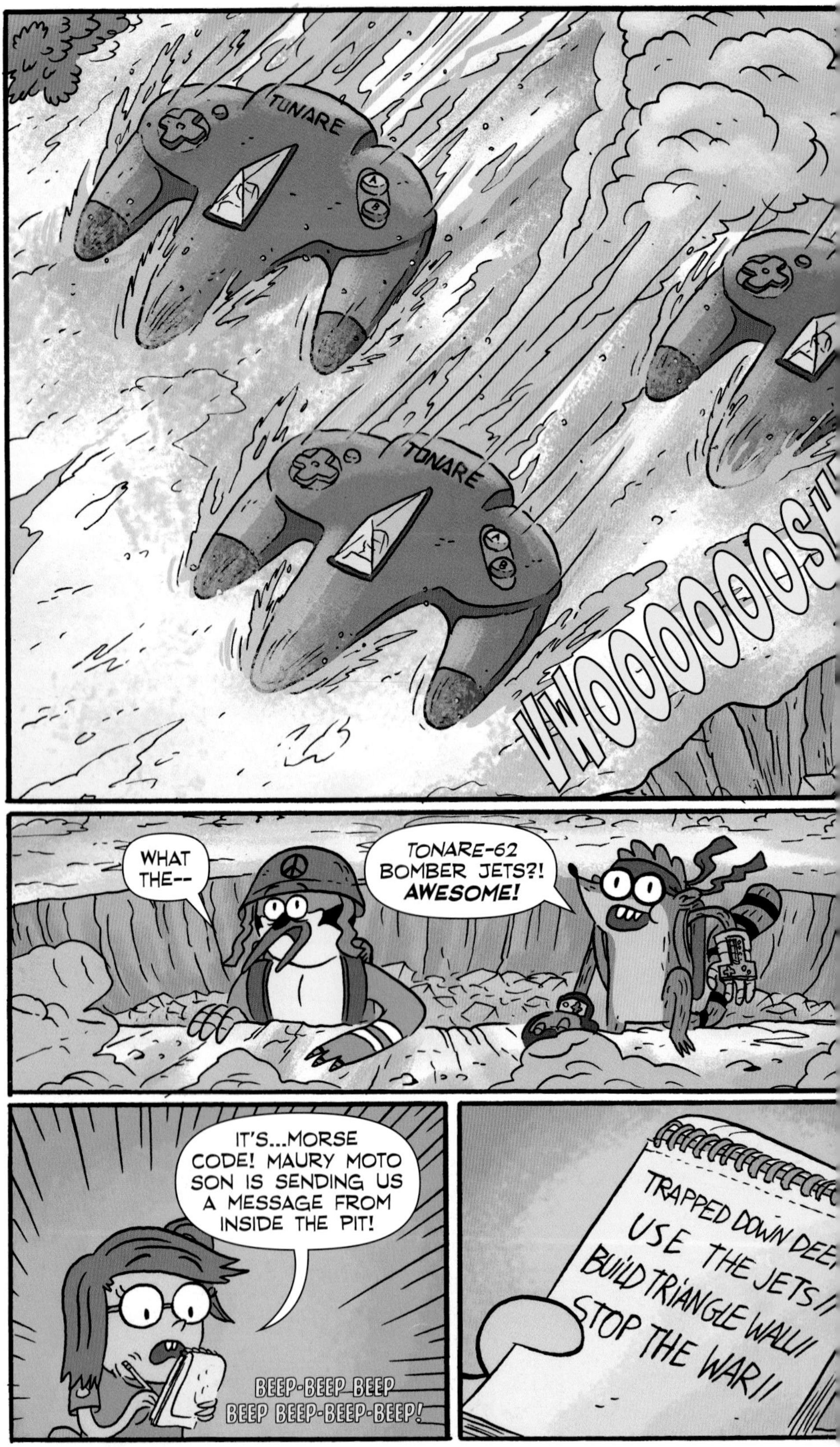
TONARE
TONARE
VWOOOOOOS
WHAT THE--
TONARE-62 BOMBER JETS?! **AWESOME!**
IT'S...MORSE CODE! MAURY MOTO SON IS SENDING US A MESSAGE FROM INSIDE THE PIT!
BEEP-BEEP BEEP BEEP BEEP-BEEP-BEEP!
TRAPPED DOWN DEE
USE THE JETS//
BUILD TRIANGLE WALL//
STOP THE WAR//

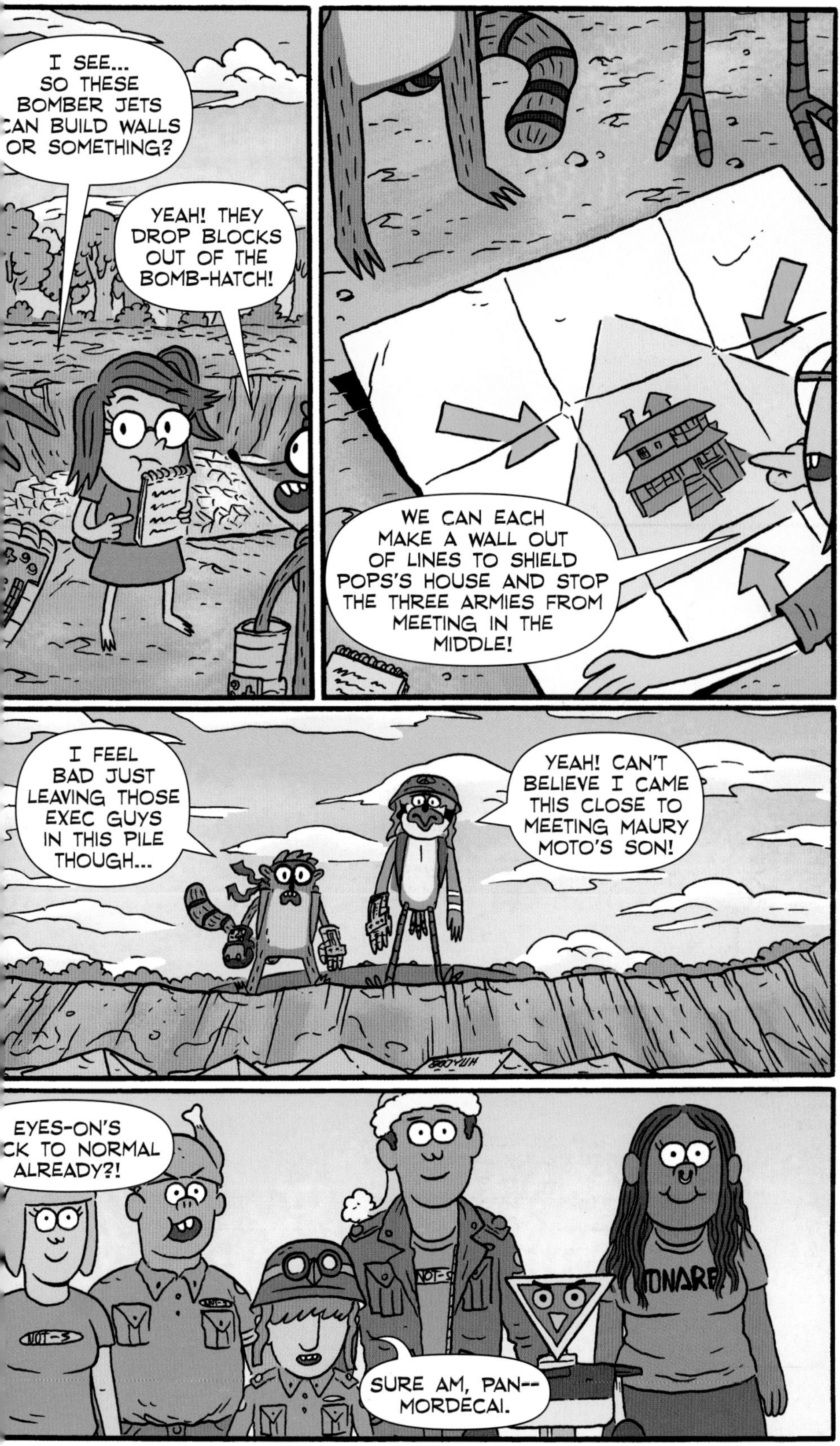
I SEE... SO THESE BOMBER JETS CAN BUILD WALLS OR SOMETHING?
YEAH! THEY DROP BLOCKS OUT OF THE BOMB-HATCH!
WE CAN EACH MAKE A WALL OUT OF LINES TO SHIELD POPS'S HOUSE AND STOP THE THREE ARMIES FROM MEETING IN THE MIDDLE!
I FEEL BAD JUST LEAVING THOSE EXEC GUYS IN THIS PILE THOUGH...
YEAH! CAN'T BELIEVE I CAME THIS CLOSE TO MEETING MAURY MOTO'S SON!
EYES-ON'S CK TO NORMAL ALREADY?!
SURE AM, PAN-- MORDECAI.

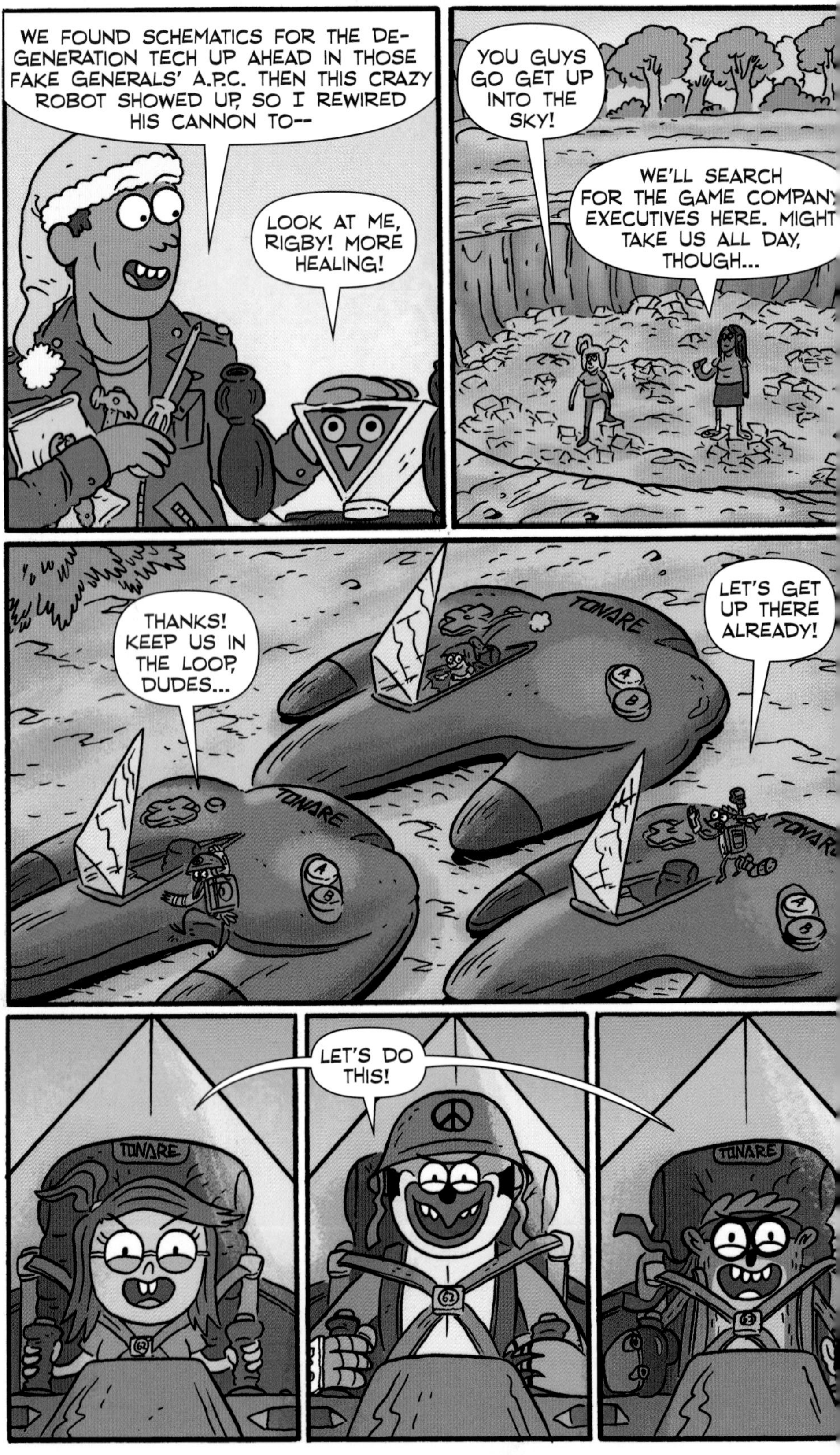
WE FOUND SCHEMATICS FOR THE DE-GENERATION TECH UP AHEAD IN THOSE FAKE GENERALS' A.P.C. THEN THIS CRAZY ROBOT SHOWED UP, SO I REWIRED HIS CANNON TO--
LOOK AT ME, RIGBY! MORE HEALING!
YOU GUYS GO GET UP INTO THE SKY!
WE'LL SEARCH FOR THE GAME COMPANY EXECUTIVES HERE. MIGHT TAKE US ALL DAY, THOUGH...
THANKS! KEEP US IN THE LOOP, DUDES...
LET'S GET UP THERE ALREADY!
TONARE
LET'S DO THIS!

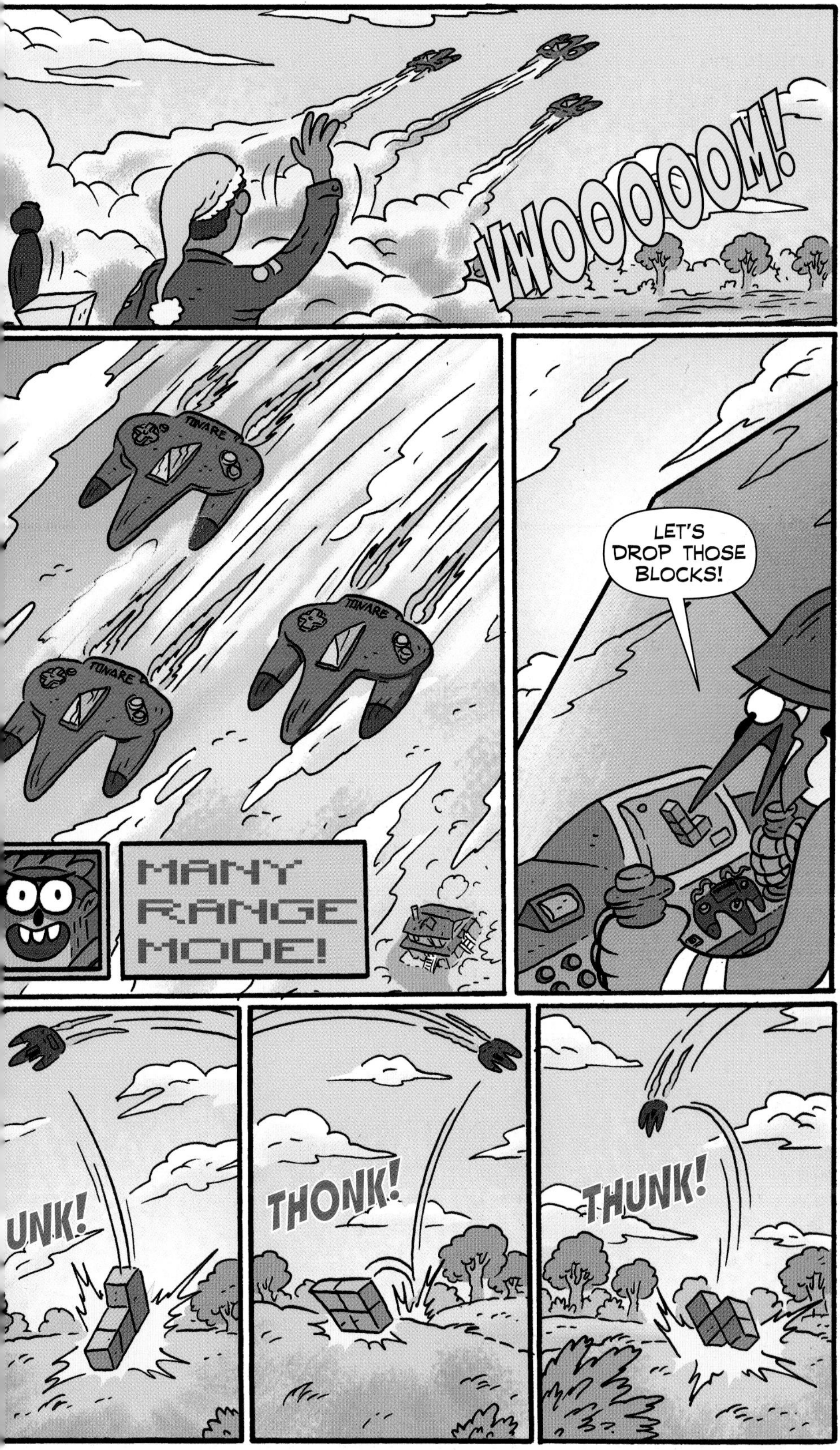
VWOOOOOM!
TINARE
TINARE
TINARE
LET'S DROP THOSE BLOCKS!
MANY RANGE MODE!
UNK!
THONK!
THUNK!

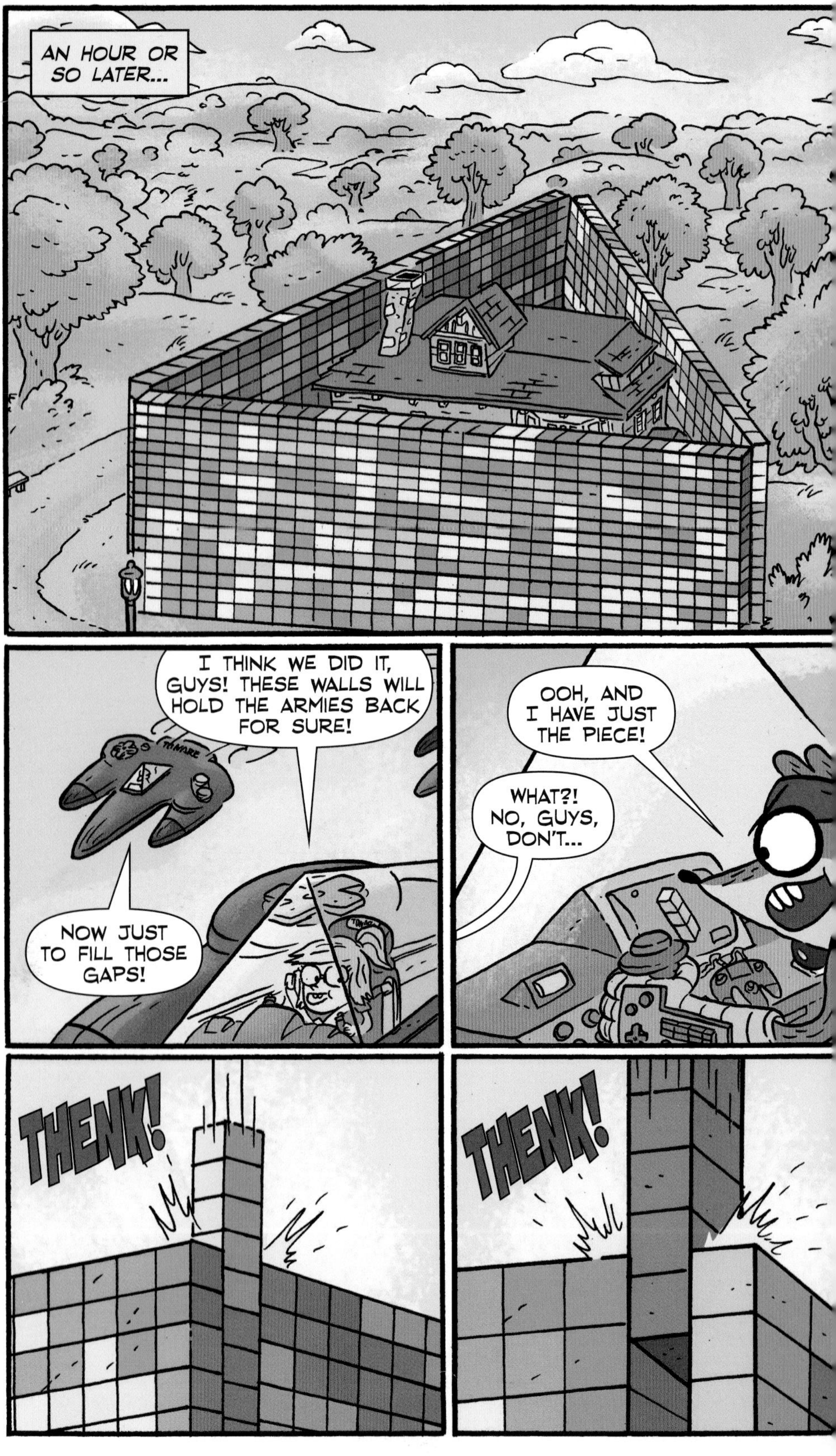
AN HOUR OR SO LATER...
I THINK WE DID IT, GUYS! THESE WALLS WILL HOLD THE ARMIES BACK FOR SURE!
NOW JUST TO FILL THOSE GAPS!
OOH, AND I HAVE JUST THE PIECE!
WHAT?! NO, GUYS, DON'T...
THENK!
THENK!

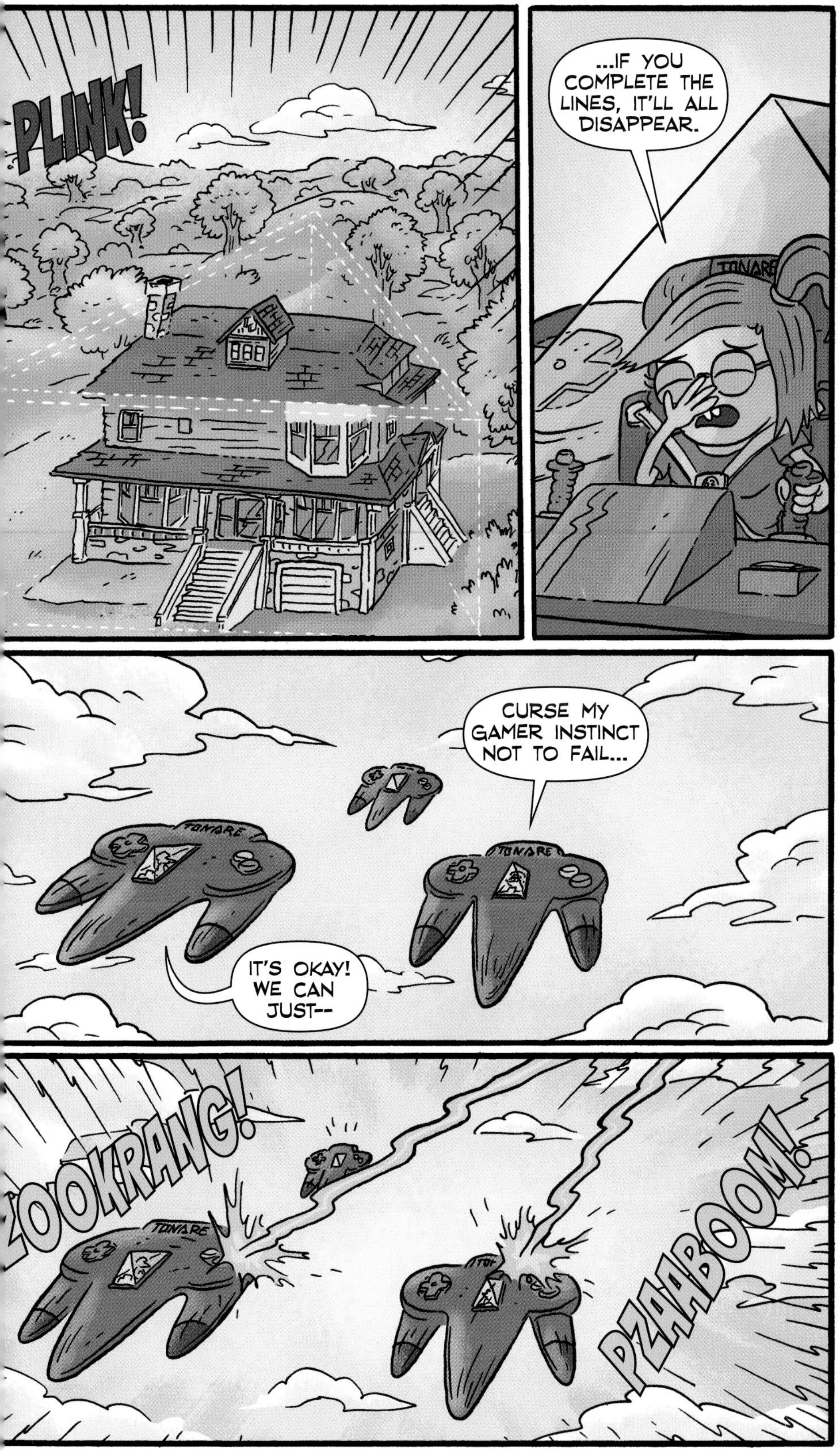
PLINK!
...IF YOU COMPLETE THE LINES, IT'LL ALL DISAPPEAR.
TONARE
CURSE MY GAMER INSTINCT NOT TO FAIL...
TONARE
TONARE
IT'S OKAY! WE CAN JUST--
ZOOKRANG!
TONARE
PZAABOOM!

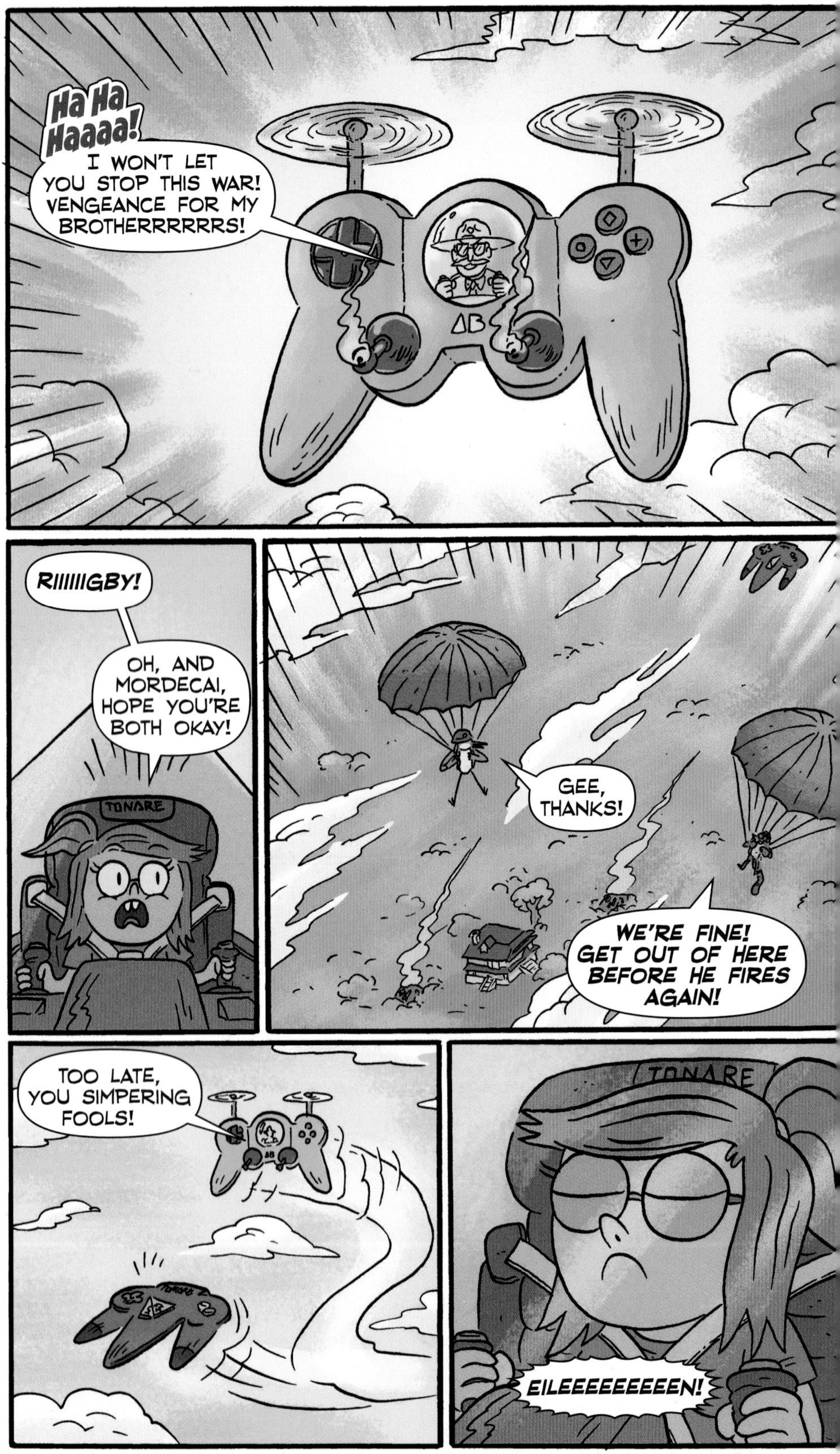
Ha Ha Haaaa!
I WON'T LET YOU STOP THIS WAR! VENGEANCE FOR MY BROTHERRRRRRS!
RIIIIIIGBY!
OH, AND MORDECAI, HOPE YOU'RE BOTH OKAY!
TONARE
GEE, THANKS!
WE'RE FINE! GET OUT OF HERE BEFORE HE FIRES AGAIN!
TOO LATE, YOU SIMPERING FOOLS!
TONARE
EILEEEEEEEEEEN!

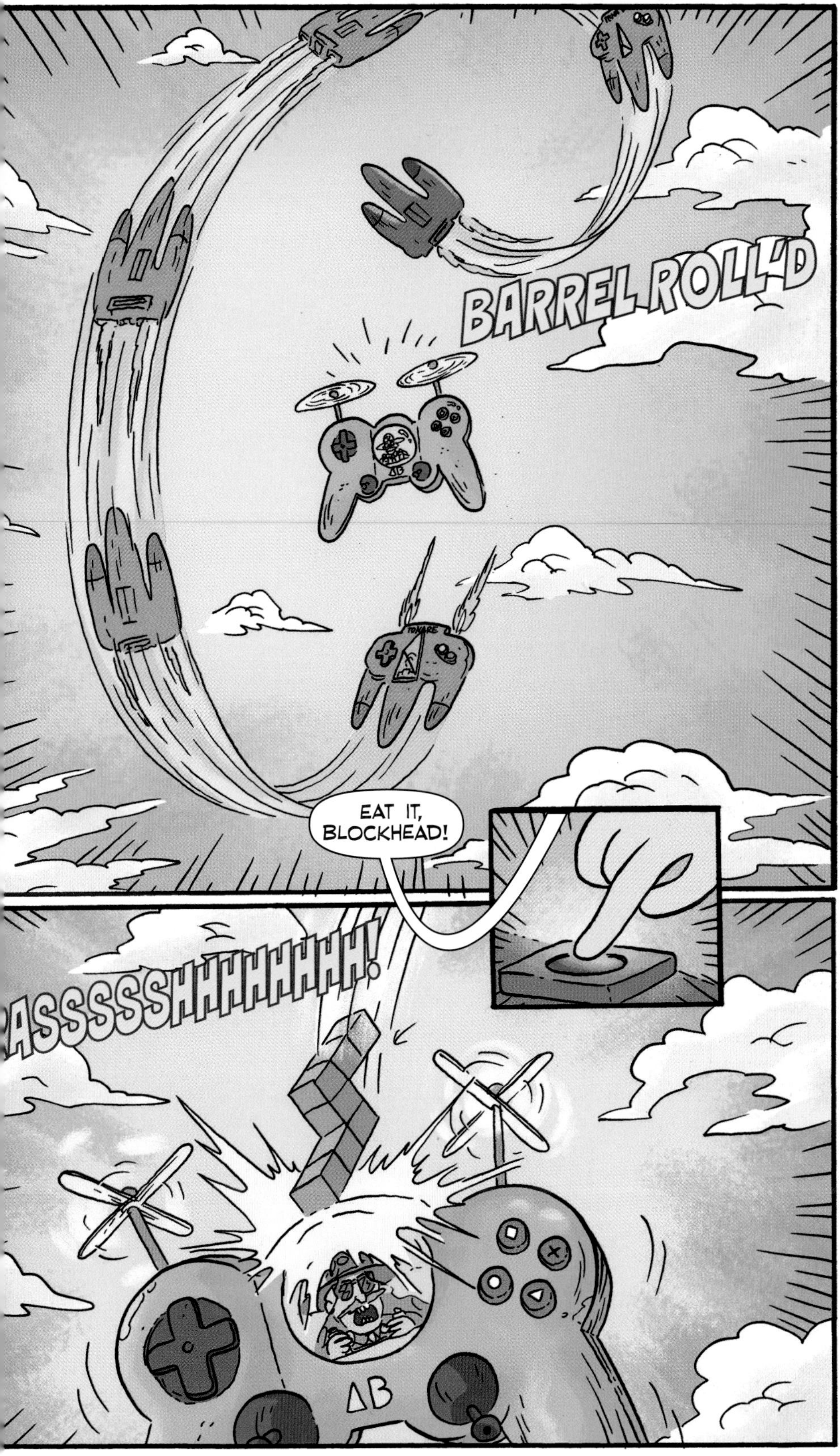

BARREL ROLL'D
EAT IT, BLOCKHEAD!
ASSSSSHHHHHHHH!

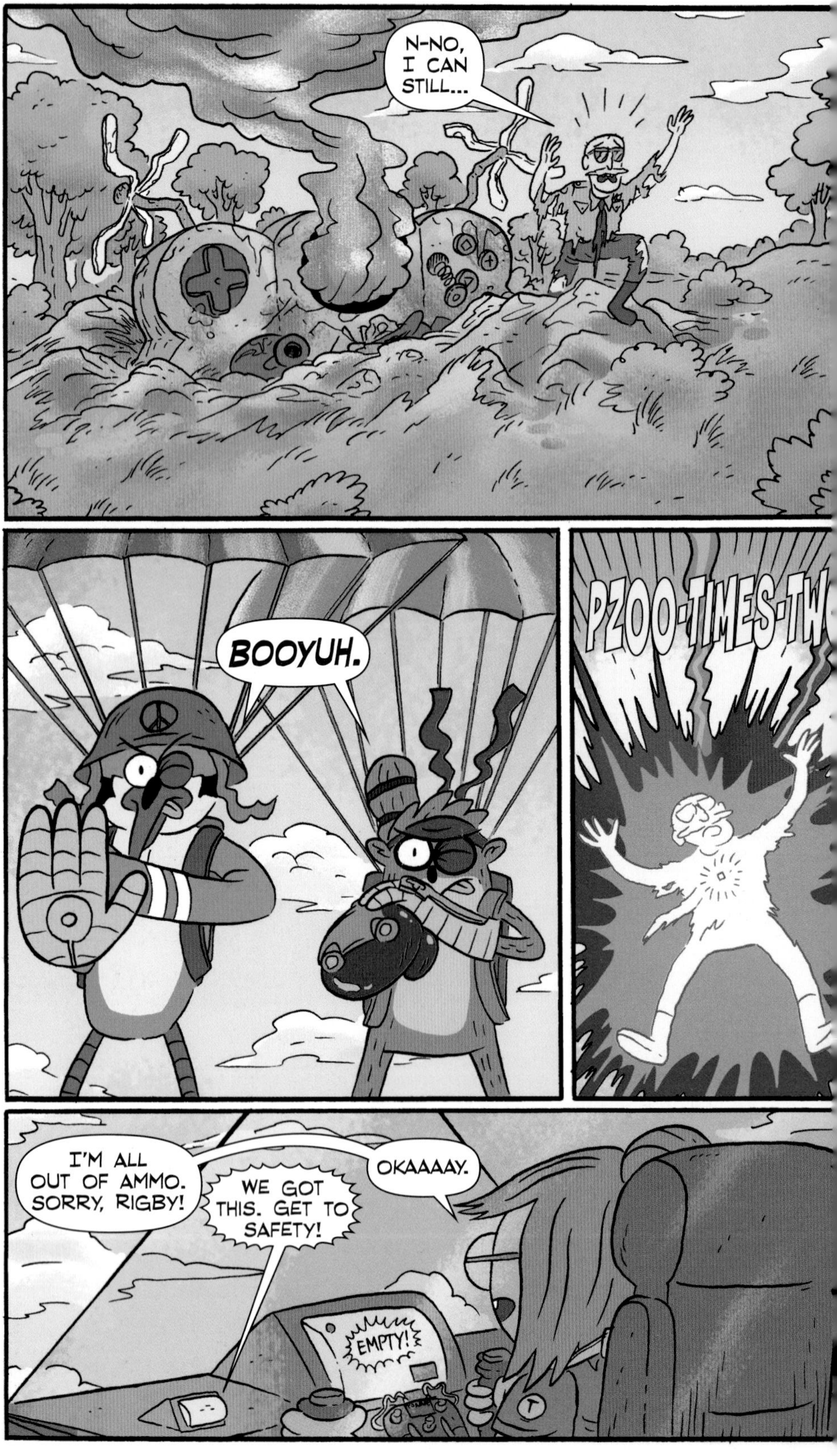
N-NO, I CAN STILL...
BOOYUH.
PZOO-TIMES-TW
I'M ALL OUT OF AMMO. SORRY, RIGBY!
OKAAAAY.
WE GOT THIS. GET TO SAFETY!
EMPTY!

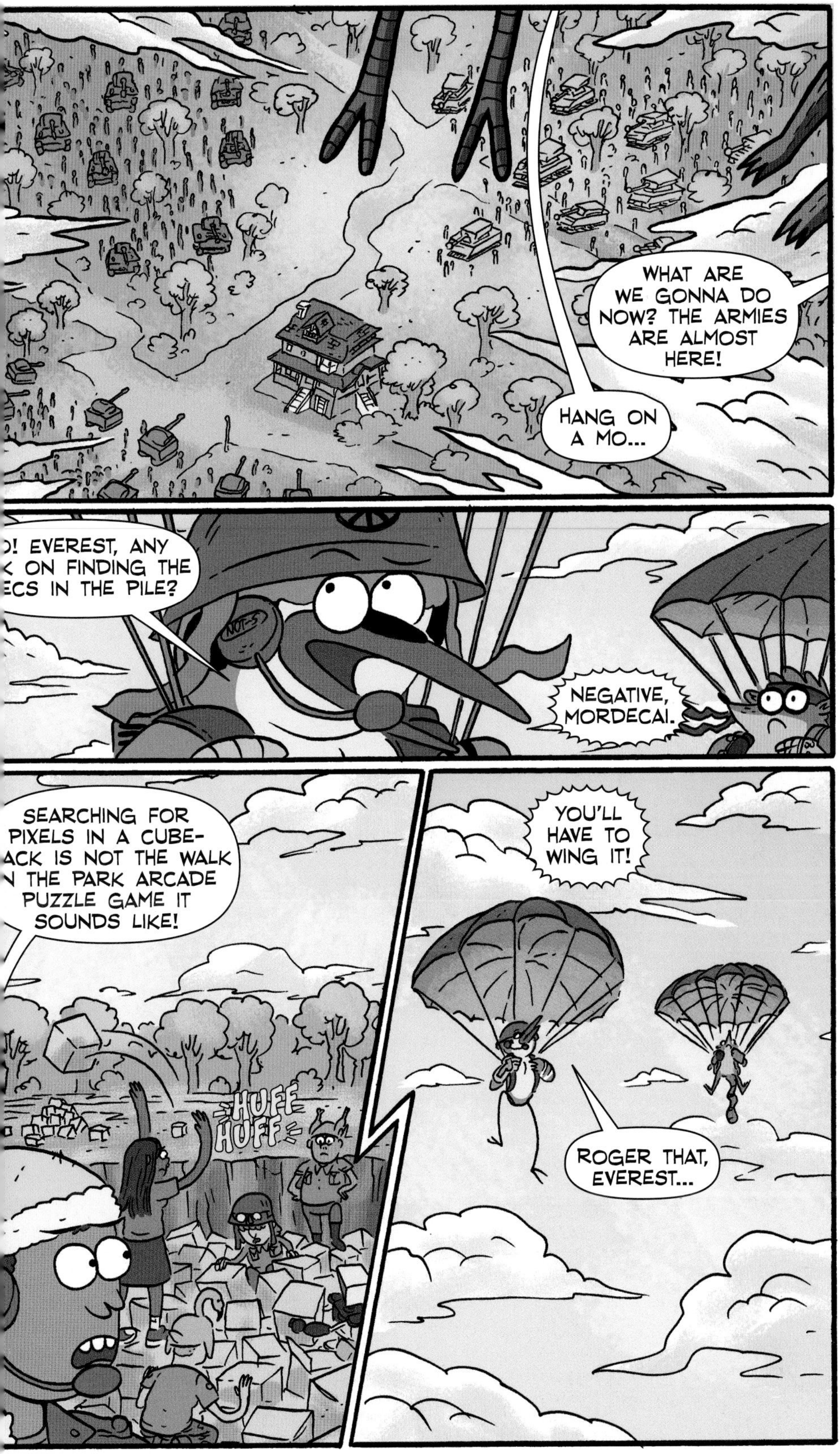
WHAT ARE WE GONNA DO NOW? THE ARMIES ARE ALMOST HERE!
HANG ON A MO...
O! EVEREST, ANY K ON FINDING THE ECS IN THE PILE?
NOT-5
NEGATIVE, MORDECAI.
SEARCHING FOR PIXELS IN A CUBE- ACK IS NOT THE WALK N THE PARK ARCADE PUZZLE GAME IT SOUNDS LIKE!
HUFF HUFF
YOU'LL HAVE TO WING IT!
ROGER THAT, EVEREST...

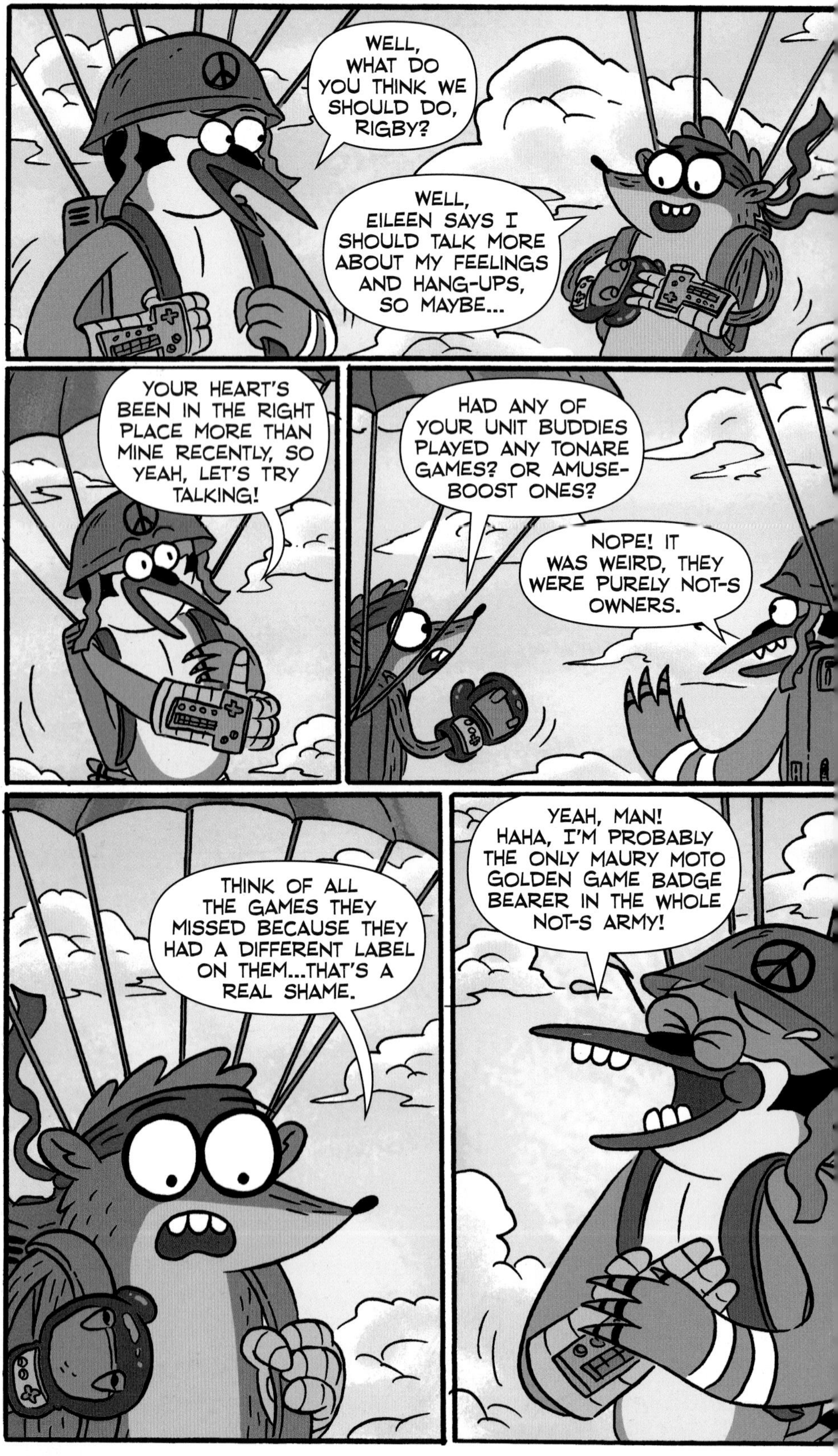
WELL, WHAT DO YOU THINK WE SHOULD DO, RIGBY?
WELL, EILEEN SAYS I SHOULD TALK MORE ABOUT MY FEELINGS AND HANG-UPS, SO MAYBE...
YOUR HEART'S BEEN IN THE RIGHT PLACE MORE THAN MINE RECENTLY, SO YEAH, LET'S TRY TALKING!
HAD ANY OF YOUR UNIT BUDDIES PLAYED ANY TONARE GAMES? OR AMUSE-BOOST ONES?
NOPE! IT WAS WEIRD, THEY WERE PURELY NOT-S OWNERS.
THINK OF ALL THE GAMES THEY MISSED BECAUSE THEY HAD A DIFFERENT LABEL ON THEM...THAT'S A REAL SHAME.
YEAH, MAN! HAHA, I'M PROBABLY THE ONLY MAURY MOTO GOLDEN GAME BADGE BEARER IN THE WHOLE NOT-S ARMY!

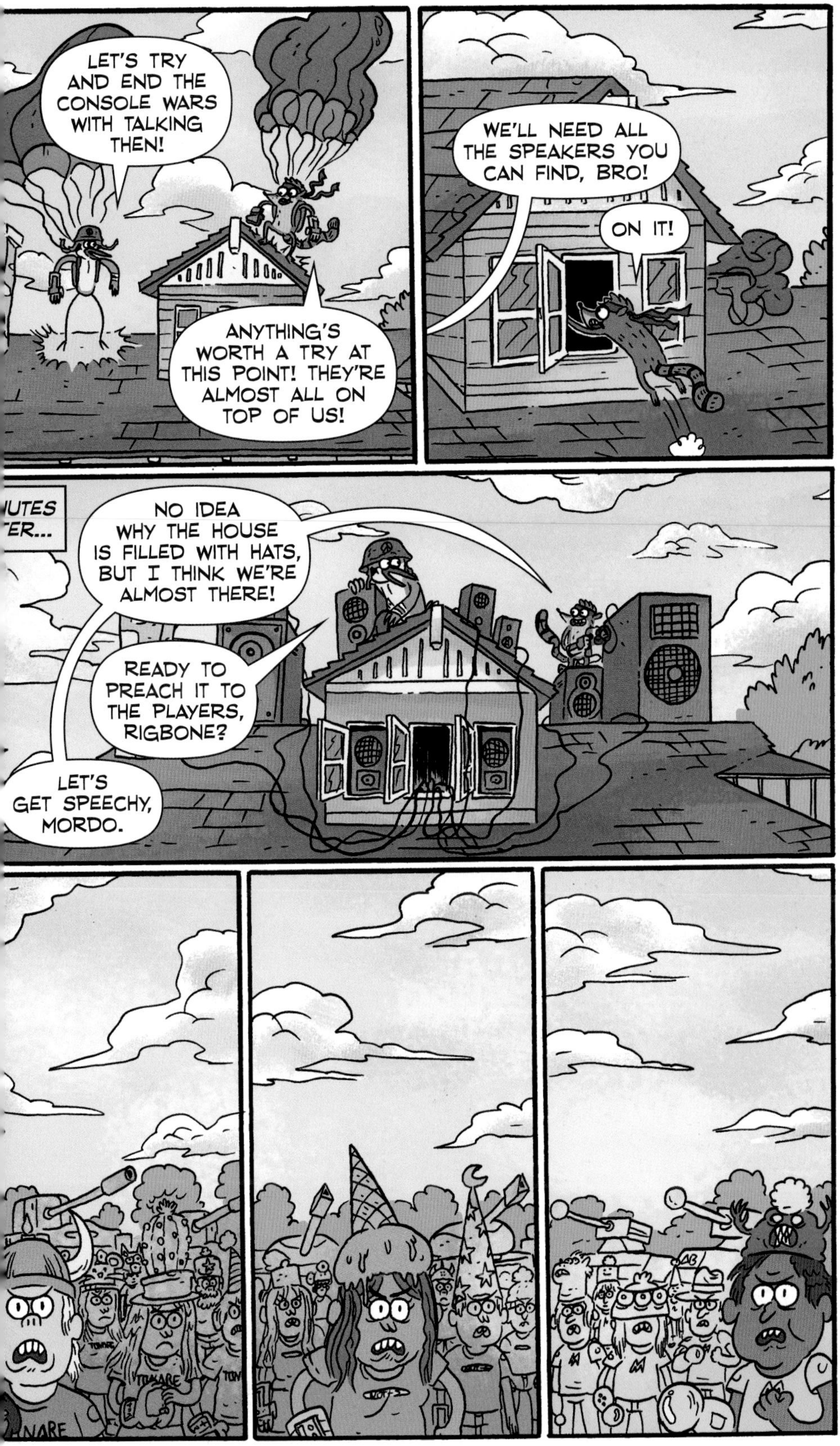
LET'S TRY AND END THE CONSOLE WARS WITH TALKING THEN!
ANYTHING'S WORTH A TRY AT THIS POINT! THEY'RE ALMOST ALL ON TOP OF US!
WE'LL NEED ALL THE SPEAKERS YOU CAN FIND, BRO!
ON IT!
UTES
ER...
NO IDEA WHY THE HOUSE IS FILLED WITH HATS, BUT I THINK WE'RE ALMOST THERE!
READY TO PREACH IT TO THE PLAYERS, RIGBONE?
LET'S GET SPEECHY, MORDO.

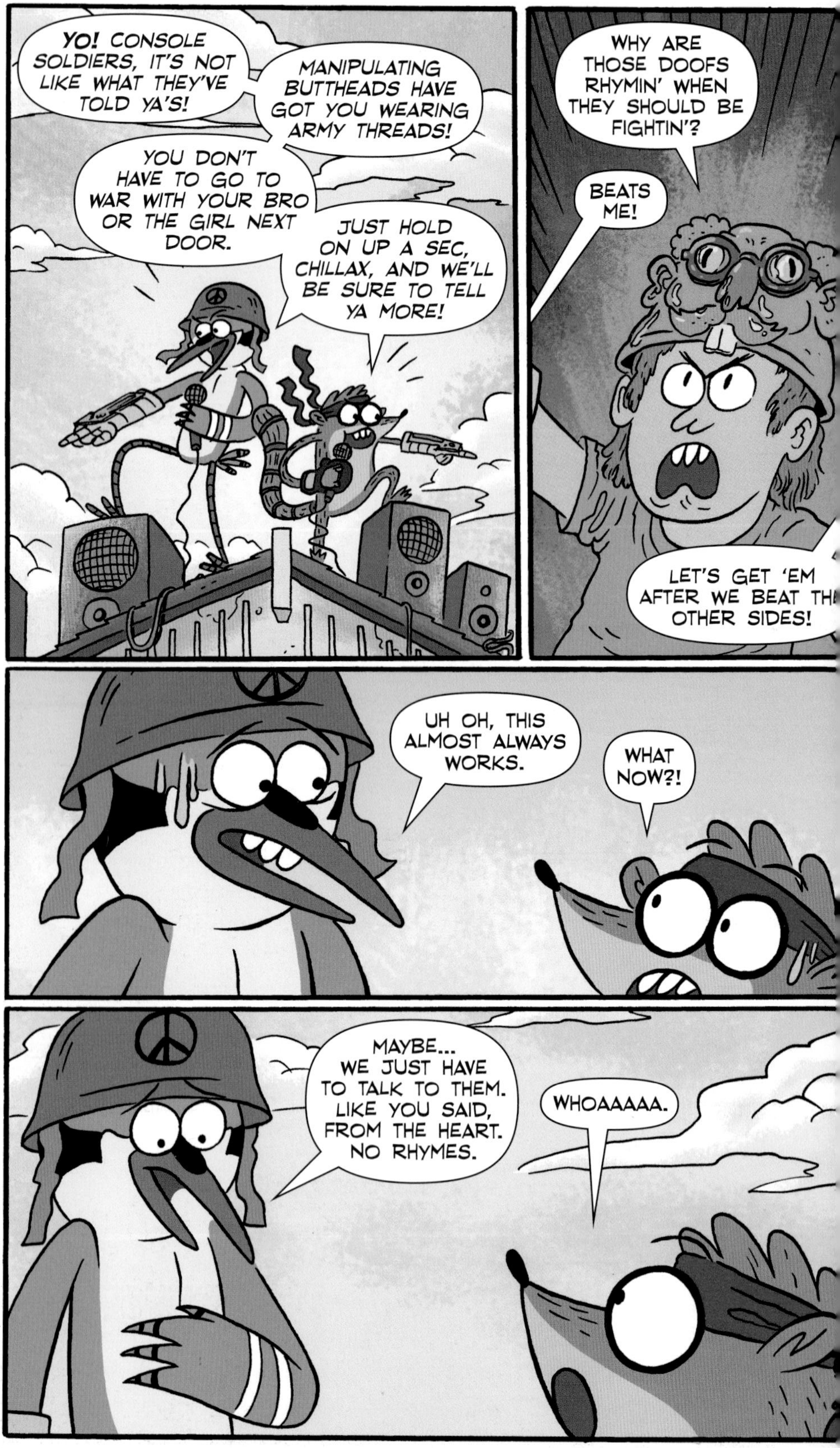
YO! CONSOLE SOLDIERS, IT'S NOT LIKE WHAT THEY'VE TOLD YA'S!
MANIPULATING BUTTHEADS HAVE GOT YOU WEARING ARMY THREADS!
YOU DON'T HAVE TO GO TO WAR WITH YOUR BRO OR THE GIRL NEXT DOOR.
JUST HOLD ON UP A SEC, CHILLAX, AND WE'LL BE SURE TO TELL YA MORE!
WHY ARE THOSE DOOFS RHYMIN' WHEN THEY SHOULD BE FIGHTIN'?
BEATS ME!
LET'S GET 'EM AFTER WE BEAT TH OTHER SIDES!
UH OH, THIS ALMOST ALWAYS WORKS.
WHAT NOW?!
MAYBE... WE JUST HAVE TO TALK TO THEM. LIKE YOU SAID, FROM THE HEART. NO RHYMES.
WHOAAAAA.

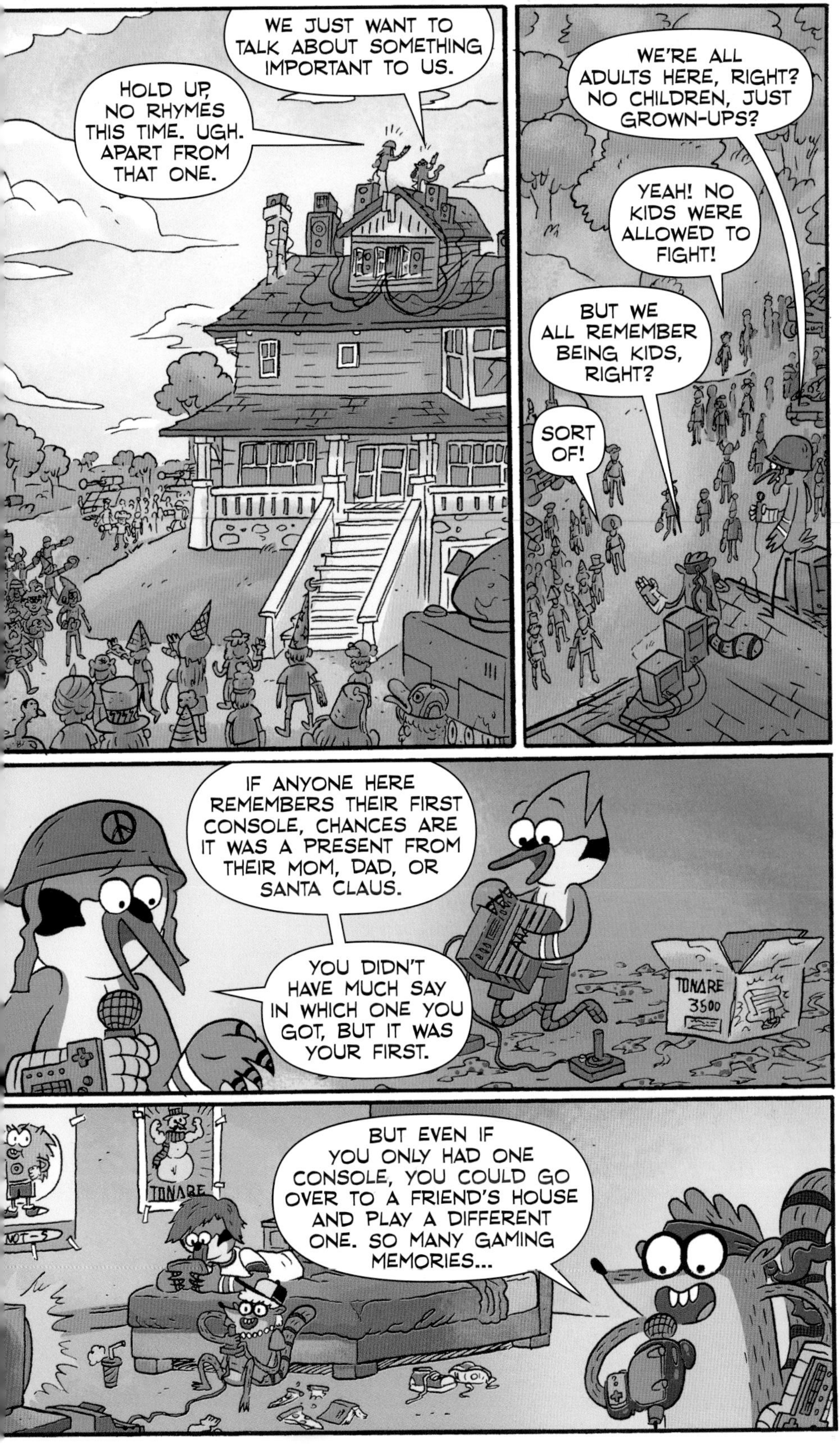
HOLD UP, NO RHYMES THIS TIME. UGH. APART FROM THAT ONE.
WE JUST WANT TO TALK ABOUT SOMETHING IMPORTANT TO US.
WE'RE ALL ADULTS HERE, RIGHT? NO CHILDREN, JUST GROWN-UPS?
YEAH! NO KIDS WERE ALLOWED TO FIGHT!
BUT WE ALL REMEMBER BEING KIDS, RIGHT?
SORT OF!
IF ANYONE HERE REMEMBERS THEIR FIRST CONSOLE, CHANCES ARE IT WAS A PRESENT FROM THEIR MOM, DAD, OR SANTA CLAUS.
YOU DIDN'T HAVE MUCH SAY IN WHICH ONE YOU GOT, BUT IT WAS YOUR FIRST.
TONARE 3500
TONARE
BUT EVEN IF YOU ONLY HAD ONE CONSOLE, YOU COULD GO OVER TO A FRIEND'S HOUSE AND PLAY A DIFFERENT ONE. SO MANY GAMING MEMORIES...

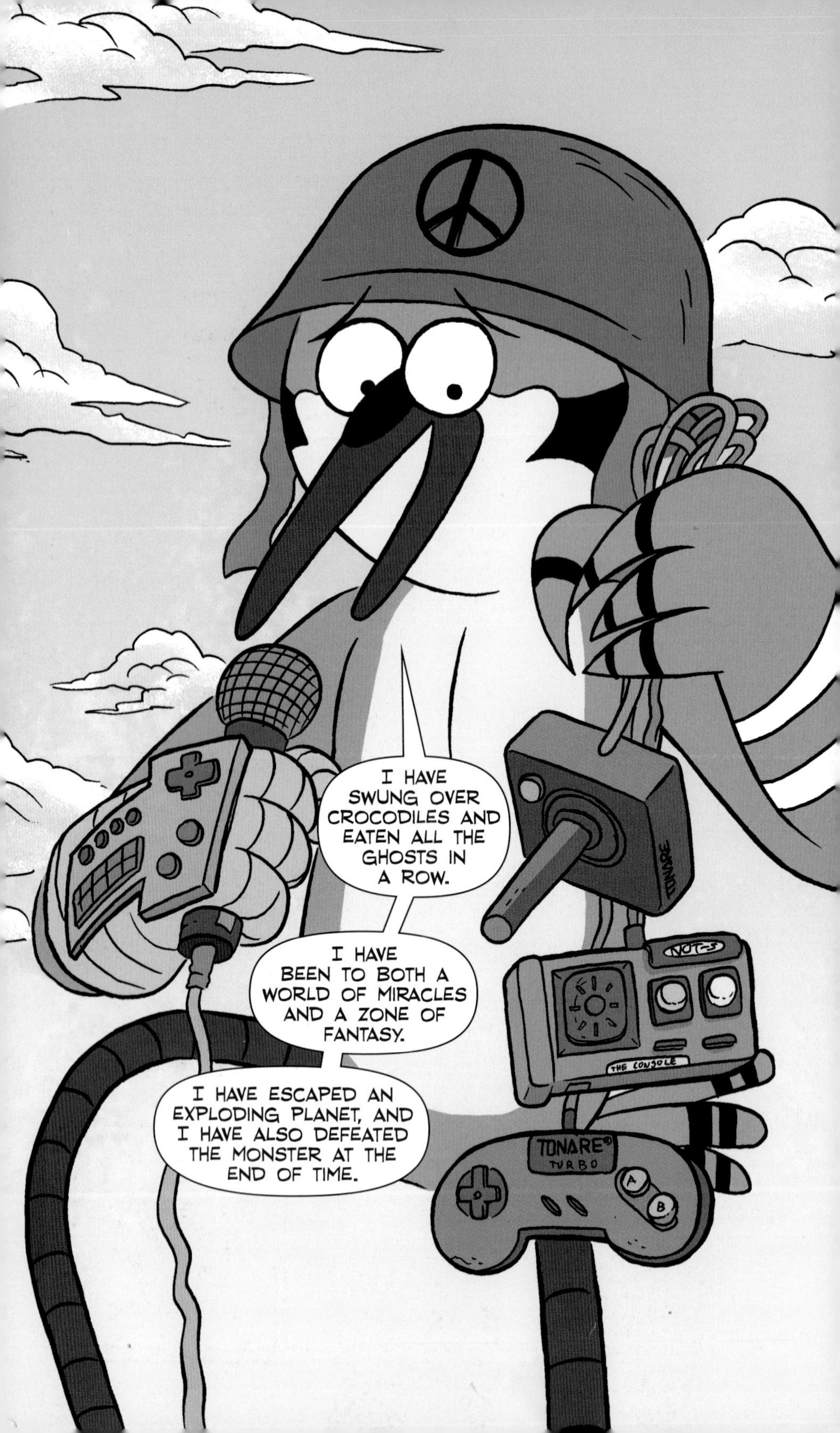
I HAVE SWUNG OVER CROCODILES AND EATEN ALL THE GHOSTS IN A ROW.
I HAVE BEEN TO BOTH A WORLD OF MIRACLES AND A ZONE OF FANTASY.
I HAVE ESCAPED AN EXPLODING PLANET, AND I HAVE ALSO DEFEATED THE MONSTER AT THE END OF TIME.
TONARE
THE CONSOLE
TONARE® TURBO
A
B

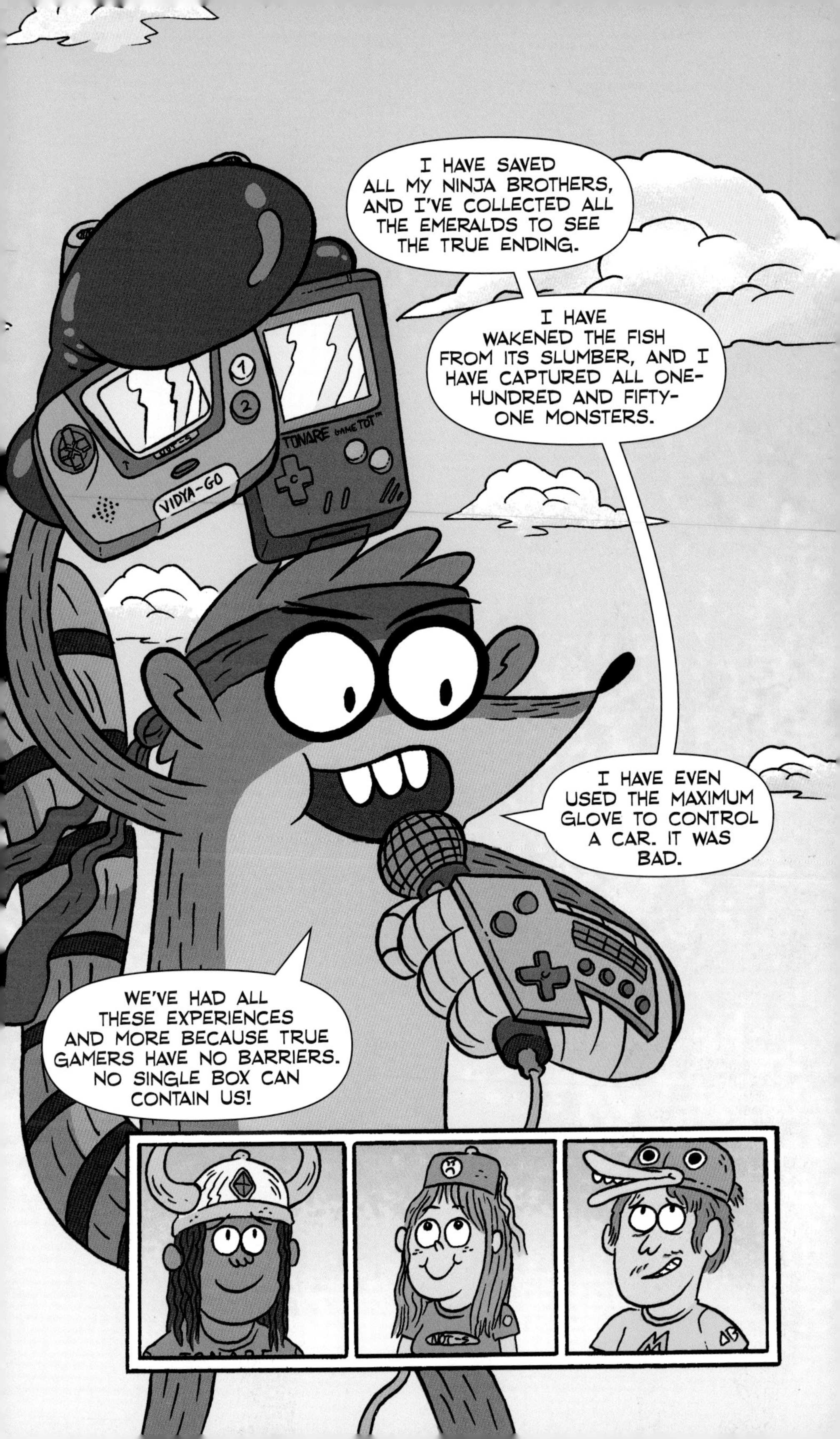
I HAVE SAVED ALL MY NINJA BROTHERS, AND I'VE COLLECTED ALL THE EMERALDS TO SEE THE TRUE ENDING.
I HAVE WAKENED THE FISH FROM ITS SLUMBER, AND I HAVE CAPTURED ALL ONE-HUNDRED AND FIFTY-ONE MONSTERS.
I HAVE EVEN USED THE MAXIMUM GLOVE TO CONTROL A CAR. IT WAS BAD.
VIDYA-GO
TONARE GAME TOT™
WE'VE HAD ALL THESE EXPERIENCES AND MORE BECAUSE TRUE GAMERS HAVE NO BARRIERS. NO SINGLE BOX CAN CONTAIN US!

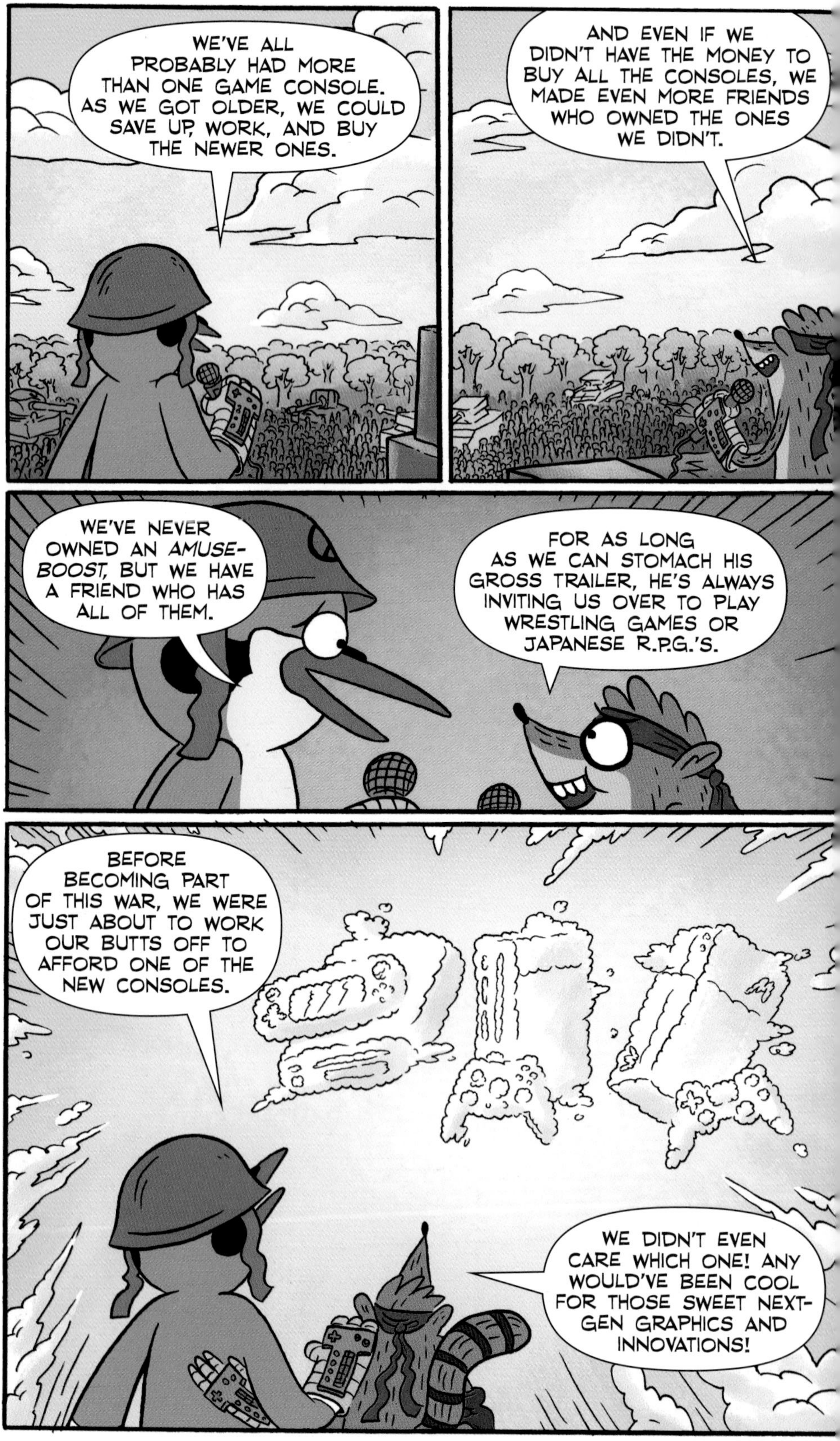
WE'VE ALL PROBABLY HAD MORE THAN ONE GAME CONSOLE. AS WE GOT OLDER, WE COULD SAVE UP, WORK, AND BUY THE NEWER ONES.
AND EVEN IF WE DIDN'T HAVE THE MONEY TO BUY ALL THE CONSOLES, WE MADE EVEN MORE FRIENDS WHO OWNED THE ONES WE DIDN'T.
WE'VE NEVER OWNED AN *AMUSE-BOOST,* BUT WE HAVE A FRIEND WHO HAS ALL OF THEM.
FOR AS LONG AS WE CAN STOMACH HIS GROSS TRAILER, HE'S ALWAYS INVITING US OVER TO PLAY WRESTLING GAMES OR JAPANESE R.P.G.'S.
BEFORE BECOMING PART OF THIS WAR, WE WERE JUST ABOUT TO WORK OUR BUTTS OFF TO AFFORD ONE OF THE NEW CONSOLES.
WE DIDN'T EVEN CARE WHICH ONE! ANY WOULD'VE BEEN COOL FOR THOSE SWEET NEXT-GEN GRAPHICS AND INNOVATIONS!

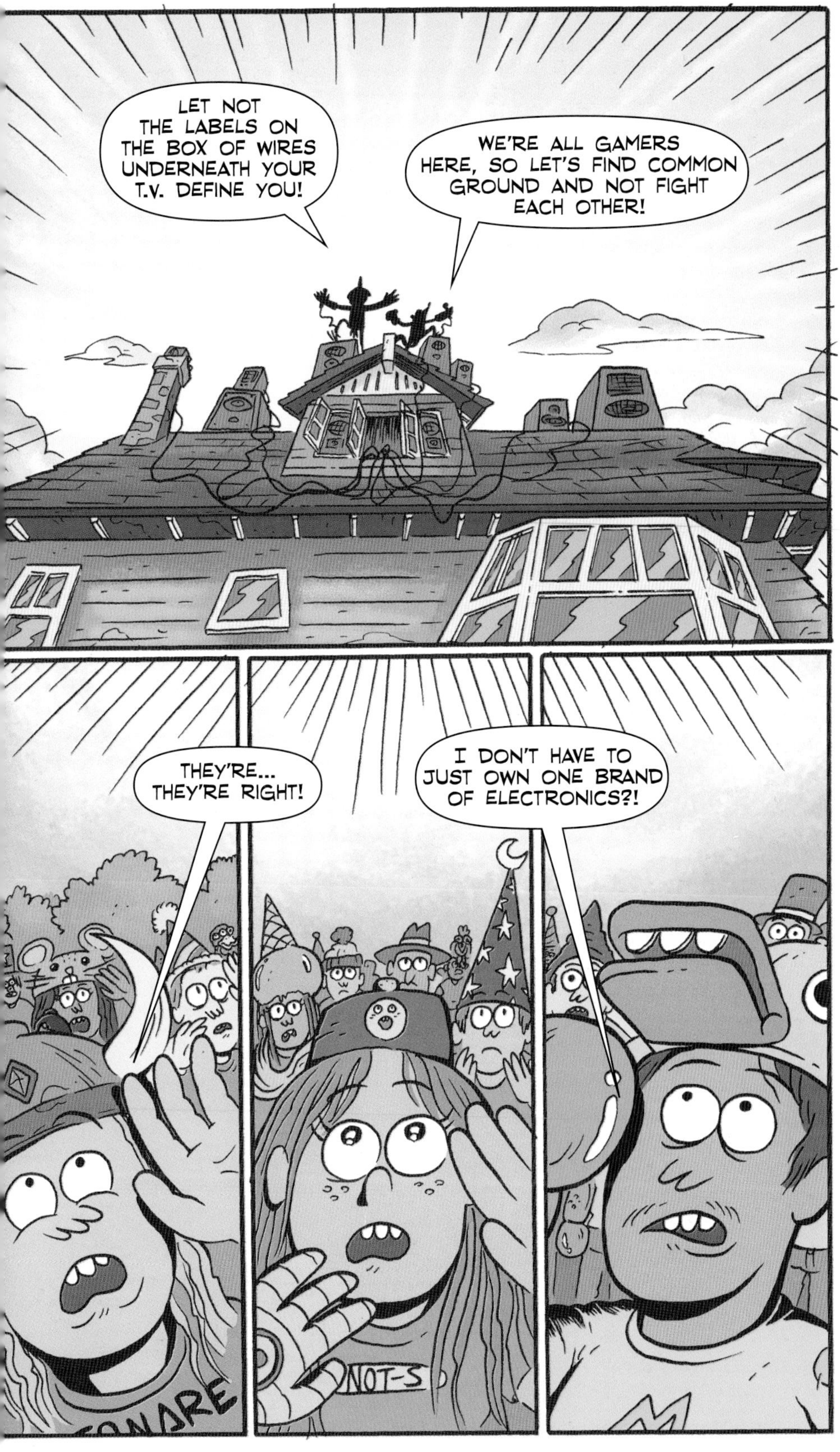
LET NOT THE LABELS ON THE BOX OF WIRES UNDERNEATH YOUR T.V. DEFINE YOU!
WE'RE ALL GAMERS HERE, SO LET'S FIND COMMON GROUND AND NOT FIGHT EACH OTHER!
THEY'RE... THEY'RE RIGHT!
I DON'T HAVE TO JUST OWN ONE BRAND OF ELECTRONICS?!
NOT-S

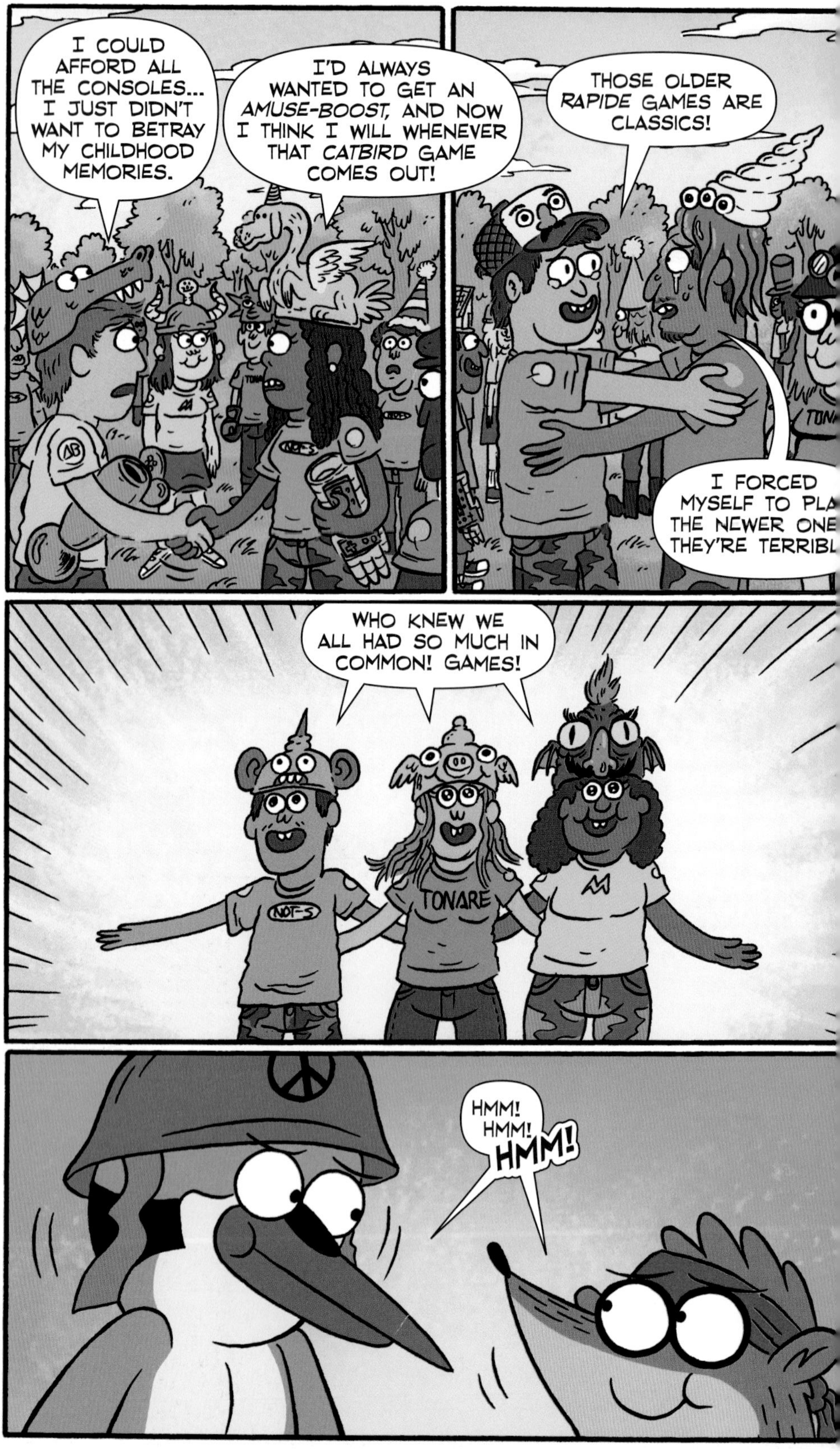
I COULD AFFORD ALL THE CONSOLES... I JUST DIDN'T WANT TO BETRAY MY CHILDHOOD MEMORIES.
I'D ALWAYS WANTED TO GET AN *AMUSE-BOOST,* AND NOW I THINK I WILL WHENEVER THAT *CATBIRD* GAME COMES OUT!
THOSE OLDER *RAPIDE* GAMES ARE CLASSICS!
I FORCED MYSELF TO PLA THE NEWER ONE THEY'RE TERRIBL
WHO KNEW WE ALL HAD SO MUCH IN COMMON! GAMES!
TONARE
HMM! HMM! HMM!

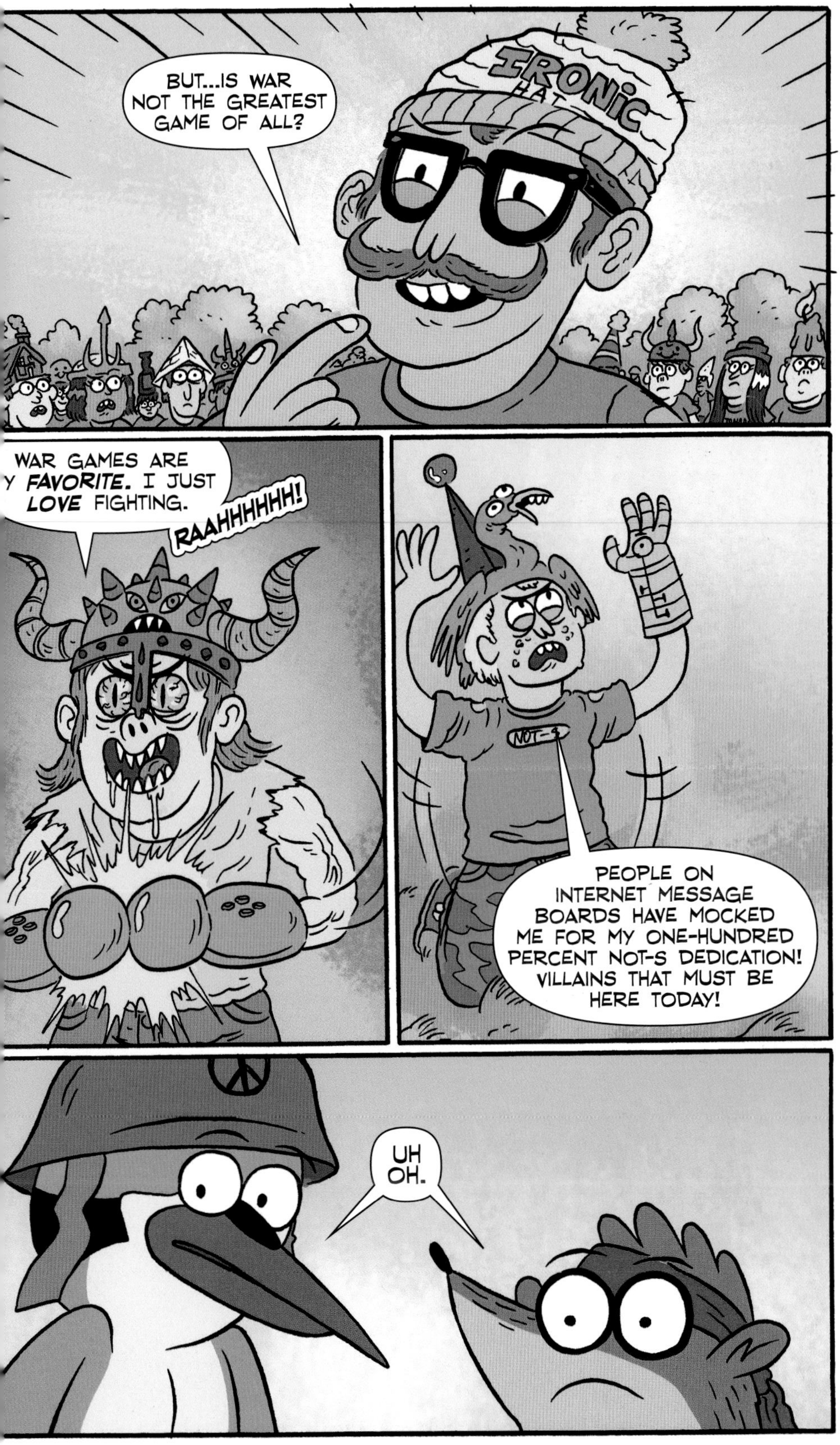

BUT...IS WAR NOT THE GREATEST GAME OF ALL?
IRONIC HAT
WAR GAMES ARE Y FAVORITE. I JUST LOVE FIGHTING.
RAAHHHHHH!
NOT-S
PEOPLE ON INTERNET MESSAGE BOARDS HAVE MOCKED ME FOR MY ONE-HUNDRED PERCENT NOT-S DEDICATION! VILLAINS THAT MUST BE HERE TODAY!
UH OH.

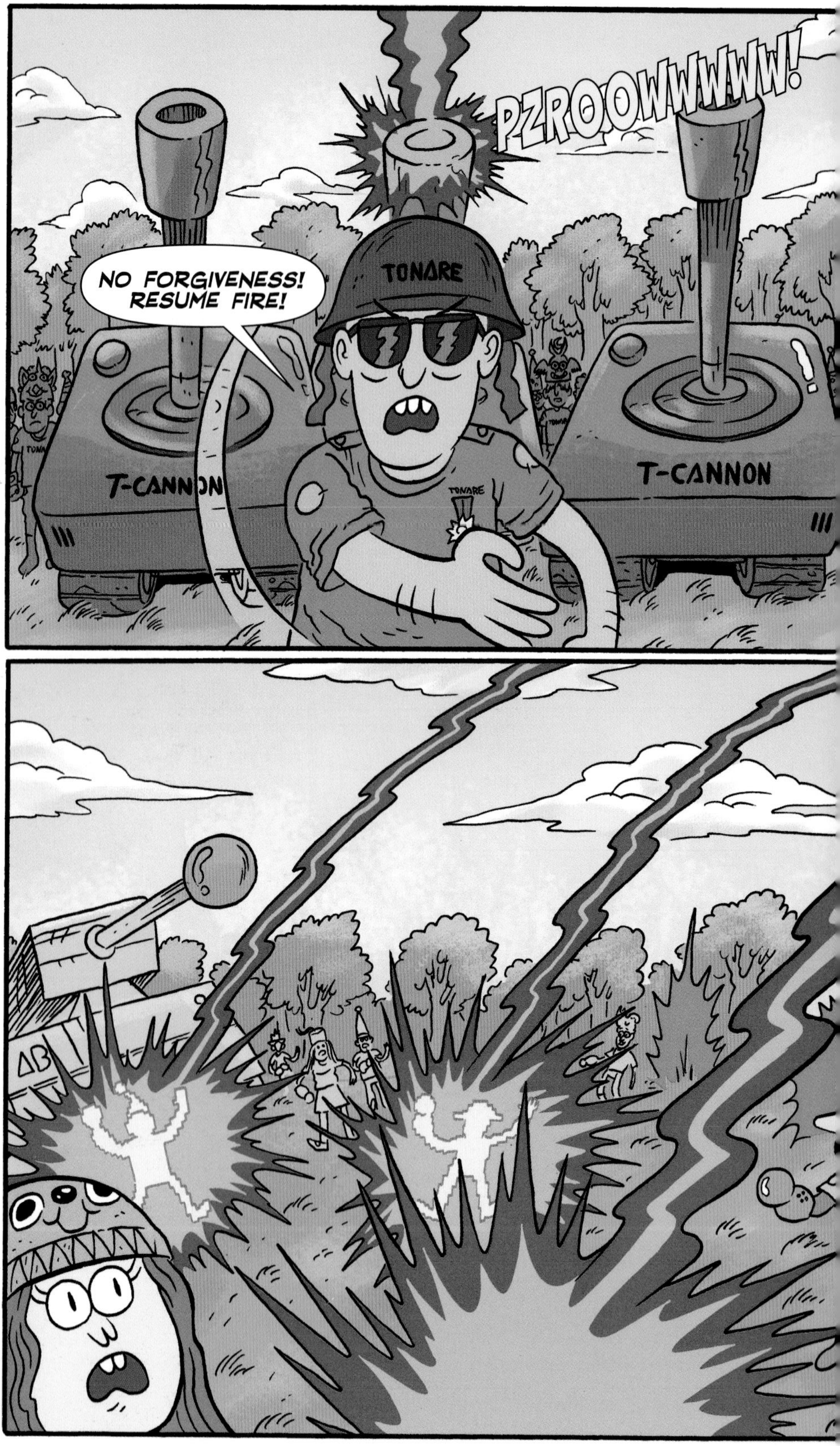
PZROOWWWWW!
NO FORGIVENESS! RESUME FIRE!
TONARE
T-CANNON
T-CANNON
ΔB

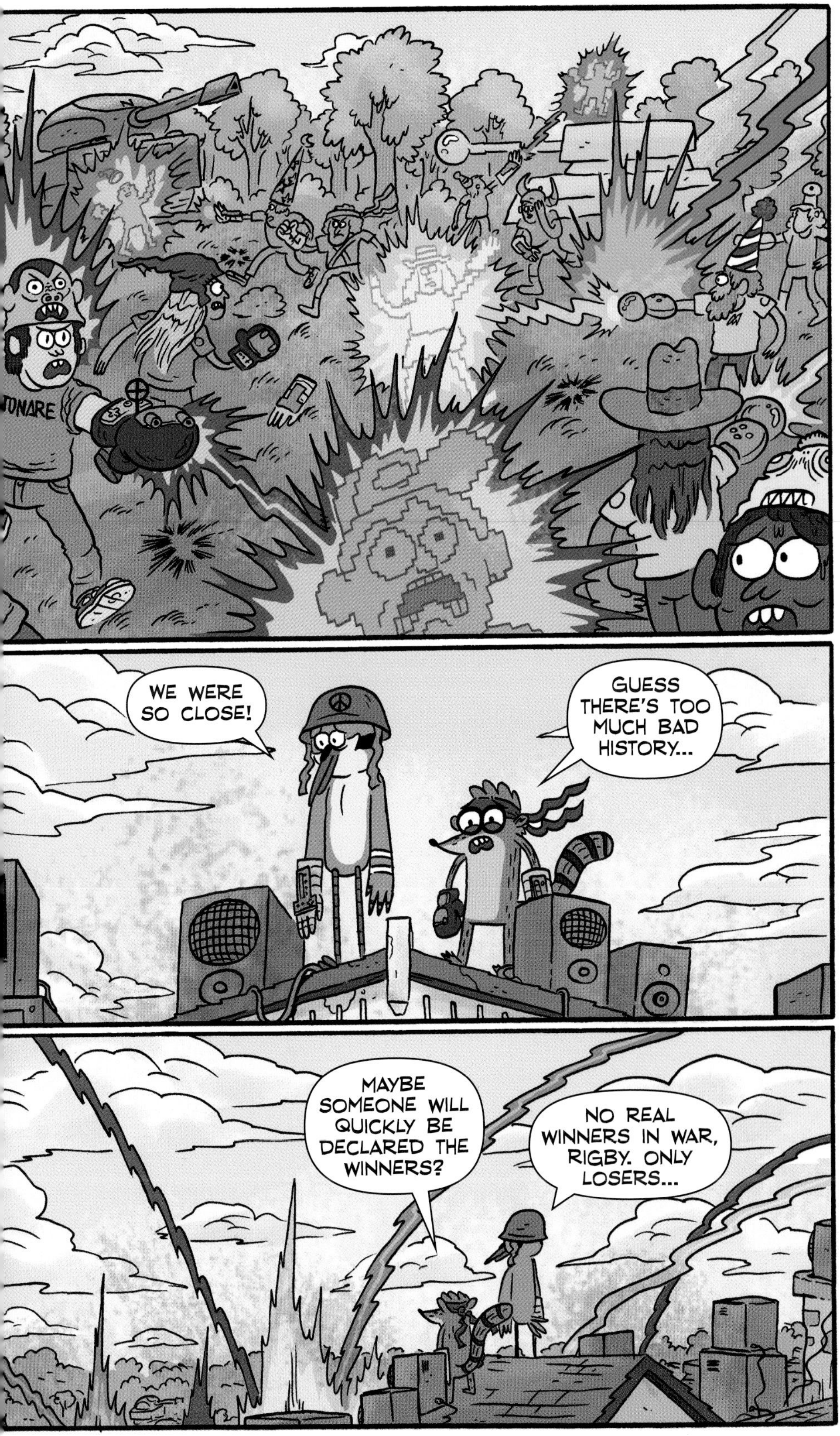
TONARE
WE WERE SO CLOSE!
GUESS THERE'S TOO MUCH BAD HISTORY...
MAYBE SOMEONE WILL QUICKLY BE DECLARED THE WINNERS?
NO REAL WINNERS IN WAR, RIGBY. ONLY LOSERS...

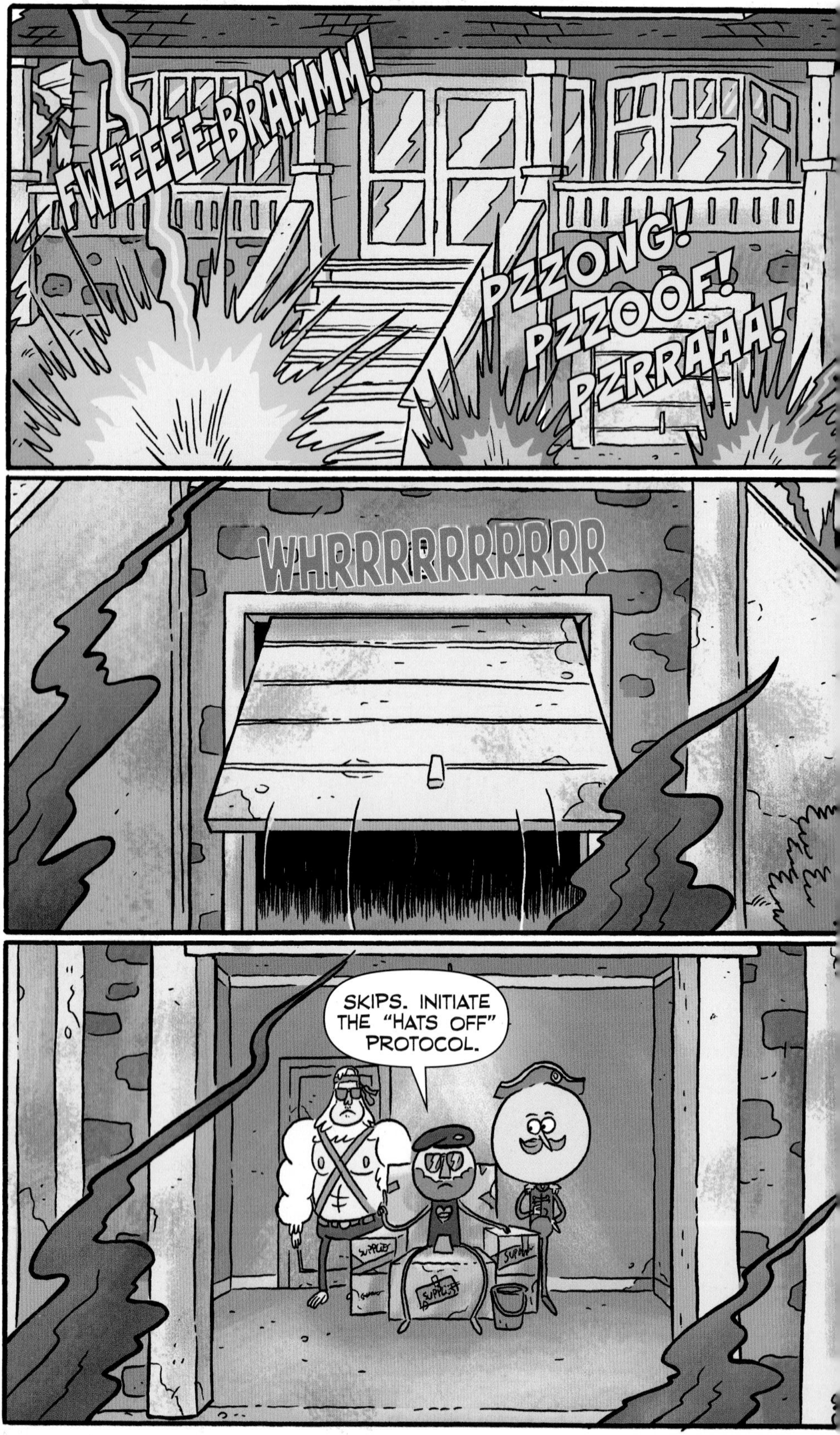
FWEEEEE-BRAMMM!
PZZONG!
PZZOOF!
PZRRAAA!
WHRRRRRRRRRR
SKIPS. INITIATE THE "HATS OFF" PROTOCOL.
SUPPLIES
SUPPLIES

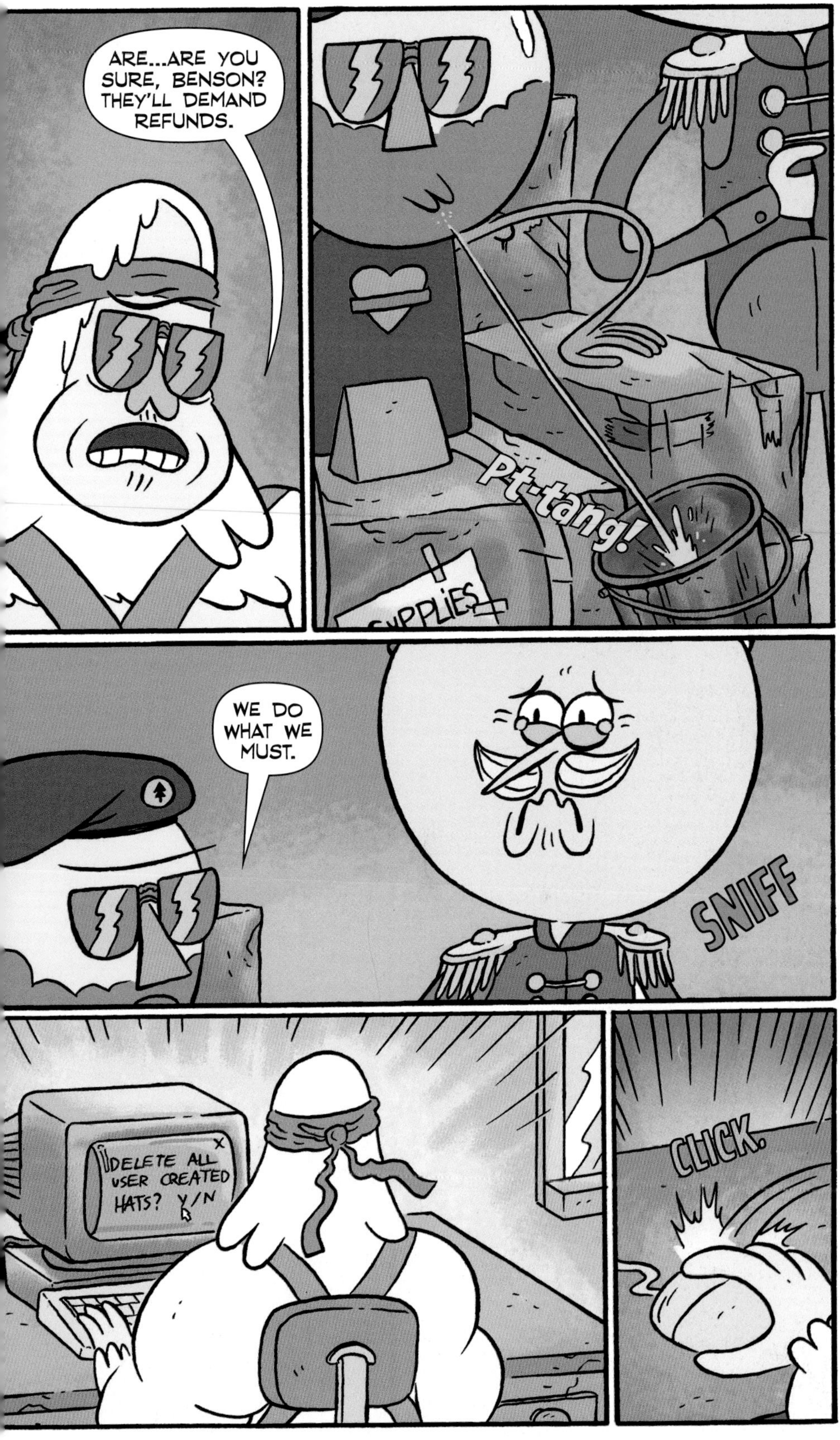
ARE...ARE YOU SURE, BENSON? THEY'LL DEMAND REFUNDS.
Pt-tang!
SUPPLIES
WE DO WHAT WE MUST.
SNIFF
DELETE ALL USER CREATED HATS? Y/N
CLICK.

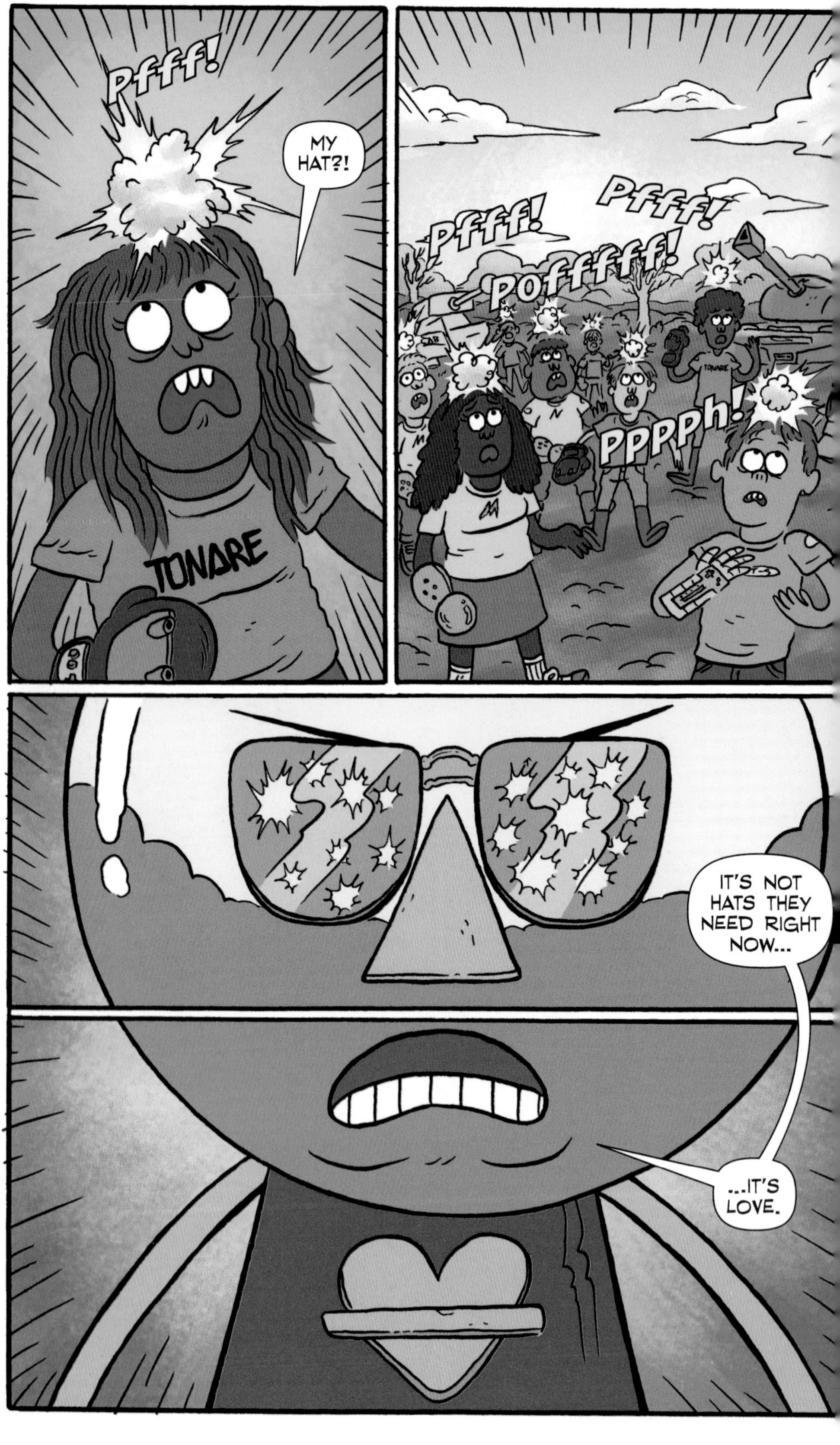
Pfff!
MY HAT?!
TONARE
Pfff!
Pfff!
Poffffff!
PPPPh!
IT'S NOT HATS THEY NEED RIGHT NOW...
...IT'S LOVE.

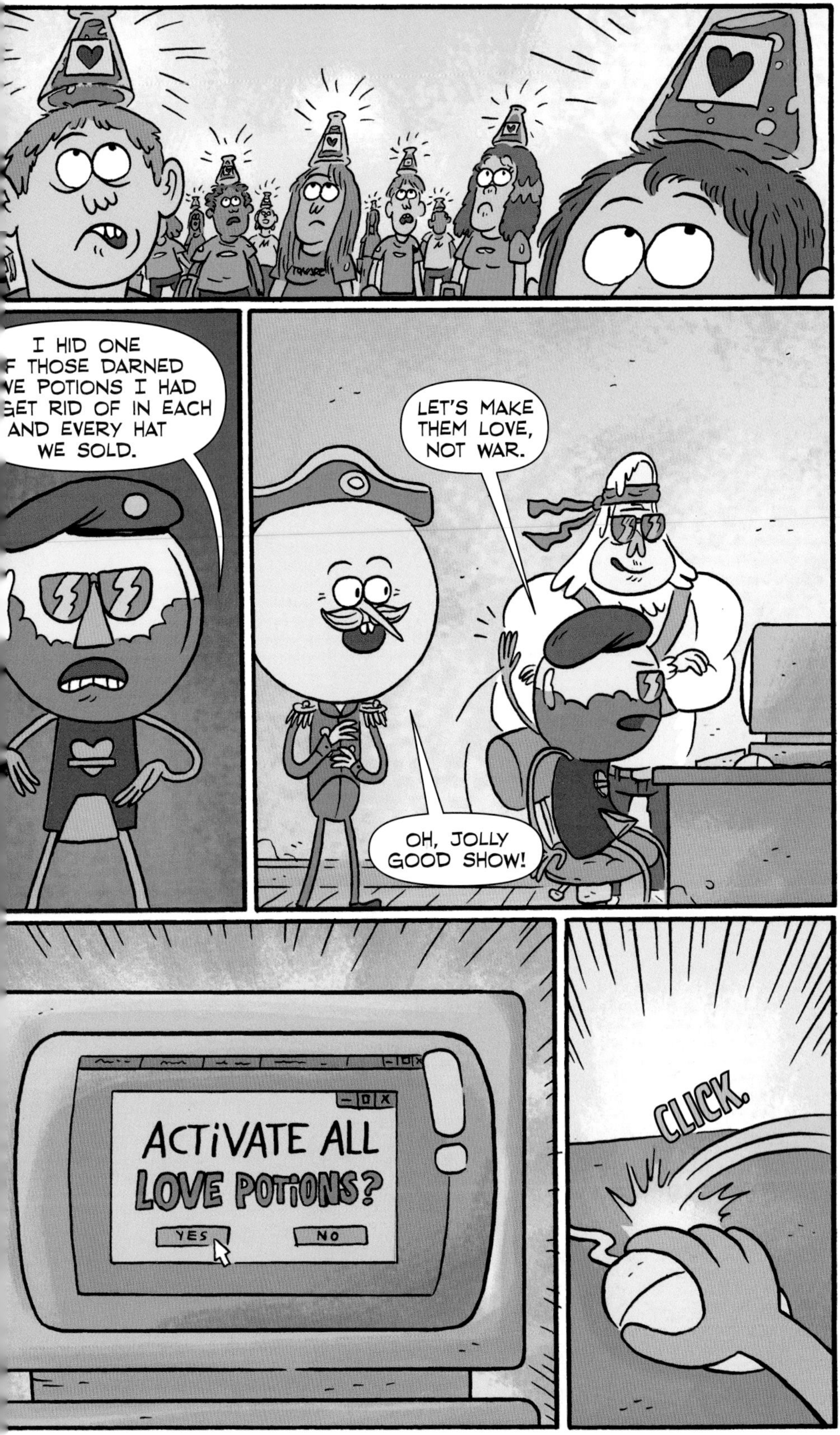

I HID ONE F THOSE DARNED VE POTIONS I HAD GET RID OF IN EACH AND EVERY HAT WE SOLD.
LET'S MAKE THEM LOVE, NOT WAR.
OH, JOLLY GOOD SHOW!
ACTIVATE ALL LOVE POTIONS?
YES
NO
CLICK.

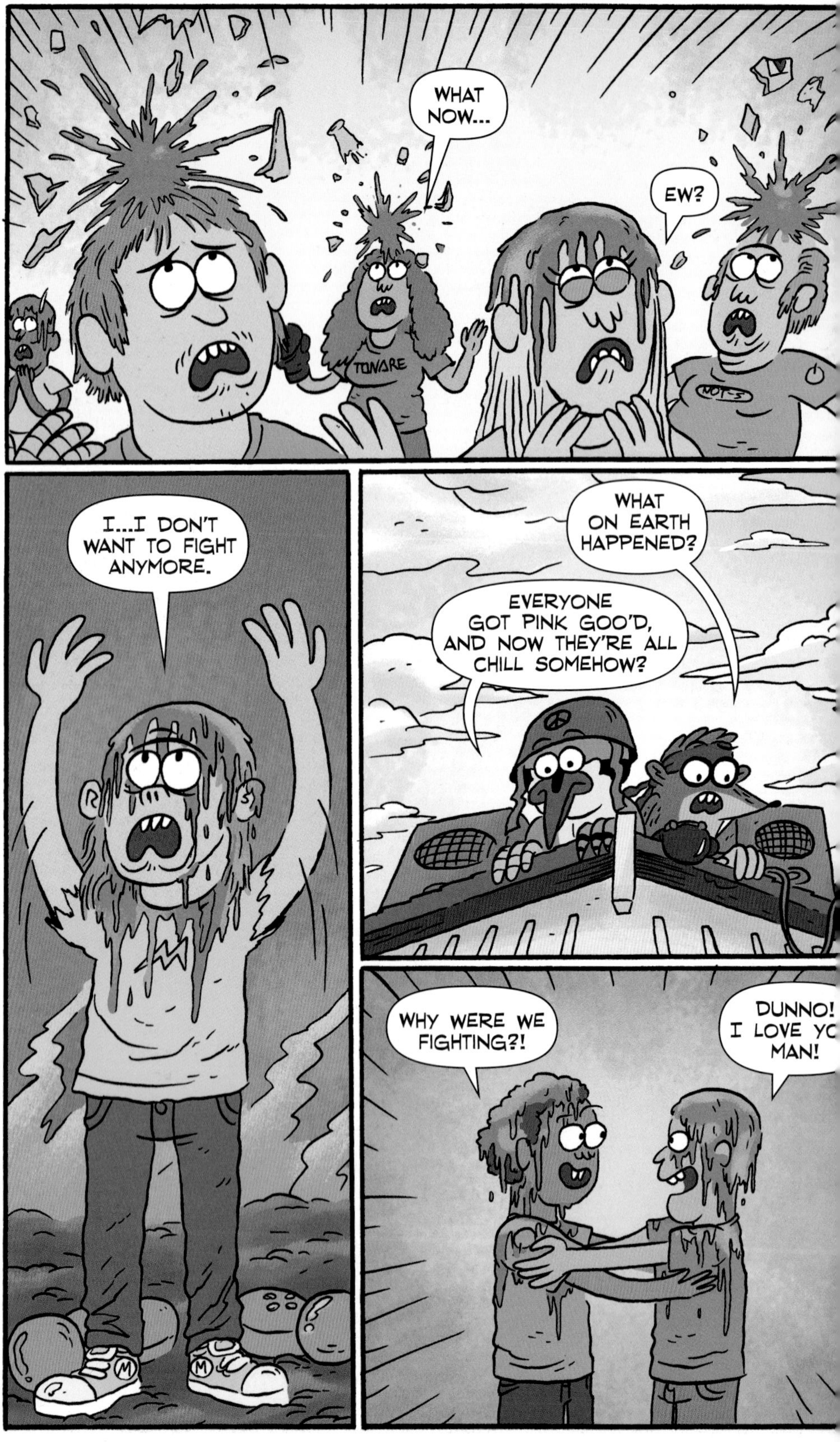
WHAT NOW...
EW?
TONARE
NOT-S
I...I DON'T WANT TO FIGHT ANYMORE.
WHAT ON EARTH HAPPENED?
EVERYONE GOT PINK GOO'D, AND NOW THEY'RE ALL CHILL SOMEHOW?
WHY WERE WE FIGHTING?!
DUNNO! I LOVE YO
MAN!

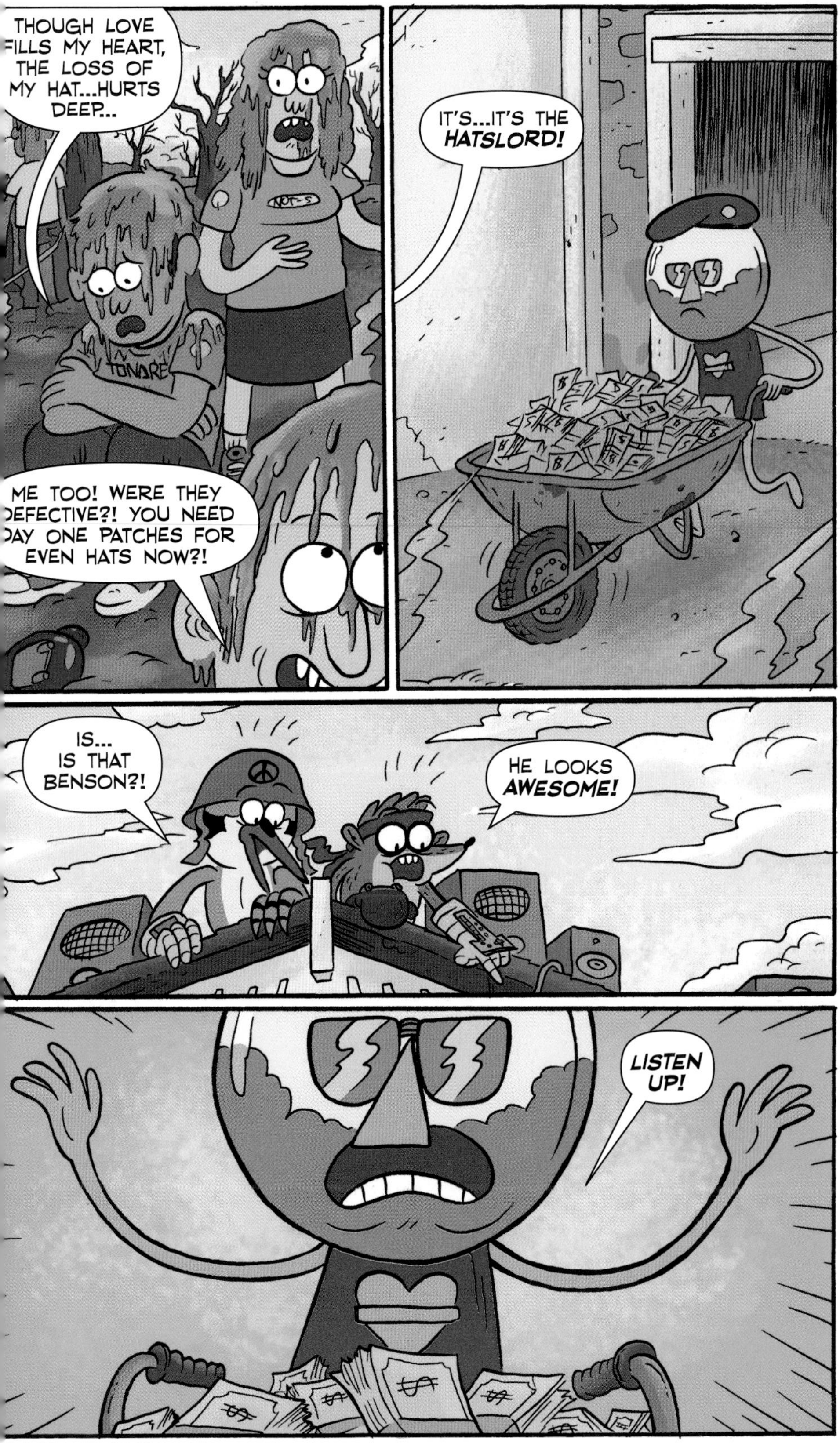
THOUGH LOVE FILLS MY HEART, THE LOSS OF MY HAT...HURTS DEEP...
ME TOO! WERE THEY DEFECTIVE?! YOU NEED DAY ONE PATCHES FOR EVEN HATS NOW?!
IT'S...IT'S THE *HATSLORD!*
IS... IS THAT BENSON?!
HE LOOKS *AWESOME!*
LISTEN UP!

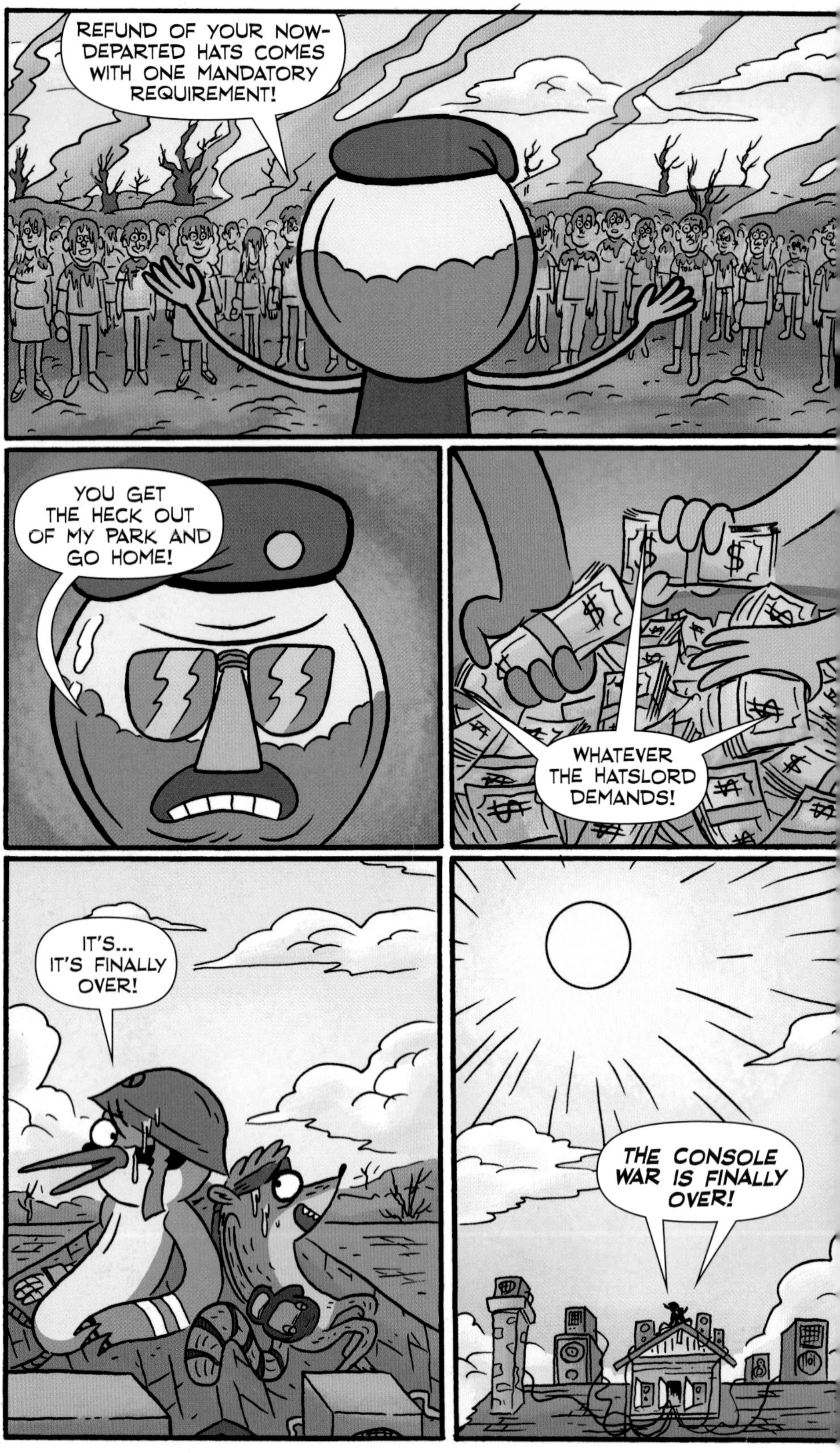
REFUND OF YOUR NOW-DEPARTED HATS COMES WITH ONE MANDATORY REQUIREMENT!
YOU GET THE HECK OUT OF MY PARK AND GO HOME!
WHATEVER THE HATSLORD DEMANDS!
IT'S... IT'S FINALLY OVER!
THE CONSOLE WAR IS FINALLY OVER!

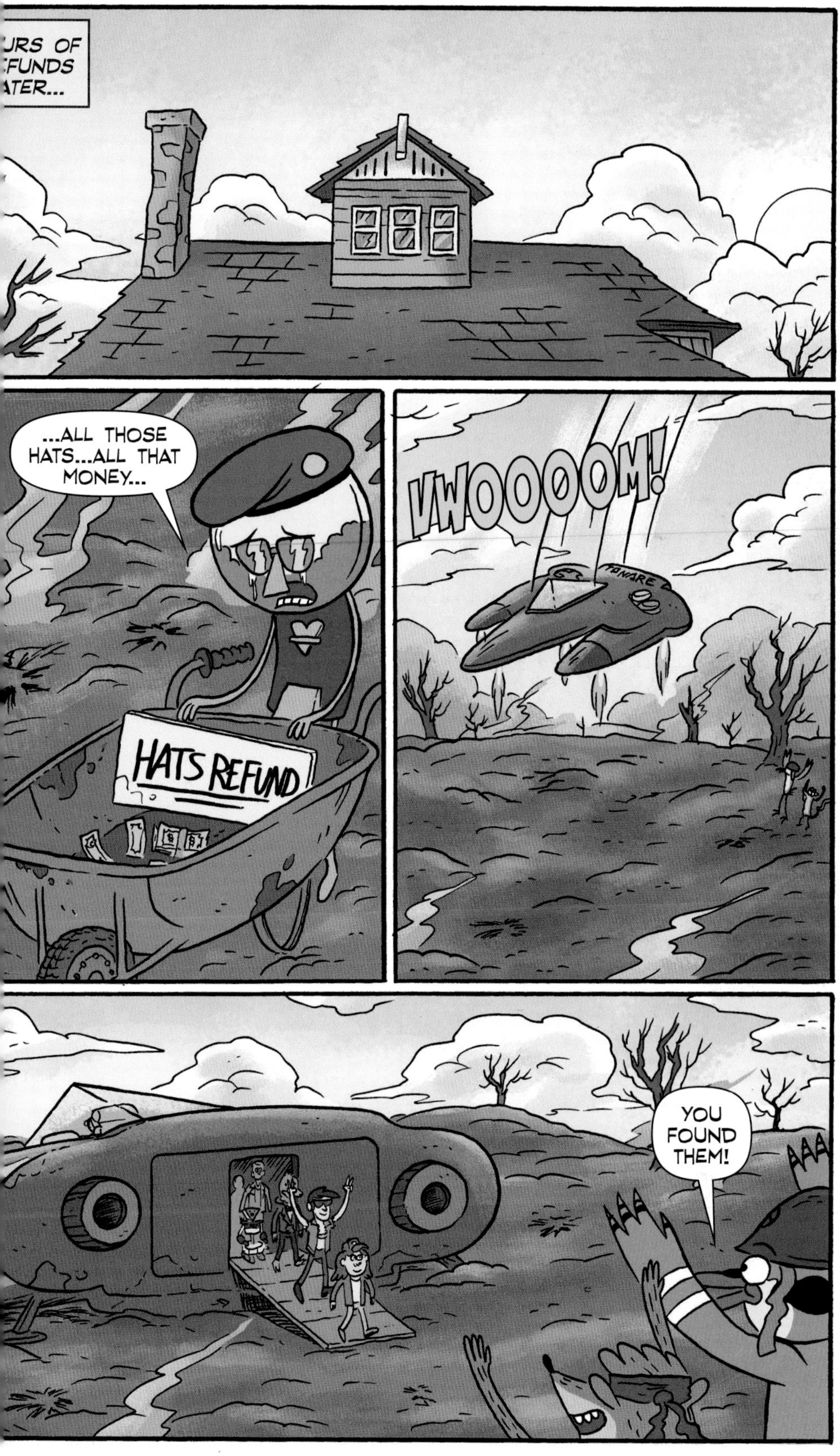
URS OF
FUNDS
ATER...
...ALL THOSE HATS...ALL THAT MONEY...
HATS REFUND
VWOOOOM!
YOU FOUND THEM!
AAA

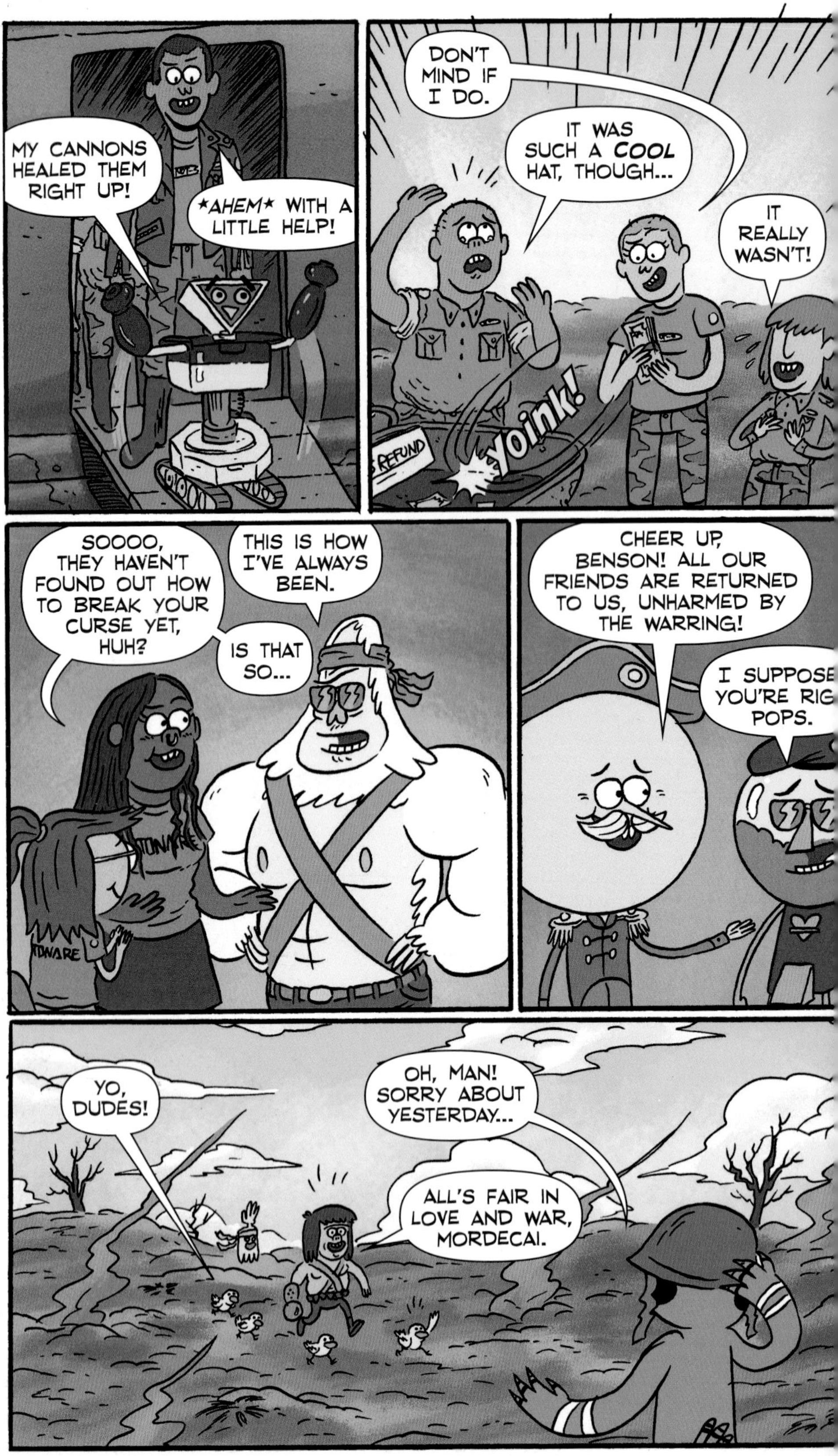
MY CANNONS HEALED THEM RIGHT UP!
AHEM WITH A LITTLE HELP!
DON'T MIND IF I DO.
IT WAS SUCH A COOL HAT, THOUGH...
IT REALLY WASN'T!
REFUND
YOINK!
SOOOO, THEY HAVEN'T FOUND OUT HOW TO BREAK YOUR CURSE YET, HUH?
THIS IS HOW I'VE ALWAYS BEEN.
IS THAT SO...
CHEER UP, BENSON! ALL OUR FRIENDS ARE RETURNED TO US, UNHARMED BY THE WARRING!
I SUPPOSE YOU'RE RIG POPS.
YO, DUDES!
OH, MAN! SORRY ABOUT YESTERDAY...
ALL'S FAIR IN LOVE AND WAR, MORDECAI.

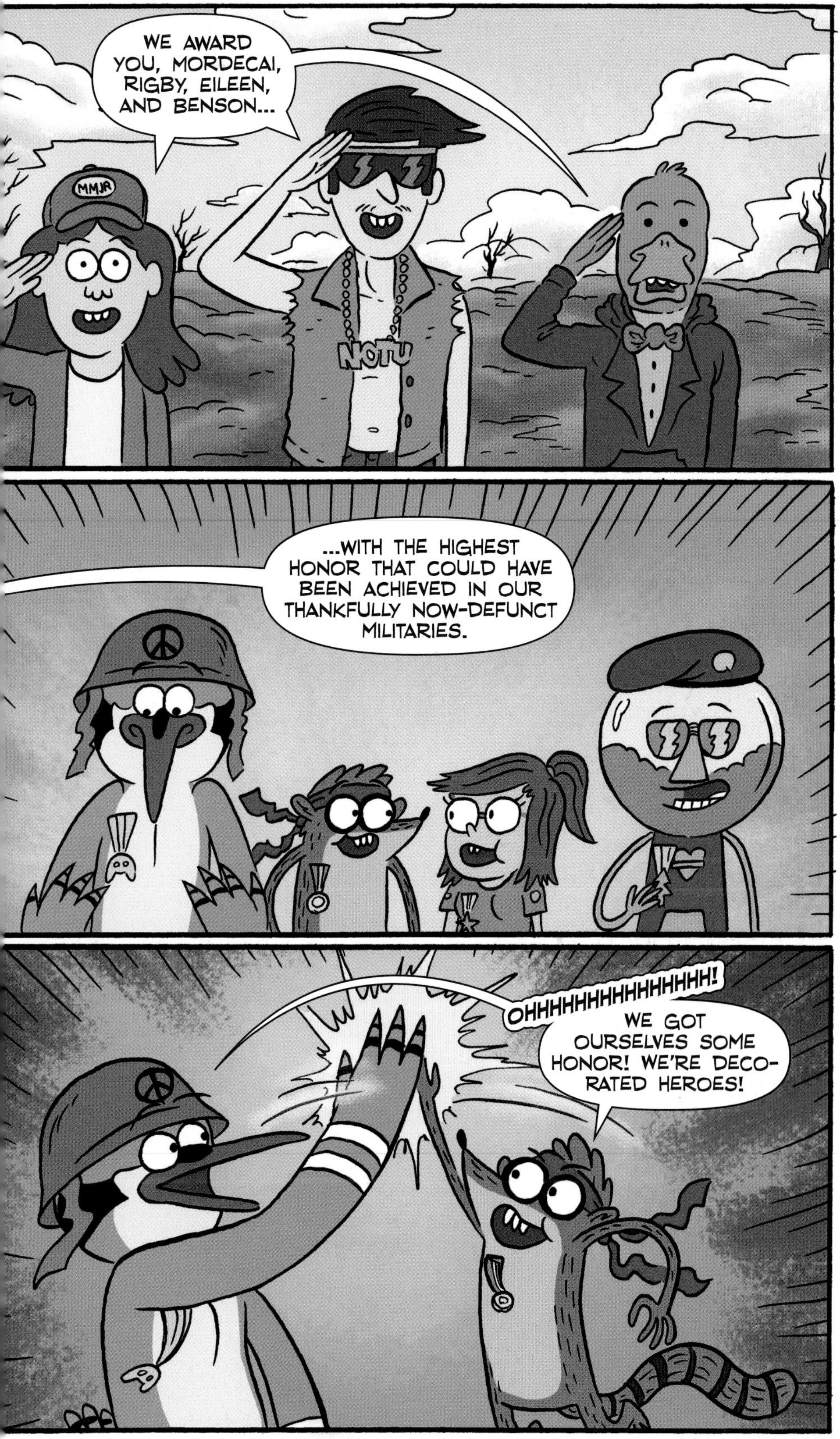
WE AWARD YOU, MORDECAI, RIGBY, EILEEN, AND BENSON...
MMJR
NOTU
...WITH THE HIGHEST HONOR THAT COULD HAVE BEEN ACHIEVED IN OUR THANKFULLY NOW-DEFUNCT MILITARIES.
OHHHHHHHHHHHHHHH!
WE GOT OURSELVES SOME HONOR! WE'RE DECORATED HEROES!

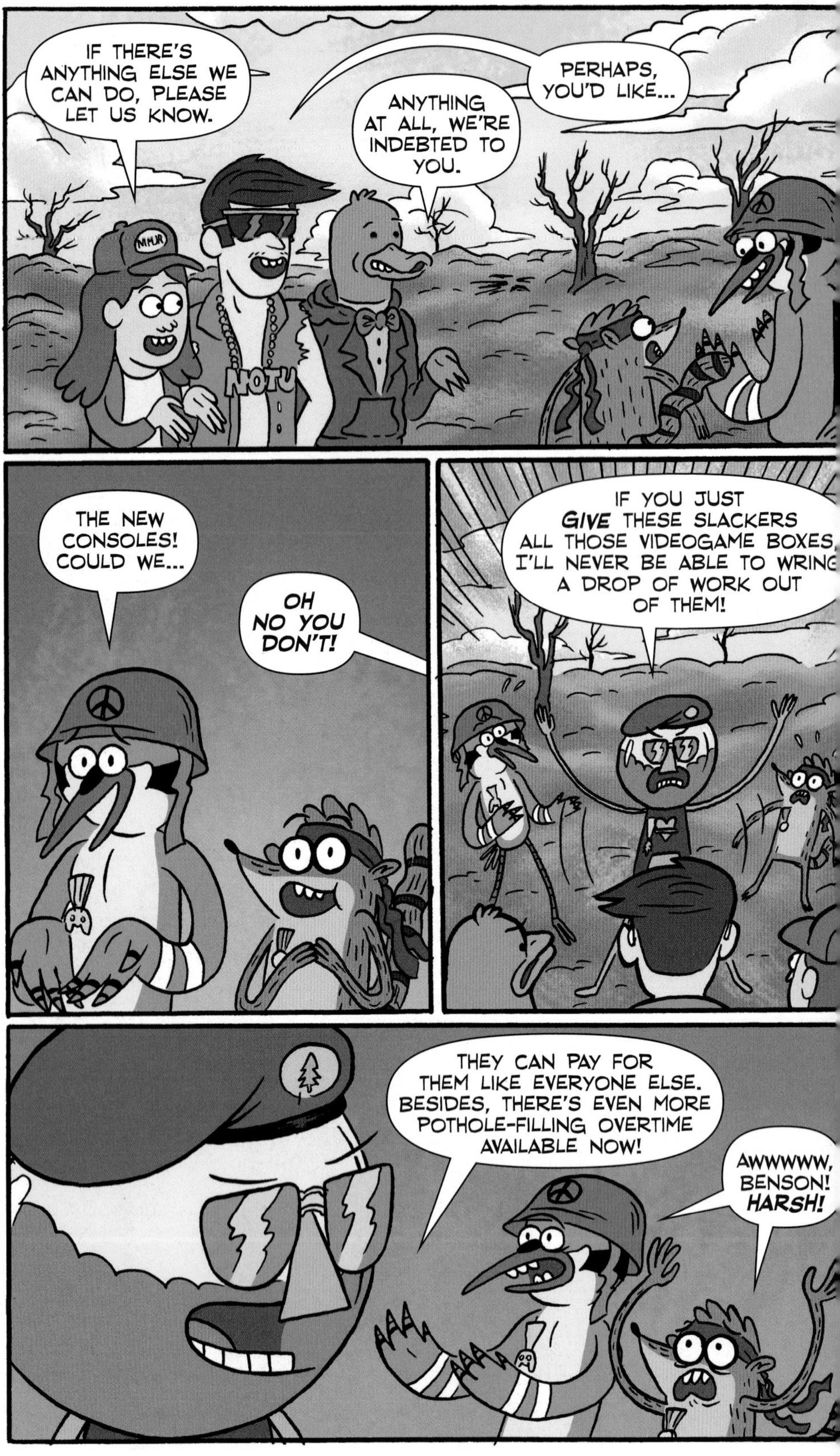
IF THERE'S ANYTHING ELSE WE CAN DO, PLEASE LET US KNOW.
ANYTHING AT ALL, WE'RE INDEBTED TO YOU.
PERHAPS, YOU'D LIKE...
THE NEW CONSOLES! COULD WE...
OH NO YOU DON'T!
IF YOU JUST GIVE THESE SLACKERS ALL THOSE VIDEOGAME BOXES, I'LL NEVER BE ABLE TO WRING A DROP OF WORK OUT OF THEM!
THEY CAN PAY FOR THEM LIKE EVERYONE ELSE. BESIDES, THERE'S EVEN MORE POTHOLE-FILLING OVERTIME AVAILABLE NOW!
AWWWWW, BENSON! HARSH!

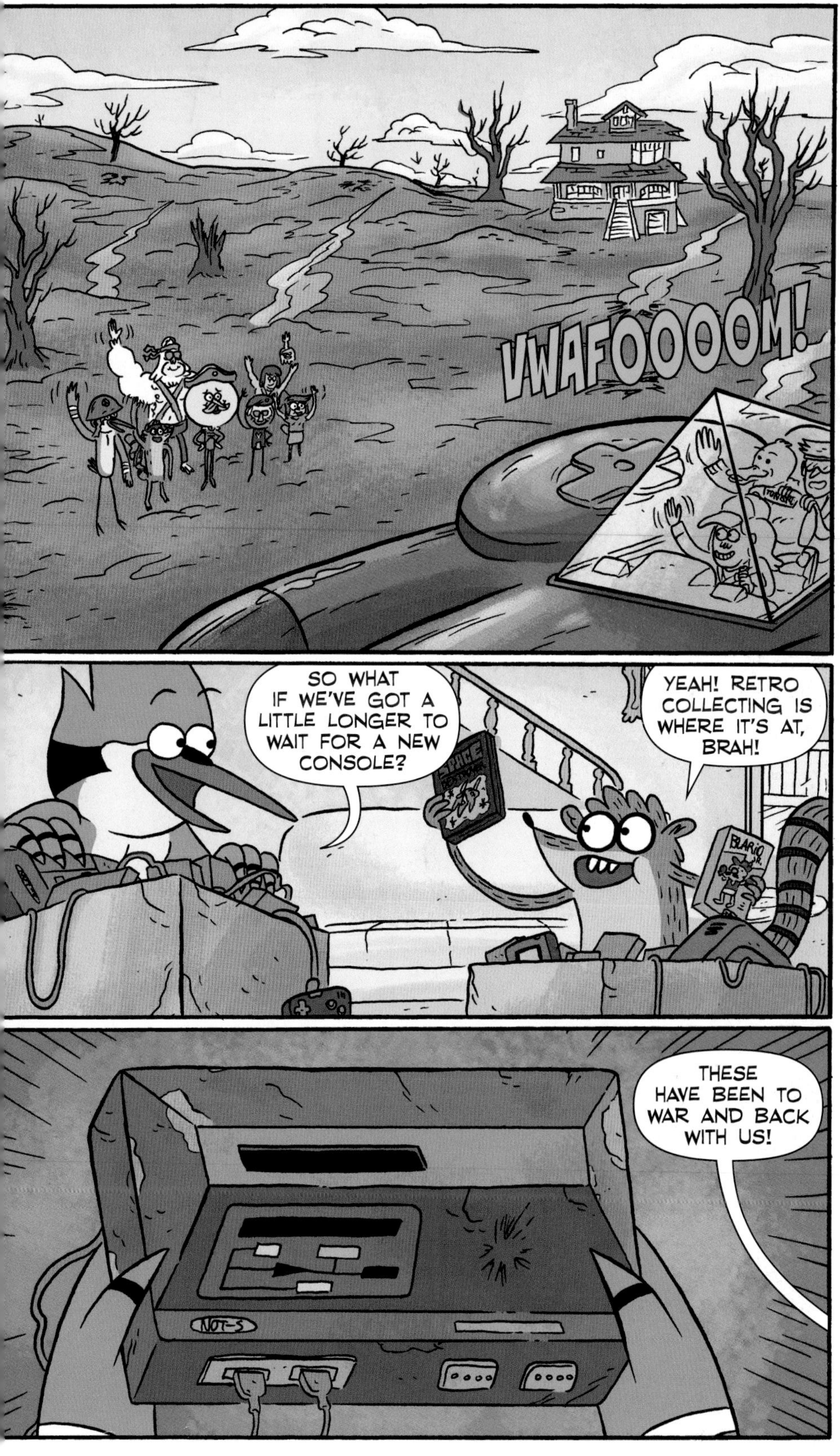
VWAFOOOOM!
SO WHAT IF WE'VE GOT A LITTLE LONGER TO WAIT FOR A NEW CONSOLE?
YEAH! RETRO COLLECTING IS WHERE IT'S AT, BRAH!
THESE HAVE BEEN TO WAR AND BACK WITH US!

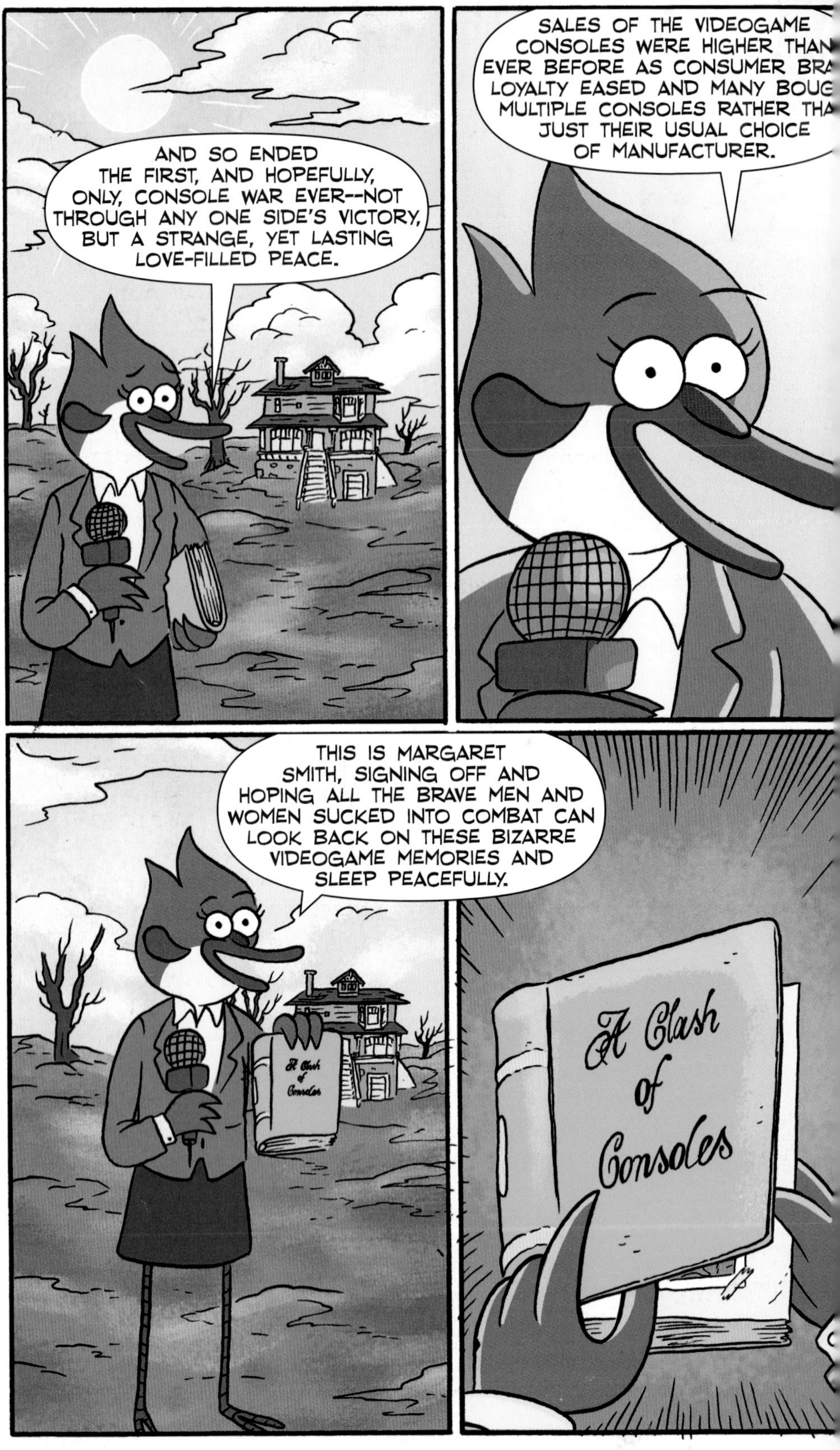
AND SO ENDED THE FIRST, AND HOPEFULLY, ONLY, CONSOLE WAR EVER--NOT THROUGH ANY ONE SIDE'S VICTORY, BUT A STRANGE, YET LASTING LOVE-FILLED PEACE.
SALES OF THE VIDEOGAME CONSOLES WERE HIGHER THAN EVER BEFORE AS CONSUMER BRA LOYALTY EASED AND MANY BOUG MULTIPLE CONSOLES RATHER THA JUST THEIR USUAL CHOICE OF MANUFACTURER.
THIS IS MARGARET SMITH, SIGNING OFF AND HOPING ALL THE BRAVE MEN AND WOMEN SUCKED INTO COMBAT CAN LOOK BACK ON THESE BIZARRE VIDEOGAME MEMORIES AND SLEEP PEACEFULLY.
A Clash of Consoles
A Clash of Consoles

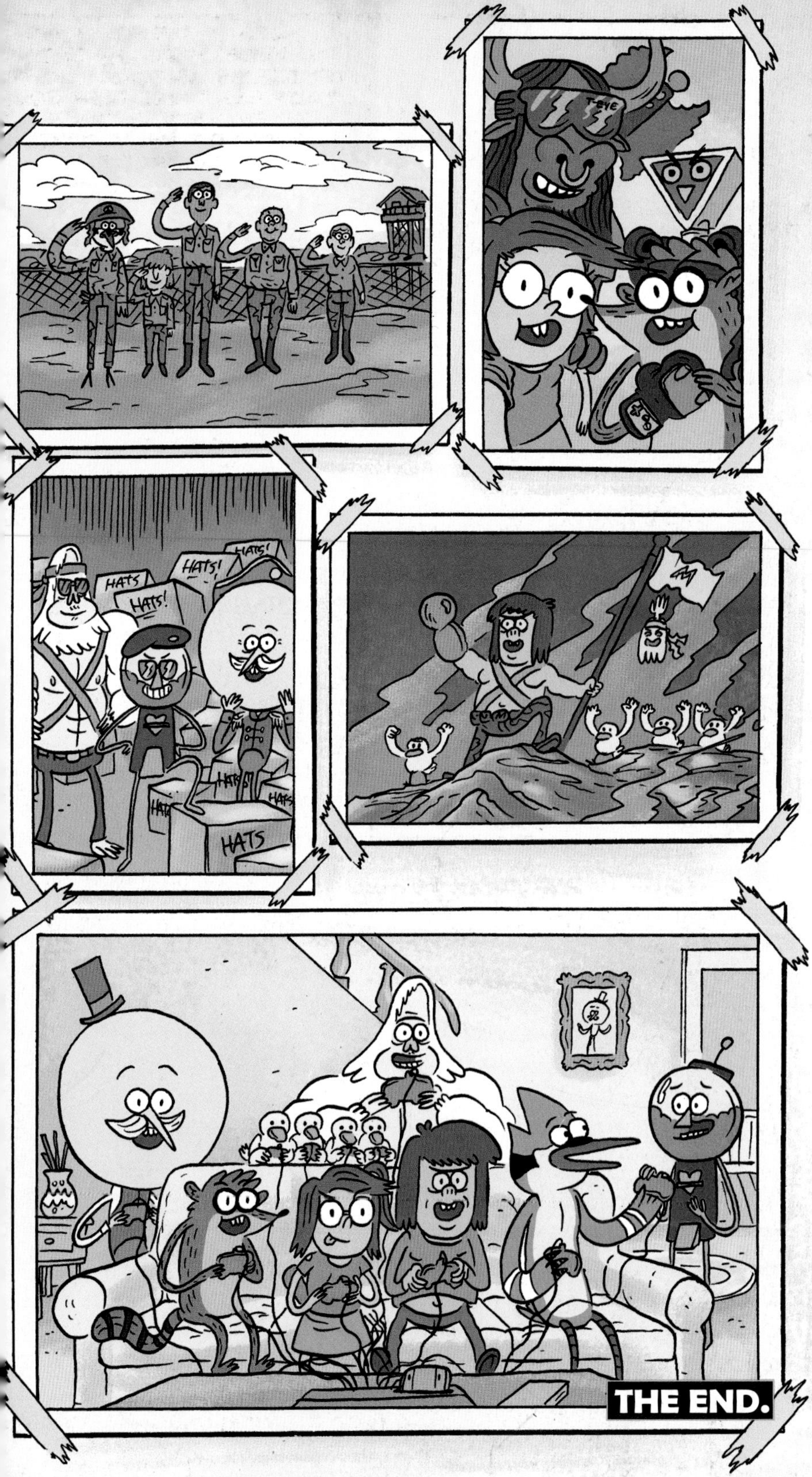
HATS!
HATS!
HATS!
HATS
HATS
THE END.

THERE'S ALWAYS MORE TROUBLE AT THE PARK . . .

REGULAR SHOW

Regular Show Volumes 1-6
KC Green, Allison Strejlau, Nick Sumida, Mad Rupert

Vol. 1 | ISBN 978-1-60886-362-4 | $14.99

Vol. 2 | ISBN 978-1-60886-426-3 | $14.99

Vol. 3 | ISBN 978-1-60886-485-0 | $14.99

Vol. 4 | ISBN 978-1-60886-709-7 | $14.99

Vol. 5 | ISBN 978-1-60886-775-2 | $14.99

Vol. 6 | ISBN 978-1-60886-841-4 | $14.99

Regular Show: Skips
Mad Rupert

978-1-60886-431-7 | $19.99

Regular Show: Hydration
Rachel Connor, Tessa Stone

978-1-60886-339-6 | $12.99

Regular Show: Noir Means Noir, Buddy
Rachel Connor, Robert Luckett, Wook Jin Clark

978-1-60886-712-7 | $14.99

Regular Show: A Clash of Consoles
Robert Luckett, Rachel Connor, Zé Burnay

978-1-60886-800-1 | $14.99

AVAILABLE AT COMIC SHOPS AND BOOKSTORES.
To find a comics retailer in your area, call 1-888-266-4226 or search www.comicbooklocator.com.

To order direct from BOOM! Studios, please visit www.boom-studios.com. Prices and availability subject to change without notice.

WWW.KABOOM-STUDIOS.COM

CARTOON NETWORK.

REGULAR SHOW, CARTOON NETWORK, the logos, and all related characters and elements are trademarks of and © Cartoon Network. (S16) All rights reserved. KaBOOM!™ and the KaBOOM! logo are trademarks of Boom Entertainment, Inc., registered in various countries and categories.